KAISA

Volume 1: A Reckoning with Love

"Я вас любил: любовь еще, быть может,

В душе моей угасла не совсем."

by

SAMUEL THAWLEY

A Kaisa Online Project

First edition

Published by KAISA

www.kaisa.online

ISBN: 978-1-7641938-6-3

Typeset in Baskerville Old Face 11pt

To all those who have inspired me along the way.

In particular to Trina—for all her love and encouragement.

And for telling me that I must finish what I start:

In this case my first attempt at a book,

a reinterpretation of The Count of Monte Cristo.

It's taken a while!

Disclaimer

Contents

1. The Sound of Falling Light

The light on the lake had that suspended, late-afternoon quality that makes it hard to tell what time it really is—neither gold nor silver—and so still that the mirrored forest looked more solid than the trees themselves.

The man fishing from the old jetty seemed part of that reflection. He was large without being heavy, his movements deliberate, his head bent low. A thin thread of smoke drifted up from the cabin behind him, catching the light like a ghost of breath. Somewhere in the woods a bird called once, then fell silent.

The man didn't seem to hear the car approach. The gravel drive curved too far from the water, and the sound was lost among the trees. But when the engine stopped and the forest sealed itself again, the atmosphere changed.

The figure sensed it before he saw anyone—just a faint disturbance indicating he was no longer alone. Then he heard the footsteps—hesitant to begin, but more determined as the visitor approached, descending the slope toward the lake.

A young man emerged from between two birches, awkward in his city jacket. His eyes scanned the clearing—as if it were the product of some dream he wasn't sure he wanted to disturb, half-fearing it might dissolve and turn into a reality even more daunting. He paused on seeing the fisherman.

"Are you Alex?"

The older man reeled in his line, slowly. "That depends on who's asking."

"My name's Daniel." The man stopped short of the jetty, as if uncertain whether to step closer. "Daniel Warren. I think you knew my grandmother."

Alex's face changed just slightly. He turned to look at the newcomer and study him carefully. The visitor must have been scarcely twenty. "Your grandmother and I crossed paths. I remember meeting you once or twice."

"I'm looking for her," Daniel said. "Even though she disappeared long ago." A gust of wind passed across the trees. The water trembled, then went still again. "She went without explanation—and even now no one can understand why."

"I was very young at the time," Daniel went on. "I scarcely recall her. But I remember my feelings—how alive I felt around her. Some part of me went missing that day." Alex looked at the young man quizzically.

"And as I grew up, this hole only got larger. I felt like I wouldn't be whole again, I couldn't move on, until I had the answer." He paused. "So, I decided to solve the mystery, myself. I would not rest until it was done." He looked down with a self-conscious smile. "I began to research, talking to family members and acquaintances—anyone really. I collected material. And when at last I finished school, I set out."

He scuffed a bit of earth at his feet. "I thought it would take some effort, but with focus I'd get results. Instead it's taken forever, and now I'm running out of ideas—and money," Daniel said honestly.

"I can't see what more is possible." The sense of hopelessness was almost palpable. "Then someone mentioned you." He looked up. "They said that you might know something—that you two had a history—that even if there wasn't much to go on, you would have the ability to investigate where others were reluctant."

Daniel slowly looked around the lake and back at Alex, taking it all in. "Whatever that meant."

Alex looked at the young man for a long time, as if weighing something neither of them could name. Then he seemed to reach a conclusion and nodded at the cabin. "You'd better come in."

The cabin was larger than it appeared from the water: two-story, log-built, filled with the faint, comforting scent of cedar and tobacco. Inside, there was order but not neatness; it had been arranged for use rather than display. A wood stove ticked in the corner, and a dog rose lazily from the hearth rug to stare at the stranger before lying back down again.

Daniel's eyes caught on the shelves—full of books in different languages. He noted military manuals, histories, novels... There was a scattering of atlases and weathered notebooks. Many he couldn't tell what they were, just foreign.

On the mantel was a single framed photograph: the back of a woman, taken outdoors somewhere mountainous, dancing in the sun, her hair windblown.

"Nice photo," Daniel commented.

"Yes," said Alex. "That was my wife." For an instant, he looked sad but recovered and gestured for him to sit. "Your grandmother—tell me about her."

So Daniel told him what little there was to tell: the car abandoned near the ferry terminal, the months of official silence and speculation that followed—about a woman vanishing into air. No remains, no witness, no confession.

After leaving school, he'd broken up with his girlfriend, given up the idea of going to college to instead chase the story of his grandmother. He'd hunted down the faintest traces—half-truths from family acquaintances, rumors of a new life, the whisper of an ill-fated trip gone wrong. All his leads—meager as they were—eventually petered out.

Alex listened without interruption. He poured whiskey into two short glasses and slid one across the table. "If you're willing to stay here a week or two," he said at last, "I'll do some investigating. In the meantime, you can rest and recover; share my meals, enjoy the wilderness, hear my stories. I'll try hard not to repeat myself." Alex grinned. "But I don't think I'm quite at that age."

"I'll even elaborate what I know about your grandmother—how we met, what happened, the little I understand about what followed. It's all a bizarre story, and I'm sorry your grandmother got embroiled in it. Maybe by the end we'll glean some new clues suggesting where she's gone, hinting where you might find her."

Daniel exhaled, half in relief, half in disbelief. "You'll really help me?"

"I wouldn't get your hopes up." Alex's voice was gentle. "The newspapers made your grandmother's disappearance seem minor, almost trivial. I feel the coverage was a disservice to such a good person, a strong woman. Any decision she made would have emerged from careful reasoning—done with the best intentions."

Alex stood, and his size seemed to fill the room. "If my investigations reveal anything, I hope—at least—it will be how sincere she was, how powerful and determined."

They sat down to eat early. The dinner was carefully prepared: venison with red currant sauce, potatoes roasted, spinach wilted in butter and nutmeg. Daniel hadn't realized until he began eating how hungry he was. The scent alone undid him. The long day had made him tired, and the wine—dark, almost opaque—lulled him further.

The older man spoke not of Daniel's grandmother, not yet, but of the land—the old logging trails, wolf sightings, the storms that could fell whole ridges of pine.

"I come here to regain my spirit," he said. "It's the only place left where silence means something positive."

Outside, the night deepened to a thick indigo. The lake reflected the last of the sky like a splash of purple mercury. Alex lit a lamp and carried it to the table. Its glow softened his features. Daniel hadn't appreciated how hard his face was in the daylight. It carried, he thought, the exhaustion of someone who had lived too long with the weight of unspoken things.

"Let me start, then," Alex said at last. "And I'll start not from the beginning, as the King of Hearts famously dictated, but from the key moment—so that it makes sense, so that you can see how things evolved and why."

Daniel leaned forward, and the dog lifted its head as if to listen as well.

"The trigger was the sixtieth birthday in St. Petersburg of a naturalized American–Mariya Asimov. She was a Russian émigrée and it was 2009." Alex hesitated as if recalling a storm.

"I won't explain it all up front. The tale quickly becomes too complex." He looked into the lamp as if seeing again in its dancing light all that happened.

"I'll just let the narrative unfold naturally, as it did, and everything will slowly become clear. The pieces will fall into place one by one, especially the connection between Mariya, me, and–in the process–your grandmother."

Daniel nodded. "Please tell everything," he said. "How you tell it doesn't worry me."

"And at some points," the man continued, "if holes develop in the story–if I fail to explain properly how someone got from A to B, or why things happened the way they did, then I'll come back and fill in those details when the timing seems best."

Daniel nodded again. "I just want to know it all."

Alex smiled and looked down. "I didn't realize at the time, but the sixtieth birthday of this émigrée, Mariya, was the catalyst for everything. It set off twin fates–like cursed knights on horseback, like figures in *The Lord of the Rings*–charging over the countryside, dueling each other to reach the end first and to claim victory over the future." He dwelled on the memory.

"Mariya's party in St. Petersburg was the hinge," he repeated, looking for another metaphor, "both the start of everything and the unraveling of it all."

Alex paused before continuing. "The resulting maelstrom was so big and so terrible that it caught up even your grandmother. None of us knew what was happening—nor, at first, why. We certainly didn't guess where it would lead. All we knew was that our trajectories had changed forever."

He stopped there to refill the glasses. The sound of the wine pouring into crystal had an almost ceremonial weight.

"Your grandmother," he continued, "wasn't supposed to be there that night. A friend canceled last minute. And as a result, your grandmother, somehow, got entangled in the whole tragic affair." At these last words, Daniel looked into Alex's eyes—suddenly nervous the unfolding story might indeed confirm his worst fears.

"You'll see as I go on," Alex noted, "how impossible it is to say where accident ended and choice began."

Later, when Daniel went to his room upstairs, rain had started. It drummed against the roof—a patter, rhythmic and unrelenting. The window looked down toward the lake, which had now vanished in the darkness and a dimly perceived veil of fog.

He could hear Alex moving below—clearing dishes, washing glasses, putting logs in the stove, opening and closing cupboards. Then quiet—nothing but the rain.

Daniel lay awake for a long time, the day's strangeness pressing on him—the long empty roads, the improbable coincidences that had brought him here—it all felt surreal. Yet the house itself was solid, reassuring.

He could smell the faint sweetness of the wood smoke. He could still taste the sharp tang of the venison sauce. Now, fresh scents of rain against dry wood and earth somehow crept into the room. And gradually his mind filled with the nebulous ghosts of conversations just begun.

His last image before sleep overtook him was his grandmother's face—not as she'd been in the photographs, smiling dutifully at events or with family, but as a woman still young somewhere in a corner of the world—chasing a dream, turning perhaps toward a sound only she could hear.

At dawn, the forest woke first. The rain had stopped, leaving the air raw and clean. Daniel woke late and opened his window. Through it came the cries of a loon, the smell of moss and cold earth. Alex was there outside already, splitting logs, his breath white in the chill.

When Daniel eventually came down, Alex was back in the kitchen.

"Sleep all right?"

"I think so," Daniel said. "It's very quiet here."

"Yes. The cabin's greatest attraction." He paused and looked outside. "It's so quiet here sometimes, on still evenings, that I almost hear the light as it falls into the lake." Alex's eyes crinkled. "Like so many shards of crystal—broken, exquisite, lost forever." He paused. "Then I simply hope that the next day will dawn despite all the ruin."

They ate breakfast—porridge, sliced apples—washed down with coffee. Alex had found a sharp Japanese-style knife to cut the fruit—which he did, Daniel noted, in quick accurate strokes.

Alex spoke little, and Daniel now found himself with time to study his host: the precision with which he moved, the scars visible when his sleeves were up, the sense that even his silences were deliberate. He recalled the hint of a tattoo on Alex's back when Daniel had looked down from his room earlier.

There was something about Alex that felt hardened—not merely strong, but disciplined in a way that had nothing to do with fishing or forestry. As if he had been severely tested and had survived. Daniel wondered about the scars, about the tattoo, about Alex's manual dexterity.

He noticed again the isolation around them—what he'd taken at first sight to be peaceful and restorative. Was he right to come alone? Daniel briefly considered whether he had been foolish, whether his host belonged to some darker part of the whole affair. He realized, suddenly and a bit late, that he hadn't fully worked out who he was asking for help.

After breakfast, Alex took out a folder from a drawer and set it on the table—his hand lingering for an instant on the cover as if in warning.

"Before we go on," he said, "I want to be clear. What I'm about to recount isn't a single tale. It's several that collided. What started as a mix of high spirits and youthful ambitions, in so many ways ordinary, pedestrian—even, shall we say, clichéd—became... something else entirely. Something a lot more personal."

Daniel said nothing. In the lull that followed he noticed the lake glimmering through the cabin windows. Alex opened his folder. Inside were old photographs—some black-and-white, others faded color. Indistinct faces, half-obscured interiors, frozen abstract exteriors.

One image caught Daniel's attention: a young woman standing by a lake, hair blown back, laughing at something outside the frame. It was his grandmother—or close enough to his memory of her that his breath caught.

"She looks happy," he whispered.

"She was," Alex replied. "But happiness, as you'll see, was the first casualty in this saga." He closed the folder with care—as if sealing it tight to prevent the contents from escaping.

"And so," he said, "I must get on with this story. Or even a week won't suffice." He paused, perhaps momentarily daunted by the idea. He procrastinated yet again. "Let's build up the woodpile a bit for the stove."

They headed out. The wind had risen once more, and clouds raced across the sky. Daniel turned toward the forest, half expecting to see someone—or something—emerge from the trees. However, nothing broke the scene: the treeline shaking, the old jetty empty—the lake now tearing at its old wooden structure, the fishing crates secure where Alex had left them the day before.

Behind him, Alex's voice came, steady and low. "The world is full of people who vanish, Daniel. Some by accident, others by will. Some despite themselves, others by artifice. The trick is working out which category your grandmother fell into."

Alex picked up a few logs to bring inside. Daniel followed his example. And once back—the door slammed shut, the woodpile replenished—Alex made some more coffee, poured them each a cup. The smell of it mingled with the resin from the fire and the scents from the disturbed lake, which infiltrated the cabin.

As the day widened, the story emerged—the real one. It had bided time as if beneath deep water—dark, cold, and enigmatic—waiting for someone to take the plunge.

"Sometimes," Alex said quietly, "truth lies buried like a ghostly treasure, which legend suggests is there but no one dares claim. When someone does, it changes everything. Sometimes the treasure redeems—other times it destroys." The saga might overwhelm Daniel, Alex mused, if the young man wasn't well prepared.

2. A Birthday Dinner

The early summer twilight stretched a luminous veil across St. Petersburg, coloring the sky in a translucent shade of blue that refused to succumb to true darkness. The city's famed white nights were in full bloom, so that even at this late hour dusk reigned instead of black.

In a cozy bistro on a winding cobblestone street, the atmosphere buzzed with conversation, clinking glassware, and the savory aroma of roasting meats and fresh dill.

At a rectangular table by the back wall, a family of three generations was celebrating the sixtieth birthday of their matriarch, Mariya. The candles flickered against exposed brick, and the low-hanging lights cast a warm, golden glow that softened the lines of Mariya's face—one used to laughter, but encumbered by the sorrows of a journey that spanned decades and continents.

Until now, the summer of 2009, Mariya had not set foot in Russia since the 1980s, when she and her husband, Ilya, emigrated with three young children under reforms Gorbachev had initiated. She'd become a literature professor in upstate New York.

The years in exile gathered quietly, one semester at a time. However, Mariya was happy in her new world and scarcely thought about returning home—to the land of her birth, the city of her childhood.

But Ilya's sudden death four years earlier, and Mariya's growing sense of unfinished business, had led her back at last, over twenty years later, surrounded by her children—Anna, Ivan, and Ekaterina—and their five lively offspring: Nicholas, Natalia, Polina, Michael, and Sasha.

All evening, they had indulged: in plates of pelmeni, in bowls of ink-purple borscht, in loaves of dark-brown rye bread topped with fresh butter and coarse salt. The children tore into the enticing dishes with unabashed relish and a tinge of curiosity: What did the 'real thing' taste like?

For the adults, shots of chilled vodka and glasses of full-bodied Georgian wine were served around the table with a generosity that matched their moods. Ivan and his sisters took turns translating the menu for the younger ones, who spoke scarcely a word of Russian despite their heritage.

Since landing in St. Petersburg, Mariya had been wound tight as a coiled spring, anxiety and a certain half-fearful anticipation mingling in her posture. The tumult of the past year, the stunning collapse of self-confidence in America with the onset of the global financial crisis, the change of presidents, the relentless wars—internal as much as external. Everything appeared to accentuate the uncertainties in her life.

But now, with the hum of friendly chatter surrounding her and the taste of home on her palate—missed for so many years—she felt herself finally beginning to thaw. Another round of shots prompted a chorus of toasts in Russian and English. The entire table continued to grow louder as the evening grew later.

"To Mariya's sixtieth birthday," Ivan announced in Russian, lifting his vodka glass high enough to catch the soft gleam of the overhead light. "And to her first return to the motherland in over twenty years!"

The refrain of "*Za vas!*" rang out around the table, quickly followed by "*Za zdoróvye!*" and finally "*Za lyubov!*" The five grandchildren giggled with the challenge of wrapping their tongues around the largely unused syllables.

Mariya clinked glasses with Ivan and then sipped the bracing liquid, savoring the sharp heat, which slid down her throat and spread its warmth to her fingertips. She felt the knots in her shoulders loosening. "Thank you, my dears," she said in the lull that briefly settled over them. "This... all of this... is more than I ever imagined when we first arrived in New York."

She paused, thinking of Ilya—the man whose high spirits had once lit up every meal they shared, who had encouraged her to keep teaching their children Russian at home so they'd never lose their roots. He was absent tonight, yet somehow more present than ever in her mind. Mariya's gaze collapsed for a moment, but she caught herself and smiled. "Truly, I can't thank you all enough."

"How do you feel, *Babushka*?" Natalia asked in English, leaning across the table. She was thirteen—caught between the last wisps of childhood wonder and the first sharp edges of self-consciousness and resistance. Her hazel eyes flickered with concern.

Mariya took a deep breath, embracing all the nostalgic aromas. "Better than I have in years, my dear. Better, and... bolder."

The waitress, a serene woman in her thirties with hair pulled back in a tidy knot, approached to clear away empty plates. Anna and Ekaterina ordered more blini—a spontaneous notion fueled by the pure joy of the evening—and the waitress promised to return quickly.

Over in another corner, a musician tuned a balalaika, and a moment later, lively notes began to dance through the bistro. A few patrons started to tap their feet in time.

All at once, Mariya pushed her chair back and stood, glass still in hand. Her children, noticing the movement, quieted their conversations. Even the grandchildren grew attentive, sensing that something meaningful was about to happen.

The sudden hush at their table contrasted with the ongoing swirl of activity around them: servers weaving around tables, the thread of balalaika music gaining momentum, everywhere the rise and fall of Russian voices in earnest desire to enjoy the evening.

"I realize," Mariya began in Russian, though she paused before switching to English for the grandchildren's sake, "some of you may not understand all my words, but I hope you will understand my heart." She glanced around, meeting the eyes of each loved one in turn.

"Tonight, seeing us all here," she continued, "I feel compelled to share a favorite passage from Russian literature. It is something I've taught many times—but never used myself, until now. It captures for me the hope we must all hold onto when life twists us away from where we thought we'd end up."

She drew a gentle breath, and in Russian, she spoke the lines:

Если жизнь тебя обманет,
Не печалься, не сердись!
В день уныния смирись;
В день веселья, верь, настанет.

Her voice trembled slightly—a mixture of reverence and raw emotion. Then she repeated the lines in English, each phrase precise and resonant:

If by life you were deceived,
Don't be dismal, don't be wild!
In the day of grief, be mild;
Merry days will come, believe.

A wave of quiet wonder passed over the table. Even the grandchildren, who had only begun to discover the contours of the Russian language, felt the solemnity in their grandmother's tone. Ivan and his sisters exchanged looks, recalling childhood memories when Mariya would recite poems in their weekend cabin near the Finger Lakes, bridging the gap between the old country and their new home in America.

Mariya's eyes glistened. She closed the book of memory in her mind and gazed around at all those dear faces: her children and especially the grandchildren, who she had worried might never see—let alone know—this land. "Pushkin, Russia's beloved poet, wrote those words nearly two centuries ago," she said, her voice still trembling.

"And yet I find them so fitting in this moment. Life did deceive me, in a way—I thought I would never return to Russia. I thought if I left, a door would close behind me—perhaps forever." She paused, letting a slow breath escape.

"And when your *Dedushka*, Ilya, died so suddenly, so unexpectedly, I felt the door lock shut in a way even I couldn't have imagined. I'd lost my partner, my fellow dreamer. I grieved. I was angry. And I almost gave up, completely, any thought of return."

She looked at the table. "Yet here we are now. 'Merry days'—they did come."

The children smiled at her, a bit misty-eyed themselves, though they were too young to fully understand the tumult of emotions roiling inside her. Nicholas, the oldest grandchild, caught Mariya's eye with a gentle nod as if to say, *I'm old enough now—I can sympathize.*

Mariya smiled through tears she didn't bother to hide. "So let that be our toast. Let us remember that times of sorrow yield to days of joy. And I—" She swallowed, raising her glass. "I cannot tell you how grateful I am for this day of joy."

They toasted, gently, each lifting a full glass—vodka for the adults; a tart berry drink, mors, for the children; wine for those who wanted to stay in-between. And in their shared silence, insulated rather than invaded by strains from the balalaika and laughter from the other diners, they drank.

A heartbeat later, the hush was shattered. A huge swell of applause burst out around the table because—in truth—there was nowhere else to go but back into the gaiety of the evening. Anna clapped her hands delightedly, beaming proudly at her mother. Ekaterina leaned across to press a delicate kiss on Mariya's cheek. Ivan, who'd always followed his mother's passions in his heart as much as he'd followed his father's advice on the surface, lifted his vodka glass higher.

"To Pushkin," he declared, a hint of mischief in his eyes, "and to Mama's sixty years—which we hope will become sixty more."

"To *Babushka*!" the grandchildren chorused. "To Mama!" Ekaterina and Anna echoed, and even some of the neighboring tables turned to see the family's newly boisterous cheer. There were smiles, a few murmured toasts from strangers in Russian. And everyone, suddenly feeling self-conscious, initiated another wave of laughter that went cascading along the table's edge.

When Mariya sat down at last, an almost giddy sense of relief spread through her. It was as if the tension haunting her since the plane landed had finally seeped away when reciting the poem—transforming her fears into something more hopeful, more forward-looking.

She glanced down the table, where plates of half-finished dumplings and stray slices of dark bread patterned the tablecloth among empty bowls of soup. The children were leaning on one another's shoulders, half-laughing, half-bickering, with the irrepressible energy of youth. Mariya, for a second, glimpsed herself as a young girl out with her cousins—nothing to restrain her excitement.

Ivan and Ekaterina turned their focus to the musician in the corner, clapping along as he picked up a faster tune. Anna was pouring more vodka, her cheeks flushed. "Mama," she said, teasing, "I'm blaming you if we close this place down."

Mariya gave a mock gasp. "Me? I think it's your father's spirit urging us on," she quipped. "Ilya would've loved this. So many voices talking at once, so many delights spread over the table. He would have devoured the moment."

Ivan nodded, a distant fondness rising in his expression. "He would've been the loudest among us, starting a debate on the importance of math—or, to tease you, the order of the greatest Russian dramatists and writers, all while convincing the children to pile more sour cream on their borscht."

At that, Polina chimed in, proudly announcing in halting Russian, "*Ya lyublyu borscht!*" eliciting cheers from her cousins. Sasha, just seven, picked up a piece of bread and waved it triumphantly. "And I love this bread," proclaiming his affection in English, because he wasn't sure of the words in Russian.

The entire family dissolved into a delighted uproar. Amid this swirl of good feeling, the waitress reappeared with a generous plate of newly made blini, steam still rising. She set them down with a smile, commenting in Russian on how the family was the liveliest group she had served in quite some time.

Mariya thanked her warmly, starting a rapid and animated exchange with the waitress that made the grandchildren blink in admiration. Their *Babushka*'s command of Russian was effortless—something they'd never fully witnessed at home in New York, where her accent and tongue were so often reined in by necessity.

The next quarter-hour was a haze of forks clinking on plates and boisterous chatter, while the musician in the corner transitioned through a set of folk-inspired tunes. This time Ivan and Ekaterina hummed along, showing off half-remembered verses of old songs that Mariya had once taught them.

Ekaterina, ever dramatic, tried to coax the more daring grandchildren into dancing in the narrow space between the tables, though they protested that it was "too embarrassing." Even so, Natalia and Polina did rise for a moment, giggling so hysterically they could barely manage a single step in time with the music.

Amid it all, Mariya found herself relaxing further in her chair, letting her gaze drift over the bright, dear faces of her children and grandchildren. She felt the faint sting of fresh tears—a contradiction to her laughter. Yet, somehow, both were perfectly aligned with her mood.

Pushkin's lines echoed in her mind. *In the day of grief, be mild; Merry days will come, believe.* The poet had written those words long ago. And, tonight, they seemed to perfectly encapsulate Mariya's winding journey. She'd known sorrow, plenty of it. Nevertheless, today was undeniably a merry day.

She silently raised her glass, too overwhelmed for more speeches. Her children and grandchildren mirrored her action, filling their table with refractions of candlelight.

And in that bright hush of possibility, they drank to the moment itself—when sorrow met laughter, when old fears bowed to new joys—and when a grandmother, at last, felt she had truly come home. But Mariya had no idea that, in returning, she had tempted fate, and everything would change.

3. The Woman in White

As if to break the moment, a towering honey cake arrived: golden, layered, and glowing under the restaurant's low-hanging lights. Mariya felt the last vestiges of tension and restraint slipping away. What was the use of holding out any longer?

The warm air of the bistro, fragrant after a long night, full of aromas that collected and lingered from the candles, meats, and herbs, seemed to melt every worry.

Mariya took a bite of the honey cake, savoring its sweet richness. It was a small act of rebellion—against her dietitian in New York and, implicitly, against the parts of her American life she still resisted. It was also a way to reach back to her teenage years, when anything seemed possible, when everything could be tasted—every sweetness enjoyed without consequence.

She let her gaze wander over the other patrons who remained about them—some chatting, others now lost to over-indulgence. Mariya idly wondered if women still hauled their comatose husbands back home by their feet along the ground, their heads bouncing to the rhythm of their wives' no-nonsense gait. The practice didn't seem to cause any longer-term damage she could recall.

It was then she noticed a young woman seated near the far wall—quiet, self-contained, the soft lamp-light accentuating the white of her skin and her voluptuous proportions. For a second, Mariya envied her youthful freshness.

The woman was wearing a blue summer dress with a white pattern of sword-leaved helleborine. A book was propped open, leaning against a vase—and she looked utterly composed, as though dining solo in a lively room were the most natural thing in the world.

"She's fascinating," Mariya whispered, nudging Ivan, who sat to her right.

"Who?" Ivan asked, pausing mid-forkful in his first piece of cake. He followed Mariya's line of sight.

"That girl with the book," Mariya said, voice low. "By the wall. She seems so at ease, so confident, reading while she eats."

Ivan peered over. "She could be a spy," he pronounced, half under his breath. "Straight out of a Cold War novel."

Mariya chuckled. "A spy? You mean a honey trap? You read far too much. It's bad for your eyes. She's obviously a poet, wandering through Russia for inspiration."

"A poet, Mama?" asked Anna, overhearing. "No way. She has the air of a pianist—look at her long fingers. She's here as part of the city's music scene to join in a masterclass."

"And I say journalist," Ekaterina interjected with a wry smile. "Look at the coat hanging over her chair. It's practical—lots of pockets, perfect for chasing leads."

The grandchildren joined in with their own theories: a princess in disguise, a magician studying ancient lore, an intelligence agent on a surveillance mission. Their eyes sparkled with the excitement. Mariya, enjoying the fun, offered a final verdict: "She's French—without a doubt. Only the French dress with such casual elegance."

Ivan smirked. "You're saying that because you want us all to go to Paris next, aren't you?"

"Maybe," Mariya said, "but I'm not necessarily wrong."

The family spun one story after another as their focus returned to the table and they slowly consumed the honey cake: at least the adults slowly, the children as fast as they could without drawing exasperated complaints from the others. Eventually, Mariya glanced at the far wall—and discovered the table now empty; the young woman had gone without drawing any attention to herself.

"Oh," Mariya sighed, crestfallen. "She's gone."

Ivan confirmed it. "Vanished. Definitely a spy. She managed it so covertly."

"She had such grace," Mariya murmured, suppressing her disappointment. "A beauty as much spiritual as physical."

"Well, that's it." Anna clapped her hands briskly. "Now we'll never know! Perhaps it's better that way."

Mariya giggled. "Yes, you're right. Some secrets are best left..." She trailed off, as her mind drifted back to younger days.

Ivan, his cheeks rosy from vodka and amusement, leaned closer. "You know," he said in a playfully exaggerated tone, "I could go find her. Ask her. The night air might do me good."

Mariya's eyes danced with mischief. "Yes, let's do that! See if she's French. If so, we'll plan our next trip immediately."

"Challenge accepted," Ivan declared, grinning. He straightened his shirt like a man about to embark on a grand quest. Anna and Ekaterina exchanged a look of disbelief, while the grandchildren burst into hysterics.

"Don't go," Anna exhorted, embarrassed by the idea.

"It might be a trap—as you suggested," Ekaterina mocked. But Mariya just clapped her hands in delight. "Hurry, before she disappears into the night!"

Ivan slipped out the door into the St. Petersburg twilight. He would find her, whatever the risks. The family craned their necks, peering through the windows as he stepped outside and scanned the length of the cobblestone street.

* * *

As Ivan stumbled outside, he blinked in the change of light. The restaurant's warm glow spilled out over the cobblestones, illuminating faint wisps of night air. He saw a lone figure some distance away, her silhouette passing under a streetlamp.

He headed in that direction, hoping the figure was their mystery woman. His breath grew ragged from the burst of energy, and soon Ivan had to quicken his pace, afraid of failing his mission and returning empty-handed. *It would be so embarrassing*, he thought.

"Wait!" he called out, increasingly worried. There was no response. "Wait!" He accelerated again in a final, desperate effort to reach his target, stretching a hand to touch her shoulder.

She turned, looking a little surprised. Nevertheless, she stopped. Ivan noticed again the book, clutched to her side.

"Sorry," Ivan managed, raising a hand in greeting, sweating from the exertion and the vodka. "It's just–it's simply... my mother wanted to know if you were French."

The woman blinked, remaining silent for a long moment. Ivan began to lose his nerve. Then the woman slowly shook her head. "French?" she repeated, considering the idea with a smile.

"No." She laughed. "I'm Finnish. But," she paused, "I suppose your mother was close enough. They both start with an 'F'." At that insight, she allowed herself a more sustained chuckle.

"Finnish?" Ivan exclaimed, both relieved and exhilarated. He liked her laugh–the deep, rumbling laugh of someone who enjoyed life. In other settings, he guessed, it might almost be Rabelaisian. "That's perfect," he replied, but for no particular reason.

"We were playing a silly guessing game inside." Ivan felt he owed some kind of explanation. He looked down with an embarrassed smile. "I'm sorry to have bothered you." He glanced at her through his lashes, then turned and hurried back to share the news, losing the last of his breath along the way.

It was only a few minutes later that he arrived back, pushing through the door with a triumphant smile. "Finland!" he announced, leaning on his mother's chair. "She's from Finland."

Mariya's mind took a moment to focus, to regain the thread. Then her eyes lit up. "Finland? Oh, I love the Finns." She clapped her hands. "They're so charming! Did you bring her back? Let's invite her to join us for some of this cake and tea!" She looked at the cake and realized, a bit late, there wasn't much left.

Ivan hesitated, feeling for a second doubtful. "You... want me to fetch her? I only asked where she was from." He was going to end up a spectacle.

"Yes, go!" Mariya urged excitedly. "Hurry. She can't have gone far." Her enthusiasm was not to be denied. "I want to meet her. I want to chat. It's my night, after all!"

Buoyed by Mariya's energy, the laughter around the table as everyone began to focus on the drama, and the lingering effects of the evening's toasts, Ivan agreed with a shake of his head. "All right. But if she slaps me..." A wave of applause and chuckles followed Ivan as he disappeared out the door again.

Once more at Mariya's urging, Ivan braved the cooling night. The street looked even more deserted this time, and the woman was—of course—nowhere in sight. *I knew it,* Ivan thought, a knot of apprehension tightening in his belly.

But she can't have vanished entirely? he half-wondered, half-wished. Ivan didn't begin slowly, but broke at once into what passed for a fast run in the circumstances.

He rounded the corner where the young woman had gone with a mix of dread and hope. And his heart leaped as he glimpsed a long way down the block the single figure, her outline framed against the light sky.

"Excuse me!" Ivan practically shouted as he neared, too excited and too nervous to hold back. "Wait!" The woman stopped and turned, her face serious once more. But seeing the man, looking increasingly ridiculous—obviously in such a state of discomfort—she permitted a wry smile, brows lifting.

"You again?" she asked, probing but amused. She chuckled, revealing once more her dry sense of humor.

Ivan skidded to a stop, panting. "I know, I know, I'm so sorry."

"Don't keep apologizing," the woman interrupted good-naturedly.

"My mother wants to invite you to join us for a chat." The woman's smile widened. "She's celebrating her sixtieth birthday—well, we're celebrating it. And...well, she says she loves the Finnish." Ivan felt slightly embarrassed by this explanation. "And it's her night—so she insists."

"We have tea, cake," Ivan continued relentlessly, "and a big, loud family," he sought to uncover a rationale that might prove compelling. "I promise we're nice."

The woman studied him under the lamplight, her breath a soft cloud in the night chill. A bemused smile crossed her face. "All right, then," she said eventually. "Why not? I'm sure you're all nice." She emphasized the word a little and smiled once more. "Lead on," she commanded. Ivan loved the inflection of her voice when she pronounced her verdict. He could already tell he was in trouble...

Inside, the family broke into cheers when Ivan returned with the mysterious woman alongside him. The bistro's ambient glow seemed even warmer now, the rooms somehow smaller and cozier.

"Oh, marvelous!" Mariya exclaimed, standing to greet her. "You really came! I was beginning to wonder if Ivan had let us down." She gave him a wink.

The young woman smiled politely. "My name is Kaisa," she said, placing her book, a Jane Austen novel, on the table's edge. "And yes—I'm Finnish."

Ivan shot his siblings a smug grin that said, *mission accomplished.* Mariya, beaming, introduced everyone at the table in a flurry: Anna, Ekaterina, Nicholas, Natalia, Polina, Michael, and Sasha. Each offered welcoming smiles, waves, or shy hellos.

"Wait," Nicholas interjected, leaning forward with curiosity, "I love new names. Does Kaisa mean anything?"

She nodded, flattered by the question from such a young gentleman. "It's basically a short form of Katariina," she explained, "which comes from the Greek meaning 'pure.' So, yes, 'Kaisa' means something like 'pure' but in a roundabout way."

"Cool!" Nicholas said, nodding. "That's neat."

Mariya continued, ignoring the interruption. "We're celebrating my sixtieth birthday," her voice alive with excitement. "Please forgive this strange intrusion—I so wanted to talk. And a woman must be forgiven everything on her birthday."

Kaisa shook off her dark coat. "It's all right," she said, sitting down. "I don't mind." She looked over the table, at the remnants of the night's feast. "I was just wondering what to do next—and I love tea."

"I suppose," she added after a pause, "I'm curious too."

At this welcome, Mariya could resist no further. "You see, recently I met this Finnish woman at the airport bus stop. I happened to be in LA at the time. She was so full of interest in the world and life. We had the most wonderful and long conversation. The bus never arrived."

Kaisa smiled, "I'm not sure all Finns are usually this talkative."

"She was traveling around the world without using any of her money, the little that she had. She recorded everything on her blog—which was so amazing. You should read it one day. People would somehow find her website and offer her a place to stay, and she would help in return. She ended up staying with us for several days before then flying over to Alaska."

At this point, Anna worried Kaisa might, indeed, need some refreshment. "There's some honey cake left," she offered, sliding a plate Kaisa's way. "I saved a piece in case you agreed to Ivan's reckless invitation. And if it's too sweet, we can find something else."

Ivan reclaimed his chair, catching his breath, then poured himself some wine. Michael and Nicholas gave him a thumbs-up for completing his "mission." The grandchildren, now emboldened, asked Kaisa all manner of questions: about Finland's winters, her travels, the reason for visiting St. Petersburg, what book she was reading.

The bistro became a swirl of close chatter and late-night thoughts. Mariya and Kaisa talking animatedly. The family excitedly planning the next day's events—the children extracting promises that they would have some more briquettes of vanilla plombir ice cream. And Ivan watching on, pleasantly exhausted, tracing a finger around the rim of his glass.

Candlelit sconces cast dancing shadows on the walls, and a musician again took up the balalaika strumming gentle notes, which drifted over to their corner. Those groups of diners still in the bistro continued to drink, engaged in increasingly passionate dialogue about the true meaning of life.

Mariya's table seemed more raucous than most, caught up in an improvised encore none of them had anticipated. It resonated with a bright, infectious energy that every now and then spilled over—drawing the attention of other customers nearby.

As Kaisa finished her slice of honey cake and everyone's cups were newly filled with steaming black tea, Mariya surveyed the gathering yet again. She couldn't get enough of this sight—the family all together in her hometown. She had started life alone, the only child of a single woman, worried how it would turn out—and here she was surrounded by a huge cradle of warmth and energy. She had built something that would continue down the years.

Mariya raised her teacup in a small toast—both to Kaisa and to the table: "To chance encounters," she said, beaming at Kaisa. "To the magical nights of St. Petersburg—which, like the best poems, never really leave the imagination."

A chorus of agreement sprang around the table—cups rose and clattered. A comfortable buzz of conversation resumed, weaving humor and curiosity into a tapestry of voices. Through the windows, the northern twilight glowed as the early hours of the morning passed unnoticed.

Inside, no one seemed in a hurry to leave. They were bound together by a sense of excitement and a willingness to embrace serendipity.

For Mariya, it was the finest gift she could have received: to be reminded at sixty that life still held surprises, that new friendships could form in the unlikeliest of ways, that letting go of old anxieties could usher in moments of pure joy.

She didn't consider that the new might unsettle, if not unseat, the old—or that a single encounter could so dramatically reorder their lives.

4. The Hermitage Museum

A crisp, bracing wind blew in from the Gulf of Finland, racing along the Neva River. Ivan and his family—his mother, sisters, and the grandchildren—made their way up the stone steps of the Hermitage Museum.

Even from outside, it commanded respect as visitors surged past the grand entry doors. The ornate façade proclaimed centuries of imperial glory. Mariya paused near the threshold, taking a moment to absorb every detail: the towering arches, the brass fixtures, the echo of footsteps along the corridor beyond.

"I can hardly believe I'm here again," she murmured, her eyes shining with anticipation. "I first walked these halls when I was scarcely older than you, Natalia. Then I came with your grandfather, and we'd lose ourselves here for hours among these treasures."

Her children listened intently, eager to hear any memories she might share. Anna and Ekaterina exchanged a quick, excited grin. Ivan, for his part, shifted closer to his mother, deeply attuned to the emotion in her voice.

Stepping inside, they entered the grand entrance hall, where tall marble columns rose like sentinels guarding the museum's secrets. Frescoes adorned the ceiling in elaborate patterns, a chandelier cast a sharp, dazzling light across the marble floors. Tourists clustered at the ticket counters, impatient voices blending into a lively hum.

Even at this point, art was everywhere: statues poised in alcoves, oil paintings arranged with regal precision, and tapestries that hinted at the countless wonders beyond. Despite the rush of people, an air of reverence clung to the space—an unspoken acknowledgment visitors were entering a realm of history and beauty.

The family advanced, passing with determination through an ornate archway leading into the first vaulted room. The Elizabethan Baroque structure, mirrored in the polished floor, revealed occasional Rococo flourishes. The combination made the palace one of the grandest in Europe, alongside a handful in France and Austria.

Sunlight streamed through tall windows, illuminating sculptures and paintings carefully arranged along the high walls. Mariya stopped again, reliving the wonder of her youth. "It's as splendid as I remember—although I believe it's even more striking than my memory allowed."

Turning to her children, she continued with a quiet fervor, "Do you recall how I once told you about the siege during the war? The curators moved countless artworks to safety, risking everything just so that future generations could stand here as we do now."

Anna and Ekaterina nodded, clearly moved by their mother's recollection. Ivan gazed about him, admiring the interplay of light and shadow dancing across the gilded ceiling. Already, the family seemed transported—each of them caught in the thrall of grand narratives: history, art, peoples.

Before they could press on, Ivan's eyes caught sight of someone near a large painting. Only a few paces away, he glimpsed Kaisa—so intent on a canvas she seemed, like the previous night, unaware of the bustling crowd around her.

And she looked even more radiant—fresh, elegantly dressed in a white blouse paired with an aquamarine linen skirt. A thin silver chain, hanging from her neck, subtly caught and angled the light.

A smile brightened her face, as though she were successfully piecing together the meaning of the painting in front of her. Ivan's heart leaped with surprise and pleasure. He slipped past a group of visitors. "Kaisa," he called, his voice hushed but full of joy. "Hey again."

She turned, blinking once. "I didn't expect to see you here," he continued.

She lit up on recognizing him. "Ivan! What a coincidence." Glancing at the imposing hall around them, she added with a soft laugh, "I just got here—fifteen minutes ago. I've barely had time to catch my breath. Everything is so wonderful. I've got no further than this painting."

Kaisa's gaze flicked over to Mariya, Anna, and Ekaterina, who were busy at a nearby sculpture, murmuring excitedly among themselves, and the children racing around—looking as much at each other as at the exhibits. "It's great to see you all again," she said, a hint of shyness in her eyes.

"What were you studying?" Ivan asked. "Your face was so earnest."

Kaisa chuckled lightly, a sparkle in her eyes. "Oh, it's just this painting..." She paused, glancing back briefly to appreciate the artistry before turning her attention to Ivan. "I think it's an incredible reflection of vulnerability and resilience. Don't you feel that art speaks to us in a language beyond words?"

"Absolutely," Ivan replied, captivated by the warmth and strength of her conviction. "These paintings almost pull you in."

Kaisa nodded, "Yes, it does seem so." Their voices remained low as they spoke, out of deference for the sanctity of the space—and maybe to savor more privately this unexpected moment.

Ivan glanced up at the ornate vaulted ceiling, then back toward the painting that had so enraptured Kaisa. In that instant—as the first room of the Hermitage enveloped him in its impressive mix of history and art—hints of past, present, and future seemed to converge.

He was struck by the sheer improbability of their two meetings. His initial encounter with Kaisa had unfolded in such an odd and unexpected manner. Yet here she was again, admiring a painting as if she had been waiting for something—in some way, for him. Maybe some encounters turned out more aligned with fate than others, unfolding long after one assumed they were over.

Without any clear signal, but with an irrepressible combination of delight and curiosity, Kaisa and Ivan began to wander the spacious galleries together—leaving behind Ivan's family as the two of them went off to make their own discoveries.

They strolled side by side along the Hermitage's corridors—every so often glancing at each other with a mixture of surprise and ease, as if to confirm that, indeed, the other was there—sharing this moment. Kaisa held a small guide in her hand. Ivan noticed her nails were painted a light blue—like the morning sky.

The conversation started tentatively with comments about how a single artwork could evoke so many thoughts, so many reactions. However, it slowly expanded into a gentle, meandering dialogue about what drew them both to art in the first place.

"There's an odd relation to time here," Kaisa remarked. "Every room feels like a portal that carries you somewhere different—ancient or modern, European or Russian, realist or contemporary. It becomes clear how much we try to compartmentalize our world when, really, it all flows together."

They passed the sculpture of a resting satyr. "Artwork is timeless. It connects us—to minds that shaped the past, to possibilities that build the future. In spite of all the innovations that relentlessly shake our world, upend our lives, something in us endures beyond time. We reread and reuse old literature. We return to classical art, rework it."

Ivan adjusted the strap of his messenger bag. "I know what you mean."

Kaisa's eyes brightened. "Art is more like a two-way mirror—it shows us who we've been and hints at who we might become." She liked the thought. "It doesn't simply preserve a moment; it links that moment to what lies ahead."

"Each visitor meets an artwork at a particular crossroads in their life. So the work becomes a kind of hinge—opening one way or another, depending on the path the beholder has taken, the prospects they're facing."

Ivan smiled. "It's like magic, isn't it?"

"These works, from hundreds of years ago," Kaisa expanded, "can still resonate in a deeply personal but unique way with you, me, others who arrive."

"And as the paintings become a subject with agency," she continued, "I wonder if they watch us as keenly as we watch them."

Ivan chuckled. "I like that idea. If so, I hope they approve of our talk."

Kaisa and Ivan exchanged a grin, then crossed into a lofty gallery devoted to the Italian Renaissance. Alerted by a crowd of visitors, they spotted one of the museum's prized exhibits. Even without the plaque, Ivan recognized the soft lines and subtle chiaroscuro that defined Leonardo da Vinci's style. It was the *Benois Madonna.*

He stopped a few paces back to absorb the scene. Kaisa, instead, went right up to the protective barrier. The image before them—Mary cradling the infant Christ—radiated an intimacy, a sense of familial love and devotion, that few artists, whether before or since, have achieved.

The baby reached for a flower Mary held, and the affection in Mary's gaze suggested a universe condensed into that singular bond of mother and child.

"Look at their expressions," Kaisa whispered, angling her head to better capture the different aspects of the painting. "It's like we're peeking into a private world."

Ivan stepped closer, allowing the sense of shared awe to envelop him. "Yes," he murmured.

"There's such tenderness in Mary's face," Kaisa continued. "Leonardo has this ability to capture the eternal essence of what is, in reality, just an ephemeral moment—like, if we blink, the child may wriggle in her arms, or Mary may laugh softly at his curiosity."

Even if in this corner of the gallery many tourists were snapping pictures with their digital cameras, the movement did little or nothing to disrupt the painting's aura. One or two were panning over the room with their handheld camcorders despite the rules.

Kaisa's gaze interrogated the brushstrokes, the finely drawn outlines of the hands, the subtle transitions in light. "My father was an artist. Did I tell you that?" she asked. Her tone suggested that she too had lost someone earlier than expected and was now recalling her childhood, not seeking a response.

"He was quite famous in his day. People admired his artistry, but struggled to grasp his ideas. My father would battle to explain his work, his vision. I would write the exhibition notes for him." After a pause, she added, "He was a great man."

There was a lull as Kaisa continued to examine da Vinci's picture. "I've read somewhere that mother and child paintings often symbolize the universal theme of nurture or growth, not just physically but spiritually." She paused. "When I look at this, I feel a sense of hope, as though every act of care we offer someone has the power to expand and ripple outward."

Ivan digested the confession and the train of Kaisa's thoughts.

"It's reassuring, isn't it?" Kaisa went on. "If a painting from centuries ago can still impart such feelings, it suggests that these quiet, profound moments—love, care, devotion—are stronger than all the noise and chaos that time can unleash."

They lingered there, neither seeming inclined to leave. The simplicity of the scene grounded them, offering a gentle encouragement to their joint exploration. Soon, however, a flow of new visitors nudged them onward.

They drifted around a corner, through an archway adorned with ornamental leaves, and entered a space showcasing the museum's Baroque masterpieces.

Their conversation flowed with each painting they passed, as they got used to each other's rhythm and perspective. Some paintings prompted loose, unstructured discussions about color palettes; others inspired musings on the artist's personal struggles.

Yet through it all, a playful current ran beneath their words, as though they were seeking out and gently exploring the contours of each other's lives—how well they matched.

From time to time, Kaisa would pinpoint a small detail, such as the reflection in a painted window or the dynamic swirl of a subject's sleeve—and Ivan would give short replies, his admiration and respect growing with every new glimpse of her perceptiveness and insight.

Eventually, one of the corridors opened into a vaulted chamber spotlighting another of the museum's most revered pieces: Rembrandt's *Return of the Prodigal Son.* The crowd when they arrived was surprisingly quiet. Perhaps they had reached here faster than others—or was it slower?

Kaisa let out a soft exhale the moment she saw it, as if the painting itself had drawn the breath from her lungs. "Ah," Kaisa said in recognition and allowed the moment to absorb her fully. "Rembrandt's *Return of the Prodigal Son.* Many believe it is among the Hermitage's crown jewels—a painting that glows with a compassionate mystery."

"See how the father's embrace of his weary child holds all our attention even when it's off to the left," she exclaimed. "The rule of thirds."

"And the figures to the right, in the background, partly hidden there in the shadows, seem to watch—each with their own emotions."

Gentle, warm light fell from an unseen source onto the father's hands, which cradled the back of the son with a powerful but devoted affection. Kaisa, encouraging Ivan too, moved closer to pick out the texture of Rembrandt's brushwork—so different from da Vinci's, even if somehow related across period and philosophy.

"How can a single image, yet again, hold so much love and emotion—only, this time, so different in character from the da Vinci?" Kaisa asked, her voice trembling slightly. "It's as though Rembrandt distilled the essence of fatherhood and the notion of forgiveness into a few square feet of canvas."

Ivan studied the son's tattered clothes and bare feet—considered how exposed he must have felt.

"This painting is so humbling," Kaisa continued. "It makes me wonder: Have I ever shown that much mercy—or been so vulnerable? Rembrandt shows the almost divine power needed to reconcile institutions with ideals, principles with feelings."

Kaisa looked at Ivan sidelong. "Maybe we're all both father and son at different points in our lives. Sometimes we have the power to forgive, sometimes we desperately need to be forgiven."

Ivan marveled at Kaisa's insight, her ability to see and condense the world. His gaze fell on the background figures. "And sometimes," he added, with sudden inspiration "we're simply bystanders, unsure whether to celebrate, envy, or resent."

Kaisa nodded slowly. "The world is complicated, which is why I love the interplay of light and dark here. It's as if Rembrandt is reminding us that compassion isn't straightforward. My brother went off to Sweden and didn't return. Now it makes no difference; my father is gone."

They fell silent, letting Kaisa's words settle. Other tourists drifted in and out. A few whispered excitedly, others stood wordless.

Oblivious, Ivan and Kaisa contemplated the father figure—someone they'd both lost, it seemed, too soon. They focused on the figure's softly lit hands—gentle and welcoming. The painting, Rembrandt's sermon on family and religion, touched a sensitive nerve.

The artwork triggered the childlike yearning in both of them for love and forgiveness—and pressed upon them the harder truth that such longing required humility and vulnerability. They could not imagine how soon life would ask this of them.

5. Dancers in Time

Once they left that gallery, Ivan and Kaisa descended a flight of broad steps lined with a regal red runner, each lost in private reverie.

Eventually, they found themselves in a more modern collection—a spirited space where avant-garde pieces leaped off the walls. Walking brought them to a light room devoted to early twentieth-century art. Here, the colors were bolder, the strokes freer, the sense of motion almost electric.

They paused at a wide canvas that commanded attention from across the room: Matisse's *Dance*—the 1910 version. Five figures—all nude—locked together in a circle against a backdrop of green and blue, caught in a primal whirl of ecstatic lines and bold reds, hands joined in a blur of motion. The painting seemed to burst with energy—raw and irrepressible.

Kaisa's face lit up. "You can almost feel the music, can't you?" she said, stepping closer as though willing the dancers to pull her into their circle. "It's so alive, so unabashed."

"I don't know why," she continued, "but this museum—here, today—speaks to me, provokes me in ways that few outings have done before." She looked at Ivan.

Not wanting to take her confession any further, she changed tack. "I love how this painting's stripped to the essentials: color, shape, movement. Nothing extraneous, no frills—just raw expression. I've always loved dance."

Ivan looked at Kaisa. "It feels like a celebration," he commented.

"Yes," Kaisa agreed, "it's the sheer joy of existing—breath and movement. They are linking arms, absorbing and repurposing the rhythm. It's a reminder that, even when life is complicated, we can always reclaim—if we are conscious and willing—an elemental sense of freedom."

Her words resonated with Ivan. He found himself longing to trace the arcs of those drawn limbs, to share in that exultant circle, to enter the painting in that moment with Kaisa. "Yes," he said in a faint voice, scarcely able to resist his thoughts. "Perhaps we forget..."

He stopped, but Kaisa waited for Ivan to finish the sentence. "We forget how simple it can be to let go," he concluded. "This painting is like an antidote to overthinking."

Ivan considered how circles applied to his own life. The familial gravity that helped him stay grounded, pulling him back for events like these with his mother and sisters. The centripetal force that he now felt with Kaisa—which threatened to pull them together, exposed and unprepared.

"It's so uninhibited, isn't it?" Ivan exclaimed, verbalizing his thoughts. "The painting urges you to join the circle, to lose oneself in the rhythm, even if it feels exposing. And yet to join demands commitment."

Ivan could even picture circles in the corporate world—structured orbits like high-swing rides at amusement parks, taking people up and down. The thought took him outside the Hermitage—back into the world and the many pressures of real life.

"What if a dancer hesitates," he said, "somehow breaks the chain?" Kaisa glanced up at the question, probing, as if sensing the undercurrents in his mind.

Even as he waited for word about his next assignment at work, Ivan's phone had been silent all morning. A bur of worry had attached itself to his thoughts. What happened when the personal and the public got entangled? Hadn't he been there before?

"Maybe that's the risk," he went on. "To dance means to lose oneself to the music, to the movement. It means to imbibe the tune and follow it—to keep going, shift as the music shifts, until the melody has finished, and the dancer can go on no more."

Outside, the Neva shone under the summer sun, flecks of light glinting off the slow-moving water and in through the windows. The day had advanced.

Worried about where things were heading, Kaisa changed tack. "This feels like the perfect juncture..." she began. "There's a poem in my language—Finnish—that I'd love to share. It might capture something of this moment."

Ivan's eyes lit up with curiosity. "I'd love to hear it."

Kaisa drew a small notepad from her handbag, flipping through the pages until she found what she wanted. Clearing her throat softly, she began to recite in Finnish:

> *Ruislinnun laulu korvissani,*
> *tähkäpäiden päällä täysi kuu!*
> *Kesäyön on ihmeellinen taika,*
> *se on suuri, se on pyhä, se on.*

Her voice echoed in the airy chamber. Ivan didn't understand the words, but the rhythm and cadence imparted a wistful enchantment. Kaisa smiled. "I'll try and give you an English translation," she said.

> A rye bird's song in my ear,
> above ripening fields a full moon glows!
> The midsummer night holds a wondrous magic,
> vast and sacred it seems.

She closed the notepad, her eyes reflecting a softness, an opening. "It's just a snippet of a longer piece," she explained. "But I've always found it speaks to how beauty can arrive unexpectedly—like a song in the night—and remind us that life is still full of wonder."

Ivan let the words settle over him, imagining what a Finnish landscape might be like: open fields, a moonlit sky, a bird's call in the quiet midsummer. "The poem's beautiful," he said quietly. "I can see why you like it—a sense of magic, fleeting in time, that nevertheless has such an immense and long-lasting effect."

Kaisa drew in a breath. "Exactly. It's the feeling that there's so much more to see or discover beyond the daily grind—beyond the mundane that meets the unsearching mind, the unquestioning eye."

Kaisa looked out the window. "Sometimes all it takes is a painting, or a poem, or a chance encounter, and suddenly the world feels immense, unknowable, and sacred again."

Ivan's gaze focused more fully on Kaisa, and he felt an emotion newly uncovered pounding in his chest. "Yes. What was the line again? *The midsummer night holds a wondrous magic*."

"Indeed," replied Kaisa as if reading Ivan's thoughts. He felt the ground tilt—spoken words blending with the unspoken, everything suddenly too close. Kaisa's hand brushed his, a light touch that sent heat running under his skin.

"Does the music have to stop?" Kaisa asked gently, her breath near and warm in the cool air of the museum. Ivan smelled a faint note of mint.

His heart quickened. He took a step forward, feeling her shoulder brushing past. *She sees me*, he thought. "Perhaps it doesn't have to," Ivan replied, his voice ragged. "Maybe we keep the circle going."

"And it becomes fulfillment." Kaisa finished the thought. Ivan swallowed, a physical act as he raced to keep his emotions under control.

However, before the situation could evolve further, Ivan's phone vibrated—sharp and insistent. He ignored the intrusion, keen to stay focused on Kaisa: her eyes, the way they matched the painting's blue hues; her face, which seemed to reflect back his own desire. But the phone buzzed and buzzed again, unrelenting, shattering the spell.

With a sigh of frustration, he pulled it out, glancing at the screen: Evelyn Marks. Eve. It was a work call—although Eve was a close friend from his earliest days at the company.

"I'm sorry," Ivan muttered, the friction building. He looked down, apologetic. "It's work. I should—"

Kaisa's expression clouded, a hint of upset flickering. "Of course. The dance does pause." She was almost cross, but with Ivan or the world it was not clear. "It must do so for reality." She stepped back, and Ivan saw her posture stiffen.

He didn't know the soreness beneath her reaction—couldn't guess the way last-minute cancellations had left her travelling alone. Ivan answered his phone, stepping aside and keeping his voice low. "Eve? This isn't a great time."

Evelyn's voice crackled through the bad reception, professional but familiar. "Ivan, congratulations! The executive committee just announced it—you're the new head of the Moscow office. Effective next year. I wanted to be the first to tell you."

The news caught him like a giant wave—ambition's reward, but laced with challenge. Head of Moscow: more potential, but more exposure to the gray zones he'd already tasted with his firm. "That's... incredible," he said, his mind whirling. Matisse's dancers now seemed to mock him, their circle of freedom all at once contrasting with his new commitments.

"But listen," Eve continued, her tone shifting to a warning. "It's tough here, Ivan. Tougher than you might think. The business, the politics—the need to interact with Russians on their terms—it will demand compromises. You'll land in the thick of it. Don't underestimate the pressure; it can break even the strongest."

Eve's words, coming when they did, brought an instant of self-doubt. *Did he really want it?* As country head, he'd have to follow a delicate line—no losing himself to wild impulses. "I appreciate the heads-up, Evelyn. Really. But I'm in the middle of something—"

"Understood," she said, betraying another note of personal warmth, one that reminded him of their history together. "Just... You must be prepared. You earned this result. You do everything with such a steady hand. Simply, Russia is different." There followed a stretch of silence as Eve waited, hoping for a response. Getting none, she just repeated her reason for calling: "Congrats again."

Ivan hung up, pocketing the phone, but the distraction lingered. Kaisa stood a few paces away, her gaze upon the Matisse. Tension was etched into her posture—annoyance visible along her jawline, a subtle glare breaking cover despite the outward calm.

"Ivan," she said, turning to him. "Is work always going to pull you away like that—even here, on vacation, in this... space?" Kaisa's hand rose to her throat, pinching the skin—gently kneading the flesh between her fingers.

She realized her words sounded harsh as soon as they'd left her mouth, but the call had disrupted the moment, and the warmth had escaped. She gave a lot. She'd always given a lot: to her father when he exhibited; to her mother when he died—even more so when her brother left; and to her ex-boyfriend as he stumbled into adult life.

Kaisa just wanted a little consideration in return—at least some of the time. However, what really irritated her was a worry that, yet again, she'd got caught up with someone who was stuck between authenticity and ambition—who could neither decide nor balance.

Ivan could feel the suppressed anger in her, that piercing ache of being let down. "Kaisa, I'm sorry." He tried to apologize and explain. "That was Evelyn, a colleague. She was congratulating me on a promotion—head of our Moscow office."

Kaisa searched Ivan's face. "It's more than that," she said. "You lit up on the news, even as it pulled you away from..." She didn't quite name it. "Ivan, be honest: is that your real world—the corporate one? Is this simply an interlude that makes the vacation more interesting, the experience more memorable?"

The intensity hit Ivan. He took Kaisa's hand, feeling an ache, a compulsion rise in him to draw her closer. "No. That world—it's important, yes, but it's not everything. I want," and here he seemed to answer truthfully, "I want a full life." Kaisa looked at him quizzically.

"Here, with you, I can see it," Ivan continued. "I want to be like Matisse's dancers—free, alive and yet somehow connected, purposeful." He looked into Kaisa's eyes. "I like that structure. I desire that rhythm. I want to share that energy—indeed I want..." His voice trailed off.

"Then prove it," she said—Ivan's words, if anything, fueling her rage. "Show me." A part of Kaisa reflected she had no real claim on Ivan, that she couldn't really make such demands on someone she had met only the day before.

He answered seriously nevertheless. "I'm still caught," he confessed, "within the grind of an office career. I still want to achieve. I can't simply let go."

Kaisa's upset softened a little in the honesty. "It's fine," she said, almost reflexively. She squeezed Ivan's hand. "But wouldn't it be great if we could commit to the dance—beyond just today?"

They stepped away from the room, letting other visitors enter, and as they did so Kaisa studied Ivan again. She suspected that in him lurked the counterweight she desired. Somehow his external conflicts seemed to match her internal ones. They wanted similar things, worried about similar dilemmas. Kaisa believed that they would, as a couple, work well together and be good for each other.

Gradually, they wandered into a smaller alcove near the gallery's edge, where a tall window offered a panoramic view of the city. The solstice sun gleamed across the rooftops of St. Petersburg, the Neva reflecting soft gold as the day inched into afternoon.

Kaisa rested her arms on the window ledge. "It's amazing how this city has altered over the centuries, yet it retains this aura—like a mosaic put together using countless *smalti*: wars, celebrations, revolutions, love stories."

Ivan joined her, leaning on his forearms, peering out at the mesmerizing play of light on water. "True."

"Perhaps," Kaisa ruminated out loud, "that's why it feels so poignant here. Everything about St. Petersburg, the Hermitage, reminds us we're part of some continuum that interweaves pain and joy. People have come before us, left their mark. Briefly, now, it's our turn."

Ivan smiled. "Yes, exactly."

"It's comforting somehow," Kaisa concluded. "Even if our footprints vanish eventually, we join the collective tale, however small our role. We get to be in conversation with da Vinci, Rembrandt, Matisse—with Russia. Just through witnessing their work—by being here—we help to keep the story alive and so, maybe, give it new meaning."

Ivan exhaled. "That's a wonderful thought."

They fell once more into a companionable silence, the city's murmur carried to their ears by a slight draft through the window. In the distance, they caught the faint, short toll of a church bell marking the hour.

They retraced their steps. Each painting they passed seemed to speak anew, as if it had found a fresh voice—even in the brief time since they'd arrived. Ivan noticed the swirl of visitors differently too—how each person paused at certain details, lingered or moved on, pursuing their own unique dialogue with the art. Some ticked an item off their bucket list; others recorded their surroundings as a story to relay later.

They emerged into another grand hall—this one a transitional space featuring a domed ceiling that scattered light like a celestial canopy. Kaisa hesitated. She didn't want the day to end.

"Before we step any further, can we pause to take this in?" she asked, her voice tinged with a mix of sadness and resolve. "I find every part of this building a revelation. The world opens up once more in this room. After compression, the release."

Ivan nodded, and they stood side by side in the center of the hall—the fluted columns rising majestically; the dome overhead projecting shades of blue, flecked with gold-leaf designs. The silence was so complete they could hear their own breathing.

Minutes stretched in a haze, elongated by the gentle mesmerizing swirl of dust motes. Then Kaisa murmured, "Thank you—for..., for sharing all this with me."

Ivan turned, catching her gaze. "I should be thanking you. I might have glanced at these pieces and had a nice time, but I would've finished in scarcely twenty minutes. You helped me engage with the museum, took the experience to a whole different level."

Kaisa offered a small shrug. "Maybe that's what this day was meant to be—a reminder that art is best experienced with an open heart, and if possible, in good company."

Ivan smiled, so widely he worried his cheeks might cramp. "I'd say it's mission accomplished."

A patter of footsteps signaled a small tour group entering from an adjacent corridor. Their guide's voice drifted across, describing some eighteenth-century architectural detail. Ivan and Kaisa exchanged glances—two travelers who'd discovered a hidden oasis and were reluctant to depart.

Eventually, they made their way toward the museum's exit, weaving through the last smaller rooms filled with decorative arts—porcelain vases, intricately carved furniture.

They walked unhurriedly as the inevitability of departure loomed ahead. Daylight spilled through the Hermitage's main vestibule with its wide staircase curving downward. The museum's grand doors were open to the courtyard outside, alive with new arrivals.

Kaisa paused as she exited, glancing back as if to commit the palace and her tour of its galleries to memory. "I feel I could spend a lifetime here and still it wouldn't satisfy me," she confessed, regret coloring her tone.

Ivan gently touched her elbow. "At least we've had this day, and maybe it's not the last. St. Petersburg has a way of calling people back—so my mother always says."

Kaisa dipped her head in agreement. "Then I'll hold on to that possibility. If we both end up staying longer in the city, or if fate draws us here again, we can plan another visit. The museum is massive—plenty left to explore, even after today's experience."

The sun was now low, bathing the Hermitage's pastel-green and white façade in a gentle luminescence. Ivan spotted his mother and sisters waiting nearby, carrying museum pamphlets and shopping bags—energized, laughing.

He waved to them, then turned to Kaisa. "I hope you'll let me return the favor of your Finnish poem with something of my own. You've set a high bar, though."

She smiled. "I'd love that. I'd love to see any sketches or notes you make from today's excursion. Even half-formed, it would be fascinating."

Ivan chuckled. "Then I'll do my best. Maybe I'll try to string a few words together about the *Benois Madonna* or the Matisse."

"I look forward to it," Kaisa looked into Ivan's eyes. "Until then, I'll keep the memory of this day tucked away—like that poem I recited. A reminder—no matter how vast the world might feel, sometimes we stand in exactly the right place at exactly the right moment."

They said their goodbyes with a gentle exchange of smiles, and Kaisa started to drift across the courtyard. Ivan moved to join his family. But then he stopped and raced back to Kaisa. "You know what, if it's meant to be—as you say the right place at the right moment—then let's make a pact." His mind raced.

"Let's meet," he proposed, "on February 10 next year, the anniversary of Pushkin's death, the day of Russian language."

"Okay," said Kaisa hesitantly. "Where?"

"In the Moscow Metro. You know, the beautiful Komsomolskaya Station along the Koltsevaya Line. Let's meet at midday. The platform sits in the center, so we don't have to worry about which side to approach it."

"Okay." She took Ivan's hand, drew him in, and gave him a quick kiss on the cheek. "Okay," she repeated. "If it's meant to be, let's meet there."

"If we're there at noon…" Ivan's voice trailed off.

"Maybe it means we're willing to risk something more," concluded Kaisa.

They parted again, and Ivan turned back to greet his family, who were now approaching him with eager curiosity. They peppered him with questions: about his time in the museum, his conversation with Kaisa, his impressions of it all, of her.

All around them, the Hermitage loomed as regal and grand as ever, continuing to welcome new visitors even at this late hour. Ivan and Kaisa would appear as just another pair of travelers, meeting together and wandering. Yet in his heart, Ivan knew there was something special about their encounter—an intertwining of beauty and emotion and destiny.

That night, back at the hotel, Ivan couldn't sleep. The city was still luminous, and the Neva remained visible behind the curtains. The Scarlet Sails festival had taken place only a few days before, and the white nights wouldn't finish until early July. His mind lingered on Kaisa and the spiraling constellation of memories from the last two days.

The ghostly echo of Matisse's dancers circled somewhere in his mind. He thought of his mother's Pushkin lines and of Kaisa's poem, as if the two women were pulling at him: one offering return, the other direction. Ivan heard his phone buzz, and saw an email from New York.

There would be a call next morning at dawn—such as it was this time of year. He hesitated before opening the message. The corporate world was clawing him back, taking him away from St. Petersburg over the country to Moscow.

Ivan suspected the results of meeting Kaisa would endure and evolve long after he'd left behind the Hermitage and St. Petersburg. What he couldn't figure out was how he would balance his burgeoning interest in Kaisa with his career or its demands.

And what he couldn't know was how quickly any kind of balance would be scrutinized and rejected—how sharply fate, having brought them together, would then redraw the lines between the two of them.

6. An Arctic Deal

High above the icy shuffle of Moscow in winter, on the top floor of a newly erected glass tower, the temporary offices of a New York–based oil & gas firm overlooked the city with its concentric circles and radial arteries. As the sun lowered, it seemed like nothing more than a spiderweb caught in the angular light.

A long table of black steel—sleek and intimidating—dominated the center of its boardroom, commanding attention. Soft indirect lighting, more at home in Taliesin West, glowed across its surface, illuminating letters embossed in gold leaf: PanEnergy.

The interior design was eclectic rather than coherent. Everything was intended to showcase success and status. The architect had sought to demonstrate ambition and focus in the steel and glass; lineage and pedigree in the Art Deco accents; and old-fashioned gravitas in the mahogany and brass.

On the far wall, a high-definition digital display pulsed with international news and global stock tickers, capturing in its pixels PanEnergy's frenetic attitude.

Ivan—the recently arrived country head—stood near the room's entrance facing toward the windows, the subtle lighting strip casting a theatrical glow over him. From his vantage, Ivan felt the capital's potential was almost tangible, as though it might be captured in a single grasp—if only the hand grasping were large enough.

Lean and confident, dressed today in a charcoal suit, he showed little sign of the hectic month he'd just weathered since arriving back in Russia. At thirty-one, he'd already cemented an image for making things happen. Yet, for all the poise, a certain tautness around his eyes suggested he was not at ease.

Already seated and relaxed was Dmitry Petrov, a powerful figure in Russia's hydrocarbon industry. His thick hair, which was more silver than anything else, and the many crevices decorating his face both hinted at an age well into the forties, if not fifties—years spent navigating the intricacies of business at a national level. Men in Russia, Ivan felt, aged faster.

Petrov had grown up among the remnants of a transformed nation—rising from the ashes of the 500 Days Program in 1990 and Shock Therapy in 1992, the failures of which he attributed to America and its special agent of disruption, Jeffrey Sachs. Petrov brought a formidable composure—the imperturbability of someone who'd dealt with every kind of hardship and risk from frontier territories to private ventures to government relations.

The two folders between them on the table bore the title: "Proposed Asset Swap - PanEnergy & VoltaGaz Holdings - African Assets: Angola, São Tomé e Príncipe, and Additional Projects."

A few chairs down the table, near the digital display, polished and bold like everything in the room, sat Eve—Evelyn Marks—PanEnergy's senior advisor for the region. She was dressed smartly in black with delicate red earrings that matched her favorite shade in lipstick and nail polish. Evelyn typed on her laptop, occasionally looking up to measure the temperature of the talks.

Her presence in this boardroom added a touch of awkwardness. Years ago, she and Ivan had dated when he was still new at PanEnergy, working in the U.S. headquarters. Ivan had even gone to visit her parents at their home for a Sunday lunch: a surgeon and his lawyer wife living in Connecticut. They were lovely but driven—he couldn't work out who was the more successful. They competed not just with the world but with each other.

Ivan and Eve had parted, amicably if not smoothly—the accidental result of diverging careers and slightly different interests that they didn't endeavor to patch up. Sometimes Ivan wondered if he had been simply an experiment—he hadn't really fit into Eve's world.

Now, after a two-year posting in Moscow, she had another twelve months left before returning to New York. Meanwhile, Ivan's recent assignment placed them both under the same towering roof.

Evelyn—poised, brilliant, and unapologetically ambitious—performed her role in Moscow with effectiveness and professionalism. Yet the slight tension in her posture and the small glances she threw in Ivan's direction suggested she might be seeing more in their newly crossed paths.

Ivan, however, needed to focus on the negotiation with Petrov. The swap in question proposed VoltaGaz buy PanEnergy's African offshore blocks, in Angola as well as São Tomé e Príncipe, while PanEnergy acquired stakes in the firm's local assets in Russia.

Petrov tapped a finger against the steel table. "Your assets in Africa are promising, to be sure. Angola, especially—fields with potential for deep-water extraction. But let's be clear, those nations come with their complexities. Political risk. Insufficient infrastructure. The occasional brinkmanship from local officials. You can't expect me to ignore that."

"You're right to address it," Ivan replied calmly. "However, we've built relationships with local governments, and we've structured deals that complement their developmental goals. The entire model we've crafted is predicated on stable, mutually beneficial arrangements." He paused.

"True," he continued, glancing at Eve, "there are occasional hurdles, but we've navigated them effectively for many years."

Petrov's gaze measured the thick sheaf of reference work in his folder. "That's PanEnergy's perspective. I'd like to see some risk assessments from a more, shall we say, neutral party. My own team has received a memo suggesting that the current administration in São Tomé might revisit existing offshore concession terms inside the year—to appease domestic pressure."

Ivan shrugged, not dismissively but with the pragmatic acceptance that this was part of the game. "Revisiting terms is something every administration does. The question is whether they'd do so in a way that actually undermines foreign investment—that would sabotage their own broader objectives for economic growth." He looked down for a second.

"More often than not, governments posture—they rarely dismantle existing partnerships, especially those well-established. They tend to protect relationships they know and trust, particularly when technology transfer or local employment is at stake."

Ivan went for a target he knew Petrov would like. "Just think of Australia with its coal, or Britain—which struggles to shut down its steel industry, let alone its aluminum works."

There was a ghost of a smile. "We'll see," Petrov said. "Then there's Angola, where questions of revenue sharing may escalate if commodity prices shift. Again, the notion of a stable environment is subjective. So tell me—what is it, precisely, you want in return? We can see if there is some kind of balance."

Ivan took a measured breath. Here was the pivot. "PanEnergy's aims are straightforward: we want more involvement in your region. You have holdings that include not just Russian onshore sites but new possibilities in Arctic waters." Ivan pointed to his folder on the table.

"We see potential, lots of it, for synergy between your business and ours. Here in Russia your political capital, in securing drilling rights or export corridors, can save us years of bureaucratic hassle. In return—our Africa business gives you a base for expansion overseas; our technology helps accelerate your development plans at home."

Petrov's eyes narrowed—an expression of something that may have been amusement or wariness crossing his features. "So you trade your solid presence in Africa for a gateway into some piece of Russia's great frontier."

Ivan lifted his chin. "We think the payoff for both sides is worth it." From where she sat, Evelyn clicked to a new set of slides, mirrored onto the boardroom's digital screen. Her refined voice interrupted, slow and precise—less about her schooling at Andover, more about her self-confidence.

She knew she could perform—and well. That was never her concern. "These figures show the forecast production for Angola's deep-water blocks. Even in conservative scenarios, the yield turns significant by year four of operations."

Petrov glanced over at her. A shrewd expression crossed his face, as if he sensed more in Evelyn's calm façade than just competence. "Impressive forecasting, Ms. Marks. Have you truly accounted for unpredictability in Angola's regulatory structure?"

She nodded. "Yes. Our scenario planning includes the potential for delays in licensing and even short-term disruptions. We have incorporated various statistical models for risk, including Monte Carlo simulations. We still see a compelling return, a high IRR, for an investor with the right political links. The project also has real option value."

Petrov let his gaze linger on Evelyn, then returned his attention to Ivan. "If these blocks are so valuable, why is PanEnergy giving them up? Why not simply expand your presence in Africa?"

Ivan's mouth twitched in a fleeting smile. "We believe that a strategic pivot is necessary." In fact, PanEnergy in New York had decided that the collapse of oil prices after the financial crisis would give them the sole opening to pursue such a deal—a brief moment when the Russians might accept relinquishing a part of their market, especially new drilling rights in Arctic waters—the sort of access Western companies almost never obtained. They'd seen the Chinese do the same in Australia's iron ore sector.

"We want to concentrate our overseas business," Ivan continued, "and have just a few major world-class collaborations. Partnering with you, here in Russia, allows us to consolidate our strengths and avoid spreading resources too thin. And if we can take a share directly in your firm, then we can still maintain an indirect exposure to Africa."

At that, Petrov leaned back in his chair, lacing his fingers together. "And how do I know you won't unload suspect assets on me, only to withdraw once I'm saddled with the risk?" His tone bore a heavy skepticism.

Evelyn advanced another slide showing a phased approach. "We propose an incremental buy-in," she explained. "You'd start with a partial share, see how the fields develop over two to three years, and expand your stake if satisfied."

She paused before laying out the exchange. "PanEnergy would acquire a minority role in your onshore Russian fields and a stake in your Arctic projects, with the option to escalate that stake depending on performance metrics."

Petrov's eyes tightened. "An incremental approach. Sensible, but still a way to shift immediate burdens."

Ivan stepped in. "We're not burying any traps here. PanEnergy has poured huge investment into these African concessions. We wouldn't do that if we intended to offload them the moment trouble arose. Our plan is to remain involved—by taking a stake in your firm. We gain from your success."

A taut silence gripped the room. Evelyn could feel the intensity simmering. She respected Ivan's unruffled presence in such settings. He was always like this: passionate yet contained, sure of his own analysis—calm, focused upon the right outcome.

She had noticed Ivan first because of his unusual past, his dual nationality—different from what she'd known growing up. But his steadiness, his willingness to keep the line, had subsequently enhanced Ivan's attractiveness.

Now, as she watched him grapple with VoltaGaz, Evelyn couldn't help recalling late nights that they had spent together at PanEnergy's New York office—poring over spreadsheets, bantering about market prices, and occasionally letting their professional fronts slip into something intimate.

Her fingertips moved lightly across her laptop keyboard. She glanced at Ivan, trying to catch his eye, but his focus never wavered from the discussion. Fragments of her old longing needled Eve. She swept them aside, reminding herself he'd made it clear on arriving the two of them should be strictly colleagues.

"After all," Ivan had noted, *"this is the tone of company policy."* Even so, the memory of his words stung. *"We have to keep it professional, Evelyn,"* he had urged. *"Our feelings belong to the past. Our focus, the company, is our future."*

She'd smiled and nodded, outwardly gracious, but privately annoyed. They had enjoyed more, and they could still aim for more. They were a great couple together: his steadiness, her fire. The day might come when company policy was more restrictive, and boards more assertive; but that day hadn't arrived yet.

Eventually, Petrov broke the silence. He studied the image on the digital display, showing the potential yield curve in Angola. "And what of São Tomé?" he pressed. "You know how quickly new governments can change the rules."

Evelyn fielded this question. "We have a close, robust relationship with local authorities. Our legal counsel has hammered out extended concessions with renewal periods that favor stable partnerships. Of course, we cannot give any guarantees. No market truly allows that. We could say the same for onshore sites in Russia, especially if foreign policy shifts."

At that, Petrov's lips curved in a half-smile. "Touché, Ms. Marks. Indeed, we both know how swiftly policy winds can change." He eyed Ivan. "So, I have to trust you won't collapse at the first sign of air turbulence."

Ivan maintained his gaze. "We're ready for turbulence. PanEnergy thrives in it. Consider our track record in other frontier regions. We navigate hiccups and capitalize on them."

Evelyn's voice, clear yet composed, interjected again. "We've run multiple scenario analyses that account for fluctuations in crude prices, local political risk, and infrastructure challenges. Even in our worst-case scenarios, the combined African assets remain profitable over the full life of the project."

"The benefit you'd gain from having us with you," she repeated, "is the local network. The partnerships are not bulletproof, but they are among the most robust."

Petrov's eyes shifted from the display back to Evelyn. He offered a nod that bordered on the courteous. "Well prepared, Ms. Marks. Ivan is indeed fortunate to have you working with him. But you know, as well as I do, that business is never purely about spreadsheets."

Before Ivan or Evelyn could respond, his phone on the table buzzed. Petrov lifted it, glowering. The room's tension, already taut, ratcheted higher as he scanned the message. The lines on his forehead tightened in concentration.

"It seems," he said slowly, setting down his cell phone, "there's some chatter about a new maritime boundary dispute near São Tomé. A reclassification of certain blocks under question. Care to comment?"

Ivan's jaw tensed; he'd heard no such rumor. He felt an involuntary twist in his gut. "I wasn't aware of any new dispute over boundaries," Ivan said dryly. "Are you certain it's credible?"

Petrov shrugged, leaning back in his chair with deliberate nonchalance. "I have sources in certain ministries who keep me abreast of potential developments. These local governments can be fickle, especially if they sense an opportunity to renegotiate."

Ivan pivoted to Evelyn, who was already tapping her phone. She stepped away from the table, voice lowered as she engaged PanEnergy's liaison. A silence stretched over the boardroom, thick with unspoken menace, while Petrov seemed content to watch Ivan squirm.

Finally, Evelyn returned, clearing her throat. "The Ministry of Natural Resources in São Tomé is always in dialogue with neighbors regarding borderlines, something that's been a point of contention since almost the start." She caught the faint curl of Petrov's lip—Evelyn knew his game, perhaps better than Ivan did.

"But our inside contacts say there's nothing new here: anything happening right now will have more to do with administrative housekeeping than a sudden new effort to target and undermine existing deals. We see minimal, if any, threat to PanEnergy's rights."

"That's encouraging," Ivan said. Then, to Petrov, "Nothing new. We'll provide official verification as soon as we receive it. It'll be a non-issue."

Petrov raised an eyebrow. "Minor, perhaps. But I can't build a relationship purely on your assurances. The real world often intrudes on the best-laid plans. And I dislike surprises. If I'm stepping into a region on the brink of a boundary dispute, I need more than a legal guess. I need a guarantee."

Ivan steeled himself. "We can't offer ironclad guarantees any more than you can promise absolute certainty in any of your territories. Energy deals are always built on some measure of risk." He looked directly at Petrov. "That risk is precisely why we all stand to benefit when the gamble pays off. Still, the issue remains: do you want a seat at the table in Africa, or do you allow someone else to claim it?"

The older man studied Ivan intently, a faint respect in his eyes. "You're forthright, I'll grant you that." He tossed the phone aside, leaving it face-down on the smooth tabletop. "But forthrightness alone doesn't close a deal."

Ivan leaned forward with a certain confidence now, but mindful of the end-game. "No. Results do. And we understand," Ivan said.

"Which is why we suggest a phased model: you invest cautiously, verify performance and stability, then expand. We stay with the project at the beginning but as a minority partner, helping to smooth out local politics where we can. Both sides share in the risk—and ultimately the reward."

Petrov mulled it over. He tapped the table, an uneven rhythm that echoed the tension in the room. "I'll entertain the concept. But if the rumored reclassification or new bidders emerge in São Tomé, I reserve the right to renegotiate the terms of this swap."

Ivan nodded. "Fair enough, as long as any renegotiation is mutual. If new sanctions or regulations impede your Europe sales or Arctic expansions, we'd expect the same courtesy from your side."

For a moment, Petrov appeared pensive. "Yes, okay. Let's incorporate some form of symmetrical clause. I warn you, though—if you stall our capacity to access the African market through endless bureaucratic excuses, we'll walk."

"Understood," Ivan replied, resting his hands on the folder. "Let's formalize our next steps."

Evelyn began typing notes with brisk efficiency, capturing every clause. The succinct clacks of her keyboard fell into a regular cadence, her eyes darting between the screen and the negotiators.

Observing her, Ivan fought a surge of nostalgia. Years before, he'd known Eve's energy in more intimate settings. He recalled the two of them brainstorming well past midnight, Manhattan's lights in the background. Ivan remembered the intensity, the laughter—how readily their professional synergy eased into a personal one.

However, after the breakup, he'd chosen to keep that door shut—even though he still recognized a faint tug in his heart and, he thought, a well-controlled yearning in her expression.

Petrov broke into Ivan's reverie with another question. "If we do finalize this, I want a clear timeline for PanEnergy's technical support, especially if we shift more capital to those fields in Angola. We can't be left fumbling about for skills and technology in six months."

"Absolutely," Ivan said. "We can provide you a technical roadmap—Evelyn can share it after the meeting. It highlights how soon engineers can transition their on-site roles to facilitate your entry."

Petrov nodded. "And about the split of costs in the first few years. I would like to suggest a cost sharing agreement—say, 60 to 40 in our favor—till the fields prove themselves."

"We can incorporate cost sharing into the deal," Ivan replied. "Though we'd expect a reevaluation once certain thresholds are met, taking the split back to a level that reflects our ultimate interests."

"Conditional on performance metrics," Petrov clarified. "Yes, I'd agree to that."

Evelyn jotted the details and turned to Ivan, eyes bright. "I'll reflect these points in the final draft. We'll need sign-off from Legal, but it's workable."

"Send me the contract by tomorrow," Petrov instructed. "I have a board meeting in three days. I'd like to provide my partners a finalized version. Then, if they approve, we can sign by the end of the week."

Ivan offered a measured smile. "We'll make it happen."

A strained silence filled the boardroom. At length, Petrov rose, his imposing figure casting an elongated shadow across the floor. "Well, Ivan, you've impressed me. We're not done, but I see potential in this. I just hope your African operations don't blow up in my face."

"We'll do everything in our power to ensure the transition works smoothly. Thank you for the confidence."

Petrov allowed himself a tight grin. "Likewise." He turned to Evelyn. "Ms. Marks, I appreciate your thoroughness. You are the pillar on which this business"—he looked at the logo on the table as though to remind himself—"PanEnergy stands."

She offered a professional nod. "It's been a pleasure."

With that, Petrov collected his coat, phone, and paperwork. His departure left a silence, which the quiet whirr of the heating and the plush carpet underneath the table seemed to accentuate—like the moment after thunder recedes, leaving a stillness charged with both relief and lingering risk.

"That was... intense," Ivan muttered.

Evelyn closed her laptop. "You handled it well," she said, her voice echoing slightly in the room. "Better than I expected. This whole deal—it's complicated. Petrov's not the type to back down if he smells weakness."

Ivan raked a hand through his hair, breaking the composure he'd maintained through the meeting. "You were indispensable, Evelyn. Thank you. He obviously respects you—and the data that you presented kept him on track."

Eve stepped closer, searching Ivan's face. "You're welcome. I—I..." She hesitated, as though weighing how to phrase what she wanted to say. "I'm proud of you, Ivan. Really. Seeing you like this, heading negotiations in a high-stakes environment. It's a reminder of how far you've come since we first worked together in New York."

He mustered a polite smile. "It's been a ride, hasn't it?"

Eve regarded him, her voice growing mellower. "You know, I recall the nights we spent prepping for those small domestic expansions back then. How we'd debate market ideas when the takeout arrived, never quite sure how to end the day once work was done..." A slight wistfulness brushed across her features.

Ivan shifted his stance, careful not to encourage the direction Eve was taking—even as he himself felt attracted to the same memories. "I, too, remember those days fondly," he said. "But they're history now. We've changed. And the times are different."

Eve's eyes hardened, conveying a trace of disappointment. "True. Still, I suppose I had hoped that us being in the same office ... you know, might have brought back a sense of what we had."

Ivan betrayed a hint of regret in his expression. "You're brilliant—fun, smart, adventurous. You challenge the world—you certainly opened my eyes. I'm worried now that I'd simply dim your flame."

He didn't know where to look. "You deserve someone whose life isn't so consumed at the office. And right now I can't offer more than work and fatigue. All my focus is on PanEnergy and its development in Russia. I don't have room for more." He paused again. "I'm sorry. I really am."

Eve forced a small smile, though her disappointment was palpable. "I appreciate your honesty, at least." This city was lonely, and the work unforgiving. She would have welcomed Ivan back into her life; it would have steadied more than just her heart.

The air hung heavy between them—not hostile, but laden with unresolved feelings. To ease the pressure, she returned to a more professional mode. "Anyway, I should finalize notes for the legal team. We still have to include Petrov's changes and reconfirm the African positions."

"Right," Ivan said, collecting himself. "We can't afford to drop the ball. The last thing we need is a second rumor about reclassifications in São Tomé."

"Exactly." Evelyn lifted her laptop. "I'll send the revised document to your inbox tonight, so that you can make sure it aligns with your thinking."

"Thank you," he said, meaning it. "Everything you've done today, everything you've done since I arrived... it means a lot. I want you to know that."

Evelyn nodded, pushing back a strand of hair. "I appreciate it, Ivan. And trust me, I do believe in our work here. It's going to be huge for PanEnergy if we get it right."

They exchanged a final glance—her eyes lingering a bit longer than Ivan's. Then she pivoted and left the boardroom. The door closed, a gentle click, leaving Ivan alone with the receding glow of Moscow's skyline.

The building's silence enveloped him like a cocoon. After a short hesitation, he went over to the wide windows. The city's grandeur stretched out below, headlights tracing their paths along the avenues, the golden dome of a distant cathedral shining beneath the sunset's first embers.

He inhaled deeply, trying to process the swirl of events: the tense negotiation with VoltaGaz, the undercurrent of desire in Eve's voice, his own doubts, the sheer magnitude of PanEnergy's next steps.

A month into his Moscow posting, and already the stakes felt immense. He would soon be juggling more than just Petrov's demands—there'd be local bureaucrats, regulatory challenges, equipment concerns, supply chain issues. And all the while, he'd have to manage the delicate balance with Evelyn, whose professional brilliance he desperately needed and wanted, but whose more personal hopes he felt compelled to discourage.

He went back for his folder, still on the table. Opening it, he flicked through the pages with a decisive speed—scanning the technical annex with its references to Angola's proposed timelines, verifying once more the data on

São Tomé e Príncipe. If everything progressed, if VoltaGaz did sign on wholeheartedly, PanEnergy would be able to recast its entire global strategy.

He closed the file. Tomorrow, he would finalize the details, phone the partners back home, and ensure no curveballs disrupted the fragile equilibrium he and Evelyn had built here. For now, the day's negotiation was done, and victory—albeit an incomplete one—was in reach.

As he stepped away, Ivan wondered how best to navigate the next weeks and months. This was the life he'd chosen: always another deal, another fire to put out. He worried it might come at the cost of everything else—including, possibly, Kaisa...

7. Celebrating in Style

The snow fell in lazy, feathered spirals outside the towering windows of the repurposed Orthodox monastery, each flake a silent witness to the night's excesses. Once a place of solemn devotion, the monastery now bore the weight of modern revelry.

Its grand halls and cloisters, previously echoing with the incantations of prayer, now resonated with boisterous laughter, the sharp clink of crystal glasses, and the muffled thump of bass from speakers hidden in the dark.

The air inside was thick with expensive perfume, cigar smoke, and the faint tang of freely flowing vodka—a heady mix that clung to the skin like an unwelcome embrace. From the walls, saints gazed down sternly, their gilded faces glimmering under the lights, heightening the sense of unreality.

These holy men and women seemed to judge the revelry below in silent condemnation, as though the decadent party unfolding in their midst were a profane mockery of the sanctity they had once guarded.

Ivan couldn't help but feel their gaze upon him, a prickling reminder of the moral ambiguity that threaded through the evening. In this place of former piety, ambition and excess danced a gritty tango, each step revealing with raw intensity the frailties of human desire.

Tonight, the monastery corridors and imposing sanctum were alive with guests celebrating a monumental business deal between PanEnergy and the Russian conglomerate known as VoltaGaz. Billions of dollars in strategic resources, infrastructure, and pipelines would change hands, sealing a new partnership that might alter entire markets for years to come.

It was a success that demanded a celebration as grandiose as the ambitions and the larger-than-life characters who'd orchestrated it. Ivan, fresh from the ratification ceremony, felt the weight of it all—the taut suspense right to the end of negotiations that had teetered on the edge of collapse. Now, amid this opulent chaos, his victory tasted a little bittersweet, shadowed by the moral grayness that seemed the inevitable cost of such pretentions.

In a cavernous hall adjacent to the former nave, chandeliers dripped with crystals, scattering arrows of gold light across a floor polished to a mirror sheen. Beluga caviar gleamed in chilled silver bowls, and smoked fish lay piled in artful designs.

Ice sculptures dotted the trestle tables loaded with food—some carved into the shapes of mythical creatures, fire-breathing dragons or soaring eagles; others molded into the logos of the newly allied corporations, their edges slowly melting in the warm air.

The monastery felt unnaturally hot—a sharp contrast to the bitter cold of Russian midwinter still swirling just outside, where the snow blanketed the world in unforgiving white.

Ivan stood at the center of it all, leaning against a tall marble column veined with gold. Only hours ago, he'd worn a pinstriped suit and delivered measured words in the formal deal between the two sides, his voice steady amid the high-stakes tension.

Now, jacket discarded and tie loosened at the collar, he let the packed heat of the moment swirl about him, a vortex of bodies and voices that pressed inward like the closeness before a storm. Ivan's short hair glistened faintly with sweat.

The room was steadily growing more intoxicated, with vodka flowing more freely than champagne and champagne more freely than cognac—and with expectations flowing wildest of all.

He had chosen whiskey—a tumbler dangling from his fingertips, the amber liquid catching the overhead lights and reflecting back dark copper hues. Ivan sipped, the burn helping to ground him. However, his mind continued to wander.

Standing by his side, letting out a deep laugh that vibrated through the lavish hall like a seismic rumble, was his Russian counterpart: Dmitry, the face of VoltaGaz. Tall, broad-shouldered—a figure with a commanding presence—he exuded the sort of triumphant glee of someone celebrating a final battle, the ultimate conquest, of a prolonged nasty war.

Dmitry wore an expertly tailored midnight-blue suit—better-pressed, sharper-looking than Ivan's rumpled attire. He held a tumbler of vodka with the confidence of a man who had stared down empires. Periodically, he raised it in a boisterous salute to passing colleagues, his movements expansive. His aura was a force of nature—seeming to draw eyes without effort, to influence sentiment without action.

"To partnerships!" Dmitry exclaimed, his voice echoing off the high ceilings. "To frontiers opened and fortunes made!"

The crowd roared back in approval—executives in smart tuxedos, advisors with notepads tucked away for the night, and hangers-on mingling without restraint, their faces flushed with excited anticipation.

The Russian accent that colored Dmitry's impeccable English lent an air of drama to every word, turning simple toasts into grand proclamations. Ivan acknowledged Dmitry's latest toasts with his own glass.

Ivan knew such alliances were fragile—prone to collapse under the weight of economic fluctuations, exposed to betrayal by the shadows of unquenchable ambition. However, tonight was not the occasion to quibble. It was a time to accentuate the positive.

By the windows, where stained glass depicted biblical scenes of redemption and fall, a DJ had set up an impromptu booth, where she mixed dance anthems and electronic tracks that reverberated through the centuries-old stone walls. The bass thumped like a heartbeat—syncing with the crowd's own pulsating movements.

Clusters of international guests moved in languid dances—some all the way from Houston with their Texan accents, others from London with their exotic flair, a few from Singapore with their driven efficiency. Only a fraction of their talk concerned expansions into Russia's north or Africa's reserves.

It was a swirl of personalities and languages—English, Russian, even the occasional Mandarin—a testament to the hardy reach of international business, where deals were sealed not just in boardrooms but in these hazy nights of intense self-indulgence.

From a side chapel along the hall boomed a karaoke setup—yet another incongruous note in this increasingly surreal evening. A small stage had been erected, and the altar now served as the unlikely stand for a screen and microphones. Revelers stepped up beneath an old carved relief to test their courage before a makeshift congregation, their voices cracking under the weight of alcohol and bravado.

At that moment, a slick-haired VoltaGaz executive, his face red with vodka and euphoria, was belting out a raspy version of a classic Sinatra tune—*My Way*, fittingly enough. The lyrics drifted upward and out, mingling—if one believed in ghosts—with the faint echo across time of monks chanting psalms.

Colleagues circled him, cheering with raised glasses, while a PR team busily snapped photographs on their digital cameras, capturing the moment for corporate newsletters or social media posts that would sanitize the excess.

Ivan winced at the absurdity, sipping his whiskey—feeling its warmth spread through him like a slow fire. The entire scene reminded him of another era—those days only two years ago, before the global financial crisis had crashed like a tidal wave. Russia's proud economy had soared on high oil prices, and lavish parties were commonplace for the elite.

He'd heard rumors about such nights—where alliances were forged in the haze of cigar smoke and the fog of whispered promises, where fortunes were partied away in less time than it took to reach an agreement. He had never seen it. Tonight he was witnessing this era resurrected, catching sight for once of the earthiness beneath the glamor: what was exposed when the shell of humanity gradually broke apart.

At his side, Dmitry gave Ivan a hearty smack on the back that nearly caused Ivan's drink to slosh over the rim, the impact jolting him back to the present. "So, my American friend," Dmitry boomed, his breath heavy with vodka, "are you ready for the real Russia now you've signed the deal? This, here, is how Russians celebrate when we win big: without apology, without restraint."

“Apparently so,” Ivan replied, raising his glass in a wry salute, though his mind raced with foreboding.

The Russian let out a booming laugh, which echoed like thunder. “Don’t worry; you’ll learn to pace yourself. Just—don’t let them trick you into a never-ending series of toasts. That’s how they assess you—see if you can hold your own in the storm.”

A woman in a glittering bejeweled fantasy of a cocktail dress drifted over, her hips swaying with calculated allure. She offered them a tray of caviar spoons. Ivan took one and thanked her.

The flavors exploded in his mouth. He savored the briny burst on his tongue that somehow offered a counterpoint to the rich mass of serious tuxedos and sequined dresses around him. Ivan studied the crowd once more—and as he gazed, one figure caught his eye: Irina, senior advisor at VoltaGaz. He could feel her presence even from across the nave. She, like Dmitry, had an almost mystical pull.

Irina, however, was a quiet force amid all the noise, sitting on a plush chaise beneath a grand archway, dressed in a shimmering gold gown that hugged her form like liquid metal. She seemed to float above the party—detached, yet observant—her sharp eyes scanning the room, precise and thoughtful.

Her long black hair fell in a carefully arranged cascade down and over her shoulders, framing a face that blended beauty with an eagle-like intensity. It summoned, unbidden, an image of the Russian Imperial Flag—with its bold, defiant symbols impossible to ignore.

The silver Orthodox cross at her throat simply deepened the impression. Her posture exuded authority, as though every conversation in the room were a puzzle she was slowly assembling, piece by piece.

Ivan found her gaze intersecting with his across the room, a brief lock that sent a prickle down his spine. Her mouth curved in an enigmatic smile. In the dim light, her eyes seemed to offer both invitation and warning, much like the luminous stare of a cat. The whole effect was disconcerting.

Irina slowly lifted her glass in salute, and brought it to her lips with a smooth, controlled grace—never breaking eye contact with Ivan, never spilling a drop.

Irina was rumored to be formidable in negotiations, her intellect a weapon honed through dealings in boardrooms and backrooms alike, adept at reading and exploiting the weaknesses of the unwary, both men and women. Was her acknowledgment now some feint in a larger game?

Ivan recalled glimpsing her fierce intellect during the day's final discussions. She hadn't spoken often, mostly content to watch from the sidelines and strategize. However, her silence had been powerful, and her presence was the kind that made or broke alliances.

"You're being watched," Dmitry now said, noticing Ivan's glance, his voice dropping to a conspiratorial rumble. "Irina is beautiful, *da*? However, be cautious. She is—how would you say it?—a chess player, one who never stops thinking about her next move. In this world, she strategizes steps ahead."

"Duly noted," Ivan replied, his tone light but his mind already churning. Irina's small nod in his direction made Ivan lift his own whiskey in a subtle toast. And yet, as he did so, Irina turned her attention to a person who'd come up beside her, her expression shifting seamlessly into a professional geniality.

Off to the side, the karaoke session reached a temporary climax, the music swelling to a raucous crescendo. A group of inebriated Americans from PanEnergy tried to belt out a famous Russian pop song, stumbling through the unfamiliar syllables with drunken enthusiasm—and much too little embarrassment. The crowd, their faces red, roared with laughter and good-naturedly cheered the effort.

One of the singers glanced in Ivan's direction for rescue, his eyes pleading amid the chaos, but Ivan merely shrugged. This was the cultural exchange that no memo prepared you for—the charged collision of two worlds, where self-respect competed with corporate needs for dominance.

A fresh wave of servers glided through the crowd like ghosts, bearing trays brimming with shot glasses of clear, potent liquid. Ivan marveled at their brash costumes. The aroma of spiced vodka rapidly infused the air, sharp and inviting. Dmitry grabbed one and thrust it toward Ivan with forceful insistence. "Another toast!" he declared, eyes gleaming with an almost manic fervor.

Ivan chuckled, the sound a bit forced amid the mounting pressure. "If I drink any more, my flight back won't be necessary. I'll simply float home."

"Ha! You Americans worry too much about tomorrow. In Russia, we savor the now," Dmitry declared, draining his shot in one swift motion, his experience showing. "Besides, we just sealed a deal that will be talked about for years—live a little, Ivan. Embrace the storm."

Just then Eve appeared in a sculpted red dress and black sash, her entrance sending a subtle ripple, a tremor of curiosity, through the assembly. For a heartbeat, the noise fell away—the sight catching even Ivan off guard. She'd chosen a darker oxblood tone for her lipstick and nail polish this time.

And, Ivan noticed, she'd put on some geometric onyx earrings he'd given her as a present one birthday. The outfit made the green of her eyes shine even brighter, more jewel-like, as they scanned the room.

He found himself marveling again at the coincidence that she should overlap his own posting in this frozen capital. He hoped they could navigate the professional waters without dredging up the past, that it wouldn't get messy. Neither had properly unpacked the tangle of ambitions, interests, and emotions that had accompanied the end of their briefly intense relationship.

As the night wore on, Ivan found himself drawn into more conversations. A London banker clapped him on the shoulder, praising the deal's ingenuity, while a Singapore investor hinted at future collaborations, her words laced with promises that, for all Ivan knew, could be real alliances or future traps.

The heat of the room continued to press in, the air growing thicker with smoke and sweat. Ivan sipped his whiskey—it was his second or third by now—and the eyes of the monastery's saints seemed to pierce ever more deeply—judging not just the party but Ivan's own role in the recklessness.

He couldn't help but feel the weight of their condemnation, their silent scolding that reminded him all such nights ended in consequences. He recalled his mother, who had inherited a fairly strict religious streak. Ivan had never consciously interrogated the implications of this upbringing. Here—facing this party—he wondered.

He felt sure that, even if the new deal between PanEnergy and VoltaGaz led to huge wealth, excessive celebrations like this attracted ill-fortune; they did little other than augur a spectacular downfall—as the history of Rome taught. He only hoped that, when punishment came—as it always did—the penance would not drag him down too.

8. A Clash of Cultures

The party's pulse quickened as the hours slipped by, the initial jubilant toasts giving way to a fiercer, more intense undercurrent that tightened like a noose around Ivan's resolve.

The cavernous hall, with its crystal-dripping chandeliers and melting ice sculptures, now felt like a pressure cooker, the air heavy with the scent of spilled spirits and overheated bodies. The DJ's beats throbbed harder, reverberating off the ancient stone walls, which seemed to shake in their foundations.

The guests had largely shed their professional façades. Their laughter turned sharper, the conversations more confidential, the remarks more pointed, as if the night itself conspired to strip away pretenses, revealing the real bodies, the skeletons beneath.

Ivan remained near the marble column, his tumbler once again empty. Dmitry had wandered off to greet colleagues, his booming voice cutting through the din like edicts.

Ivan's mind couldn't stop churning. The deal with VoltaGaz was sealed, but at what cost? The excesses he was witnessing gnawed at him: careless whispers in shadowed alcoves, raw hedonism skirting legality, the unbridled, almost senseless, chase of indulgence for its own sake.

An image of Kaisa surfaced—and instinctively he locked onto it, as if to a distant beacon. Her promise to meet in the Metro seemed to offer a safe path through the quagmire before him.

He saw Evelyn approach, her steps measured amid the swirling crowd, her red dress clinging ever more tightly in the heat. She carried two glasses of whiskey, offering one to Ivan with a smile. "I remember you like whiskey," she said. A peace offering, Ivan guessed.

Their fingers brushed as he took the glass, a touch that lingered with old familiarity, stirring pleasant memories—and a little unease. "To your triumph," Eve declared, her voice earnest. "You did it, Ivan. Our presence in Russia—the Arctic fields, the pipelines—it's done."

She stopped mid-smile noticing Ivan's earnest countenance. "But you look exhausted, as if you're still carrying the weight of it." She nudged him, gave him a dig in the side. "You've got to celebrate the moments when you can."

Ivan shook himself and smiled. He clinked glasses, the sound crisp amid the chaos. "It's a lot to process—that's all. The party's... relentless."

His gaze landed on a nearby group of executives. He noted Jake Laskin, the company's local director of business development, dressed in a tobacco-brown woollen suit and iron-blue shirt. The suit looked nice but had shaken loose over the course of the evening. Jake was laughing loudly, with a boisterous energy—his arm sliding down a young woman next to him whose minidress left little to the imagination.

Jake's eyes met Ivan's for a moment, registering the silent condemnation, and shot back a look of resentment—anger that had only intensified since he first learned Ivan had beaten him to the desirable Moscow role. Jake saw Evelyn and rolled his eyes. Already tipsy and inclined to have fun for at least tonight, she suppressed a laugh.

Ivan felt the moment as a small betrayal—not of him exactly, of something more general: the principle that decency should be able to survive success. He realized this city would question him not in combat but in conscience. Ivan wondered how Kaisa would handle all this: past relationships, office intrigues, questionable displays of corporate morality. He felt daunted by the impossibility of it all.

Evelyn followed his gaze, interpreting his introspection as something she needed to fix. "Jake's always been a loose cannon. But in Moscow, that's almost an asset. Yulia—you know, Markova who looks after HR—says as much."

Ivan's continued silence encouraged Evelyn to talk more. "Yulia's sensible. Useful to have around. She's all about the company's good, even if it means turning a blind eye." She sipped her whiskey with appreciation, her green eyes probing Ivan's face for a reaction. "You shouldn't get upset about these things. We must work within the system. And this—tonight—what you see before you now, is the system. I'm sure Markova would tell you that poking the bear, as people love to say, only causes trouble..."

Evelyn's attempts to resolve the situation, to lighten Ivan's frame of mind, only worsened his composure. He sensed a weakness in it all—the moral ambiguity behind their ambition, the readiness to succumb, the general lack of interest in finding another way.

"I don't know what to do," he murmured truthfully, his voice low. Eve had always been a confidante since the start at PanEnergy, and he felt a need to unburden himself. "The evening's crossing lines—all I can see is debauchery. Acts that we simply wouldn't tolerate if our own families were involved."

He looked at Eve, almost beseechingly. "It's moving beyond a celebration, and becoming a liability." Again he wondered how he could possibly introduce Kaisa to such a world. "Let's test fate," she'd said. Ivan wondered if seeing this would destroy anything destiny had in store for them.

Eve's hand touched his arm gently. "I know you, Ivan. You're the one who, despite appearances, refuses to bend. You try to make everything right—to make it somehow all fit together. But sometimes it just doesn't." She paused.

The alcohol was slowly stripping away her reserve. "Everyone thinks you're simply one of the guys. But they haven't seen you with your back against the wall—not like I have." She gazed at him.

"Here, bending keeps you in the game." Eve's words carried a plea laced with the barest hint of frustration. Ivan pulled back slightly, the contact stirring old regrets. And the party's intensity continued to press in—a London man he half-knew staggered past, slurring something about "unlimited potential." Meanwhile Dmitry's laugh continued to boom from over the hall, always drawing the crowd. Ivan found it increasingly grating.

And to crown the moment Irina appeared before them, gliding between the revelers, her gold gown dancing. She joined the two of them there—her eyes assessing the moment. "Ivan, Evelyn," she said, her voice a velvet blade, her gaze unerringly grasping their history and tracing its path to the present day with a certain relish.

She studied Ivan with a bluntness that made his pulse quicken, almost daring him to look away and feel a coward for doing so. "Enjoying the fruits of our labor?" she asked him simply.

Not waiting to see Ivan's consternation, she turned to Evelyn. "You should try to calm Dmitry. He's getting a little noisy, and I've noticed, strangely enough, he respects you more than others who are here at the party tonight."

As Evelyn headed off, Irina put her hand on Ivan's arm. Her strong perfume invaded his senses. "Dmitry speaks highly of you, Ivan," she commented. "But," she continued, "I wonder if you're ready for these deeper waters—the compromises that seal true partnerships." She looked at him, waiting for some response. "I think you might be too—how shall I put this?—too brittle."

Her fingers tightened around Ivan's arm. "I'm learning," he replied, coming to his senses, his tone measured. "Give me time." But even as he said the words, he felt inside the doubts continue to swirl and grow. Was this the cost of ascent—sacrificing integrity for the greater good?

Ivan felt increasingly exposed. He'd glimpsed the scale of Jake's resentment. Eve's lingering affection tugged at him, but her talk about Yulia and pragmatism had set him on edge. And Dmitry's constant one-upmanship was rattling him. Ivan worried these various threads wove a web that might ensnare him if he weren't careful. Irina's mix of charm and calculation only exacerbated everything.

Briefly overwhelmed, Ivan excused himself and headed off into the throng, moving a little clumsily—gasping for air. He glanced back and saw Irina watching him, her fingers brushing the Orthodox cross on her necklace.

He spotted Jake again, now deep in conversation with Dmitry, their heads bent close—a sight that spiked Ivan's paranoia. What were they discussing? Would their close relationship complicate his efforts to succeed in Russia?

The music swelled, the bass thumping like a warning. Eve caught up to him near the windows, her expression fraught. "Ivan, wait. About us... I didn't mean to push earlier. This promotion—head of Moscow—it's yours. But I have to say again: It's tough. The assignment demands many things."

She continued, worried that Ivan wasn't listening—not truly. "Results are all-important. You do well here, and the future opens up. Don't let ideals blind you—not here."

Eve's words, sincere and urgent, did nothing either to douse the embers of his old feelings for her or to soften the pain he was experiencing. Ivan nodded dully. He couldn't see anything but trouble as desire and ambition bumped up against reality. "I won't," was all he managed to say.

Dmitry appeared again, having followed Eve across the floor. A part of Ivan marveled at how Eve cast a spell on everyone. He didn't have time to dwell on it, however, as Dmitry gave Ivan's back another big slap and flagged down a waiter.

"One more toast, my friend! To the many storms we'll weather together." The group raised their glasses and downed them in one go. As the vodka burned his throat, Ivan thought again of Kaisa's words: *risk something more.* They echoed in his mind. Was this what she meant—not ambition, but integrity?

9. A Long Night

For the last time that evening, Irina appeared beside him, her sequined dress catching every stray beam of light. Her expression was calm and inscrutable, her dark eyes gleaming, as he realized they always did.

"You look as though you've seen enough of our revelry for one evening." She smiled. "Would you like me to arrange a car? I know your hotel isn't far, but the cold outside is deadly."

Ivan hesitated. He wondered if leaving early would damage his standing—these gatherings often served as an informal extension of the day's negotiations. Then again, it was well past the hour when work finished. Now it was simply a swirl of indulgence, and the night pressed on him.

"Yes," he said, deciding. "I think it's time."

Irina simply nodded, her posture flawless. She caught the eye of an attendant and murmured instructions for a driver. The world around them still pulsed with colored disco lights and the occasional echoes of laughter. They moved toward the exit.

Someone tried to grab Irina's arm—perhaps mistaking her for a waitress, perhaps seeking another drinking partner—but she brushed him off with a polite, if icy, smile.

As he exited, Ivan looked back at Evelyn. She'd taken off her heels and was now carrying them by the straps, her face also lined with fatigue. She appeared far more glamorous tired than he did. Their eyes met and lingered. Evelyn offered him a wan smile of acknowledgment.

Ivan saw a hint of relief in her glance, as though she too had recognized the party's end and welcomed it. Any business had been done, and the evening had crossed into territory neither of them wished to navigate. Ivan gave her a slight nod, his gaze communicating that he understood her exhaustion—and her unspoken longing to escape.

In the background, someone clambered onto the stage for one last drunken rendition of a classic Russian ballad. A few guests clapped half-heartedly, but the energy was at last starting to dwindle.

Ivan and Irina emerged into the chill Moscow night. A mix of car exhaust and building ventilation danced in the glow of exterior floodlights, and a subtle but frigid wind dispersed any lingering clouds of alcohol and sweat hanging in the entranceway.

A polished, black sedan idled by the curb. Irina led Ivan to the passenger door. "After you," she suggested, half invitation, half challenge. He didn't refuse. Irina sat down beside him, her gold gown dazzling, her silver cross briefly visible against her chest as she entered.

The sedan glided through Moscow's snow-dusted streets, its plush leather upholstery and warm interior a contrast to the stark cold of 14°F outside. Ivan sank into the cushion, the celebrations fading in the rearview mirror like a mirage of the night, a fever-dream.

Despite the fresh air, the party's residue clung to him—the sweat on his brow, the smoky tang of cigars in his hair, the accumulated weight of watchful eyes on his shoulders. His whiskey tumbler was long gone, but the burn lingered in his throat. Moscow thrived on blurred lines. He knew that. However, the scenes he'd witnessed were now seared as afterimages in his mind.

He wanted darkness and a chance to recover. But Irina's dress shimmered so brightly. Ivan wondered how it was possible. And her perfume—a floral scent with bold notes of sweet spice—continued to assault his senses, filling their confined space as powerfully as her presence did.

Irina sat with poised elegance, one leg crossed over the other, her hands folded on her lap. Her silence felt deliberate—an effort to calm the night down from the frenzy of the party.

Even so, Ivan's pulse raced—not least from the undeniable heat of Irina's proximity, the dangerous pull she exerted. Ivan worried about her exact intentions. In the monastery's haze, she'd watched him closely, her sharp eyes dissecting his unease amid all the excess.

He shifted, his loosened tie twisting in the collar of his shirt, and glanced at Irina. "Quite a night," he said at last, aiming to get a better handle on the situation. The words felt a little inadequate, a thin shield against the tension coiling in the car.

Irina turned her head slightly, her long black hair catching the interior light. "You handled it well," she murmured, her tone—as always—velvet but probing. "Not everyone can navigate such... excess the first time without losing themselves. But I take it not your style?"

The question hung, as if Irina had already summed up her mark. Ivan's mind raced, replaying the party's gritty underbelly. Could Irina read his thoughts? Could she see his feelings? Or was she simply fishing for gain? A faint buzz pulsed behind his eyes—fatigue, confusion, or something darker.

"I'm not used to celebrations that feel like battlegrounds," he admitted, his voice somewhat gravelly. "The deal's a victory, but the rest—it becomes a liability when it goes so far." He shifted, trying to edge himself away, but the car's confines trapped him.

Irina smiled gently. Was she an ally or adversary? Ivan asked himself. Perhaps both, he wondered, depending on the situation.

"You see it clearly," she said, leaning closer, her hand grazing his as she moved to adjust her gown. The contact was fleeting but sent a shiver through him, a mix of unexpected desire and fierce suspicion.

"But you need to be careful. To paraphrase one of your countrywomen, you're not in Kansas anymore." Irina's advice felt constructively meant. However, her closeness—her warm breath, her overwhelming perfume—challenged him. Was this a test, a trap, or genuine concern?

He noticed his hand resting near hers on the seat, and felt a compulsion to either pull back or draw closer. Both seemed to hold out risks. He kept his hand where it was.

Irina tilted her head, her gaze piercing. "Moscow is a chessboard, and you're a knight—bold, but exposed." She leaned forward, her shoulder brushing his, the heat of her presence continuing to distract him.

"You can lead in Moscow, truly lead—from above. You can give full rein to your ambitions. Russia rewards those who learn not to flinch. And you are capable." She paused, looking him squarely in the eyes. "However, you need more here." Irina put her hand over his heart, pushing lightly. "More heart. You must not end up all alone."

The touch and the challenge hit Ivan squarely. It took him a moment to recover. "I must be myself," he said at last. "Or else something erodes… something essential." He felt the confession exposed him, opened a crack in his corporate armor. However, Irina's gaze softened. Was it a flicker of solidarity? Ivan wondered again.

"You're not like the others," Irina said, her tone softer, almost intimate now. "That's why I noticed you. But survival here means adapting—playing the game." Her hand rested on his for a heartbeat, cool and deliberate, as if no more than an affirmation of her statement and her support. Even so, Ivan's breath caught.

He thought of Evelyn's lingering glances, Kaisa's pure connection—and now, Irina's touch. They all stirred him in different ways. He felt caught in a repeated dance, something primal, an infinite loop between attraction and denial. Part of him wanted to scream—to find a path forward, or be done with it.

Before he could regain his bearings or digest the situation, the car slowed, pulling up to his hotel. The doorman's umbrella loomed outside, keeping away the snow. They got out.

Irina leaned across, her breath against Ivan's cheek, and delivered the Slavic triple kiss—left, right, left—each touch leaving him reeling. "Choose your steps wisely, Ivan," she whispered, pulling back, looking into his eyes. "We'll meet again."

Her farewell caught some echo in him—the way Kaisa, too, had said, "we'll meet again," only with heart and faith instead of calculation. Moscow, Ivan felt, had a way of turning hope into foreshadowing.

And with that Irina got back in the car, her gown whispering against the seat, and the driver shut the door. The sedan vanished into the snowy fog, red taillights fading like a last warning. Ivan stood under the doorman's umbrella for an extra minute, the cold biting through his shirt.

Then, concluding that the night had proven well beyond his capacities, he entered the hotel lobby and returned to his suite. The stillness now felt almost disorienting. The lamps cast golden glows on plush linens, and a tray of midnight treats lay as a gift from hotel management on the oversized desk—fruits, chocolates, a bottle of cognac.

Ivan moved to the window—Moscow's skyline frosted in white. Irina's words echoed. Again he wondered if she would be an ally, or simply part of the machine. He thought of Kaisa, her promise of the Metro meeting, a light to guide him forward.

And all the while, the saints' eyes from the party lingered in his mind, like symbols of judgment, hinting at a betrayal he couldn't yet see.

Even as sleep beckoned, Ivan's mind churned—all the elements swirling and merging into an ominous scene. The deal's triumph felt precarious, his triumph hollow. Somewhere beneath the snow and silence, the city had its truths buried—waiting for someone reckless enough to dig them out.

He sensed danger, as if some monstrous spider, cold and patient as the Moscow winter, rested on some edge of the great city's cobweb structure, waiting to bind him tighter in the threads it had spun.

10. Speaking Up

Morning broke dark and pale over Moscow, still trying to bleach the excess of the previous night. The meeting room at PanEnergy glowed warm underneath the shielded light of an Art Deco fixture that characterized the whole office.

The floor-to-ceiling glass walls would normally showcase the city below. Today, however, the snow continued to beat hard against it—winter in Moscow.

The interior design—a successful mix of American tropes now in fashion—felt worlds apart from the ancient grandeur of the repurposed monastery where, just the previous night, a different kind of spectacle had unfolded.

At one end of the oval glass table sat Ivan Asimov, a rising star in PanEnergy. He wore a three-piece silver-gray suit. Although his posture was poised, tiredness marked his eyes with red streaks and dark rings. The effort to focus tightened his face, a tacit acknowledgment of a tough recovery from the night's decadent celebration.

The memory of it clung to him like a lingering perfume—heady, invasive, and slightly nauseating. Despite the office ventilation, the atmosphere felt stifling.

Opposite him, Yulia Markova, head of PanEnergy's local HR department, radiated a composed sort of authority. Her sleek chignon framed a face of cool elegance, and the sharp cut of her blouse and pencil skirt underscored her efficiency.

Spread before her lay a contract that, in Ivan's state, seemed overly bright—a bundle of papers that outlined his new role. Markova's neat, polished English had a faint Russian lilt, giving a melodic edge to all she said. "As you can see," she was saying, once Ivan had settled.

She tapped a manicured finger on the contract. "As you can see, this role includes greater responsibilities as well as enhanced compensation." Markova pointed out the relevant sections. "We've adjusted the package, the salary and benefits, to reflect your seniority." Aware of the celebrations, Markova paused to check that Ivan was following and that all was clear so far.

"You will receive additional allowances for hardship and travel," she added. "Naturally, living expenses are all paid, and you'll have a dedicated driver; Moscow's roads can be treacherous, especially for newcomers—although, of course, you're not quite a newcomer." She smiled.

Ivan nodded, trying to appear attentive. Beneath the table, he gripped the edge of his seat. He felt a little dizzy. Events from the night before kept playing like a loop in his mind—the opulent chaos of the monastery, the mix of alcohol and laughter, the private rooms offering space for questionable encounters, and the disquieting knowledge that some of his own colleagues had indulged perhaps too deeply in the night's illicit amusements.

When Markova glanced up from the pages, she caught the flicker in his gaze. "You look distracted, Mr. Asimov," she noted—her voice betraying neither sympathy nor judgment. "Is everything all right?"

He hesitated. The standard corporate script called for a polite deflection, maybe an innocuous reference to his hangover, the pressing demands of business. But a part of him—one that had propelled him through the ranks—refused to keep silent.

"Actually," he said, choosing his words with care, "there is something. About last night's celebration."

A subtle shift entered Markova's gaze, like a door quietly swinging: open or shut Ivan couldn't tell. "I'm listening."

Ivan's heart thudded as he sat forward, hands braced on the glass tabletop. "Look, I understand the reason for last night's party. Finalizing the deal, turning us into a player in the Russian market, was a massive achievement, and I'm proud to have contributed. But what I witnessed last night..."

He paused, scanning the room's sterile surfaces, as though seeking validation from their icy precision. "Some of the senior executives engaged in behavior that wasn't just risky—it was unprofessional. The kind of conduct that, if it got out, could tarnish reputations, compromise deals, and destroy careers."

Silence stretched between them, a taut thread. Markova regarded him with an inscrutable expression, dark eyes steady. Encouraged by her quiet, Ivan pressed on.

"This is a professional environment, or so it should be, with a clear set of company policies," he continued. "People look up to these leaders. If employees see their executives disappearing behind closed doors for, shall we say, questionable entertainment, it sends the wrong message—and it compromises us when dealing with our partners. I'm concerned about the moral and legal implications. If a scandal erupted—"

Markova lifted a hand, halting his words. Her manicured nails gleamed in the artificial light. "You're direct, indeed bold, in speaking up," she said, voice pitched low. "Most would not, especially not in this city, at this level."

He drew a measured breath, pulse fluttering. "I'm not trying to be bold for its own sake. But this can't be healthy for anyone—especially for a company like PanEnergy, which has just landed one of the largest deals in its history."

A glimmer of something passed across Markova's face—amusement maybe, or something akin to curiosity. "Mr. Asimov," she said, an almost imperceptible upturn gracing her mouth, "do you know why PanEnergy's board recommended you for Moscow, why VoltaGaz welcomed it?"

He opened his mouth to answer, his mind flashing to reams of performance evaluations, praise for his negotiations, the trust that the board in New York had placed in him. "Because of my work on this project," he ventured.

Markova placed her elbows on the table, steepling her fingers. "In part, yes. Your skill in orchestrating the deal was remarkable. But there's more. We see you as someone able to navigate complexities—a leader able to manage the inherent contradictions of a market like Russia, particularly given your background, your upbringing. You must understand: business here isn't the same as in New York. The rules are subtler—the lines are more nuanced."

Ivan felt a ripple of frustration. "I get that cultural differences exist. But there's a clear line between adapting to local norms and ignoring ethics altogether."

Markova's smile broadened, though it held no warmth. "Ethics. A fine word. But whose ethics? Yours? The board's back home? The Kremlin's? In this arena, many consider 'ethics' a luxury. A first-world problem, they might call it. A Westerner's effort to keep the rules of the game in his favor."

"Then perhaps they've lost sight of something important," Ivan said, his words coming out sharper than intended. "We can't just discard integrity because it's inconvenient."

"Did you ever read *The Chrysanthemum and the Sword*?" Markova asked. Ivan shook his head.

She sighed, tapping the contract. "Your conviction is admirable—truly."

"But consider this," she went. "You talk of moral codes and reputations, yet our reality is that deals in the Arctic, or anywhere in Russia, depend on relationships built on trust, loyalty—mutual obligation. The executives you saw indulging last night, they understand."

She looked at Ivan again to make sure he was still following. "They know the local players, the politicians, the unspoken rules; they are treading the paths expected of them."

"That doesn't make it right," Ivan retorted, heat creeping into his voice.

Markova eyed him for a moment, impassive. "I never said it did. But it might be unavoidable. My advice: choose your battles carefully. You must decide which battles are worth fighting. If you try to confront and expose these men, you might find yourself outmaneuvered." Ivan let out a snort, mocking the suggestion.

Markova continued regardless, "This city does not react well or kindly to moral crusaders, especially local ones; and you are not truly seen here—how shall I put it?—as an American. You should watch that film, the one with

Baryshnikov—a long time ago. *White Nights.* You should watch this film if you haven't already seen it."

A knot tightened in Ivan's stomach as he recalled some of the debauchery from the night before: a senior colleague, red-faced and almost giggling, vanishing into a side room, returning his clothes in disarray. He forced the image away. "So, I'm to ignore it?"

Markova angled her head, posture shifting as she leaned forward. "I'm telling you that if you stir trouble, you may not just lose alliances—you could jeopardize everything, including your position here. PanEnergy is counting on your subtle, diplomatic touch. The newly signed deal is precarious. Internal fighting, however valid, could unravel long months of negotiation."

Bitterness coiled in Ivan's chest. He recognized the subtext: stand down, or risk your career and achievements. The thought stung. He'd built his status making tough calls—not skirting them. Yet a threat was there. "I'll take that under advisement," he said a little too stiffly.

Her mouth tightened, acknowledging his discomfort. "Very well. Now," she said, shifting tone—keen to conclude. "Let's finalize the contract details." Markova slid the papers forward, pointing to specific clauses. "For instance, here's your updated salary figure reflecting local allowances. Here's the language concerning your additional benefits. Does it appear to be in order?"

Ivan skimmed the text, the words out of focus as his adrenaline ebbed and headache reasserted itself. He tried to read, seeing references to an expanded budget, a personal driver, health coverage in a place known for bureaucratic mazes. All the perks of a leadership role to sweeten the burdens.

"Yes," he managed, "the numbers are in the range I was expecting."

"Excellent," Markova said, her demeanor entirely businesslike. "You'll note we've also structured performance incentives around continued growth in our Russian footprint and progress on the Arctic initiative in particular." She paused.

"Achieving certain outcomes will trigger bonuses, stock options—those sorts of benefits." She tapped a final paragraph, then halted, meeting his gaze squarely. "This is your next step up the corporate ladder, Mr. Asimov. A big step. But it doesn't guarantee anything."

She reorganized the papers into a neat document. "I hope you have the resolve—and the pragmatism—to keep ascending."

Ivan breathed in slowly. "I appreciate the opportunity."

"And PanEnergy appreciates your talents," Markova said smoothly before standing.

"Sign here, initial there." She handed Ivan a gilded Montblanc pen, a relic from some prior ceremony in earlier days. He accepted it, hands hovering over the dotted lines. His mind returned to the swirls of vodka, the music, the doubtful gatherings of the previous night. He wondered: Was this the price for success—turning a blind eye to moral hazard, to gray zones? Had it always been like this?

Still, he set the pen to paper, scrawling his name in decisive strokes. The act felt strangely intimate—less a signature than a surrender. The pen's scratches seemed to have a finality about them. Every contract was a covenant, but this one seemed more than a simple transaction. It was almost a confession, an admission.

He set the pen down, blinking at the paper now with his signature. Markova nodded, sliding the document away. "Congratulations. It's all done. Your driver will be at your disposal immediately. You have a meeting with Petrov, yes?"

"Yes," he said, voice taut. "I do."

She offered her hand, and he shook it. Her grip was cool, solid, unwavering. "You've proven you know how to navigate the storms, Mr. Asimov. But do not forget: a storm can also be harnessed if you understand its force."

With that, she stepped around the table, leaving Ivan to gather his thoughts. He heard the door hiss open. Before it slid shut, Markova turned. "Let me say this. Moscow is bipolar. It respects power, tramples weakness. It rewards ambition, punishes naivety. It chews up the nice, the conciliatory, the good without mercy. The result is everything."

She held the door open a moment longer. "You're here to lead, but first you must learn. Leadership isn't universal. What offends you may be how things get done. It's a dangerous game—sure. Yet it's the only one we have."

The hush that followed Markova's exit pressed against Ivan's ears, an almost mocking silence. Rising from his chair, he moved to the panoramic windows. He felt, for the first time, the full isolation of his new rank.

As the snowfall ended, the skyline of Moscow emerged below—sun breaking through to light up gilded spires and slate towers standing in stoic defiance against an unusually tough season. Just last night, he'd glimpsed the private forces driving this city. Now he had a contract binding him more deeply to those same forces—ones that swirled continuously in the dark, unseen, and—he imagined—ready to exploit any sign of hesitancy.

He placed a hand on the cool glass, watching his breath create an irregular circle—almost amoebic, he thought. The memory of the partying executives haunted him like an unwanted specter.

He considered Eve and her ambitions, Dmitry with his love of the spotlight. Yet it was the solitude that awaited him when he walked away from all the opulent chaos that unsettled him the most. Yulia's words echoed: *You must decide which battles are worth fighting.*

Outside, a gust of wind rattled the windows, flinging needles of snow across the glass. They sounded unusually loud, and he flinched. Ivan could sense the precariousness of his position—as though standing atop some ledge on a skyscraper, the potential for relief or ruin awaiting his decision.

The city beckoned below, ancient and modern, layered and alluring. Would he step back—or step off?

It was near midday on February 10—the anniversary of Pushkin's death—when Ivan stepped onto the marble platform of Komsomolskaya Station on the Koltsevaya Line of Moscow's Metro system. The subway pulsed with ceaseless energy—a symphony of echoing announcements, rumbling trains, and shuffling commuters in winter coats.

Grand baroque-inspired pillars rose like silent guardians, gilded mosaics celebrating Soviet triumphs gleaming above ornate chandeliers. The air carried a metallic tang, mingled with the damp scent of old stone and the faint, acrid bite of rusting machinery. Ivan clutched the strap of his dark leather case, his breath steady but his mind churning.

According to the station's large clock, it was 11:43 a.m. Kaisa had seventeen minutes, depending on how you counted the crawl of time in a place like this. They'd agreed on noon—a precise pact. He checked his vintage Omega watch, the one he'd bought in New York after his first big promotion at PanEnergy, and felt his chest tighten. The minutes dragged, amplifying every hope and doubt.

At the Hermitage last summer, standing before Rembrandt's *Return of the Prodigal Son*, Kaisa had teased him: *You look like a planner—structured, purposeful. But when do you take a chance on the unknown?* Afterwards, in a moment of impulsiveness, he'd proposed this midday rendezvous on February 10—half-serious, half-defiant against her gentle pigeonholing, her annoyance at his work interruption.

And she'd agreed, with that amused bow of her head, that deep laugh which had unraveled him since their first encounter. *If we're there at noon,* she'd said, *maybe it means we're willing to risk something more.* The agreement felt more sacred than any boardroom deal.

Yet all morning a whisper gnawed at him: *What if she didn't show?* No contact number, no email—he was acting on faith and hope. A Finnish woman had smiled and laughed, and in doing so pierced his guarded world.

Another train roared in, screeching metal on metal, the high-pitched wail now scraping his nerves. Ivan stepped back, letting passengers flood the platform: men with cases, women cradling bouquets for home or as tributes to Pushkin, families navigating the underground labyrinth. None was Kaisa.

As the train departed, a gust ruffled his coat, carrying the chill deeper into his bones. 11:47 a.m. He shoved his hands into his pockets, fingertips brushing the small velvet box. Crazy, too soon. And yet the lure of *maybe* had gripped him.

His mind, unwilling to idle on hope alone, drifted to the shadows that had trailed him these last weeks. PanEnergy's Moscow office had turned a bit strange after that wild party. He'd witnessed too much. And Jake Laskin had been among the worst—red-faced, staggering with a woman on each arm, giggling like a schoolboy, tie askew.

Ivan had pulled him aside once, murmuring a warning. Jake had laughed it off: *Lighten up, Ivan. This is how it's done here.* Ivan realized later that Jake had not welcomed or forgiven the criticism, his face screwed up in a mix of anger and resentment whenever he believed Ivan wasn't looking.

The next day, hungover and haunted, Ivan had gone to Yulia Markova. He had laid it out—as gently as he could, without names at first. And Yulia had listened, her expression a mask of calculated professionalism.

Ethics, she'd replied, *is a fine word. But whose ethics? In this arena, it's a luxury.* She'd warned him: *Choose your battles.* Yet he'd pressed, pointing obliquely at Jake, insisting the firm couldn't afford the risk.

Yulia had sighed, steepling her fingers. It wasn't what she'd wanted to hear. *I understand,* she had said. *But remember, Ivan, leading here isn't the same.*

Since then, the atmosphere in the office tower had shifted. Whispers in the corridors, sidelong glances during meetings. Jake avoided him, his usual boisterous greetings replaced by curt nods, his eyes shadowed. Had Yulia spoken to him? Or maybe worse, had Jake heard through the grapevine, believing Ivan not just a rival, but a threat?

Jake had a vast network in Russia, beginning with Dmitry. His role put him into daily contact with entrepreneurs, companies, authorities. His sociability made him likable to everybody. One word from him to Dmitry—or others at VoltaGaz—and things could sour fast.

Dmitry—that towering Russian counterpart with his booming laugh and midnight-blue suits—had slapped Ivan's back at the party, toasting their alliance. But Dmitry thrived in the gray zones, his conglomerate built on unspoken compromises. If Jake confided in him, or if Yulia felt Ivan's intemperate crusade jeopardized the partnership… Ivan shivered, and not because of the platform's draft.

Then there was Eve—Evelyn Marks, his ex, now his colleague in this frozen world. She'd approached him at the party, her red dress hugging curves he once knew intimately, her green eyes alight in the flames.

"Seeing you like this," she'd said, "it reminds me of New York." He'd rebuffed her gently, insisting on professional boundaries. "My life's about PanEnergy now," he'd told her. "I don't have space for more." Her disappointment was palpable, a wounded pride that lingered in her gaze during briefings.

Eve handled the data—local research, field reports, sensitive projections—all the files that could twist into evidence if someone sought leverage.

Was she upset enough to turn against him? Or worse, could she somehow align with Dmitry, who'd always eyed her with appreciation? Evelyn knew Ivan's vulnerabilities; a scorned associate in this cutthroat world could be deadly.

11:52 a.m. A knot tightened in Ivan's stomach. He scanned the platform as unease crept in like a chill. Was that man in the scarf lingering too long? Was the teenager tapping his phone signaling? The city's ancient spires and slate towers above ground seemed to conceal a network of surveillance below. Ivan felt Moscow's underbelly pressing closer.

Yulia's words echoed in his mind: *If you stir trouble, you may find yourself—unfairly or not—outmaneuvered.* She'd signed his contract that day, but her eyes were cold by the end.

Ivan knew Yulia prioritized the company's good—PanEnergy's footprint in Russia, their billions in the Arctic. A troublemaker such as him, fresh from New York with his American ideals, could unravel it all. If she saw him as a liability, whispering to Dmitry or others... He imagined Yulia in her office, weighing options: *Ivan's conviction is admirable, but impractical. Better to sideline him before he causes real damage.*

This wouldn't be so extraordinary to imagine. Ivan had seen it happen elsewhere where cohesion was a priority—discussions regarding foreign executives in Japan.

The floor vibrated with another approaching train. Ivan squared his shoulders, heart pounding. What if this was all connected? His complaint rippling out, alerting Yulia's pragmatism, shaking Jake's indulgences, needling Eve's pride. Somehow, for reasons of his own, Dmitry might get involved—seeing a power play, a new lever for future machinations.

And a deal as big as theirs didn't tolerate loose ends. Would Dmitry see Ivan as a risk? He felt exposed. The Soviet heroes on the ceiling appeared to condemn his protest against the country's traditions and feats—while at the far end of the platform a bust of Lenin stared his way, ready to pass judgment.

11:55 a.m. He exhaled. The wait for Kaisa wasn't simply romantic; it was a lifeline amid the storm. She represented an alternative path, something pure, untainted by boardrooms and fights. But even here, doubts gnawed. Would she really enjoy his life? What if his troubles spilled over and affected her?

No. He pushed the thoughts down, focusing on the clock. Five minutes... The platform buzzed—lives intersecting in a constant but inchoate rush.

And still the shadows lingered. Jake's flushed face at the party, Eve's glances, Yulia's steely advice, Irina's ambiguous presence—they all formed a noose, tightening with each tick. Dmitry's toast rang hollow now: *To new frontiers!* But whose?

Ivan glanced over his shoulder, sensing eyes on him. Was this just a sudden paranoia, or instinct? In this city founded on power and ambiguity, trust was a luxury he could no longer afford.

11:58 a.m. Two minutes. The velvet box burned in his pocket—his lone point of certainty in the shifting dark. He would propose, damn the risks; seize the unknown, exactly as Kaisa had challenged.

Yet as the next train screamed into the station, he felt the weight dragging him down: PanEnergy's strange turn wasn't coincidence. It was a signal.

The ornate series of Soviet heroes and martyrs, in their configurations of *smalti*, shimmered above him like a jury. He knew every choice carried a price. The question was, who would determine the consequence?

Ivan told himself it was crazy to ask—too soon, too bold. Nevertheless, he couldn't resist. If she felt even a fraction of what he felt, maybe they could imagine a new world together, something liberating as the first Soviets may have felt. But if she laughed—or if she never arrived at all...

12. Kaisa

The loudspeaker announced another train. Ivan quivered. Could Kaisa have changed her mind—or had something happened? A family illness, perhaps. A delay. Maybe she was elsewhere—on another platform. Moscow's Metro was famous for its grandeur but notorious for its ability to confuse tourists.

However, a voice inside him insisted that if she truly wanted to come, she'd find the right exit, the right platform, the right moment. And if she didn't... well, maybe that was answer enough.

The sense of finality felt daunting, as if an invisible hourglass trickled its last grains of sand. He stepped closer to a platform column to avoid the crowd, to calm his racing pulse. Overhead, many in the city were taking a moment to remember Pushkin and mourn his death. Underneath, it was all about a small private gamble.

11:59 a.m. The floor vibrated with the arrival of another train. The clock hand ticked forward, second by second. Ivan clenched his fists. The train's doors slid open, and passengers poured onto the platform. This time, he resisted the urge to push forward. If she was there, she'd find him. He tried to steady his breathing, counting silently: One... two... three...

Then, through the swirl of movement, he glimpsed a slender figure with pale blonde hair carrying a small tote bag. Her eyes darted over the station, searching. A hush pressed against Ivan's ears. A surge of hope shook his balance. Ivan stepped away from the column, willing it to be her.

Kaisa. There she stood in a thick cobalt-blue coat, a color that enhanced her eyes and, he noticed once again, her nails. She'd paired it with a white scarf and dark cerulean pants. The ensemble looked simple but striking.

The crowd parted just enough for her to see him. Their gazes locked—her eyes meeting his with relief and welcome. She navigated through the crowd. By the time she reached Ivan, the overhead clock had shifted to 12:00 p.m. exactly.

For a heartbeat, neither spoke. Around them, the station buzzed as countless lives went about their midday tasks, oblivious to the charged moment unfolding beneath the chandeliers and Soviet mosaics. Ivan's chest tightened in pain, a mix of extended anxiety and now raw joy.

"You're here," he managed, voice taut with amazement.

Kaisa's smile was soft, tinged with something uncertain. "I nearly got lost," she admitted, lifting the tote in a small shrug. "Komsomolskaya is... big. I grew worried I'd miss you."

Ivan laughed, the sound a release of pent-up tension. "I was about to lose my nerve." Then, more quietly: "I'm glad you came."

Kaisa's gaze wandered over Ivan's face, then back to his eyes. "Me too," she said simply. The swirl of passing commuters forced them closer. He caught the faint scent of winter mint, perhaps from her hair.

For a second, neither spoke. The question hung in the subway breeze: *What now?* They'd set up this meeting as a test—of faith, of commitment—of readiness for something bigger than just a fleeting conversation in a museum hallway.

Kaisa took a measured breath, as though steeling herself. "We talked about it at the Hermitage, you remember? That moment when you decide to see if life can mirror art, if we can break from the conventional scripts we're prone to follow. So," she hesitated, "what's next?"

Her words echoed the points Kaisa had made before, the gentle prodding about his future. Ivan swallowed, feeling the weight of the tiny box in his pocket. But he decided to hold back. *Not yet.* "Maybe you could help me figure that out," he said, aiming for a lightness he did not feel.

Kaisa regarded him with a half-smile. "That's a tall order, Ivan Asimov."

"We don't have to decide everything now," he said, voice low. "We can... start small."

Behind them, another train came and went in a swirl of air and screeching metal. Another wave of passengers left the platform, scattering into the station's vast halls. Despite the constant tide of people, Ivan felt curiously alone, insulated by his focus on Kaisa—just the two of them—as though suddenly transported back into a corner of the Hermitage during the height of summer.

"Okay," Kaisa murmured. "I've got the rest of the day free." She glanced at him, a brightness in her eyes. "Would you like to leave the station and find somewhere quieter? Maybe lunch, or just a walk by the river?"

Ivan felt a dizzy swirl of relief. "Yes—yes, I'd like that."

In the lull that followed, he noticed her hand trembling slightly, perhaps from the cold or the enormity of this leap they were taking. Without overthinking, he reached out, gently threading his fingers through hers. The soft feel of her skin sent a current through him, a reminder that some connections transcended logic.

A final glance at the station's clock revealed it was only a few minutes past noon. The rest of their lives, or at least the next chapter, lay just beyond these subterranean walls. Now turning his back on Lenin's bust and weaving carefully through the waves of people, Ivan left behind judge and jury. Together with Kaisa, he ascended the grand marble steps leading back out and into the world.

The velvet box inside Ivan's coat remained a silent witness to his hopes and fears. There would be a right moment, and he would know when it came—when the bond between them felt powerful enough to bear the weight of his question. For now, the victory was she'd come. Kaisa had chosen to meet him in a place as resplendent and complex as the feelings within his chest.

They emerged out of the cathedral of the Metro and onto the bustling Moscow street, the bright cold of midday enveloping them. The wind conveyed a lingering chill, and city traffic bustled between the grandeur of Moscow's buildings. Kaisa paused, drawing in a breath. "Where to now?"

Ivan couldn't resist a grin. "I have something... unexpected in mind. This way."

Not yet ten when his parents fled Russia for New York state, Ivan had grown up straddling two worlds. At home, his parents spoke Russian and upheld certain old Soviet values. Outside, East Coast traditions shaped his schooling, and a certain preppie culture shaped his early ambitions.

Returning to Moscow for PanEnergy's expansion had stirred something in him, something he hadn't suspected—a longing to reconnect with the roots Ivan only half-recalled. Coming to St. Petersburg for his mother's birthday, seeing her love for the motherland, meeting Kaisa at the Hermitage—they'd catalyzed within him a new sense of purpose.

Parked at the curb stood a sleek, vintage-black Chaika limousine, its chrome accents gleaming dully under the overcast sky. Kaisa's eyes widened in astonishment. Ivan opened the door with a slight flourish, heart pounding as Kaisa slid onto the leather seat.

"This is not quite what I expected," she said, an undercurrent of laughter in her voice. "Where on earth are we going?"

"You'll see," Ivan replied, entering from the other side. He shut the door, and the driver, an old local who'd grown up on the outskirts of the big city, gave a courteous nod before merging into the traffic.

They went onto a highway, and soon the frenetic energy of Moscow's center gave way to quieter districts. Ivan stole glances at Kaisa as the journey progressed, her profile lit softly by the car's interior lamps. She gazed out at the passing scenery, curiosity mingled with a touch of apprehension.

"This isn't lunch in the city," she observed wryly.

He smiled. "No," he admitted. "I'm hoping it's better."

The limousine sped along the route until eventually they turned off and began more sedately along winding side roads heading deeper into the countryside. At last they found a narrower lane with birch trees lining its sides. A short drive farther and they reached a traditional-style Russian country house, a dacha, its welcoming lights already shining in the early dusk—like a promise.

Ivan felt a burst of pride, but underneath his nerves were jangling. He had gone to tremendous lengths to get this property. His parents used to visit during the mid-1980s; the stories they'd told had fueled his imagination. He could just remember it himself.

He was keen to find the dacha again after relocating to Moscow. He thought it perfect for today—a thread of continuity with his parents and a piece of old Russia he could share with Kaisa.

***

When the car stopped, Ivan hopped out first and opened Kaisa's door before the driver could get there. Ivan offered his hand. The cold air whipped his cheeks but a cozy, amber light spilled out the dacha's windows promising salvation inside.

Kaisa's wide-eyed expression spoke volumes as they went through the door. The warmth embraced them like an old friend waiting for their arrival—a blazing fire crackled in a stone hearth, its shadows dancing across the floor.

The interior combined a wonderful mix of aromas: from the cooking that had taken place, from the birch in the fireplace, from the pine that entered with them, escaping from the woods that encircled the dacha.

"You did all this?" Kaisa asked quietly, surveying a table laden with pirozhki, smoked fish, duck, cabbage, a bottle of chilled vodka. Ivan shrugged, attempting to look casual even as his pulse hammered. "It was a little tricky, but... it was more than worth it."

"And," he added as a woman appeared from the kitchen, "of course, I had a lot of help from Natasha here." The woman smiled, and after putting some bread on the table, returned behind the kitchen door.

Kaisa's eyes shone. "Ivan, this is... incredible," she said, voice quiet with wonder.

They shed their coats, and Kaisa hung up her scarf. Once again, Ivan was struck by her figure, her sense of style. She had this aura, he couldn't describe it any other way, that bewitched him. Kaisa's dark blue shirt and pants played off the earthy colors around them: the honey-brown and chestnut of wood, the cream of painted fixtures, the pale flax of handmade curtains.

She went over to the table, as if needing to confirm it was real. Ivan fetched two plates and laid them out.

Once they'd sat down, he poured small glasses of vodka. "To unexpected journeys," he said, lifting his glass. Kaisa returned his toast, eyebrows arching playfully. "And to surprises," she said.

They sipped, letting the liquor's heat spread through them. The meal was straightforward but comforting—a taste of traditional Russia. Kaisa listened, enthralled, as Ivan spoke about his earliest memories, his childhood in New York, his trips to the lakes.

He explained how being here in Moscow felt like reconnecting to a legacy he'd barely understood—what he'd inherited from his parents, from their tales and old songs, their superstitions, their love of literature. She watched as he ran his finger along the rim of his glass and talked about poetry.

He paused more than once, hand brushing his pocket where the small velvet box lay hidden. *Not yet,* he kept telling himself. She was leaning forward, curiosity brimming in her gaze, so he recounted how he had tracked down the dacha. "My parents came here ages ago," he explained. "A quiet spot where they could dream about a different life. It took me weeks to find the current owner and strike a deal."

When Kaisa looked at him quizzically, Ivan replied. "He gets a month at my apartment in New York, and I get tonight here with you."

She laughed—a rich, clear sound. "You're full of surprises, Ivan." The hint of admiration in her voice emboldened him.

After dinner, he cleared the dishes and beckoned her outside. "There's one more thing, but you'll need to layer up." Kaisa followed him, bundling once again into her coat and scarf, her breath condensing into white puffs as they exited into the sharp cold. A large bonfire blazed nearby, ringed by wooden benches on which lay piles of fur blankets.

"Did you plan this too?" she asked, awed.

Ivan nodded, patting a bench for her to sit. They nestled under a thick blanket, the heat of the flames casting shadows over their faces. Beyond the fire's glow, the sky gleamed under scattered clouds and stars. For long minutes, they savored the hush—a stillness punctuated only by the crackle of burning logs and the low hoot of some night bird serenading them in the distance.

Finally, Ivan turned toward her, heart hammering. "Kaisa," he murmured.

She met his gaze. "Yes?"

He slipped a hand into his coat pocket, fingers curling around the velvet box. His throat felt tight, but a surge of conviction pushed him onward. "I know this might feel sudden," he began, voice low and earnest. "But every time I'm with you, I realize how much I don't want to let you go."

Gently, he produced the box, opening it to reveal a slender ring with a single diamond sparkling in the firelight. It had been his mother's engagement ring, and at least her mother's before that. He drew a breath—the swirl of cold air and bonfire smoke stung his eyes. "Will you marry me?"

For a heartbeat that felt like an eternity, Kaisa stared at the ring, her face a blank—the flames suddenly intense, the shadows suddenly deep. Ivan worried for a second he could no longer see her eyes. *Was Kaisa in doubt? Had he misunderstood?* Then her face brightened into a soft laugh, overflowing with tenderness. "Ivan, yes," she whispered. "Yes—of course I will."

Relief and elation coursed through him as he picked up the ring and slipped it onto her finger. He pressed his forehead lightly to hers, overwhelmed by the rush of feeling. The bonfire glowed and crackled, brightening their small space.

An occasional pop from the resin or moisture trapped in the wood seemed like fireworks; the stars behind the clouds like blessings. In that instant, all the tensions of Ivan's business life, the swirl of doubt that had haunted him on the Metro platform dissolved—replaced by the generosity and love he'd found in Kaisa's acceptance.

They stayed like that for a moment, cocooned in shared awe, until another crackle of the fire coaxed them back to reality. Kaisa raised her hand, twisting the diamond so that it caught the light, and smiled at Ivan with a quiet joy. "This is our new journey," she said.

Ivan nodded, his heart brimming. "Yes," he replied.

They huddled closer against the chill, staring into the fire. For an instant, as the wind hissed through the pines, Ivan thought he heard something—perhaps a faint echo, like the creak of distant rails. The sound vanished, but it left him with the odd sense that the world was still out there, waiting.

A gentle snowfall began. They laughed, gathered the fur rugs, and moved indoors.

13. The Scarf

They went across the room and dropped their fur rugs into a loose heap before the fireplace. The commotion raised a faint, earthy aroma, which mingled with the wood smoke.

Natasha had cleared away everything that remained on the table although left the candles, which still flickered, spreading their light seductively over the main room. Ivan now went into the kitchen to thank her for such a splendid evening. He felt nothing but the most intense elation. The future stretched new before him—once more open.

How wonderful it was to be here—so far away from the grinding determinism waiting back in Moscow—amid the warm scents of roasted duck and homemade berry pie, which lingered in the air, sweet reminders of a meal savored to the last bite.

Ivan did worry briefly that this elation might not last, that it might be no more than an unconscious effort to avoid the teleology of an ordinary career. But it was not the occasion to dwell on negative thoughts.

Kaisa had thrown off her jacket and kicked off her shoes, and was waiting for him on the sofa. He quickly followed her example, and they wrapped themselves together in a thick blanket—combining their warmth in front of the fire.

Kaisa rested her head against Ivan's shoulder and stared at the window. She could see the snowflakes start to accelerate, appearing in sudden white flurries out of the dark. Their whisper against the glass recalled winters back home—thick, heavy, and solitary. Here it felt different—a shared storm.

"Can you believe how it all started?" she whispered, a dreamy nostalgia overtaking her. "That stumbling encounter in St. Petersburg."

Ivan let out a low chuckle, its vibration rippling across the two of them. "That dinner was indulgent—and there I was, sprinting after you down those narrow streets. I don't think that I've ever done anything so foolish before."

"And yet," he said, altering his tone slightly, "the moment I caught sight of you—a presence both so ghostlike and so powerful—I knew. When you disappeared, I would have to get you back—and God, as if he were listening, smiled down on me."

Kaisa laughed—was Ivan simply rewriting their story to mask his impetuous desires? She recalled again the improbable invitation from a stranger with an unexpected but resolute charm.

"Somehow you succeeded in making the reunion of an unknown family seem like a fleeting chance to peek inside another world—to taste an unconnected life—like a voyeur who gets to see without getting involved, without the pain or risk. Something, in the instant, I couldn't refuse."

"And I'm convinced," Ivan murmured, pulling her closer, "that you were always meant to be there. Like a spiritual twin, like that movie *La Double Vie de Veronique*—or perhaps it was just me being too stubborn to let you slip away."

He felt Kaisa smile. "Then meeting you again at the Hermitage the following day," he continued, "it was like destiny refused to let us part."

Ivan pictured the moment. "Despite all those paintings staring down in all those grand rooms," he said, looking at Kaisa, "you were the only thing I could see." It was like a confession. "I forgot the art and noticed only you."

Kaisa angled her face up to meet Ivan's gaze, candlelight reflecting in her eyes. "Each room we entered felt like it existed for us," she said. "The corridors, the halls, the paintings—everything seemed to arrange itself as a frame for us to explore and talk."

Ivan smiled. "And you pointed out such tiny details—things I would have missed." His fingertips brushed back a strand of Kaisa's hair. "It was overwhelming. Each step," he went on, "felt like the gradual unfolding of some new story."

An edge of the blanket fell off Kaisa's shoulder, drawing his attention. Ivan took her hand, their fingers interlocking with easy intimacy. "And here we are," he said, "days and nights of chaos evaporating into this single evening."

A surge of possessive happiness washed over Kaisa. "Yes."

Ivan gazed back at Kaisa's eyes. "That night in St. Petersburg, I saw you sitting there. You looked so confident despite the noise. Unaffected and radiant—reading your book. It was the most captivating vision."

Kaisa's pulse quickened at the memory. "You had such confidence, too. As though you'd chase after me for a hundred miles if I tried to slip away."

Ivan's voice cracked. "I would have. I did. In the early hours of that morning after you'd finally gone—back to your hotel. I thought I had lost you; I cursed for waiting so long to declare myself." It had been an opening, he felt sure, to escape the claustrophobia he increasingly felt.

Kaisa leaned over and, capturing Ivan's lips, kissed them with a tenderness, a repeated softness that caressed his mouth, that gently licked at the edges of desire, sharpening its contours. She strengthened her embrace, never losing touch, until both of them were breathless and temporarily exhausted.

Ivan caught once more the elusive fragrance of mint, reminding him of their first days together. "Every second I have spent with you," he said at last, "has felt like the unfolding of some fantastic tale."

"I can't get enough." He felt overwhelmed. His hands slid to Kaisa's waist, as if struggling to keep afloat, helpless on the surface of a dark ocean, torn between the thrill of surrender, the welcome of the void, and the innate fear of losing himself entirely.

A fundamental caution gripped him—some hesitation that interrogated his recklessness. What if the void were empty? What if there were no return? Like a drinker over-extending or some tired creature fighting against sleep.

The snowstorm outside strengthened, its patter against the window growing more insistent. Sitting on the couch, Ivan felt the cold descend—noticed the shadows intensifying—and for an instant felt cut off and isolated once again.

Then the fire popped, snapping him out of his reverie—its light offering his body sanctuary, his mind a point of refuge. "And I want more too," Kaisa declared. "More of this... more of you... more of everything."

In one fluid movement, Ivan recovered—slipping his arms around her body and lifting Kaisa off the sofa. A soft, delighted gasp escaped as she was carried across the room—and Ivan, kneeling, placed her gently amid the furs heaped before the fire.

The flames bathed their silhouettes in fierce hues. Ivan remained there a second—his knees against her body, as if in prayer—his eyes tracing Kaisa's form with reverence. "You are—so beautiful," he intoned.

The words were like a release; the prayer a call to action. Kaisa didn't wait to hear more, but stretched out to unbutton Ivan's shirt. Intending to do it with care, she grew impatient and pulled Ivan over. She rolled on top and ripped open his shirt—the way she used to unwrap presents early Christmas morning on her bed...

The sudden excitement was surprising. It had been years since she'd taken something for herself, and softening, she decided to trace a freckle near Ivan's chest, an accidental mark of the man she was just discovering. Kaisa wondered idly what other secrets this body held.

She leaned forward, the scarf ends brushing the floor. Her fingers explored his body, tracing the ribs like a steel comb in a cylinder music box, responding to the various peaks and furrows. Her hands could feel the heat rising, steady and alive.

A shiver ran through her—not from the cold, but from the surge of emotion. "I won't unravel you too fast," she teased. She was older now—sufficiently mature, she was convinced, to savor her presents slowly. Ivan raised his head and his lips found Kaisa's forehead, which he kissed gently. His grin was mischievous, his eyes full of anticipation.

"I intend to explore every secret you hold," Kaisa went on. "I'm going to map your body. I believe that understanding is important. Understanding and appreciation."

Kaisa kissed Ivan's nose and made a path slowly over his lips and chin to his throat, eliciting tremors of pleasure. She placed her hands on his shoulders and arched upward, catching sight of the rafters: the rough-hewn birch beams and wooden planks. A rush of exhilaration almost knocked her off balance. Her nails grazed Ivan's skin as she sought to steady herself, suddenly gulping for air.

"It is just us," she now whispered a little hoarsely. "The world outside can vanish, but we shall remain here—a moment insulated in time."

Ivan reached up for her blouse, fumbling at one of the low buttons. Kaisa's attention returned. "Don't be so hasty," she declared, her voice betraying a tremble. "I haven't concluded my exploration. We haven't even reached the unboxing. I just want to look at you for a second," she said, pinning Ivan's hands against the floor.

"You mustn't move. I like the opening to be slow. And I want to admire you—like a painting. One of those masterpieces at the Hermitage. As you know, paintings don't move." Ivan smiled. "And they don't smile." Kaisa bent over to kiss his eyelids shut. Unwrapping the scarf, she took it off and gently tied it around Ivan's eyes.

"Keep them closed." Behind her, a little red ember fell onto the grate. "For you, this is a dream—and you can only dream fully when your eyes are shut." Ivan nodded. She caressed him once more, then drew her fingertips down his chest, bringing them to rest at the top of his pants.

Kaisa ran her fingers gently around the inside rim, measuring its fit, before returning her focus to the central button. She undid it—slowly, deliberately—and kissed him softly. "Don't move," she repeated.

Kaisa stood up and loosened her blouse, taking her time—bit by bit undoing each button—then delicately slipping it off and letting it drop with a subtle swish.

She stepped out of her pants, exposing her skin to the firelight as she lingered before the flames. She looked down, admiring the faint rise of goosebumps along her smooth legs as the air—at once warm and cold—swirled around her. The fur rugs caressed the sensitive arches of her feet. Every nerve felt awake.

She caught a glimpse of herself in the darkened windows—the fire painting her body in red and orange, sharpening her figure. Light and shadow accentuated every curve. She seemed almost statue-like but alive and fluid. For a second it reminded her of Melisandre, the Red Woman. Kaisa appreciated, now more than ever, this character and her appetite to resolve the world in light and flame.

Ivan lay still on the ground, her scarf around his eyes. She pulled away the last of his attire. She was ready—she knew. The instant had arrived. Slowly, carefully, she knelt astride Ivan and sat there—acknowledging the pulse in her body, absorbing it all.

Everything felt heightened. She could feel Ivan's heart, see his breath going in and out. The earthiness of the fur rugs beneath her knees grew even more intense. The saltiness of Ivan's skin persisted on her tongue. Every sound reached her more sharply: the rush of air sustaining the fire, the snowflakes dissolving against the window panes.

She leaned over and whispered in Ivan's ear, "Welcome to the new world." And with that, she guided him into her rhythm, took him down all the paths she knew and cherished.

"If I lose myself in this new land, I shall at least die happy," Ivan confessed. And so they moved together, the warmth of Kaisa's skin against Ivan's, the heat of the fire creating beads of sweat that sparkled in the semi-darkness like so many little diamonds.

As Kaisa reached her first peak, she jerked with almost violent bursts—no rhythm, just raw, seemingly random thrusts—first one way, then another—abrupt spasms that rattled Ivan's teeth and knotted his stomach. When the tremors calmed she lay her chest on top of Ivan's; rested her head on his shoulder, looking at him—her mouth curved in a dreamy smile.

There was a silence, which stretched. For a moment it appeared the storm outside had stopped, but it was just a pause between gusts as more snow returned to beat against the windowpanes. Eventually Ivan spoke. "I have craved you since the moment I first saw you."

Kaisa grinned and sat up, removing the scarf from Ivan's eyes. "Show me," she demanded, face alight with renewed desire. "At the Hermitage you said you wanted to be like Matisse's dancers—free, alive, connected."

"I challenged you then," she said. "And I challenge you now. Prove how much you crave me."

She grabbed Ivan tightly, rolling herself back onto the rugs. As she did so, her nails grazed Ivan's back, compelling him closer—whether to consume him entirely or to pull him down level with her—she couldn't tell.

Kaisa scarcely cared. Letting go, she lifted her knees. And Ivan obliged, pressing her deeper into the pile of rugs.

Behind them the fire continued to radiate heat, sending off sparks that fell on their spirits as upon dormant embers—reigniting them. The flames of their passion, finally released from constraint, melted everything.

The night became a blur of light and motion. Consciousness rose and sank like shapes drifting in a lava lamp, each burst dissolving back into the dark. Just once, Ivan paused long enough to hear the wind howling—to wonder if somehow it were objecting.

Later, after they had at last admitted surrender and allowed their hearts to relax, they lay entangled on the rugs—wrapped in each other's arms and faintly trembling, as if their muscles failed to recognize the action had ended.

They laughed a little breathlessly, teased, and succumbed for a moment to more kisses, an encore of caresses. Ivan winced slightly as he noticed the scratches on his back. Kaisa's eyes lit up. "Just so you know," she joked, "I have marked you as mine."

Ivan laughed. "Can you believe how fast it's all happened? It seems like yesterday we were strangers… and yet, somehow, we've lived a thousand stories already."

"Come here," Kaisa chuckled—almost the same laugh that had attracted Ivan the first night—and placed a languid kiss on his forehead. "You should be exhausted from the pace. But how good it is to feel alive!"

Their eyes locked, the ardor of their newfound closeness slowly reigniting and spreading once more over their bodies. "We're like two wandering hearts that finally found a connection and fused," she said at last. "We are two echoes," she extemporized, still searching for the right image "that emanated from the same magical breath, ricocheting down a canyon—two echoes that finally met as the canyon opened to the world beyond."

"I can't help thinking of *The Princess Bride*," Ivan replied, more simply. "The surprises, the travels…"

He heard again Kaisa's bright laugh. "Life will never be boring for us!"

"Absolutely. It will be a continuous voyage." Ivan brushed his hand through her hair. "Let's take what we can before the world remembers us."

"Let's see the world stop us!" she declared. "The grand experiences. The everyday magic."

Ivan hoped that the passion would last. He did… But he worried. They would face battles: in the city, in the pedestrian challenges of daily life. Outside, the winter night spread its hush across the powdery landscape, the snow stopping at last. Would Kaisa ever love his world—even when he no longer did?

14. Silly Worries

Light crept through the blinds, thin and colorless. The last embers in the fireplace had turned to ash. As Kaisa moved, stretching her legs, her foot struck the cold iron grate, scattering a tiny puff of gray powder.

She pulled her leg back in, under the rugs, and wrapped herself lazily around Ivan, who lay there peacefully, still deep asleep.

Half-dozing in the late morning, Kaisa caught a faint mechanical hum rising somewhere outside, distant but rhythmic—like an engine idling beneath the snow. She registered it vaguely, guessing a snowplow was warming up for the morning.

As the pale light deepened through the windows—a gentle sun following the night's snow—she recalled Ivan's fleeting glances toward the window, as if searching for shadows beyond the frost, as if interrogating the possibility of their future happiness.

How silly his worries! The two of them were, after all, perfectly matched—this was how the world should be. Complementary pairs, kindred spirits, finding each other despite geographies and cultures. They would face any challenges together.

And yet now she heard the sound of a car outside—a door slamming, footsteps nearing. Had Natasha returned too early to put the dacha back in order? Kaisa would make Ivan answer the door when she knocked; the warmth of the rugs before the dead fire was too comfortable to leave at once.

Instead, the front door flung open and heavy boots echoed across the quiet. Before either of them could stir, the living room door burst apart. Men marched in, clad in dark suits presenting severe faces, full of authority and menace.

Kaisa opened her eyes as two men crouched and grabbed Ivan. "Get away from him!" she cried out instinctively, her voice raspy with sleep as she blinked the drowsiness from her eyes. But her words hung fruitlessly in the air as the men focused solely on Ivan, who was still in a dazed slumber.

They seized him, their movements swift and well-trained—allowing no time for thought or resistance. "What—what's happening?" Ivan said, eyes snapping open as they yanked him from the softness of the rug. He reached for something—anything—but the grip on him was iron.

"Let go!" he cried as they hauled him upright and out. The speed was brutal—designed to stun before ideas could form.

For a moment, sound and reason fractured. "Ivan!" Kaisa screamed at the men who continued dragging her fiancé of scarcely twelve hours toward the door. "What is this? Why are you doing this? Stop!" The words collided in her throat—raw, useless panic.

Ivan turned once, eyes wide. "Kaisa, I—" A shove to his head cut him off, hurling him, bent over, through the door. Kaisa tried to lunge after him. However, her limbs tangled in the rugs that had covered them just moments before, and she end up on all fours.

In an instant, Ivan was out of sight and bundled—naked, as he was—into a sleek black car waiting outside, its dark windows reflecting the morning light. A cold jolt tore through Kaisa's chest as she finally realized what was in progress. It was all too surreal, a scene torn from a film that was somehow unspooling real time in her own life.

"Stop!" she screamed again. "You can't—He's my fiancé." She did not care how it sounded—giving voice to whatever thought emerged first. She rose at last from the fur rug, her body still unclothed and vulnerable, the chill of the air biting at her skin.

Adrenaline kicked in, as it had last night. However, this time the emotions were darker and tinged with dread. A desire for Ivan to be there with her exploded across her body. But it was a painful and destructive longing, not a pleasurable one—as though she already knew, somehow sensed, Ivan had gone irrevocably beyond her grasp.

She ran to the window just in time to see the driver slam the car door shut, the tires screeching backwards. Ivan lunged toward the car's darkened window, his face appearing spectral against the black as if rising from the depths of a tempestuous sea—a mix of fear and desperation, his hands clawing at the edges of the door, grabbing at the window control as he tried to call out. Kaisa saw dark gloves pulling him back.

The roar of engines as the black car sped away drowned any more words—if they existed—leaving Kaisa standing in the dacha, without Ivan and feeling utterly bewildered. In the lull her mind turned back to her own predicament.

The scent of Ivan lingered everywhere on her skin. And she could feel the soreness that evidenced their night together—her hips, her breasts, her back. Kaisa could still feel his body against hers.

She suddenly realized how exposed she remained. Indeed agents were still in the house and some turned their attention to her now, their looks unyielding.

"Get dressed," one ordered.

As confusion swirled inside her, she struggled to find a voice. "Where's he going? What's happening?" Kaisa demanded, her heart racing as she sought to piece together the fragments of her shattered reality. But the men offered no answers, their eyes cold and detached.

As fear gripped her insides, Kaisa remained frozen in place by the window, the chill of this new morning so incongruous, so different from the warmth of the previous night.

The last men left—not interested in Kaisa, or what she might do. A silence descended. Kaisa's mind raced to grasp the incomprehensible. She went back, picked up a throw, and pulled it around her shoulders, aiming to calm herself. It offered little comfort and even less shelter.

As she slowly looked around, she now glimpsed a small, blinking device in the corner. It had, quite possibly, recorded everything.

As the full implications of what had just transpired crashed down upon her, she began to shake violently, a delayed shock overpowering any effort to stay in control.

Why had this been allowed to shatter their world? She recalled Ivan's offhand joke about 'eyes everywhere' while in the car. Had it been—in reality—a warning, disguised as flirtation?

Kaisa's gaze wandered once more over the mementoes of the night before. In some ways, the room looked scarcely disturbed—the dead fire, the fur rugs, her scarf off to one side. They were all as they had been. Only a clump of dirty snow disrupted the picture, slowly melting on the floor.

Last night Ivan couldn't see her; now she'd lost him. She glanced at the device in the corner—it too, once seeing, had stopped blinking.

15. Prisoner Swap

The room was unremarkable, yet it hummed with a subtle, potent energy. Claire Bennett sat behind a desk, with its two screens and a single jug of water. A half-full glass stood off to one side. Claire wore a close-cut black suit and structured jacket over a black blouse, an ensemble that directed the focus to her words and actions.

Claire knew every corner of her room by heart: the gray walls—bare of any art or ornament—the single clock perched above the door, its rhythmic click underscoring every discussion that took place within these walls.

If anything, the starkness of her room served its purpose well: no one came here for diversion or comfort. No one came here for a chat. They came to make decisions that altered lives.

Over the years Claire had grown accustomed to the near-silence of her office. Now in her mid-forties, she'd climbed the ranks in an agency notorious for its old-boys' club culture. She'd long ago traded idealism for procedure, telling herself duty was its own form of belief. It had taken unwavering grit, nerve, and calm that some colleagues found intimidating.

She was one of the agency's few senior women, heading a critical division that intersected with both intelligence gathering and strategic operations. Every meeting she chaired bore the weight of watchful and critical eyes at the highest levels.

Across from her desk, two men sat in simple, functional chairs. Both wore well-tailored suits that whispered authority more than shouted it. The older of the pair was balding slightly and his efforts to hide it suggested he didn't particularly like the development. The corners of his eyes further betrayed his years and experience. He radiated a sense of quiet wisdom.

The younger man beside him, all sharp cheekbones and a perpetual half-smile, exuded an artificial composure. He'd pursued his place here to progress more efficiently after some early years in the field. The two men had joined Claire for closed-door discussions several times—on each occasion, the stakes seemed high. Today was no exception.

A soft knock broke the uneasy calm. Claire lifted her gaze above the pair of computer monitors facing her. "Come in," she said evenly. Her tone carried well: an understated command that organized without drama. After all, that was her style—no wasted words, no theatrics.

The door opened, and another woman stepped through. She appeared to be in her mid-thirties, wearing a dark-brown blazer over a knee-high skirt of similar color, an outfit that spoke of meticulous, if conservative, taste. An ID clip was the only decoration.

She moved gracefully, but an undercurrent of steel suggested she too had faced her share of high-stakes situations. Her eyes darted over the room, noting the assembled presence of Claire and the two men before talking.

"May I join you?" she asked. The cadence of her request conveyed both courtesy and the urgency that had brought her here.

Claire inclined her head. "Please, take a seat." She indicated an empty chair alongside the two men, creating a semicircle about her desk. The woman shut the door and crossed the short distance, smoothing her skirt as she sat. With her arrival, the atmosphere shifted from mere discussion to a more intense focus, as though a council was at last fully assembled—bracing itself for weighty decisions.

Claire sat back in her chair. "Let's get to it," she said, folding her hands on the desk. She paused, measuring her words with the precision of someone used to orchestrating things from behind the scenes.

"We've received an overture from Russia—from Kostov's administration. They want to propose an exchange of prisoners: a number of Americans they have for a high-value Russian asset we have."

The older man, flipping open a leather-bound folder, spoke first. "This latest overture comes through back channels in Turkey that've opened up as a result of our Gulf operations." He paused. "I guess they're wanting Mikhail Orlov."

"That's right," Claire confirmed, keeping her expression cool. "He's been locked away years now for espionage. If you recall, his arrest proved a significant victory for us—enough that it rattled their intelligence apparatus. Trading him away wouldn't be a trivial matter."

The younger man's eyes gleamed with curiosity. "So, who do they offer us for Orlov? Which Americans are they dangling as bait?"

Claire sighed. "They've provided a list of nine detainees of varying profile: businesspeople, tourists, alleged 'spies.' Some cases are straightforward; others are more complicated. Well," she corrected herself, "a swap is never simple."

The second woman—who had just entered—cleared her throat. "I can guess the angles. Kostov wants to look magnanimous internationally, show his regime in a softer light, especially if pressures at home are escalating. And if he can bring Orlov home, it would bolster the regime's morale. For us, of course, it's about whether we can justify handing him back."

Claire tapped a button on her left-hand monitor, turning the screen so the others could view a roster of names. "We need to decide who, if anyone, is worth the trade." She paused.

"Let's walk through the potential exchange. We have to weigh not just the value for us of each detainee but the risk of making Orlov available to the enemy. Let's be honest: the optics of this, if it happens, will be substantial."

The older man's brow furrowed. "Indeed. Orlov's a high-level intelligence operative. Even if he's been out of the game for years, he still knows the protocols, methods, maybe even cells that have escaped our clean-up work."

"Orlov's a big fish—like Vadim Krasikov in the 2004 mega-swap. Releasing him could reopen old networks, especially with his cyber expertise. Letting him go would be seen as a major concession."

The younger man nodded in agreement, flicking through pages of notes. "So, who's on their side of the ledger? Which Americans are they listing?"

"Here," said Claire, scrolling to an itemized summary on the screen. "We have Ethan Gray, a former Agency contractor locked up on espionage charges. We have Jane Donovan, a journalist whose reporting angered the Kremlin." She paused again.

"Then we have Robert Jennings, arrested while managing his venture capital firm. Emily Tran, a young student who stupidly got herself swept up in anti-government demonstrations."

"We've had similar situations," the older man added, "where detainees were hit with treason for a minor act, like donating to a charity. Another time they arrested some activists congregating to highlight the impact of climate change on water availability."

"Then we have Mark Hampton, an ex-diplomat," Claire continued. "And one or two others who are less high-profile—accused of hacking, or petty smuggling, or drug-taking."

Claire scanned her team before concluding. "However, there is also..." She paused, dwelling on the possibility for a moment. "Ivan Asimov."

The second woman angled her chair closer to the screen. "Let's see him. We keep hearing rumors, but the details have stayed—despite every effort—murky."

Claire's fingers flew over the keyboard, pulling up an enlarged photo: a man in his early thirties, dark hair, intelligent eyes. "Ivan Asimov," she began, "a U.S.-Russian dual national, was arrested three years ago—outside Moscow."

"At first, the charges were vague, something about unauthorized access to corporate data in the oil and gas sector. Then it escalated to complaints about treasonous remarks regarding the President and rumored connections to political dissidents."

The older man exhaled, a slow, deliberate gesture. "He was an executive in the energy sector, wasn't he? With PanEnergy, no? He had some involvement in activities that rubbed VoltaGaz or Russian authorities the wrong way."

"Precisely," Claire affirmed. "Officially, the Russians tried him twice. The second trial was held in secret, resulting in a twenty-year sentence. Ultimately, a third set of accusations landed him in a Siberian labor colony—possibly for the rest of his life."

The younger man hissed out a breath. "Hell of a place to end up. So we don't know how he's holding up."

"No," Claire confirmed grimly. "The embassy's had no contact since the second trial. We were fortunate to have the access we did, given that he's Russian by birth and remains a dual national... He's now in a maximum-security penal colony somewhere in Siberia—cramped cells, no insulation, floor toilets, you name it. He will have deteriorated badly, as we've seen elsewhere."

"Like the Karelina case," the younger woman interjected.

"We've heard that Asimov has become something of a wildcard in prison," she continued. "The Russians claim he stirs up trouble—both religious and political. We suspect many of the charges are fabricated, but we can't fight them."

"Yes," said Claire. "Some intel suggests he's been proselytizing in prison—declaiming from the Bible or something. However things developed, his predicament is dire."

The second woman shifted in her seat. "If we leave him there, we're almost guaranteeing he never sees daylight again. But is it wise to trade Orlov for a man who might have acted recklessly—or, at worst, genuinely compromised himself? The details do remain opaque."

"You see our conundrum," Claire said. "We have more straightforward detainees—the student or the journalist—who garner a sympathetic press. Meanwhile, Ivan's case is complex. The question is, do we consider him a priority?"

The older man scratched his jawline, which he did whenever in deep thought. "He's an American citizen, that's priority enough for some. However, from a purely pragmatic standpoint... we must weigh how the White House and the press will interpret it."

"If we rescue him," he went on to explain, "or indeed some of the others—does it embolden Russia to grab more Americans simply for leverage in the future?"

The younger man nodded, his expression contemplative. "Yes, we should consider the bigger game. How does Orlov's potential release impact the intelligence playing field? Could Kostov's regime gain a new advantage from reinstating Orlov's expertise?"

The second woman folded her arms. "Then there's the moral dimension. If we ignore Ivan's plight in a Siberian camp, it sets a grim precedent. We've historically prided ourselves on not abandoning our citizens. In this context, leaving Ivan behind might cause some backlash, especially if details of his suffering leak out."

Claire said nothing for a moment, letting the swirl of arguments fill the air. "Of course, the press will've forgotten him already," she mused out loud. "They've a short attention span." She opened a drawer and brought out a file, undoing the cover to reveal a sheaf of reports all typed in tight fonts.

"We'll approach this systematically," she stated evenly. "Let's discuss Orlov's immediate and long-term threat if we do return him to Russia." She looked at everyone to get their consensus.

"Then let's gauge the relative value of each American detainee. Once we have that matrix, we can see whether Ivan fits into the recommended swap list or remains an outlier."

They spent nearly an hour dissecting Orlov's history: from his infiltration of U.S. defense networks to the advanced cyber tactics he allegedly pioneered. The younger man brought up details of Orlov's rumored personal network in Russia's security services.

The second woman stressed how letting him go might risk revealing U.S. intelligence methods gleaned from his arrest. Even Claire, stoic as ever, let a hint of concern shadow her eyes.

Eventually, they switched to the list of nine Americans. Each detainee's name conjured an entire microcosm of salient factors: moral, diplomatic, strategic, image-related.

Jane Donovan, the journalist, had already attracted substantial sympathy in the media. Robert Jennings, the finance entrepreneur, had been tried for alleged money laundering and hints of related activities, as though America worked just like Russia.

The arguments varied. Was it best to free sympathetic figures who might encourage positive press—or someone constructive from a functional perspective, for example with useful knowledge that might help national security?

Then came the matter of Mark Hampton, a former diplomat. The older man noted retrieving an ex-diplomat might boost morale in the Foreign Service—proof indeed that the U.S. "takes care of its own." But the younger man worried that overshadowing simpler humanitarian cases might look cynical—a sort of two-tier foreign policy. Emily Tran's youth and innocence made her a cause célèbre among several big advocacy groups.

Halfway through the meeting, one of Claire's male aides arrived with mugs of fresh coffee and a small plate of cookies. Claire took a mug gratefully. It was already past noon. They had begun early that morning, and the conversation showed no sign of concluding soon.

With each detainee discussed, the group reiterated the same points about Ivan: his plight was among the most severe, yet also the murkiest. The uncertain allegations of treason, the rumored proselytizing in prison—both complicated his public image.

"You see how hard it is to get the release of Kenneth Bae from North Korea," the younger man noted.

Claire nodded and continued. Did Ivan deserve rescue more than others, or would the administration prefer a less controversial detainee to champion? Would there be any positive coverage from saving him—or would it just lead to rehashing old debates about who deserved America's attention overseas?

Claire listened carefully to the ensuing debate. "In any case, we should keep speculation separate from what we can confirm. This is about more than an individual—it's about showing U.S. support for citizens entangled in foreign machinations."

The older man nodded. "And yet we might need White House input before finalizing anything about Ivan." He massaged his temples for a second. "This is a more complicated than average swap."

The younger man agreed. "Yes. PanEnergy's probably lobbying, too."

Claire's expression hardened. "I've heard nothing official about PanEnergy or the oil and gas association, but I'd be astonished if their back channels were not active."

"You're right," the older man confirmed. "PanEnergy has lobbied Capitol Hill, much like Baring Vostok did for Calvey—pushing to include Asimov in any future deal to avoid more bad news hitting our oil & gas sector." Claire smiled. She knew how things went—where people's sensitivities lay; how they responded.

The second woman flipped through one of the thick set of printouts on her lap. "I still can't ignore the moral dimension. If we leave a man to rot in Siberia because his arrest doesn't fit an easy narrative, that might blow up in our faces. Both politically and ethically. I'm not saying he's top priority. However, we should keep him in the discussion."

There were nods all around. "Let's record that. For now, Ivan is a maybe." Claire's gaze swept the room as she summarized. "We either find more intelligence about his status and the credibility of the original charges, or we proceed with the assumption that he's an American forcibly entangled in Russia's political machine."

"We can't finalize the recommendation today," Claire went on. "However, we can position him as a fallback or a possible secondary candidate if negotiations expand. Indeed if we push to include Ivan, we might end up with an even larger exchange."

"Yes," agreed the older man. "Think of the Fyodorov swap. That took more than a year to coordinate and involved half a dozen countries. Deals on that scale can't become routine."

Claire nodded. "Washington took a beating for trading that many targets at once. No one here wants to repeat that—not unless the situation calls for it and the rationale is unambiguous."

Her words carried a gentle finality, reminiscent of a conductor steering an orchestra to a temporary pause. Everyone in the room sensed it: the conversation had reached a useful lull, although it was far from truly settled.

They moved on to formalizing their recommendations for the four detainees they felt most confident about: Jane Donovan, Robert Jennings, Emily Tran, Mark Hampton.

The second woman reviewed the arguments for each detainee, ensuring that no detail was overlooked. She realized the team had favored the clear-cut detainees offering relative simplicity and ease—in contrast to Ivan. And she recognized the logic: it was almost impossible to reach a solution that was impervious to criticism. However, that didn't mean they were relieved of all duty towards those left behind.

They added bullet points with the motivations—from public sympathy to political benefits. The younger man typed notes into a device he had brought with him.

At length, Claire tapped on her keyboard with a few purposeful strokes, putting together her version of the conclusion. "We'll pass these recommendations along to management. The National Security Council will want input, as might the Secretary of State. Then we'll see if Russia's approach has momentum."

The older man closed his folder. "At least we've clarity about the main candidates. Although," he ventured "clarity is such a relative term, considering the swirling geopolitics."

The younger man suppressed a wry smile. "Isn't it always with Kostov's Russia? One day they posture, the next day they pivot. At least we're prepared."

The second woman reorganized her papers. "So we're done for now?"

Claire met her eyes. "Yes, for now. Let's plan on reconvening in a week's time, pending further intel or a White House directive. I'll push for more information regarding Ivan's situation. If we get anything new, I'll share it promptly."

Everyone rose to leave, offering polite goodbyes. The younger man lingered momentarily, as if wanting to say something, but one glance at the older man and the second woman sliding out the door reminded him time was running on. He simply nodded at Claire and followed them, leaving her alone.

A quiet descended on the room accentuating the presence of the clock as it ticked on relentlessly. Claire noticed the faint lines that the overhead lights cast across her polished desk.

Her gaze returned to the computer monitors. She reopened Ivan's digital file, scrolling through bleak paragraphs describing his sudden arrest, convictions, rumored transfer to a notoriously harsh penal colony in Siberia for lifers.

His initial arrest involved a pre-dawn raid at a dacha, where presumably FSB agents burst in and dragged him away—the suddenness of it all much like the Calvey case a few years back.

She studied his latest photo: hollow-eyed, visibly thinner, his face etched with frustration and despair. His deterioration had been quick. Claire shuddered slightly.

Three years. That was how long he'd languished in the Russian system. He'd become one more name lost in the overwhelming maze of foreign relations. It was a world that only disciples could navigate, much like Tenar in Claire's favorite book from childhood, *The Tombs of Atuan.*

For a fleeting moment, she indulged the possibility: What if they put Ivan on the priority list? Would it make the negotiations with Russia unmanageable? Could it sabotage the entire deal? The bitter truth was that the most pressing decisions rarely had neat solutions. She reached for her coffee, found it cold, and took a small sip anyway.

Finally, with a resigned sigh, she clicked out of Ivan's profile. She pulled up an internal memo that needed her signature, shifting to a more administrative concern. Life in the intelligence world rarely granted the luxury of reflection.

She had a job to do—coordinate with officials, parse intelligence briefings, weigh human lives against national interests. If the preliminary recommendation kept Ivan as a "maybe," so be it. That might change if new evidence arrived—or if a push from Capitol Hill or the White House demanded a different stance.

Claire noticed a tension in her shoulders. She told herself it was nothing. That the meeting had been standard procedure. That she'd overseen countless negotiations of similar importance, many of which ended in heartbreak or stalemate.

But something about this case stuck with her. Maybe it was the possibility Ivan was an ordinary citizen who had become an unfortunate scapegoat—caught up in the swirl of power politics, indicted not so much for data or espionage but for speaking out, for resisting the monstrous inertia of an authoritarian regime.

Or maybe it was a sense that, beneath all the spreadsheets and diplomatic jargon, a human story, more tragic than normal, was at stake. She allowed a moment of sympathy, a brief recognition of Ivan's plight—as she had done during active service when something went wrong: an instant to acknowledge before moving on with the operation at hand.

Claire printed the memo, then closed her eyes, as if to summon composure. *A week*, she thought. *We'll revisit Ivan's fate in a week.* With that, she turned off the computer and let the room's authority settle upon her again.

In the world of black-and-white decisions, Ivan's fate was yet another shade of gray. They would decide how dark a shade they were willing to tolerate—and that decision might see Ivan liberated from the Siberian ice, but might, just as easily, leave him in place to the mercies of a brutal system.

For now, all Claire could do was ensure that his name remained an option, that a flicker of hope existed in some corner of the intelligence apparatus guiding the nation's secrets and moral undertakings. The question whether Ivan's exile would stretch into a lifetime was precariously poised.

Claire picked up the folder on her desk. Then, with her left hand, she grabbed an elegant black walking stick with a silver lion's head. It had been resting against her desk.

She limped out of the office with a certain style and refined ease: to pick up her memo and to speak with others—keep them in the loop about today's progress. She hesitated at the door, glancing at her room and its desk. The system could not save everyone. However, she regretted those outcomes when someone had to be sacrificed.

16. Fate Beckons

The morning light had that pale, rinsed quality Paris often wears after rain—soft enough to turn stone to pearl. Irina sat by the window of the café on Rue de Bellechasse, a scatter of crumbs near her saucer, an untouched second croissant growing cold. Outside, the traffic passed in almost episodic fashion, a series of vignettes: a delivery van finding its way, a cyclist lifting his collar against the chill, a woman tugging her reluctant dog.

She gazed through the glass as though it were a screen between worlds: the city outside over reflections inside, the street's movements layering over her own face—half real, half apparition. Steam curled upward from her coffee. Somewhere behind her, the waiter adjusted the radio, and the faint notes of Charles Aznavour trembled through the air.

Her fingers, almost absently, moved to the silver cross at her throat. The small Orthodox charm, slightly tarnished, bore the slanted lower bar and a faint engraving worn smooth by time—*спаси и сохрани*. Save and protect. Her mother had given it to her during adolescence, pressing it into her palm with a look both fierce and tender. "It will remind you," she'd said, "that every gift is also a test." Irina had never removed it, though she told herself she kept it for habit, not belief.

Her mother had been the believer. A woman of omens and instincts, born in a caravan outside Rostov-on-Don. The kind of beauty that carried both grace and risk—black-eyed, swift-tongued, both adored and feared. She would read cards for neighbors and whisper warnings no one wished to hear.

Irina's father had been one of those men who arrive by chance—determined, increasingly powerful, leaving mostly disorder in his wake. A rising politician then—still exposed to the vagaries of fortune, already married, but eyes full of ambition. He had not yet lost his sense of fun, but already his attitude hinted at a boundless desire, a deep sense of entitlement. It's partly what made him so attractive. He spent a single night with Irina's mother; the next morning he was gone.

That seemed the end of the story—until, of course, Irina appeared. There was nothing to commemorate her birth but a note that arrived one day: a promise of "arrangements." And, perhaps surprisingly, arrangements had come.

An apartment, school tuition, a discreet monthly envelope, which became a discreet monthly transfer. But there was no acknowledgment, no name. Her mother used to say, "A man can hide a child, but he can't argue with fate."

Irina grew up between two vocabularies: superstition and statute. Her early life was spent either in the open fields, surrounded by the scent of herbs, or at home, pervaded by the aromas of incense and wax. Over time, this life merged into the administrative structure of schooling, the bureaucratic order of government forms that her mother had to complete to maintain her life.

As a girl, Irina oscillated between wanting to summon fate—protect love, restore justice—and wanting to outwit it, to create her own freedom, choose her own outcomes.

She entered university young and, when still nineteen, she joined the civil service. It was, she believed, a way to tame chaos—her own inheritance of passion and unpredictability. She was diligent, sharp—for some almost too sharp—and soon recruited into the more discreet departments of state, the ones that demanded silence and loyalty.

She liked her work: the order, the procedure, the clean geometry. It made life appear measurable and moldable. Yet, beneath the rational surface, another current persisted. It was like a ghost world, filled with spirits and half-truths.

Sometimes, in long meetings, she would hear her mother's voice: destiny waits for recognition; it doesn't require belief. Did Irina's work influence events or just provide an illusion?

She'd learned not to flinch when her father's name appeared in the news—an older man now, more seasoned, no longer touchable. To others, he was a symbol of Russian endurance; to her he was a cipher, the absence underlying every decision.

He'd never seen her or spoken to her, yet someone facilitated her progress, smoothed her path: a scholarship here, a promotion there. A ghost-hand guiding her upward while pretending not to exist.

In her teens, one time, she visited her mother's childhood friend—the latest representative of an illustrious dynasty of local fortunetellers. Irina had participated in a ceremony—a spontaneous decision, almost an indulgence for her mother's sake. They had been fighting, and Irina felt guilty.

The woman shuffled her cards then laid them out with the gravity of a priest as Irina looked on dubiously. After studying carefully, she looked up and stared into Irina's eyes. "A man will decide your future," she said. "A man who is neither clearly good nor entirely bad—someone who is both more, and less, than he aspires to be."

Irina had laughed. "Decide? Do you mean my father? That much is already clear. I can't escape him, whether I want to or not. Or do you mean I wed?"

The woman only smiled, the creases of her face deepening. "Not every life is a story about marriage or partnership. Sometimes it is a tale about interaction or conflict: between ambition and fulfilment, between who you pretend to be and who you are."

Since that afternoon, the phrase had settled in Irina's mind like a shard of glass—impossible to remove without bleeding out. *A man will decide your future.*

She had tried to interpret it rationally: perhaps the old woman did mean her father, but she hadn't responded positively to the suggestion. Or did she mean a superior when Irina started her career. But when, several years later, she met Ivan in Moscow—naïve, stubborn in a world that rewarded only power and the outcomes it wrought—he seemed to match the fortuneteller's words. Ivan's presence felt like the key to a story already written.

After his downfall, she'd told herself that the prophecy was fiction; that if it did have some merit to begin, the destiny it predicted had ended with him. But memory had its own stubborn gravity. And lately, sitting alone in cities that felt increasingly temporary, she couldn't help but feel a wheel turning. Despite the years of discipline, the old voices still whispered when the world grew quiet.

Her phone buzzed, disturbing her reverie, a message from a colleague in Brussels about an upcoming symposium. She ignored it, letting the screen darken. The world of work—the clean, impersonal language of reports and coordination—felt remote here.

What remained immediate was the hum beneath the ordinary: the idea that destiny walked the streets and turned common lives, dull clothes, simple stories into something special with new possibilities and different outcomes.

Irina looked down. Her thumb was rubbing the cross again, unconsciously tracing the tiny angles of the slanted foot bar. She forced her hand to the cup. The café au lait had gone lukewarm, yet retained that sweet, rich aspect that people lost when drinking Italian coffee. She drank it slowly.

Outside, the morning had brightened. A film of sunlight slid along the wet pavement, doubling the images—passers-by floating like spirits. And then, among the phantoms she caught a movement that did not seem to belong, that triggered her intuition: a tall figure, head slightly bowed, crossing the street toward the académie—one of the many in Paris.

She blinked, but the reflection persisted—the side of a face, a nose, an outline, a look. The heart in her chest gave a sharp, old-fashioned twist. Her rational mind questioned the conclusion—was it coincidence, projection, resemblance?—but already the word fate had thrown itself into her thoughts.

Irina set down her cup. The bell over the café door chimed as someone new entered; the waiter turned, greeted them. She no longer heard the words. Through the watery reflection she saw the figure pause, adjust a scarf, then continue down the sidewalk.

Her mind took note, quiet but functional, like the winding of a precision clock toward an hour she'd long avoided. Fate, she told herself quickly, is a choice we pretend not to make.

She stood, slid a few coins on her saucer, and headed to the door. The bell above gave another metallic tremor as Irina stepped into the open air. The morning had cleared entirely, the clouds thinning into a pale, bone-colored sky, and the city's pulse had strengthened. Traffic, footsteps, the peculiarly French mix of haste and indifference—Irina surveyed it all as she prepared herself to act.

She paused at the curb, drawing her coat close against the lingering chill. Across the street, the figure she'd seen in the reflection was already half a block ahead. For a heartbeat she hesitated, uncertain whether to trust her eyes. Then her mind decided—it was necessary to confirm. She gave chase.

The first moment of pursuit always felt foolish. She was aware of her heels striking the pavement, of the waiter still inside glancing after her, of the ridiculousness of following a stranger through the city. But the silhouette—tall, powerful, perhaps a little stooped now, gray at the temples—had an energy that she recalled from Moscow years ago. The memory was like a scent carried on a gust of wind.

And if pursuit felt awkward at the start, Irina always enjoyed it. The chase after a quarry not only energized her but felt like progress. When dealing with people, she always finished with a useful result. It was the spiritual that got her all entangled. Irina kept the man in sight as he walked passed a boulangerie, turned right behind the Musée d'Orsay, then left toward the Quai Voltaire.

"Wait," she ordered, though he could not possibly hear.

He crossed at the corner, weaving through traffic with an ease that made her think he knew this part of the city well. She followed, ignoring the horns, the cyclist's curse as she stepped onto the road. She forced an e-scooter to stop suddenly, the rider stumbling off.

By the time she reached the opposite pavement, her quarry was heading toward the river's edge. The peculiar light caught him in flashes, turning his overcoat silver.

The booksellers were setting up their stalls. The smell of river silt, old paper, and wet plastic rose in the air. For a moment she trailed him past the green boxes, her mind working over the puzzle. It could not be him, and yet Irina recognized something—*was it the posture, or was it something less tangible?*

He paused at one of the last stalls, picked up a volume, and turned it in his hands. She watched him, saw him in profile again—the set of his eyes, the angle of his jaw—and the resemblance struck her like a blow.

The person could indeed be taken for Ivan—an older, worn version. Her gaze narrowed. The world seemed to condense to the width of the quay. Everything else—the tourists, the vendor's mutter, the hiss of buses—fell into silence.

She took a few steps closer. She could almost hear her mother's tone, half warning, half dare: *When fate calls, you answer.* However, a rational voice inside suggested that what she'd find wouldn't be destiny—what she'd end up with would be something a lot more mundane.

Even if she found Ivan the revelation might just be the uniformity of man's relentless fascination with power and wealth, or the inability of men to see beyond their immediate challenges.

Then, as if he felt her gaze, the man looked up. Their eyes met across a few meters of gray morning. Time slowed to a pulse between them. He blinked once, as if to confirm her reality.

Irina froze. For a moment, she imagined the city itself was watching them, the river pausing its flow to see what would happen next. He closed the book, set it down carefully, and turned away. A car horn erupted behind Irina.

She snapped out of the trance and started after him again—weaving through pedestrians, her shoes slick against the damp stone. He moved fast now, heading toward the Pont des Arts. The bridge was just about empty at this hour, its wooden planks still wet from the earlier rain.

"Ivan!" she called at last, her voice raw in the open air.

He didn't turn. The sound vanished into the wind sweeping off the Seine. She lengthened her stride, the cross bouncing lightly against her chest. She couldn't be sure the man heard her.

Midway over the bridge he slowed, glancing over the railing. The weak light fell along his shoulders. She was close enough now to see the texture of his coat, the lines on his face. The similarity was remarkable—leaner, more tired, older, but somehow so familiar.

"Ivan!" she said again, louder.

The man's attention was caught by the sudden appearance of a group of students, surging past him with their cellphones, taking pictures or reels, laughing and jumping, their voices scattering the stillness. By the time they had gone, he was already moving off the bridge onto the far bank. Irina, cursing under her breath, ran after him.

The pursuit took her through the Musée du Louvre, then through a cluster of narrow streets that smelled of roasted coffee and diesel. She caught glimpses of him turning corners, always just ahead, never out of sight long enough for her to doubt her direction.

Her rational mind cataloged every detail—his gait, his attire, the way he kept to the shaded side of the street—as if documenting evidence. Yet beneath it all ran a current of disbelief so sharp it felt like awe. She recalled once more her mother's friend, the fortuneteller: *A man will decide your future.* This man. Or the ghost of him.

But was it him? And was this the moment she had been walking toward her entire adult life? The absurdity of it struck her even as she chased after him. But she couldn't stop now. Fate, once glimpsed, never released its hold. Or, at least, Irina wouldn't until she had answers. She wanted to know, had to confirm—above all—whether the world was rational or not.

The man crossed into the arcaded courtyard of the Jardin du Palais Royal, then out the other side into Rue de Montpensier. There she lost him. The street was almost empty. A delivery truck rumbled by, obscuring her view; when it passed he was gone.

She walked quickly to the corner, scanning the possible directions. Nothing. The sound of her own breathing filled her ears. She leaned against a wall, steadying herself. All around, life continued with infuriating normalcy: a man locking his scooter, a woman buying flowers, a child dragging a backpack along the ground.

Irina pressed her fingers to the cross, feeling its shape as though it could anchor her in the present, provide her answers or at least guidance. Her pulse was calm, but her mind was tumbling over questions with no beginning or end. Had he seen her? Was it him? Had he chosen to vanish once more—or was it all simply random?

A gust lifted her hair, carrying with it the faint scent of incense from a nearby church. She turned toward it instinctively. The small chapel, almost hidden between two shops, had its doors half-open. Within, candles flickered from inside shallow red cups.

She entered, more to collect herself than to pray. She saw a curtain move at the back, but it was just the wind from her entrance sweeping through the contained space. The air was cool, and she noticed the aromas of stone and polish mingling with the incense.

A parishioner entered, bought a candle, and after lighting it, placed it in the big round sand tray in the center. Irina watched, temporarily distracted. The parishioner crossed herself twice, bowed, and silently mouthed a brief prayer before repeating the cross and walking out.

Almost spontaneously, Irina followed her example, lighting a candle and watching the flame tremble.

"You send me riddles," she whispered under her breath, though she was not sure whether she meant God, her mother, or the pattern of life itself. "But I will answer them. There is always a solution." She paused, then continued as if in explanation. "It is my life to control."

Outside, the bells struck eleven. She straightened her coat, crossed herself, and left the chapel. Only as she did so, did it occur to her that the church was Russian Orthodox.

The street had brightened during the time she was inside. A tourist stopped along the sidewalk to ask her directions; Irina answered best she could. A child laughed, coming out of an alleyway. The city had resumed its pattern.

Irina once more scanned her surroundings as if she half-expected the air itself to rearrange and reveal her quarry—as it seemed to do earlier that morning. However, the instance did not repeat itself. There was nothing. Just sunlight and the groups of tourists making toward one sight or another.

She tucked her necklace under her blouse again, feeling the cool weight against her skin. Was it attracting fortune, or warding off evil? She didn't know—but perhaps, indeed, the wheel of fate was turning again.

She started walking back. She'd return to her office now. The future might belong to chance or to will. But she would find out and dictate her own conclusion. She had seen a man; and whether he was Ivan or the ghost of him, his story was something she had to confront once more—a puzzle remaining to be solved.

The office was cavernous—designed to project power, not offer comfort or functionality. Its walls were lined with black-and-white portraits of previous occupants, all male—reminders of past structures and continued influence.

A massive oak desk commanded the space from the back wall, its surface inlaid with a dark leather finish. The desk held simply a planner, a Caran d'Ache fountain pen, a paper-thin laptop, and a jug of water with a single glass.

Claire Bennett, now Director of the National Intelligence Coordination Agency (NICA), sat behind the desk—though occasionally she wondered whether its size was truly necessary. Was there a joke about men and big desks?

The agency's name was low-profile enough not to provoke questions. However, the power it wielded cut across multiple jurisdictions—defense, intelligence, diplomatic liaison.

Claire remained one of the agency's top stars, rising from a departmental oversight role just over a decade ago to the top seat today. She was now approaching her late fifties, and her hair had gone silver-white. She kept it short.

A tailored ash-gray suit and white blouse gave her an air of cool authority, while a pair of platinum cufflinks, shaped like stylized eagles, revealed a small yet personal and patriotic flourish.

She settled in her chair, the old functional one she had liked so much and decided to keep, scanning a fresh intelligence report on her tablet. The silence in her office was absolute—a thick carpet underfoot absorbing every echo.

The portraits watched rather than intruded, and the wall-length windows admitted the room's only natural light, filtered through half-closed blinds. Today an early fall sun arched across a humid afternoon in Virginia.

A knock at the door, measured yet firm, broke the silence. Claire lifted her gaze to the door, her face betraying nothing. "Come in," she said, her voice calm but carrying a quiet edge that demanded respect.

The door opened, revealing Colonel James Calloway, her adjutant, a longtime colleague. He carried himself with the confidence of a man who had spent decades in service, first in military intelligence, then in the Agency's equivalent division. He had accepted his fate—the incipient baldness—and shaved his head completely.

His uniform—simple, dark green, with minimal adornment—testified to a career spent in shadows rather than on parades, bearing the insignia of a senior rank that few outside the military would recognize these days. Despite the increasing weight of years, his posture remained crisp.

"Director," Calloway greeted, closing the door behind him. He stepped toward the desk, stopping precisely where protocol allowed—close enough to hand her documents, far enough to keep a respectful boundary. Their mutual familiarity was tempered by the rigid hierarchy they both respected.

"Colonel." Claire set her tablet aside, motioning for him to sit in one of the high-backed chairs opposite her. "What do you have for me?" There was a faint click as Claire removed the cap of her pen.

Claire had learned long ago the most dangerous introductions, whether spoken or implied, always began with "you need to see this." Calloway sat and placed a slim folder on her desk.

Inside were several photographs, a handful of typed pages, the distinctive outline of an official memo. Calloway flipped to the key document: a grainy image from an airport security camera.

The man appeared to be in his mid-fifties, with hair that was more silver than black, and a neatly trimmed beard that lent him a composed, worldly look. His features, though not unusual, held a certain confidence, if not defiance—maybe the self-assurance of someone accustomed to a world of influence.

"These images just arrived this morning from our Dulles airport security feeds," Calloway began. "The passenger triggered an alert during routine biometric screening under the IDENT/HART system."

"The one that the Department of Homeland Security manages?" Claire asked.

"Yes," Calloway confirmed. "The entrant was traveling under the name Alex Volkoff on a Swiss passport issued eighteen months ago." Calloway paused.

"He has dual citizenship in Azerbaijan. Both passports came back clean—fully valid, issued through proper channels. He landed on a flight from Zurich, connecting from Baku."

Claire's sharp eyes lingered on the photograph, waiting for the crucial detail. "And the reason this is on my desk?"

The colonel's jaw flexed as he spoke. "They cross-checked with the FBI—and got a secondary match through the NGI facial-recognition layer. The match is partial against one identity, with a confidence level in the low sixties—above the candidate threshold... An individual we believe to be dead." Calloway drew a breath. "Ivan Asimov."

A near-imperceptible shadow crossed Claire's face. She recognized the name. Asimov had been a major puzzle for her—a U.S. citizen arrested in Russia under murky, likely fabricated, espionage charges. Eleven years earlier, in 2013, she'd supervised a team that considered his inclusion in a potential prisoner swap.

Ultimately, the government had decided not to prioritize his case. Officially, the Russians claimed Asimov died in Katorga-6, a brutal Siberian labor camp, seven years later. It was a chaotic time. Covid was taking both the old and the infirm—those with existing conditions or needing treatment. No corpse was ever returned, just ashes from the cremation. However, official documents left little room for questioning, and no one was interested in pursuing further.

"Asimov is dead," Claire said, her voice level. "That was the file we closed. Are we certain there's no mistake?"

Calloway shook his head, the tendons in his neck going taut. "We're not certain of anything, Director—the biometric match is sufficient to raise questions. We double-checked with CBP. The man, Alex Volkoff, traveled here on business that appears legitimate. He's extremely wealthy, rumored to be a billionaire, riches built on commodities and telecoms. Domestic tabloids in the Caspian region call him the 'Invisible Oligarch,' whatever that means."

A cold hush settled. Claire went through the details she could recall about Ivan Asimov: arrived from Russia with his family as a young boy in New York state, did well at a prestigious U.S. college, landed in the energy sector, and took a posting to Moscow.

His arrest in 2010 at age thirty-one had caught attention but never garnered enough momentum for rescue or diplomatic compromise. By 2013, she'd labeled him "not essential for swap," a tiny detail on the global stage where national concerns pushed and pulled in a never-ending, emotional tango. Seven years later, the Russians declared him dead.

Now, long afterward, a man arriving in Washington, D.C.—more precisely, in Virginia—matched his biometric profile. Claire picked up her walking stick and crossed to the window, her limp sending a familiar twinge of pain along her leg. It was a pain she had long since learned to master. Some days she used it to provide clarity.

"Remind me," Claire said, her voice still neutral, "what exactly was the official cause given for Asimov's death?"

Calloway flipped to a typed summary. "Complications subsequent to a knife incident. The Russians reported it to our Embassy, offering a typical set of documents: the initial FSIN certificate, a one-page medical conclusion, and the official death certificate from ZAGS."

He paused before continuing. "Our own analysis couldn't disprove it. The ashes provided no DNA. We marked it as probable death. No contradictory data ever surfaced—until today."

"And now—maybe—he's waltzing through Immigration under a new identity," Claire said, her tone cutting. "Tell me more about this alleged Alex Volkoff."

Calloway retrieved another page. "He's kept a low public profile for years but is rumored to have begun his business climb amid the chaos of post-Soviet privatization. He invests in everything: energy, telecoms, tech, finance. Wealthy enough to gain control of entire firms if it suits him. The official story is that he's in the U.S. to discuss potential expansions in his initial field of energy, digital banking, and AI." Calloway let the picture sink in.

"He's also said to have tangential connections to certain American political figures—board memberships, that sort of thing. However, nothing overly suspicious. Everything is squeaky clean, almost—in some ways—too perfect."

Claire tapped a manicured finger on her stick. "A comprehensive rewrite of identity, maybe. If Asimov did survive, it stands to reason he'd require deep cover—and deep resources—to return to the West."

Calloway paused. "Director, this could become complicated. If Volkoff truly is Asimov, it implies a major operation. Someone in Moscow or elsewhere may have orchestrated an elaborate ruse—faking his death, facilitating a new persona, creating a powerhouse oligarch."

He went on to emphasize the counter-proposition. "But we could be dealing with a misidentification. The question is: which scenario is worse?"

Claire leaned forward and rubbed the silver lion's head of her stick for a moment before taking a slow tour around the room. Calloway remained quiet, waiting for her conclusion.

At last she spoke. "We can't have an American detainee, presumed dead, strolling around the country under a false identity," she said, "not if we can help it."

She came back around her desk. "At the same time, we must tread carefully. If the Russians discover we suspect Volkoff is Asimov, they might clamp down, go to ground." She sat down and rested the stick by her side. "Where do we stand in terms of next steps?" she said, looking across to Calloway.

He straightened. "No immediate arrest or confrontation. We have no legal cause—his papers check out. We can, however, observe discreetly. I have already set up a small watch detail. They'll track him but maintain distance. If he is Asimov, we need to confirm without tipping our hand."

Claire's eyes narrowed. "Yes, do it. And we need a complete review of the man. Everything on Asimov from 2010 to now, including his alleged death."

"If someone's been distorting the truth," she continued, "we want to know who—and why. We must also work out whether this Volkoff is alone, or if he's part of a bigger strategy. By tomorrow, I want a working group in place—quietly. No rumor-mongering."

"Yes, Director," Calloway said. "Anything else?"

She studied the photograph one more time, a host of memories tugging at her. She recalled the 2013 deliberations in her smaller, more functional room, going over Asimov's case multiple times—his file ending: *Deceased. No further action required.*

Something about the whole event had lingered in her mind for years—a faint shadow in her mental ledger, a small weight upsetting the balance. "Colonel," she said quietly, "we made choices back then—myself included."

"If we find out that Asimov endured all those years—that we were misled—it could break open a maelstrom unlike anything we have experienced here to date." She paused, before voicing her conclusion. "We proceed with caution. We must have the answers before taking action."

Calloway gave her a solemn nod. "Understood. I'll coordinate our internal teams. Additional resources may be needed from other agencies, but I'll keep it to a minimum. The last thing we want is a diplomatic incident—or a media fiasco. We know how well the President reacts to bad publicity."

Claire let out a measured breath. "We walk the edge, as always. Thank you, Colonel. Keep me updated the moment new intel arrives."

With that, Calloway stood and organized the documents back into the file. Claire indicated for him to leave the folder. He offered a slight bow of respect and then left the office, closing the heavy wooden door behind him.

For a long moment, Claire stared at the wall opposite. The hush of the room pressed in again, broken only by the faint hum as the HVAC system started up. She recalled the afternoon when she'd signed the recommendation that Asimov—then thirty-four—was of secondary importance in a prisoner swap.

She'd done so with cold logic: Asimov was mired in too many uncertainties, and his situation was overshadowed by easier detainees with clear value. There was no desire to push a wider-ranging swap—not after the previous effort. But if that had sealed another decade of suffering... She steadied herself. Dwelling on regrets served no purpose. She was the Director now, and the stakes were higher, the responsibilities heavier.

The Agency, and the powers above it, had decided no. She must deal with the situation as it transpired. A man had today entered American territory identifying as a wealthy magnate named Alex Volkoff; someone who could yet be Ivan Asimov. The idea was beyond improbable—but so were many realities in the intelligence world.

Reaching for the folder, she skimmed its contents one last time. Official disclaimers, flight itineraries, financial snapshots. If Volkoff truly were Asimov, someone had orchestrated a plan of breathtaking scale—faking a death, forging new fortunes, concealing him for almost half a decade, ultimately unleashing him on the global stage. Why?

Her eyes flicked to the secure laptop. She opened it up and waited for the security prompt. With a firm press of her hand on the trackpad, she logged into the system, a swirl of encrypted data populating the screen. She typed swiftly, drafting an urgent briefing order. Then she paused, staring at the text. The difference between knowledge and ignorance could be the difference between life and death. She knew. Claire typed a final sentence in her email: "Director to be informed of any findings immediately."

She closed the laptop. The reflection on its surface revealed a small frown creasing her brow. She gave it a little rub, rose, and slowly walked over to the windows again, her stick supporting her.

Outside, the late-afternoon sun bathed the complex in pastel hues. *We tell ourselves we're secure because of order and routine*, Claire thought. *However, isn't that just a confidence trick?* A second question followed, almost logically in the circumstances: *What if Ivan had survived?*

She wondered what pain might have done to him—and what this pain might still do to them all.

She turned away from the view. Another meeting awaited, another grain in the shifting sands that made up each day. Tomorrow would bring fresh insight; and Claire would know, she hoped, just how deeply this ghost from the past threatened to undermine the well-packed foundations of national security.

She strode to the door, her stick sinking into the thick carpet that muted her steps. Maybe it was time, she thought before exiting, for something a bit less forgiving. She didn't like loose ends. They weren't just unprofessional—they were dangerous.

Irina gazed out over the lights of Paris, the city's nighttime glow as enchanting as ever. She was wearing a saffron top, rose-toned skirt. From the balcony of her quarters in the 7th arrondissement, the Eiffel Tower stood out, luminous against the dark September sky.

She leaned on the ornate railing, the air cool against her face. The low hum of passing traffic drifted up from the streets. Despite the postcard-perfect view, her mind was tense. She'd almost grown accustomed to this city—she'd lived here quietly for a while—but her work never left her at ease, no matter how charming the façade.

A muffled buzzer sounded from inside. That would be her contact, on schedule. She slipped back into the apartment, crossing a living room whose tasteful décor projected an air of casual wealth. Her surroundings were curated more than lived-in, but served Irina well. She pressed a small button set flush on the wall, and the building's secure front door clicked open downstairs.

As she waited in the foyer, she could hear her visitor climbing the stairs—a bit labored. A moment later the doorbell rang. She checked the security screen, then unbolted the heavy front door. It had one of those locks that turned and turned, designed to make the apartment impregnable.

Irina found the visitor—a neat, slight man in ordinary clothes—removing his hat and scarf. "Come in," she welcomed. The strong entrance light illuminated his tousled hair, and for a moment, his features looked drawn.

"I trust you haven't been followed," Irina said, her accent faint if discernible, the remnants of her Russian roots carefully modulated to match the refined Parisian surroundings.

"Of course not," he replied, closing the door behind him. "I've been very careful. No one will know we've met."

She nodded and led him deeper inside, gesturing to an armchair by a coffee table stacked with books about French art. The curtains were drawn tight. A single lamp shone, offering the pair a small intimate circle of light in which to speak.

"You said on the message bank you had something," Irina prompted, standing rather than sitting, arms crossed in subdued impatience.

He cleared his throat. "Yes. I do. We've intercepted some chatter from the Americans. You'll appreciate the news. Their intelligence community suspects that an old acquaintance may have reappeared in the United States." Irina waited.

"The man known as Ivan," he revealed.

For a fleeting second, Irina's composed mask slipped, replaced by a note of genuine surprise. She steadied her features at once. "They suspect," she echoed. "How can they suspect anything if he's already dead—four years ago in that ghastly prison?"

"That's just it—they don't know," the informant clarified. "They have simply a partial biometric match at passport control—with a similarity score around sixty-three."

Irina's jaw tensed. She recalled her last picture of Ivan in Russia: the image of a battered, half-starved prisoner on a file. "I'm not sure 63 convinces me. He's been officially dead for years now."

"I know the files were minimal, and the follow-up perfunctory. But even we accepted the story—eventually. There was no Ivan in the system. I checked myself." Her voice took on a sharper edge. "How do the Americans explain this?"

"They can't," the informant admitted. "They only suspect," he repeated. "And—you know—once they start, they just don't stop suspecting." Irina couldn't help smiling at their inside joke. It dated all the way back to the legendary Alger Hiss.

"The partial match flagged the entrant, but there's nothing to go on. The man who arrived has a clean identity and, of course, plenty of wealth. They are still in the dark."

Irina pursed her lips. "A new name. Wealth. Possibly a thorough rewriting of his life. But if it's him..." Her pulse quickened. She recalled having already seen someone like Ivan there, in Paris—perhaps the same man. She pictured again the moment when their gaze had met, when she'd suddenly thought, *He's alive.*

The realization Ivan might still exist had churned in her mind, conjuring an undercurrent of conflicting emotions—confusion, relief, a strange sense of betrayal at his apparent resurrection.

She forced her focus back. "And who is this new identity? If it's only a partial match, who is the doppelgänger?"

"Volkoff," the informant replied, consulting his notepad. "Alex Volkoff. Claims to be Swiss-Azerbaijani. A tycoon with extensive business interests in energy, telecom, finance. Officially, he's in the United States to scout for expansion opportunities. No criminal record. The American data can't poke holes in his background." He paused.

"It gets more interesting. They're nervous also because he has tangential connections to certain U.S. political figures—serious enough to raise a few eyebrows. Still, so far, everything he does checks out as legitimate."

A silence took hold. Irina stared at a point on the wall, her mind recalling the man on a bridge across the Seine. She had recognized something in him, although at the time she'd refused to take it any further. Now it seemed her first instincts might have been correct.

Ivan had returned. But—if so—how; and—more seriously—for what purpose? Irina hid her turmoil behind a veneer of composure. "I want all background on this Volkoff. His movements, finances, associations. I want it all. If he is indeed the man I once knew... well, we need to know what it is he intends."

The informant nodded gravely. "Of course. I can gather more. But it won't be easy. Whoever engineered this identity did so meticulously. Some of our

sources are unsettled by the scale and precision of this operation. No one has found anything concrete—not enough to trigger action. It's all just instinct at the moment."

Irina's expression hardened, her gaze darkening. "Do whatever it takes. We must confirm the truth behind Volkoff's life story—when it began, how it developed, who helped him. In the meantime, we'll uphold the official story: that Ivan Asimov died in Siberia."

The informant rose from the chair, nodding his head. "I'll begin at once. You'll have preliminary data within forty-eight hours."

Irina inclined her head, almost a regal motion that ended the meeting. The man got his things, stepping back into the foyer. As he left, she locked the door, the chunky click designed to convey reassurance, echoing in the silent apartment and the corridor beyond.

Alone again, Irina let her professional mask fall. She walked again over to the window, pushing aside the drapery to stare once more at the night skyline. Her reflection in the glass revealed a woman who appeared both older and sharper than she once was.

The knowledge that she was a top-level Russian intelligence officer never bothered her, a second layer subsisting under her outward persona. In her mid-thirties, she'd already reached a rank others would court for decades. The files said 'merit.' She knew it was more choreography—her competence meeting someone else's design.

Now, confronted with the possibility that Ivan—once the object of a chaotic arrest and brutal prison experience—might not only be alive but crossing oceans with questionable aims, she felt a tremor of urgency.

For Irina, he was the one who would settle what determined outcomes: fate or rationality. She had appreciated her mother's way of life, but more as a relic from the past. Yet was the fortuneteller right? Or were the true drivers of world events just common sense and realpolitik? She thought the debate had been settled. Instead it had resurfaced, like the undead that circled her mother.

The fortuneteller had warned her about him: a man with torn allegiances, uncertain commitments, and a deep capacity to love—or to hate. Irina had concurred with this intuition when she met Ivan at the signing party.

Tonight, looking out, she felt the dark strangely menacing. In a few days, new intel might confirm or disprove her concerns. But a hunch told her Ivan Asimov was back. Regardless of the partial match in America—or the official stance in Russia—she had seen him with her own eyes.

Her mind turned over more questions. What did Ivan want: revenge or redemption? Or something else entirely? If he had orchestrated his own survival and transformation into a powerful oligarch, it spoke of a cunning she didn't realize he possessed. Irina thought of the fortuneteller's words: *someone who is both more, and less, than he aspires to be.*

As the lights twinkled outside, Irina swore she would unravel his secrets—whatever the cost. The years had taught her to be patient, to move quietly but with focus. In her line of work an old ghost reappearing was not a good omen, and she had additional reasons to find out what everything meant.

If destiny were orchestrating it all, she wanted to know what her role was in this story—and she'd make sure the conclusion suited her. Irina closed her eyes. Whatever mask he wore, she would strip it away—not just out of duty, but out of need.

19. Fall Gala

The façade of a stately Beaux-Arts edifice glittered faintly in the early fall dusk, as if burnished for an audience. Rows of decorative lights twined around entrance columns—their reflections dancing on the sleek paint of black limousines as one after another pulled up.

From the back door of the latest one, Kaisa emerged. A rush of evening air greeted her—edged with a coolness that marked the end of summer. The building's ornate sconces lent her ivory cloak a deep, rich glow and picked out, beneath it, the fine silver threads of her dress.

The building proudly displayed its heritage at the entrance: Metropolitan Trust. *Ah yes,* Kaisa thought, *the annual New York gala.*

A slight breeze teased strands of her frost-honey hair, arranged in delicate waves that brushed lightly against her cheeks. The diamond studs at her ears gleamed with each turn of her head. She paused at the curb, one gloved hand adjusting the hem of her cloak, which had turned up, then ascended the broad marble steps to the building's entrance.

Inside, huge signs marked the event as the annual gala for the ballet while towering ballerinas formed an entourage guiding arrivals into the main room, an enormous space reminding Kaisa briefly of Grand Central. Two huge display screens placed at the back of the room projected the company's best performances from the last year.

The swirl of conversation had already begun. The clink of champagne glasses and the ring of silverware on plates formed a steady melodic undercurrent, punctuated by bursts of laughter. The ballroom chandeliers bathed everyone in a golden haze.

The end of summer and the return of cooler weather to New York seemed to have enticed out socialites, executives, and others—Kaisa guessed a mixture of bankers and entrepreneurs—ready to indulge themselves in another flourish of charitable extravagance.

She had read somewhere that while charity giving, in total, was expanding substantially it was largely the big players giving to causes at the top end of town. Nominal dollars went up, but it hid what was occurring underneath.

Looking around, now, she considered the men in their perfectly tailored suits and women in their formal gowns—the ballet dancers in their costumes so elegant and attractive. Her eyes briefly followed one lithe man as he demonstrated his ability to pirouette. She counted six or seven turns. His performance was certainly eye-catching.

It all merged into an animated sea of celebration, ambition, and display. For a fleeting moment, Kaisa was struck by how this entire tableau felt like a marvelous stage set—designed with grand gestures and sublime illusions that only partially concealed the more selfish aims beneath.

A nearby server offered her a flute of champagne. She accepted with a polite nod, letting the first sip settle her nerves. Then, from somewhere across the throng, a voice called her name:

"Kaisa!"

She turned, spotting Peter threading his way toward her, a tumbler in one hand containing a honey-yellow liquid, not quite amber. *Tequila*, she guessed. He wore a burgundy-red suit, and his easy grin lit his face. Tall, solidly built, he exuded a worldly charm that matched the environment perfectly.

"Peter," she greeted, returning his grin with a subtle acknowledgment. They exchanged a brief, light embrace.

"How's the year treating you?" he asked, his tone suggesting genuine interest rather than mindless small talk.

She shrugged elegantly, her accent—a trace of Finnish lilt—coloring her words. "It's been... interesting. But tonight is about celebration, I suppose."

He read the soft deflection in her eyes, chuckling as he took a quick sip of his glass. "I'm glad you could make it. You look stunning, as always. I'm surprised others attend such events, knowing they must compete with you." He paused as Kaisa smiled, pleased at the compliment.

"Here. Let me introduce you to some people. It makes the evening more pleasant." And without waiting, his gaze swept the crowd with the efficiency of a natural networker.

It landed on a man standing somewhat apart at the edges of the room, near the marble columns. "Jake," Peter called, brightening at the sight of him. "Come meet Kaisa—you'll like each other."

Kaisa's stomach gave a tiny jolt. His name landed like static over a memory she'd tried to seal away. Nevertheless she controlled her expression and pivoted gracefully, following Peter's lead as they wove around various cliques. The sound of ballet music rose above them for a second; a burst of light from somewhere shimmered overhead, reflecting off crystal chandeliers and half-empty champagne flutes.

When they reached Jake, he turned slightly, revealing sharp features and a tailored suit. His dark hair was combed with purposeful precision, but there was a stiffness in his bearing, as though he were never fully at ease.

"Jake," Peter said, laying a hand on the man's shoulder, "this is Kaisa. Kaisa, meet Jake Laskin—CEO of PanEnergy. He's leading some pretty big projects right now. Pipeline expansions, wind farm initiatives, you name it."

Jake extended his hand, a broad smile on his face but a certain guardedness in his eyes. "A pleasure," he greeted.

Kaisa returned his handshake with a poised smile, holding his gaze a fraction longer than might be normal. "Likewise," she said, her tone betraying nothing. She had heard rumors about his ascent, of course, but their paths had never crossed, at least in such an overtly social setting.

Peter, evidently pleased with his hosting duties, launched into another grand summary. "Kaisa's a consultant—markets, finance, capital. She's brilliant at cutting through the noise. Jake's riding the wave of green energy, while at the same time pursuing a pipeline that's unavoidably... complicated." Peter let out an amused chuckle. "You two should talk."

With that, Peter offered a quick wink to Kaisa and a solid pat on Jake's shoulder, then was gone, drawn back into the shifting dance of the party.

Kaisa and Jake found themselves momentarily alone in a corner of the gala, forming a little bubble apart from the swirling lights and general bonhomie. She tilted her head slightly. "Wind farms and pipelines," she echoed with a soft smile. "Quite the combination."

Jake gave a thin, guarded smile. "We're diversifying. It's been a turbulent year in energy, so we have to keep options open. Renewables are creating opportunities, but politics still chokes the pipeline."

Kaisa nodded, taking a sip of champagne. "Politics is an ever-present factor, especially in your sector. And PanEnergy's had its fair share of challenges, from what I gather."

"Challenges—yes, but also success." An edge of pride crept into Jake's voice. "We're forging ahead on expansions, including South America. I only hope global tensions don't derail what progress we've made. Venezuela's probably the biggest issue there." He paused, then gave a slight shrug. "Enough about me. You're the markets guru. The looming uncertainties of an election year must keep you busy. How's it going?"

She offered a wry smile. "Let's just say I've no shortage of calls from CEOs stressed about the risks, especially in terms of policy. They're all frightened of one candidate in particular."

Jake smiled. "That woman from Texas," he hazarded.

Kaisa nodded. "They're so used to the current trajectory—they've assumed it's inevitable—and they've made so many statements in public to ingratiate themselves either with Capitol Hill or with the media establishment. They're scared shitless." She laughed.

"Live by the sword, die by the sword," she continued. "In any case, the outcomes are increasingly polarized. Everyone recognizes it. What that means in a concrete sense..."

Jake nodded. "Everyone's an expert until the numbers don't add up or the current's heading the wrong direction, and then they want a consultant to transfer responsibility. But it's interesting, seeing how it all shifts, especially in terms of geopolitical alliances."

The conversation hung in the air, neither of them quite dropping their guard. After a moment, Kaisa inclined her head, voice dropping slightly. "Will your wife be joining the festivities?" she inquired.

Jake's face tightened imperceptibly before he answered, "No. She had other commitments."

Kaisa only nodded. "Well, I hope the year is treating you both well." A flicker of strain passed across Jake's eyes.

Kaisa noticed the tremor, but said nothing. After a moment of silence, she gave a polite murmur—"I think I need a refill"—and departed. Jake smiled and nodded, remaining in his corner.

As Kaisa approached the bar, a swirl of gala energy encircled her. Someone toasted the current season—calling it the best ever—regretting only that the much shorter fall program remained. A pair of jovial guests burst out in shrill laughter. And a group of donors admired the lavishness of the décor, the strength of this year's ballet troupe. "Simply stunning," she heard behind her. "Too gorgeous this year."

Kaisa handed her empty flute to a bartender who promptly refilled it with some fresh champagne. She took a short sip, savoring the umami flavor, letting the effervescence steady her thoughts. The sudden meeting with Jake had unsettled her.

And that was when she saw him—or thought she did.

Kaisa looked away for a second—as if to clear her mind. *It must be a head-fake*, she thought—her subconscious triggered.

The man had just collected his drink and was stepping away from the bar. The profile, his bearing, the casual grip on the glass—it had all struck her, a bolt of recognition.

Her mind stuttered, heart racing, as a name echoed through her memory: *Ivan.* The sound of it—like a forbidden chord—vibrated through her being. Her Ivan. The man who'd vanished years ago, leaving her with an avalanche of unanswered questions and an ache that never quite went away.

The second expanded as she froze, her pulse hammering in her ears. It couldn't be him. It was not possible. He'd gone. It was one of those daytime nightmares.

She'd spent countless nights replaying—voluntarily or not—the last time she'd seen Ivan, wondering what would become of him, and eventually resigning herself to never seeing him again. He'd died. The State Department had sent her a formal note—one which indicated, in passing, that his ashes had been conveyed to his mother.

Now what was she to think? How was she to reconcile this man here with the explanation she'd curated? She stood still a while. The swirl around her seemed to distort, the golden lights turning surreal. She felt like she wanted to scream, but found herself speechless. Kaisa touched her throat as if to check words were still there. At last she turned back only to see the solitary figure drifting away from the bar, moving into the crowd.

Some primal force now spurred her forward. She abandoned the champagne on a counter and quickened her pace. Every step felt fraught with a mix of longing and dread. Reaching the spot where the man had been, Kaisa found it empty. She scanned desperately among the throng, but he was gone. Just like that.

Relief and disappointment warred in her heart. Maybe the gala spirit, with all its costumes and illusions, had conjured an impossible vision. The unreality of the instant weighed on her. Another flute of champagne was offered, and she accepted gratefully—her second or third. She needed to calm the tumult erupting in her thoughts.

Yet Kaisa couldn't shake the prospect that Ivan was there, in the same place, so long after he'd vanished. Ivan, the man she'd once agreed to marry, who had dissolved from her life as though swallowed by the earth. It was Orpheus and Eurydice, only reversed.

The underworld had taken Ivan from her, and when she dared to look back he'd vanished for good. The big screens around the hall had switched to a new spectacle—Pina Bausch's work leveraging Gluck's music. Maybe this had pierced her subconscious—a cruel echo, mocking her loss. She took another restless sip from her glass, the bubbles tasting bitter this time.

The sea of tuxedos and ballgowns—groups leaning close, smiling, laughing—hindered any proper search. Acquaintances she passed offered polite nods or half smiles, but Kaisa barely registered. She drifted as a phantom, driven by a half-formed hope.

Then she spotted him a second time, or so it seemed. He was near the far side of the room, heading out to the coat check. The man's outline, his bearing, the confident yet unhurried stride—they were impossibly familiar. She felt her heart lurch and hurried faster over the marble floor, weaving past clusters of merrymakers.

A woman in a sparkling gown abruptly crossed her path. Kaisa murmured a perfunctory apology. The press of bodies felt like an obstacle purposefully designed to slow her.

Ballet dancers crisscrossed her way. She swallowed the impulse to call out. Logic told her she was wrong—causing a scene wouldn't help. Her pace quickened, the crowd's gaiety and the bright notes of another ballet suite fading into irrelevance.

At last, the crush thinned. The corridor leading to the coat check was a quieter, more discreet space. However, the lighting was subdued, and it was harder to make out shapes. The man was nowhere in sight. An ornate archway led outside. Kaisa rushed through it, hoping he'd gone that way.

The sudden coolness of the night startled her. Breathing raggedly, she halted at the top of the building's broad steps, scanning the sidewalk and the street beyond. Cars edged past, horns tooting in the congested traffic. Well-dressed guests eddied along the sidewalk, waiting in a jovial, relaxed fashion for their rides, the lights of the building's lampposts picking out their glamorous dress and well-groomed features.

But of the man who might be Ivan, there was no sign. Kaisa felt her chest tighten. Perhaps he'd never been there at all, she reasoned again, simply a ghost conjured out of an unusual evening: her longing, Jake's presence, the ballet performance. It had provoked a sudden nostalgia.

So much time had passed. And yet so many questions had never found closure. The night breeze made her dress swirl around her legs. People jostled past, exchanging farewells and goodnights, each lost in their own worlds.

She lingered there an instant, biting her lip against a renewed sense of sorrow. Yet, whatever had just occurred—whether it was real or only an illusion—she wouldn't find resolution by pacing these steps.

She gave one last glance up and down the busy street. There was no tall figure in a dark suit waiting at the curb, no trace of the outline she had glimpsed twice inside. She drew a long breath and turned back toward the building.

Kaisa re-entered the ballroom with her composure barely restored. The intense light, the decorations, the ballet sets and costumes, the refined currents of discussion—it all now seemed a parallel reality. In a corner of her mind, an uneasy possibility had taken hold that Ivan might still be alive.

She wanted to believe—and yet dreaded the implications if it were true. She steeled herself. A passing staff member offered her another drink, and she saw her hand going out to accept it before she'd even reached a conclusion.

The music had restarted, and a ballet couple were engaged in a seemingly spontaneous display, spinning about a small stage demarcated on the floor.

She caught sight of Peter with another circle of acquaintances, animatedly discussing some philanthropic venture. Jake was nowhere in sight.

The next hour passed in a haze of courtesy and forced sociability. Kaisa nodded at conversation partners, responded to questions about work, joined in a toast to the ballet company. However, all the while, her mind was churning over the past: the man she'd accepted a future with, the abrupt end of that dream, the sudden feeling of emptiness.

She recalled fleeting references to him in the news, often articles about the nastiness of the Russian law. But Kaisa had filled the years since with another life. She had worked out her own form of therapy—homemade, patchwork, one that dealt with each pressing issue as it arose. And it had worked, at least to some extent. The life she'd cobbled together suited her fine, even if she did have occasional misgivings. She'd succeeded in finding a modus vivendi.

The dissonance between the gala spirit around her and the unsettled storm in her chest seemed nearly unbearable. Yet she squared her shoulders and reminded herself of what she always did: survive and adapt.

If the man she'd seen were truly Ivan, she'd find him. If not, she'd bury this fresh challenge, this new disappointment, as she'd once buried the pain of his disappearance.

Kaisa let out a slow breath. A group of night owls appeared at her side, eager to show their faces and catch a late taste of the gala event. Kaisa resolved to slip out. With a tired acceptance, she acknowledged that the mystery person was unlikely to reappear that night.

The coatroom staff, bright and courteous as always, handed her cloak across the counter, murmuring their good wishes. She left a decent tip and stepped back into the corridor, head full of swirling, unresolved questions. She could still feel the gala going strong behind her—the music and laughter, the ring of glasses.

Outside, the city lights flared against the streets. A dusting of leaves drifted down. There was a brief hush, almost poignant, teasing secrets she couldn't quite grasp. It was like wandering around a dream, a fantasy. And then the sound of engines and conversations returned, reminding her that the world kept turning, no matter what personal ghosts materialized.

Her driver approached, inclining his head. She nodded absently, heart still pounding. The man—Ivan—was out there, or maybe not. But if he was, she wanted to know where he'd been all this time. What tangled web of secrets explained his abrupt reemergence, his resurrection?

Pulling tight the collar of her ivory cloak, Kaisa descended the steps and slipped into the waiting limo. As the car pulled away, merging into New York's lively traffic, Kaisa let her gaze drift, her mind turning over what she'd seen.

Something deep inside her refused to dismiss the possibility that he'd come back—however improbable. The imprint of that profile, the way he held himself… it was too real, too haunting. Even so, the mirage had chosen a hell of a moment to reappear.

Pulling her phone from her purse, Kaisa opened a blank screen, ready to type a message. She stared for a moment, then locked the device again. Better to wait, get some information, keep her emotions hidden behind the same composure that had shielded her all these years.

The limo rounded a corner, and she caught a fleeting reflection of herself in the glass partition—eyes shining with a raw intensity that did not match the elegant calm of her attire. For a second she felt unmoored, cast adrift from the world with nothing but darkness around. What was out there? Kaisa didn't have the answers.

But seeing this darkness, she felt a tiny shiver of anticipation. Whether or not it was just a memory, she'd find the specter and shine a light on it so relentless that nothing would stay hidden. She settled back against the seat and controlled her breathing.

Amid the city's autumnal cheer, she held onto a single idea—as a ballerina before launching into a great leap: Ghosts only stay buried if you let them.

21. Executive Meeting

The 65th floor of PanEnergy Tower offered a tremendous view of the New York skyline, today stretched under a pale September sun. The limpid air gave crispness to the cityscape, a combination of architecture at its best and nature in the fall—replete with reds, oranges, and golds.

The walls, paneled in a deep, rich mahogany, exuded authority. Recessed lights dotted two sides of the ceiling, casting deliberate halos on the black marble conference table in the center around which clustered leather chairs. Several individuals were already sitting—some talking, others reading their notes or looking at their cell phones.

When Jake Laskin, PanEnergy CEO, walked into his boardroom, shadows already stretched across the floor. The afternoon had progressed. To Jake's left, he saw the single high-resolution photo of an offshore oil rig, which had always been there—a blazing testament to the industry's power. The picture's russet sky matched the seasonal colors outside especially as dusk arrived and enriched them with its warm light.

On his right, opposite the picture, was the boardroom's screen and video-con facilities. Jake wouldn't need to connect anyone today. The key people were all gathered there.

He was almost fifty but still remembered how the air felt charged when he first entered the company's old boardroom as a young man. These days PanEnergy's boardroom seemed more functional than mythic. However, he still got a charge from entering.

As he walked over to his chair, he noticed two new pot plants standing like silent guardians at the far end—injecting an organic note into the otherwise sterile tableau.

Outside, he saw again the Empire State Building, glowing like a beacon—an impressive symbol, eternal. Slightly to its right was the Chrysler Building. He lingered on the vision.

The Empire State would change colors at night while the Chrysler's point—its spire and crown of triangular windows—would light up a bright silver. He still found the view powerful. One day, he wanted PanEnergy to occupy a similar point on the skyline, a similar niche in the general psyche. Each era deserved its own symbols.

The enthusiastic voices of his team echoed off the paneled walls, but fell away quickly when Jake arrived. He wore a well-tailored suit and a muted blue tie, exuding a controlled confidence. Yet, his gaze hinted at a certain impatience beneath the deliberate composure.

Today's meeting was crucial for setting a framework. The year-end strategy off-site was approaching, and he intended to waste no time.

Jake sat down at the head of the table. "Let's get to it," he said, his voice slicing through the residual murmur of unfinished side conversations. "We're not here to admire the view or compare restaurant ideas. First item—Logan, pipeline update."

Logan Briggs, robust in build and sporting a faint Texan drawl, had a talent for dealing with red tape. He cleared his throat. "The Northern Connect pipeline is around 40% complete. However, we're facing fiercer opposition every week." He paused.

"Environmental groups keep filing lawsuits and stirring protests, painting us as corporate villains. The negative media coverage is beginning to bite." He shook his head.

Jake's finger tapped a soft staccato against the table. "That's become the norm. Fallback plan?"

"We're deploying more legal resources and lobbying state governments for support. But each delay drains cash. Even the unions are starting to show nerves."

Jake nodded grimly. "Keep me updated. We need to stand firm. Emily, you're next."

Emily Shore, VP of Renewable Energy, pressed an app on her tablet. "Our Cedar Ridge Wind Farm is set to become the largest in the state. And in contrast to Logan's pipeline project we get little trouble from the authorities."

She laughed heartily. "There are some local reactionaries—who want to save their beautiful surroundings. And, of course, there are implications for wildlife habitats. Yet, here as elsewhere, they'll cut down forests for wind farms with scarcely a second thought."

"I think terminology helps," a colleague joked. "Describing renewables as natural and projects as farms makes them feel congruent, even harmless."

Jake gave a weary sigh. "So we're heroes to big-picture environmentalists, but villains to local communities?"

"Exactly," Emily replied with frustration edging her tone. "They back renewable energy on a ballot, then balk when turbines appear in their backyard. It's maddening. But no different from other policy fronts. And," she paused, "this is the future."

Jake massaged his temples. "Okay. That just means we push hard with our community outreach programs. We can't let such NIMBY sentiments gain momentum. Fortunately, these stories—about preserving views and beauty—tend to be headlined in the Republican press, which encourages the present administration to ignore them."

From the other side of the table, Vince Kramer, Head of M&A, cleared his throat. "While we're on the topic of challenging situations... Expansions in the Permian Basin aren't looking promising either. High premiums, falling productivity, low oil prices. Firms are either hoarding assets or overpricing them. My scouts have found nothing that appropriately balances the cost or risk."

Jake's scowl deepened. "We need a big move, Vince, something that actually shifts the dial. We must bolster our bottom line as well as our status. Too often CEOs focus just on their public standing or their media reputation. It's a real trap. And we should be more demanding."

Vince nodded. "Understood."

Jake swept his gaze around the table. "All right. Let's pivot to the long-term outlook. Katherine, talk to me about future opportunities."

Katherine "Kat" Meyers was Head of Business Development. She paused before answering. She had long ago discovered that this simple tactic made her proposals sound more considered and powerful. "We have some good opportunities for growth, but each with their own risks." She looked slowly around the table and then fixed Jake in the eyes.

"First, offshore wind in California. Federal subsidies mitigate start-up costs, but uncertain permitting is a challenge. Second, geothermal—if we partner with a cutting-edge R&D outfit, we might fast-track the technology. Last, we have compact nuclear power in the form of SMRs—that is Small Modular Reactors."

A murmur ran across the table. Nuclear always produced controversy. Some people feared it, others saw in it a cure-all, the solution to everything.

"SMRs," Jake echoed. "Intriguing. Go on."

Katherine took a measured breath. "SMRs are basically smaller, versatile reactors. They can be built fast with fewer regulatory hurdles than a huge plant, though the rules still aren't trivial. The potential is enormous: a steady, low-carbon power source to complement our renewables. Government spend is ramping up, and if we get in early, we could corral a chunk of that money."

Jake's gaze narrowed. "Risks?"

Katherine's response was quick. "Public perception, for one. Many still equate nuclear with meltdown disasters: Chernobyl, Fukushima leap to mind. What a mess that was."

"Then there's the approval process and specialized workforce needs. On top of all this sits party politics, which never goes away. But longer-term? If SMRs deliver on their promise, we could dominate a sector that underpins our energy growth for the distant future."

Jake steepled his fingers. "This resonates with our pivot to cleaner energy. But it's a moonshot. We'll need a feasibility study. Let's do it. Katherine—gather your best team. Show me licensing frameworks, cost projections, and any synergies, for example with existing grid capacities. I want a thorough report by next month."

An undercurrent of excitement rippled through the senior staff. SMRs as a central plank in ensuring the company's future was sure to make headlines.

Jake let the moment settle, then scanned the table once more. "What about carbon capture and storage? It's pricey and forever in development, but it could be a game changer for our image and for actual emissions reduction."

"Expensive," Emily interjected, "but yes, the potential's huge."

Katherine nodded. "Yes," she agreed. "*If* we master carbon capture, we position ourselves as a leader in net-zero oil and gas. But there's the rub. The technology's always been shaky. No one's pulled it off—not for want of trying. Any breakthrough might pay off exponentially, but the paradigm-changing moment never quite arrives."

Jake made a note. "It wouldn't be the first time in industry—or technology. All right, let's keep that in mind."

He paused and scanned the faces around him. "We are at a turning point. PanEnergy's not an oil & gas company or even a wind farm—it's an energy giant, bridging the transition from old to new. Let's seize that narrative." He gave the table a little thump.

He felt satisfied with the progress made. "Any last thoughts before we wrap?"

Katherine hesitated. "One last topic: the Arctic JV with VoltaGaz. The initial data from the Arctic Basin looks more promising than we expected—reserves that could rival OPEC fields. But a rumor's circulating—they want us out." A chill fell over the table. All eyes turned to her.

Jake's voice emerged cold. "VoltaGaz wants us out of our own joint venture? That's not an arrangement we entered lightly."

Katherine shrugged. "They're not openly stating it. However, they're hinting we should consider withdrawing before it is too late. We hear that some official in Russia's Ministry of Energy has drawn up a scenario for 'strategic realignments.' This sees the phased withdrawal of foreign participation in Russia's unique assets. If we refuse to deal now, they may force us out later."

"And how would they do that?" Jake asked, a little unkindly—as if the idea were nonsense.

"They could portray us as an unreliable partner or as not technically capable or, more seriously, as malicious—forever locking out PanEnergy as a suitable candidate in Russia and opening up scope for reparation claims."

Jake inhaled slowly. "We've poured years of capital and effort into that region. Let them try to push us out. We'll see who blinks first."

The tension crackled as Jake's gaze swept the room. "We'll discuss this more once we have concrete intel—something actionable. In the meantime keep the lines open with VoltaGaz, and do nothing that suggests weakness. If they want a confrontation, we won't go quietly."

Silence fell, thick and loaded. Then Jake nodded sharply, concluding the meeting. "Let's call it a day. Time's precious. Go make things happen."

Jake got up and went over to the window. The weakening sunlight cast ever-longer shadows across the room. Chairs scraped against the floor as the executives gathered their notes and headed out the boardroom doors. A few managers congratulated him in passing on a "solid meeting." Jake gave a silent nod but felt no relief.

Despite his conviction and the company's forward-looking slogans, Jake knew that diverse pressures endangered their future. He stared at the metropolis below, thinking of how fleeting success could be if they didn't innovate as fast as the market changed.

When the last of the executives had gone, the door reopened. Kat stepped in, a stack of documents cradled under one arm. She wore a pensive look.

"Jake, got a minute?" she asked.

He turned. "Of course."

They stepped together into the corridor outside, and dropped their voices in the hope of not drawing attention to their conversation. The hallway was all glass and polished marble, providing another panoramic view that impressed visitors.

Kat continued. "About VoltaGaz," she said. "I just got an internal memo from our liaison in Moscow—the business context could be changing and changing fast. Russia's so-called 'strategic shift' may be the first step in an effort that nationalizes resources and cuts out foreign influence. If we're not completely on top of this, we could be forced out of the Arctic."

Jake's jaw set. "We can't let them claim those fields outright. If the reserves are bigger—substantially bigger than they've already let on—I'm sure they'd want to get them back cheaply. We can't let that happen."

Kat nodded. "They're making veiled threats about turning to other actors, foreign partners, if they need more advanced technology. We face competition not just from our larger peers but more likely from China's state-owned enterprises."

"Let them try," Jake said, voice steely. "We'll fight this in the courts if we have to." What he didn't say—what he wouldn't admit—was that the maneuver felt somehow personal, as if it were some kind of business karma.

"Besides," he continued, "it's not so simple to swap a partner at this point, mid-development. Our technical data is locked behind NDAs, and we can tie them up in contractual disputes for years."

Kat flicked through the folder, her face stern. "I'll coordinate with Legal. We will prepare for every outcome. Meanwhile, we should keep pushing that pipeline synergy we'd planned, see if that influences public perception at all."

Jake gave a nod. "Good. Also, while you're at it, can you discreetly gather intelligence about who's behind VoltaGaz's shift in attitude. If it's a power play from someone high in the government, we may need diplomatic help."

"Understood. I'll keep you informed," she said, her eyes reflecting a mix of pressure and resolve. She turned, her footsteps echoing across the polished floor as she departed.

Jake took a small breath. The synergy of old and new energy was more than a corporate slogan—it was an existential goal. PanEnergy had already staked claims in fossil fuels and renewables—and would not stay a bystander in any nuclear future. The Russian Arctic was an important element in their longer-term plans, one that suddenly seemed at risk of being yanked away.

He returned to the boardroom to gather a few final notes he'd forgotten. The silence in the once-animated space felt almost eerie.

The chairs stood scattered around the table as forsaken witnesses to the day's excitement—some tucked in, others randomly strewn. He picked up the lost folder. He noted a single laptop, still humming, that an assistant had left and closed it gently. Jake snapped off the lights and exited.

Back in the hallway, a clock showed five-thirty. He realized he'd hardly eaten since morning, running on coffee and momentum. His mind wandered to the ballet gala barely a couple of weeks prior—the music and champagne, the polite small talk with Kaisa.

Her curious gaze and poised questions evidenced how much Kaisa had, at last, recovered from those years after the global financial crisis. If only such gatherings were the greatest challenge he faced. But instead he had to deal with real life: pipeline controversies, wind farm execution, potential nuclear ventures, an uncertain global market, finding a stake in the Permian Basin, and now tension with VoltaGaz.

Jake exhaled. Next year's strategy was just taking shape, and it promised to be a crucible for PanEnergy. The old model of drilling, refining, and distributing might endure, but not unopposed or untransformed. And every pivot, every strategic gamble, carried huge risks.

Jake allowed himself a rare moment of reflection. A decade ago, PanEnergy had been smaller, more narrowly positioned. Now it stood, under his lead, on the threshold of epic change.

As he strode toward his corner suite, he heard the faint hum of conversation from staffers in adjacent meeting rooms, each tackling a piece of the growing puzzle that was PanEnergy's empire.

The phone in his pocket vibrated with an incoming text—likely an update on some legal detail or a stock movement. The day never ended.

And yet this was how he wanted it. He thought briefly of his father. How he'd been shuffled around the country in this or that job, never properly recognized, never promoted to a real position despite his capabilities and achievements. He'd been too passive, too accepting. And Jake had been there to witness the results.

What aggravated this memory, what irritated Jake more was that his mother—out of all of them—had been the most formidable with her relentless energy and insight.

She had engineered the family's biggest accomplishments. And yet she had been the dutiful housewife. Her tremendous spirit had burned brightly and to everyone's benefit, but it had scarcely touched the rest of the world.

Jake almost slammed the door on entering his office. He'd compensate for the treatment of his father, make up for the injustice to his mother. Jake paused to allow himself a moment to recover. He forced his mind back to the company and its core challenge as he saw it.

Wind turbines might soon pepper distant fields, nuclear SMRs might hum quietly in rural landscapes, and carbon capture might relegate emissions to memory. However—for the present—oil, pipelines, and geopolitics would still shape PanEnergy's business, underpin the firm's bread and butter. The question was how to interweave all these threads into a harmonious future.

His moment of solitude was brief. There came a knock at the door: Logan Briggs again, wanting a quick clarification on a pipeline budget. Jake motioned him in. Together they pored over financial spreadsheets on one of the office tables.

Lines and lines of data danced under the overhead lighting, and Jake's mind was on top of it all, shifting from high-level strategy back to daily numbers. This was the reality of his role: it stretched him in both directions—it asked for macro vision as well as operational insight.

He recalled a former boss, now retired, who had asked him which was more important, and he had argued strategy—the big picture. The boss had said it was attention to detail, and so Jake had missed out on the promotion. It was a serious promotion, and the outcome hurt. It was only much later that Jake realized the right answer was both.

Finally, Logan departed, leaving Jake alone again. He went back to his desk and collapsed into his chair, massaging the bridge of his nose. The hush of the office seemed to amplify the swirl of half-finished ideas in his mind. He pictured his trip to the sub-zero expanse of Russia's far north, bursting with rumor and potential.

Jake clicked open an email from the in-house legal team: a first draft about how PanEnergy might respond if VoltaGaz moved. Terms like "binding arbitration," "bilateral investment treaties," and "sovereign risk" dotted the paragraphs. His lips pursed as he skimmed it. The gist was clear: it could rapidly escalate into a major, direct confrontation.

This was the new normal—a global scramble for energy market dominance. PanEnergy was determined to remain at the forefront. If that meant clinging to fossil plays a bit longer or stepping into nuclear development a little more quickly, so be it. If that meant matching Russia's maneuvers and forging new alliances with government-level programs, they'd adapt. They would survive. Better than that, they would thrive.

An hour slipped by in focused reading—signing documents, responding to emails. By the time he noticed, the sun had shifted from a late-afternoon gold to a reddish black. A mild ache in his shoulders reminded him he'd been at it nonstop since dawn.

Finally, Jake rose, pacing to the window. The city below started to glimmer, headlights weaving in the streets. The cool glass of the window pressed against his fingertips as he stared out. The year was nearing its final stretch, and the stakes were only increasing.

Yet he was confident. He was no stranger to big gambles, and people always underestimated him—that's how he'd ascended to the CEO role in the first place. People often remarked on his cool under pressure, but few recognized it was his relentless desire to secure what he wanted—whatever the risk—that helped him get places. By unfolding a new blueprint, he'd ensure PanEnergy didn't just perform but soared.

As darkness fell he resolved to tackle the last phase of his work day. Some final meetings, follow-up phone calls, and preparatory emails—the endeavor, no doubt, stretching into the night. Each step was integral in orchestrating PanEnergy's destiny. The race for energy supremacy never let up. And Jake Laskin, CEO, was determined to come out on top.

Heading out to find Emily, Jake did have a sense the world was tightening around him—competitors, governments, whole regimes repositioning for advantage. And he knew their agendas would collide with his soon enough; collisions were part of the job.

What he hadn't registered—what wasn't part of the job—was the latest force bearing down on him. And by the time he noticed, it would be a scramble just to recover.

22. Office Encounter

It was pitch black by the time Jake Laskin returned to his office and clicked shut its polished door. The noise reverberated slightly, highlighting the emptiness of the building at this hour. Night had settled over Manhattan, and the city lights twinkled outside the windows.

Jake inhaled slowly, savoring the momentary peace. This was the only time he had to reflect, late at night, to map out the vision he had for the company and its place over the next decade.

He didn't turn the lights on, but instead walked to the glass wall overlooking Midtown. Down below, tiny pulses of white and red beat a frenetic rhythm. Sometimes, in rare cases of weakness, he wanted it to stop. He thought more calm might be nice. *What was everything for?* Then he corrected himself. He knew what it was all for.

The day's gossip drifted around the edges of his mind. Most of it would be false—rumors like any other that popped up in the market. They sprouted every few weeks, supported by the damp mist of speculation clinging to his industry and keeping it perpetually uneasy. Jake exhaled. It wasn't worth more effort tonight—he'd had enough doomsaying for at least a couple of days.

Instead, he let his thoughts linger on the future he coveted: for himself, for PanEnergy. He saw a chance to guide the company into an era that blended conventional and cutting-edge energy solutions.

Something inside him—his relentless sense of ambition, his desire to make up for the bad things in his life—stirred at the idea of shaping his sector's evolution. Let the cynics chastise him for dreaming big; he intended to turn those dreams into reality.

A faint sound drew his attention. He turned, and his heart jolted in a different kind of recognition.

Eve stood there, leaning against his lacquered walnut desk, her figure illuminated by the ambient light. Though the rest of the building had descended into after-hours quiet, she appeared anything but subdued.

Jake saw she was attired in lightweight black cotton that moved with her as she stepped toward him. Thin straps shaped a neckline that drew his gaze lower.

Jake didn't recognize this outfit—it must be new, he guessed. The ensemble highlighted all he liked best about Eve: confidence and elegance. A daring split to the waist up one side exposed a length of pale thigh. Too enticing for a room meant for business.

Her long glossy hair framed her face and shoulders in loose waves, and her lips were curved in a slow, mischievous smile.

Seeing her dressed like this in his office—their office once, back in Moscow—sent a pulse of heat through him. He'd divorced his first wife—briefly sorry about what it meant for the children, whom he almost never saw these days. And he'd married Eve—later, after winning the top position at PanEnergy.

Eve had lost her professional track at the firm as a result. But they'd both welcomed their new life, he recalled idly—embraced its possibilities.

Now, the passion that had fueled his desire to possess her in those early Moscow nights seemed more contained. Eve caught his eye, raising one sculpted brow. "You're working late—again."

He scowled slightly, crossing the room. "You know me, Eve," he said, a note of excuse, if not explanation, in his tone. "I wanted a moment to think. Sketch out where I'm taking PanEnergy over the next decade, how to merge old and new energies. The board's behind me, but it's a tightrope. And I—"

She tilted her head, cutting him off with a playful hush. "You can strategize tomorrow," she murmured, taking a step closer so that her perfume—sweet, exotic—filled his senses. He should have noticed it when he first entered but Jake was too distracted. "Right now, I want to remind you that you're more than just a CEO."

Eve's gaze studied Jake—the tired lines around his mouth, the tightness in his shoulders. He'd loosened his tie hours ago, leaving the collar open at his throat, which lent him an air of weary magnetism. She brushed a hand over his chest, her arm slender and radiant in the reflected light, and moved to undo a button near his sternum Her actions were unhurried and provocative.

Jake swallowed, the hush of the near-empty tower intensifying the moment. "Eve," he warned in a whisper, though his resistance sounded half-hearted. The memory of their earliest days in Moscow, the stolen hours of ferocious intimacy, clashed with the new reality of endless meetings and updates. Eve was giving him an opening, a brief chance to liberate himself from the worry and pressure.

"I miss my husband," she said, voice low, each syllable carrying an invitation. She slid onto the edge of his desk, crossing her legs—a slow, unapologetic display. Her dress, revealing a stretch of soft skin, hinted at the nakedness behind the shadows, distracting his focus. The flimsiness of her outfit—its shoulder straps scarcely keeping place—suggested the ease with which Jake could meet Eve's desire.

He stepped forward, torn between exasperation and want. "I'm sorry," he managed, adding a gruff note to his voice—both to put off Eve's ambitions and to convince himself that he wasn't interested. "I get consumed by these ideas. It's the only way I know to keep everything afloat."

"And who keeps you afloat?" she countered, letting a hand grasp his tie and tug him nearer. "All day, you're juggling the pipeline expansions, the wind farms, the new frontiers, the next big partnership. However, you forget about your project here with me; you forget the partnership you already have—present before you." Her voice went husky, and her lips parted in the wisp of a smile.

Jake tried to retort, but any words tangled on his tongue as Eve's free hand trailed down the buttons of his shirt, catching the rim of his pants, pulling him closer. Behind Jake the city glittered with thousands of lights, as people came and went, but in that instant he felt suddenly alone. The hum of the building's HVAC and the new, still faint, sounds of the night cleaning crew only accentuated his discomfort.

Eve leaned forward, the warmth of her breath teasing the side of his throat as she kissed him, her breast pressing into him, and for a second Jake was back in the Moscow office—the dark windows, Eve pressing his body against cold glass, the giddy danger that had energized them. "Look at me," she ordered, her voice suddenly serious.

She moved with a languid grace, the thin strap of her slip sliding down one shoulder, exposing more of her body. "I thought that we needed to catch up," she said, a bit like a medic with a patient. "Relieve some of your stress before you begin to unravel." Her voice took on a lighter note, one she'd used to entertain—even if she felt heavier these days, less optimistic. "You remember how it used to be," she said, masking the ache.

Jake inhaled, forcing his attention onto the work still piled on his desk. "I remember," he said, each word tight. It was hard to forget their early abandon—the few years before he got entangled in PanEnergy's complexities, before he got caught up in its future.

Jake closed his eyes. The pursuit of ever-greater success consumed him almost completely these days. "Things are different now," was all he said.

Eve arched an eyebrow and moved her body against his in an unspoken invitation. "Different, sure. But we're still us." She undid another button from Jake's shirt. "We are more than just business partners." Eve looked hard at Jake. "We are bound together, for better or worse. Or was that an illusion?"

He swallowed, resisting the pull in her voice—the hint of a threat. She traced his Adam's apple above the parted collar, feeling the heat of his skin rising. Once, that contact would have detonated any sense of reason. Now, Jake was too focused on expansions, projects, and a business empire, areas she could no longer penetrate.

He gently caught her wrist, stilling her. "I'm too tired, Eve." The confession felt stale, but it was true. *Too tired of everything,* he thought again. "We'll talk tomorrow. I just need to get these numbers sorted, then I will... Perhaps I'll reach home in time."

A wry laugh escaped her. "Another promise, right?" She pulled back, and her slip's other strap fell off, momentarily revealing her top before she slowly lifted it back up.

Once upon a time, he would have pulled her into an embrace without hesitation. Now he seemed oblivious, her words seemed to echo in some empty chamber that wanted no new burdens; as if the furnishings and decorations had been sold but the structure was still there—void, waiting. Waiting for what, she suspected, neither of them knew.

Jake combed a hand through his hair, seeking to appear calmer than he felt. "It's not that I don't—" he began, but she cut him off.

"I know," she said, voice edged with a mix of resignation and anger. "You're the CEO now, bigger responsibilities. The man who chased me through the corridors of Moscow is gone." The lingering softness in her eyes was mingled with a growing fire. "You're exhausted, and I'm... stuck."

A prickle of guilt tugged at him. "We'll figure it out," he said, although he felt the words sounded hollow. Their wedding in New Jersey, the vow they'd made to build something extraordinary together, felt so far off. Jake pulled away from Eve, his gaze wandering over the spreadsheets and projections neatly organized in piles on his desk alongside market outlooks and private consultant reports. This was his constant backdrop.

She studied him, her face tightening as burning frustration fed off the embers of unfulfilled desire. "Jake, we can't let it all slip away. Those nights when you could barely keep your hands off me, when you promised me the world. Look at us now—distinct atoms, almost strangers, in the same room." A fierce undertone, a razor edge of latent fury, laced the words.

Jake forced himself to meet Eve's gaze. He couldn't allow the situation to deteriorate too far or they'd enter territory from which they could not turn back.

"I haven't forgotten. But these negotiations, the expansions... The company needs me. I have a bigger dream for PanEnergy—merging renewables and oil, forging the next decade of energy leadership. There are rumors about Russia. Of course, they come and go." Pausing, he rubbed his temple. "I can't just set that aside for—for an hour of—whatever this potentially is, no matter how tempting."

Eve stared, heartbreak flashing across her features before she masked it. "More like two minutes these days," she retorted a little venomously. She calmed down. "Perhaps I should go," she said quietly. "Clearly I'm only in the way."

Jake said nothing, the silence heavy. He wanted to protest, to summon some fragment of the once-blazing feeling he'd had for her. Instead, he found himself nodding. "We'll talk at home," he murmured, knowing he wouldn't be home for hours yet.

Eve turned away, gathering herself together; a final ripple of her curves in the low light. She straightened her slip across her back. "Keep these. I won't be needing them." Eve extricated some lingerie that had been lying there in the darkness, hidden on the desktop—a pair of deep red panties.

Jake recognized a present from the boutique he enjoyed, *Baby Likes to Pony*. Eve tossed the panties up in frustration, and they dropped back, tumbling onto his desk, spoiling his neat piles of paper.

Then she walked to the door, each step slow and measured. She paused at the threshold. For an instant, he saw the ghost of the fearless woman who had seduced him against that frosty window in Moscow.

In contrast, Eve, glancing back, struggled to find the man she had conjured up in Russia—one, she believed, could turn into something. He had been a disheveled middle manager easily distracted—too little focus. She'd envisaged a man who could, in future, straddle two worlds: public and private.

Now, she realized, Jake could not. Her push had simply moved his interest from the private world to the public. Now he was just like any other ambitious executive—typical of someone who had achieved success at the top level. Predictable, self-important, and counter-intuitively, unimaginative about life and its possibilities.

He reminded Eve of nothing so much as her parents. At least he was rarely smug. She could see little that worked for her in the new persona. Once again, fate had shortchanged her. She pivoted and vanished out into the hall.

And there it was: she had gone. Jake sank into the leather chair behind his desk, staring at the ceiling. The silence of the tower closed in around him, augmented by the weight of regrets, resentments, and neglected discussions.

He did up the two buttons on his shirt and reached for his computer, feeling a moment of unease before rational thought reasserted itself. PanEnergy. The ten-year blueprint. He forced his mind to visualize the bullet points. He had to prepare and plan. It was his duty, after all—bigger than his or Eve's personal interests. And this recognition would help them through the storm they were now weathering.

He caught sight of Eve's red panties lying atop his disrupted papers, feeling a twinge of something akin to annoyance and self-loathing. He gently lifted the lingerie off his paperwork.

He appreciated their design again—inhaled their various layered perfumes, Eve's fragrance rising above the rest. Then he set them aside with quiet care, as if they might ignite and burn the fragile illusions he had built around himself. After straightening his desk, he returned to the keyboard and started writing.

Part of him had wanted to chase her, to recapture a semblance of that insane passion they'd once cultivated. Another part felt... nothing, as if the bright fervor of that romance had been consumed by a relentless drive to transform PanEnergy into a global titan.

He had now chosen the corporate path. Indeed he had always prioritized his career. For a moment the two had converged in Moscow.

He sent his email, a reminder to Finance about tomorrow's meeting. The action felt like another small nail in the coffin for what used to be a love, both irrepressible and reckless.

Midnight approached. The stillness—that space between one day and the next—could have offered something different tonight: romance, risk, display. Instead it was just lonely. He had swapped the possibility of one for the certainty of the other. That, he guessed, was the price behind his success.

Regret and resignation briefly warred inside him, but there was no time to indulge such feelings. They just deflected and undermined. He had an empire to construct, deals to close, a decade's worth of transformation to orchestrate. Jake resumed typing, burying any sadness underneath the metrics of another day's business. There would be time enough to fix his private life.

23. Ivan and Alex

The hush of a damp Paris morning cloaked the gardens outside Irina's office where leaves edged the stately shrubs, and a shallow fountain stood empty at its center.

Irina, a senior Russian intelligence officer, stood by the tall windows, gazing out. The stone courtyard below was silent as a photograph—its gray serenity at odds with the tangled puzzle unfolding in the lamplight behind her.

She turned from the glass, breathing in the faint aroma of black tea. Sergei, Nadia, and Mikhail—her three most trusted operatives—waited at the table. Laptops hummed; dossiers lay open, thick with notes.

They'd reached a crossroads in the investigation, from which every path led only to deeper uncertainty. Irina had no patience for unknowns.

Her voice carried the authority of someone long accustomed to working in the shadows. "We have a man traveling under the name Alex Volkoff—his passport flagged at U.S. customs. Yet physically, he matches Ivan Asimov, who by all accounts was sent to a Siberian labor camp and died there." She paused.

"Or at least, that's what we believed until I saw him, or someone similar, on the streets of Paris last month. The question we face: is it Alex—or is it Ivan?"

Nadia brushed a strand of chestnut brown hair away from her glasses to consult a slim binder. "Officially, the name is Alex Volkoff. Valid passport, no obvious forgeries. He's traveled from Switzerland to America—a well-known Azerbaijani entrepreneur with a difficult history." She gazed at Irina to see if she recalled the history, but Irina's face remained neutral. "The intelligence from our office is Ivan Asimov died in the camp," Nadia went on, "from a knife wound—or at least complications from a serious injury.

Mikhail took up the thread. "The man turning up in the U.S. bore a physical resemblance to Ivan, with a similarity score above sixty triggering secondary screening and cross-referencing against the FBI's NCIC and NGI databases." He paused.

"Of course, we can't confirm it's the same person. The local analyst review did not reach a conclusion."

Irina added her point of view, "The man on the Paris streets looked awfully like Ivan." She leaned against the edge of her desk, and crossed her arms. "Yet—if it's the same man—how is he not dead? How did he get out of that labor camp?" She looked around at her team.

"Why assume a second identity? Or if it's truly two men—where's the other one? Did one escape while the other stayed behind—buried quietly in the Siberian permafrost?"

Sergei, older and gray-templed, glanced up from a dossier. "Let's recap. Ivan Asimov: dual national, working with PanEnergy in Moscow. Arrested for data misuse, one of our more sweeping laws—possibly stepping on the wrong toes. Ended up in Siberia on political charges."

"Meanwhile, Alex Volkoff," he continued, "was an Azerbaijani businessman who, you may recall, was abducted in Istanbul." He paused, rummaging for the correct file. "The Istanbul operation was another of the public ones our directorate likes so much." He smiled.

"We wanted to show no matter how secure our citizens believed themselves, whatever escape or loophole they found, we could still get them. You recall Litvinenko—and our willingness to ride the fallout over fifteen years." Sergei looked up to check everyone was with him.

"Anyway, in this case, operatives bundled Alex into a van, took him across the border to Russia."

Mikhail tapped his screen, bringing up a grainy black-and-white video. "From the hotel's security feed. Late night, minimal foot traffic. Alex's private security detail, mostly female ex-military, were caught by surprise. Our team wore business suits, concealed syringes with neurotoxin."

Mikhail ran his finger along the frame to fast forward the action. "Here he's seen stepping out of his suite. An operative feigns a drunken stumble, and that's the moment. Alex is injected, the security detail is neutralized, and the target is carted away."

Nadia sighed. "A well-orchestrated public statement. Alex, the wheelchair, the blanket over his lap." She paused. "Cameras caught everything. All to emphasize intentionality and power."

"We marched him out to the van as a sleeping cripple, staff none the wiser. And the end result? Alex vanishes from sight—to a labor camp, as everyone correctly assumed. Sent for reeducation."

Irina's jaw tightened. "And that labor camp was the same one housing Ivan Asimov. Now one has emerged—Volkoff—traveling under a legitimate passport, yet physically recalling Ivan. Official records claim Ivan is dead. So who truly left?"

Sergei drew a breath. "We have to consider how they managed to clear each man's digital footprint. That might be the key: how one man's passport lived while the other's vanished."

Nadia's brow furrowed, flipping open a second dossier. "That's where it gets ominous. For Volkoff, one of our cyber-operations units at the time worked to systematically erase him from the internet following the abduction. All his emails, social media, news articles, etc.—all gone." She smiled at the irony of it.

"The method was advanced, not a simple deletion, but a rewriting," Nadia explained. "Metadata replaced or obfuscated, references changed to vague placeholders like 'an unnamed entrepreneur.' Photos doctored using AI to remove or distort him. The brilliance was that it didn't scream 'erasure;' it merely suggested he never existed."

Mikhail added, "I spoke to a contact in the hacker division. He called it white-out infiltration—they didn't smash every mention, they just layered confusion over it. So if you searched for 'Volkoff' you would find almost nothing useful. It was erasure by misdirection, not force."

"If you tracked old links," he continued, "you'd see broken pages or partial references—you'd find diverse names. Someone might suspect foul play, but only if they truly knew what they were looking for."

Irina's eyes narrowed. "That would then demand a major operation to bring Alex Volkoff back into play. But why lock him away—if our man is indeed Volkoff—just to let him reappear now." She briefly looked out the window.

"And if it is Ivan, did he willingly adopt this new identity or was he forced into it? The permutations multiply." She reconsidered the puzzle she'd studied for days.

"All I know," she began again, "is that I glimpsed that man in Paris. Then, I'm calculating, he turned up in the States, passport in hand."

She recalled the chase. The memory gave her a brief thrill. She'd seen a man, stirring instincts that told her nothing was so coincidental. The subsequent chase reminded her why she had entered the intelligence world in the first place.

"So either the real Volkoff was allowed to exit, or—more likely—Asimov is traveling under Volkoff's name. Whichever scenario is right, it provokes many questions—and leaves at least one man's fate still to be reconfirmed."

Nadia leaned forward, her hand playing with the edge of her file. "So how do we begin to unravel it? We don't have direct access to that Siberian labor camp. Even for you, Irina, that region is not susceptible to digging around."

Irina nodded, acknowledging the reality of her own constraints. "We'll have to work from the outside in. We follow up every trace from the date of Volkoff's disappearance in Istanbul. Who initiated the abduction? Where did we source the operatives? Meanwhile, we cross-check rumors about Asimov's imprisonment. Did a body appear? Did an inmate vanish? Guards talk. A single slip in a personal conversation could reveal everything."

Mikhail typed swiftly, lines of data flowing across his screen. "I'm searching for anomalies in travel logs. If the man now traveling as Alex Volkoff has a valid passport, it must have a history. If something doesn't fit, is the problem in Switzerland or Azerbaijan? We can check whether his identity is newly recreated or leveraging older resources."

Sergei looked up. "And if we confirm it's genuine? He might have the means to bribe or manipulate consular channels. High-level corruption could grease the wheels of any identity shift."

Irina paced near the windows, her silhouette emerging in the glass as the sky outside darkened. A storm was coming, and the first patter of rain had started. "Let's focus on the overlap between the two men. If this traveler is Asimov wearing Volkoff's persona, someone orchestrated it. We must uncover who put the wheels in motion and why."

Silence followed, as each operative weighed their next steps. Nadia spoke first. "Let's revisit the digital cover-up. There may be something that our team overlooked. It's possible that someone didn't finish their job properly."

Mikhail rubbed the back of his neck. "We are looking at layers of deception. But, you're right, perfect illusions rarely exist. Some backups offline or other, mirrored sites might reveal a clue."

Irina's gaze hardened. "Find them. Clues do exist in minor details—like a mismatched event date, an unexplained face in group photos, personal acquaintances who recall his presence. That's how we unravel illusions." She paused.

"And for Asimov, we do the same. Look into PanEnergy's internal comms, older social media footprints, or personal contacts who might still talk off-record."

Sergei rose to refill his tea from the side tray before commenting. "In any case we'll attempt to confirm if it's physically the same man in Paris and in America. That means cross-checking faces in feeds from security cameras around Paris with the U.S. customs image. If the match is good, we have a suspect. Then we deduce which identity is at large."

Irina nodded. "We're confronting more than the enigma of a missing prisoner. We're facing a method of controlling narratives at the highest level. If the entity here can swap or merge identities, it can also manipulate reputations, undermine networks, or jeopardize operations. The arrival of this man could reflect the rolling out of new power plays."

She set down her teacup, its steam long gone, and noticed the weather was continuing to worsen. She returned to the desk. "You know your assignments. I want news. Let's see how far this so-called erasure extended—whether it can, in fact, shield our target from detection."

Nadia, Sergei, and Mikhail murmured their agreement. Nadia's pen made fresh notes while Sergei closed one dossier just to open another. In the surprising darkness, the desk lamp cast shadows across all their faces—grim lines of focus as they planned how to peel away the illusions around Alex Volkoff.

Irina let out a tight breath. Her eyes dropped to a photo pinned to the file on her desk: a figure out of focus in the crowd. The face half-turned. She tapped it lightly, as if challenging the person to reveal himself. *Ivan Asimov? Alex Volkoff? Or a man forced to wear both names?*

The talk had ended. The operatives started on their tasks. Rain hammered the windows. Irina resolved that no matter how cunning the erasure or how deep the Siberian cold, she would keep poking around. Stirring the dead had never scared her family.

24. Kaisa Searches

Wind scoured the quiet cemetery in a New York borough, forcing Kaisa to tug her scarf closer. It pricked her cheeks as she walked among weathered headstones, her boots crunching on the path. She noted, again, that summer had finished. Above her, clouds whipped across the sky.

She stopped in front of a modest stone marker: Ilya Asimov, Ivan's father. A fresh bouquet of lilies lay on the damp earth, their white petals glistening. Kaisa's heart constricted. *Someone's been here. Last night?* Perhaps it was no one special—just a family friend or pious passerby. But maybe... it was Ivan.

She felt the thought catch in her chest. If Ivan had come here—if he were in fact alive—he'd have left some clue, left her a message, right?

Clutching her scarf, she turned toward the small Orthodox church beyond the cemetery gates. Its onion domes glimmered faintly, its gilded crosses reflecting a sun struggling to break through the gloom.

Inside, the heavy wooden door groaned as Kaisa, the scarf now covering her head, pushed it open, stepping into a still atmosphere resonant with the smells of beeswax and incense. Votive candles flickered—ghostly stars along the walls, illuminating richly painted icons. A man in a black cassock stood near the altar, methodically arranging hymnals.

Kaisa took a breath, crossing herself out of instinct—three fingers for the holy trinity, right shoulder to left—before speaking. "Excuse me," she said, her soft voice echoing in the vaulted space.

The man turned, lines of age and kindness marking his face. "Yes, child? How may I help you?" His Russian accent was faint but unmistakable.

She produced a small photograph from her coat pocket—a worn snapshot of Ivan from years ago. "I'm looking for someone—Ivan Asimov. He used to come here."

The priest studied the photo, brow creasing as if summoning faces from a distant recess. After a moment, he shook his head. “I’m sorry. That name doesn’t ring a bell. Perhaps it was before my tenure.”

A twinge of disappointment crossed Kaisa’s face. “I understand.” She managed a subdued nod.

His gaze lingered on her, full of empathy. “We have a new head of the parish, Father Nikolai. He took over just last month. Maybe he’d know something. If you’d like, I could show him the picture when he returns.”

Kaisa felt torn—her caution battled her desperation—but in the end, desperation won. “Please do. This is very important to me.”

He took the photo gently and tucked it into his pocket. “Come back tomorrow. I’ll speak to Father Nikolai tonight. We’ll see if he has any insight.”

She whispered a quiet thanks. Back out in the cemetery, the wind stung her cheeks anew. *Ivan... where are you?* she thought.

Her phone buzzed, yanking her away from her thoughts. Glancing at the screen, she saw it was the private investigator. “Any progress?” she asked, stepping through the iron gates, which squeaked in protest.

“No sightings yet,” the P.I. replied, his tone matter-of-fact. “I checked his old PanEnergy office, the gym he used to frequent. Zip. I’m heading to the last apartment listing we have for him.”

Kaisa sighed, gripping the phone hard. “All right. Thanks! Let me know.”

The line clicked off, leaving her alone in the city’s hum that greeted her once back outside the cemetery. She stopped and stared around the buildings in the neighborhood, her mind a tempest of worry and determination. Even the golden domes of the church behind her seemed to hold secrets.

Then her phone buzzed again. She blinked at the caller ID: Caleb Warren, her husband. Senator Warren. She braced herself—took a deep breath. Without waiting too long, she pushed the green button to pick up. “Caleb... Hello.”

"Kaisa," he greeted. She detected the usual undercurrent of urgency. "I just wanted to confirm you're ready for the upcoming fundraiser. It's crucial for our donor outreach."

She held back a moment before answering. "What do you need from me?"

Caleb's voice carried that familiar charm, honed through endless politicking. "We have a table of key figures, potential supporters for our campaign. Please keep them happy—engaged. Make them feel part of something big. You're good at that."

Kaisa gave a faint sigh. "Fine. Which VIPs exactly?"

"Several, but among them is Ambassador Lane," Caleb said, dropping his tone slightly, as if imparting sensitive intel. "We need his endorsement—not just to attract the media coverage, but so that I can reach across party lines; leverage his non-partisan image. I have to appeal to a wider range of voters, including those independents and undecideds."

She clenched her jaw, recalling talk of Lane's notorious ego. "Understood. Consider it handled."

A burst of relief colored Caleb's laugh. "You're a true lifesaver, Kaisa. The dinner is pivotal, you know. Our alignment with Hawthorne's campaign is a risk, but a calculated one, and if this event goes well..."

She cut him off gently. "I know. I'll be there, I'll do my part."

"Thank you. You really are amazing." He paused, then added with his usual bright sincerity, "I might be home late tonight—meetings stacked. Don't wait up, all right?"

Kaisa forced a tiny smile. "Sure, talk tomorrow." She ended the call, the senator's parting words dissolving into the frigid air.

For a moment, she stood there—phone still in hand, the wind tearing again at the scarf around her neck. It was another event—*yet more donors, with more of the same talk.* She cataloged the day's frustrations: Ivan's cold trail, the church's uncertain lead, her husband's endless demands.

Tugging her coat, she made her way toward the avenue, where cabs passed, splashing water onto the curbs. Just once she glanced back, noting the church windows, which still reflected the dawn light, pale and unyielding.

Where did the flowers come from? she wondered. In her mind's eye, she saw again the humble grave with fresh lilies. *If Ivan's returned... I will find him.* The vow coalesced in her mind like the damp chill around her.

Whatever game he'd started, she would work it out—step by step, lie by lie—until she'd cornered him and got an explanation.

25. Finger Lakes

The late afternoon sun bled through the trees flanking the rutted dirt road, casting restless flashes of light across Kaisa's windshield as she drove into upstate New York's wilderness. Fall was still young, but an icy wind blew, reminding her that winter was next.

The area was so pretty at this time of year; the colors of a sienna palette dappled the landscape. Among the various trees, Kaisa recognized birch, aspen, and pine. They recalled her childhood.

Even so her hands tensed around the steering wheel, knuckles pale against the car's dark interior. The cabin she sought wasn't listed anywhere official—only half-remembered from a photograph and Ivan's scattered tales.

Her heart hammered with the certainty that this was the closest she'd ever come to tracing Ivan. However, she no longer knew whether she was pursuing a man or a memory—or just a part of herself that had disappeared with him.

Ivan's words from fourteen years ago still echoed vividly in her mind. "Off the grid," he'd said, eyes alight with excitement. He had shown her the photo: a simple, weathered cabin in the wooded fringes of the Finger Lakes, no power, no cell service, just a quiet lakeshore.

"Dad put it together on some land shortly after arriving," he'd told her. "We used to come every summer. I want you to see it, Kaisa. Show you everything it means."

She had teased him then, half in jest, and that jest had become a clue. Her search for the cabin had been anything but straightforward. She'd stumbled on the photo again while sorting through the items Ivan had left behind at the dacha.

Kaisa had pieced together the property's location near Keuka Lake, cross-referenced Ivan's old stories of summers spent fishing. And, in the end, she'd found an outdated parcel map that identified an "I. Azimov" as the owner.

She steered onto a gravel path, and the little stones that the tires threw up onto the chassis made a quiet percussive sound as she advanced. Before too long, there it was: the cabin, smaller than she'd imagined but unmistakable. Gray clapboard siding, moss patches on the roof, a modest hand-built deck stretching lakeward. It seemed locked in time, as if waiting for some visitor who never returned.

Turning off the engine, Kaisa let the silence of the forest reclaim the space. Her ears took a while to adjust. The air hung thick with pine, falling leaves, and damp soil. She stepped out onto the gravel, which scrunched loudly in the stillness, and scanned the cabin for any sign of recent presence—a boot print, a fresh scuff, anything.

The front door stood ajar, and a thread of alarm snaked through her chest. Carefully, she pushed the door wider open. The interior lay dim and cold, only a weak shaft of daylight cutting through the grime-caked windows. Dust motes swirled in the faint glow. She noticed footprints across the neglected floorboards. Her breath caught.

Inside, a sense of disturbance greeted her: an overturned chair, a half-empty coffee cup, a worn leather jacket draped on a small table. The jacket wasn't obviously Ivan's—too generic, she decided—but it proved someone had been there not long ago. Her pulse quickened.

On a rickety bench near a window, she spotted a stack of papers and maps, red circles marking certain spots. A battered notebook lay open, the style resembling Ivan's neat but hasty scrawl. Her fingers trembled as she flipped a few pages, unsure if these notes were recent or old. *Please let it be him,* she prayed, unsure whether it would give her peace or ratchet up the disconnect she increasingly felt with her life.

A sound in the next room froze her. A faint shuffle on the boards. She clutched the edge of the table, heart pounding. "Hello?" she called. Her voice sounded intrusive in the silence.

Mustering courage, she edged toward the back room. This door too was slightly ajar. Kaisa opened it more. Inside, gloom reigned. As her eyes adjusted, she saw a camp bed and a backpack spilled over the floor—clothes, tin cans.

On the cot lay an old and battered paperback: *I Capture the Castle*. The sight of the book, one Ivan had recommended to her, sent a shaft of hope and dread through her. He's here. Or was.

Suddenly, a twig snapped outside the cabin, making her jump. Someone was out there. She moved to one of the murky windows, peering through a gap in the old curtain. A shape hovered at the edge of the treeline, another shadow in the waning light. She felt her body tense as the figure stepped out, a metal glint in his hand.

Heart hammering, Kaisa rushed outside, ignoring the sudden, savage throb of panic. The small clearing seemed to contract around them as the man broke free of the trees. But this was not Ivan—too tall, wearing a well-cut suit that felt out of place in the rustic setting.

Kaisa wouldn't have recognized him. Irina had sent two of her team across to New York: Sergei to unearth Ivan's history and Nadia to review Alex's acquaintances. Sergei had found the cabin and had begun sweeping the area. Kaisa saw a silver cell phone in his hand.

He noticed her glance and smiled thinly. "It doesn't work out here. No coverage." Kaisa didn't find the knowledge comforting.

"I hope I didn't frighten you," he continued, his voice smooth but unnerving. "I'm with the Azerbaijani embassy. We're looking for a citizen named Alex. We believe he passed through here recently."

Kaisa blinked, her thoughts reeling. Alex? She hadn't encountered any Alex. Maybe Ivan was using an alias. "I don't know an Alex," she managed, forcing the words out. "I'm here for my ex-fiancé, Ivan. He—he might have come to this place."

The man's gaze sharpened. "Ivan, you say?" He weighed the name—neither confirming nor denying familiarity. In the end, all he said was, "Curious." The man studied Kaisa's face, as if deciphering whether she was a potential ally or just a random soul. "This region has many secrets," he continued. "People wear masks when it suits them."

A chill crept over her, intensifying with each breath. She took a cautious step back, unsettled by the man's presence. The air pressed in around the pair, the sky picking up darker colors as dusk approached. "I—I don't understand what you mean," Kaisa managed.

Sergei's mouth curved slightly—perhaps a smile, perhaps something else. "If you hear anything about Alex... or Ivan, contact me." He produced a neat business card from his suit pocket, pressing it into her hand. The name read Farid; the title "Second Secretary, Administration" above the embassy logo. There was a Manhattan phone number. "We'd appreciate any help you can give us."

Her fingertips brushed his hand, and an electric prickle raced across her skin. Something about this man was not right, choreographed. She considered his graying hair. It looked unusual for a typical second secretary. "Thank you," she whispered.

He glanced at the cabin, then back to her, a hint of warning in his voice. "Be cautious. Nothing is quite as it appears in these parts." Then, with eerie grace, he faded back into the treeline, vanishing as swiftly as he'd arrived.

Left alone in the clearing, Kaisa's heart pounded, the business card weighing heavily in her grip. The last rays of daylight were sinking behind the trees and the cabin began descending into darkness. A quiet blanketed the scene, thick with unspoken threats.

She turned slowly, her gut clenching with a new apprehension. Farid's questions forced their way into her mind. *Who was Alex*? she wondered. *And why was an embassy operative seeking him?*

She stepped back inside the cabin, now almost dark, retrieving what courage she had left. The place felt, if anything, more menacing. She switched on her cell flashlight. "Ivan, where are you?" she called. Her demand fragmented in the gloom.

The half-worn footprints, the scattered notes—it all told of a story in progress, pieces she couldn't quite fit together. Was Ivan truly the one behind it? Or was there someone else?

The evening deepened, the hush outside broken only by distant night birds. Despite searching the rooms one last time, she found no clues. Anxiety gnawed at her, the fear that she'd stumbled into a web more dangerous than she'd imagined. Carefully, she closed the cabin door on her way out, as though preserving a crime scene.

The sun gone, darkness had enveloped the quiet lakeshore. Kaisa returned to her car, the flashlight reflecting off its windows. Each step weighed more heavily than the last.

She'd hoped to be nearer a conclusion about Ivan. But every move created only more riddles. And it had revealed another world—one full of risk. Searching for Ivan in hidden corners, even in a state that she had come to know well, had unleashed strange encounters and unexpected threats.

She started the engine, the car headlights piercing the trees, highlighting the shadows beyond. The night felt charged with mysteries she could barely name. *I won't stop*, she told herself, as she accelerated out. *I won't let him slip away again.* Yet in her heart, an unsettling dread pooled. Farid's presence—his talk of "Alex"—underscored how much she had encroached upon sinister forces.

The cabin's shape was soon swallowed by the dark. And it was only later, when the trees had thinned out, that Kaisa noticed the moon—low and swollen behind the forest. It appeared to hang there—too heavy to rise any farther. A Blood Moon.

She had the feeling someone, somewhere, was watching her go. *So be it*—Kaisa was too far in to retreat now. She'd see it through, whatever the cost.

Jake stepped out of the SUV and into the crisp air of a Brooklyn street that still clung to its industrial past. The warehouse before him loomed like a weathered cathedral, its corrugated metal façade pockmarked with rust. A few patches of graffiti—both calculated and careless—decorated the walls around the entrance, alongside a planter of weeds that looked deliberately left to overgrow.

"Jake," a woman greeted him before he'd spotted her, voice as polished as he knew would be her appearance. The gallerina—but what a gallerina.

An avatar of cool precision, she was wrapped this time, he saw, in a camel coat that brushed the tops of her sleek boots. She smiled—a calculated curve—and extended a hand adorned with gold rings. She was a symphony of golds and umbers.

"Charlotte," Jake replied, taking her hand with a grin equal parts charm and challenge. His own black coat hung open to reveal a dark cashmere sweater; casual but elegant. A faint hint of cologne escaped to mingle with the metal and brick of the area.

The two stood in the street a moment, trading small talk about the weather—a nice change—and about how the neighborhood had "come up" in recent years. Behind them, a delivery truck honked, squeezing past and rattling the glass windows of a nearby bar.

"Shall we?" Charlotte said, gesturing toward the warehouse door.

Jake followed her inside, and the air shifted immediately. A blast of warmth hit them—carrying with it the smells of turpentine and varnish, oil paint and glue.

The space was vast, a cavernous expanse of corrugated metal, concrete, and steel beams. Paintings leaned against walls and sat on easels in every direction. The artworks ranged from severe geometric abstractions to lush, almost indecent landscapes. It was a cacophony of styles and emotions.

In the far corner, a man in paint-splattered overalls hunched over a canvas. His brush moved in tight, deliberate strokes as a soprano voice floated through the air, piped in from a pair of battered speakers mounted on the wall.

For a moment, Jake stood still—surveying the scene, taking it all in. The rawness of the room. The sheer, unapologetic vanity of the artwork. The incongruous opera, dramatic and soaring in this rough-hewn setting. He guessed it might be Allegri's *Miserere*. Mozart had famously copied it on hearing the piece just once in the Vatican's Sistine Chapel.

Jake concluded that if anything united the set-up it was a certain audacious ambition.

Charlotte didn't stop but kept moving ahead, her heels clicking against the concrete. Jake watched her cross the space. Her coat slipped from her shoulders as she neared the artist, revealing a silk blouse that caught the fluorescent light like a whisper of gold. She bent down and spoke to the artist, her profile a study in casual elegance and untouchable invitation. A quiet laugh rose up.

Jake slipped his hands into his pockets and grinned. This was the kind of theater he enjoyed—chaos, beauty, and power, just waiting to be spun into something special. "Nice place," he said, mostly to himself, as he began to stroll deeper into the room.

Jake was halfway across the space, when the artist straightened up from his canvas and looked over. He wiped his hands carefully on a rag, leaving streaks of vibrant blue and ochre to join the myriad colors already there, and waited for Jake to reach him.

"So," the artist began, his voice gruff but not unfriendly, "you're here to buy some art for your office."

Jake grinned, easy and assured. "That's the idea. Big office, lots of walls. They need a serious upgrade. No more oil rigs in the dusk."

The artist nodded, his gaze appraising. He glanced at Charlotte, next to him, her expression attentive but unreadable. "How many pieces do you have in mind? And what kind? Big or small? Abstract? Figurative? As you can see," he said with a sweep of his arm, "I have everything."

Jake shrugged lightly, his hands still in his pockets. "Honestly, all of the above. I inherited from my predecessor the art we've got now—stuffy landscapes, industry portraits, bad corporate modernism, you name it. I feel it's the equivalent of elevator music." Jake laughed.

"It's the kind of stuff that screams beige conformism. I want something different. Something with guts. And for my own office... Something grand. Something people won't forget."

The artist crossed his arms, the faintest smirk tugging at the corners of his mouth. Charlotte took a step back and folded her arms too, as if thinking. Jake briefly noted her long, elegant fingers, which rested lightly against her sleeve.

"Well, you've come to the right place," the artist said. "But first let me show you something—what I've got in the next warehouse." He led them past a back room and heaved open a huge sliding metal door. It jammed once or twice because the panels had warped and the runners eroded. However, eventually he revealed another huge storeroom.

Jake let out a brief gasp as it appeared. A vast, dust-flecked space lay beyond. And above, on the ceiling, was an oval hole through which light streamed and hit the interior, leaving a bright shape in constant flux, now partly on the wall and partly on the floor. "It's by Gordon Matta-Clark," the artist said. "He was an architect who carved buildings apart as sculpture. What a vision! So far ahead of his time. Now if only I had his creativity..."

"Astonishing!" Jake affirmed. "We could all do with his vision: ripping open old structures to create something new and beautiful." He paused. "From what I've seen, I'd say your art does just the job: it's provocative and driving. Precisely what my office needs."

"Right," said Charlotte, looking at the artist and giving a flick with her head.

"Sure. Let's start with what's in the main room where we met." He gestured back toward the sprawling collection of works spread over the room behind them.

Jake nodded, and the trio returned to the main studio where they walked around the artwork. Charlotte led the way, explaining the provenance of particular items in her cultivated tone. She paused at a large, striking abstract in bold reds and blacks.

"This one," she said, her voice smooth, "is from when the artist was younger, based in LA. The piece is called *Conflagration.* It's about transformation: destruction and renewal." She glanced over her shoulder at Jake. "It could make quite the statement in your reception area."

Jake tilted his head, considering it. "It's bold," he admitted, "but maybe a little too... apocalyptic. I'm trying to inspire our visitors, not terrify them."

Charlotte laughed, brushing a strand of hair behind her ear. "Fair point. Let's keep looking."

They moved on, pausing at a series of smaller impressionistic works that Charlotte described as "playful" and "lyrical," then a monumental piece depicting a stormy seascape. Jake dismissed the seascape with a wave of his hand.

"Too much like what I've already got. I want something that feels alive. Electric."

The artist exchanged a glance with Charlotte, his brow furrowing. "I've got a lot more things in various back rooms," he said. "Stuff that's not out here yet. Might be closer to what you're looking for."

Jake raised an eyebrow, intrigued. "Lead the way."

They followed the artist into a smaller, more intimate space. The back room was dimly lit, with only a few spotlights highlighting works stacked against the walls. The paintings here felt rawer, often more experimental—pieces not yet polished for the market, if they were ever heading there.

"This," the artist said, pulling out a huge canvas layered with thick, dynamic brushstrokes of gold and deep blue, "is something I've been working on for months. It's untitled, but it's about… ambition. Grasping for something just out of reach."

Jake stepped closer, his hands on his hips. Charlotte came to stand beside him, their shoulders almost brushing.

"It's got presence," Jake murmured.

"More than presence," Charlotte corrected. "It demands attention. It could be exactly what you're looking for." She knew how to soften a sale.

Jake turned to her, his grin sly. "You're good at this, you know." He wasn't sure whether he meant selling art—or reading him.

Charlotte shifted her gaze toward Jake, a gentle smile lighting her eyes. "I recognize what people want."

The artist cleared his throat, drawing their attention back to the painting. "There's more," he said. "If this one doesn't grab you, I've got others. But if you're serious about making an impression…"

Jake nodded slowly, still studying the canvas. "I like it. But let's keep looking. I want to see all my options."

Charlotte leaned closer, her voice barely above a whisper. "You're thorough. I like that."

Jake chuckled, the flirtation subtle but unmistakable. "You'd better. It's why I'm so good at what I do."

The artist rolled his eyes and moved to retrieve another painting, leaving Jake and Charlotte to linger just a moment.

As they continued sorting through the paintings, the trio settled into a certain rhythm. Charlotte would pause to point out details in a piece—the sharpness of a brushstroke or the layering of colors—while Jake asked questions varying between genuine curiosity and casual dismissal.

Jake paused in front of a large, textured canvas with streaks of ochre and indigo that seemed to ripple with movement. He gestured at it. "This painting's got something... kinetic about it," he said, then glanced at the artist. "So, how's your mom doing these days?"

The artist didn't flinch or hesitate. He nodded. "She's holding up. Busy, as you'd expect. Polls have been... well, they're polls. All over the place lately." He pulled a smaller painting from a stack. "There's this one too."

Jake ran a hand along his jaw, studying the canvas. "Right. Can't trust polls much anymore. What about internal surveys? What's the situation there?"

The artist leaned the smaller painting against the wall and gave a shrug. "The party's confident. Internals suggest the opposition's struggling, especially in certain demographics. But, you know, campaigns are never a done deal until the last vote's in. Can't be complacent. Hillary showed that."

Charlotte, standing nearby, chimed in with a knowing smile. "Especially these days. Messaging is everything."

Jake nodded in agreement. "What about volunteers," he said. "You can't fake grassroots. What's the plan there? Got enough boots on the ground, or still scrambling?"

The artist smiled faintly, as if he'd expected this line of questioning. "Always a need for more volunteers."

Jake tilted his head, thoughtful. "Good to hear. And contributions? They coming in strong, or still playing catch-up?"

"Always a need for more contributions as well. Campaigning isn't what it used to be—it's a full-time arms race now. But we're pulling more than the others." Jake weighed every answer against what he already knew.

"That's a good sign. Money flows tend to reflect views about outcomes more than anything else. At least that's what I think..."

"Yeah. Me, too. I've always been a little cynical," the artist replied evenly, pulling out another artwork. This one was a bigger painting—a luminous abstract in gold and crimson. "But every little bit helps. There's no such thing as too much in politics."

Jake gave a low chuckle, his hands sliding into his pockets as he surveyed the latest suggestion. "Well, I hope she keeps her role. We need more people like your mom—strong, visionary. She's particularly good on climate. Either we protect our future or we don't have one."

The artist straightened, his voice carrying a note of firm agreement. "If the other team gets in, forget the future. We're heading straight back to the dark ages."

Charlotte nodded, her expression composed but her tone carrying subtle pull. "True leaders don't just react; they build. And she's done it all with tact."

The artist turned to her with a grin, his voice teasing but with a thread of sincerity. "You're a poet as well as a gallerist. I believe we could almost fashion a haiku out of that statement. That's why I like and admire you so much."

Charlotte returned his look with a wry smile, her eyes bright. "Thank you."

"Here," the artist continued, setting another canvas upright. This one was bold and sprawling, a riot of blues and whites, like a storm captured mid-motion. "Let's see if this one fits the bill."

Jake stepped forward, his gaze sharp, Charlotte once again close by his side. They studied the piece without saying anything, just as the speakers began a short rendition of Pergolesi's *Stabat Mater*.

By the end of the afternoon, twenty or so pieces had been chosen. The artist's backroom seemed emptier while the chosen paintings were positioned carefully against a wall of the main studio. Jake stood back, surveying his selections with a satisfied nod.

"So," he said, turning to Charlotte and the artist, "can one of you deliver these to me sometime during the next week or so? The sooner the better."

Charlotte and the artist exchanged looks, a silent agreement passing between them.

"Sure," the artist said, brushing his hands against his jeans.

"I'll bring them around," Charlotte added, her tone matter-of-fact but with a flash of amusement in her eyes.

Jake's smile widened. "Wonderful. Let me know when you're coming. I'll make sure you get access to the loading dock."

He turned to leave, his coat swaying as he moved toward the warehouse door, but then paused, pivoting back toward the artist.

"You've been to Azerbaijan, haven't you?" Jake asked, his tone casual, as if discussing the weather.

The artist blinked once, again showing no surprise at the question but waited a moment to gather his thoughts. "Yeah, I've been there. Really nice place. Baku's something else—those Flame Towers, just like something from a sci-fi film. Amazing food, too. The landscapes outside the city are wild, with the mountains and deserts. I've visited several times. I was there recently to see the F1."

Jake was intrigued but still nonchalant. "Do you know a guy named Alex Volkoff? He's been in contact with our office."

The artist hesitated again, but only for the briefest second. "Sure. Alex is a nice guy." He leaned against a table and put his hands on his hips—a habit that often left paint stains on his work pants. "Sharp, knows how to get things done. And, god, does he know how to party. You won't forget a night out with Alex, that's for sure."

Jake laughed. "But is he trustworthy? Did you have constructive experiences in dealing with him?"

The artist's expression grew thoughtful, but he nodded. "Yeah. Can't recall anything particularly negative about Alex. If you're going to Azerbaijan, he's definitely a useful guy to know. Well-connected, resourceful."

Jake held the artist's gaze for an instant longer, then gave a slow nod, his smile shifting into something more opaque. "Appreciate it. Thanks for the intel."

He turned toward Charlotte, his expression softening. "Let's get a drink to celebrate, and talk a bit more about all this art I'm paying top dollar for."

Charlotte's lips curved into a subtle smile, her voice dipping just slightly into playfulness. "I'd like that. I'll teach you some more about painting—the use of negative space."

Jake smiled and opened the warehouse door, holding it as Charlotte passed. They stepped into the fresh evening air, and their conversation continued—the flirtation easily weaving through discussion of business, art, and whatever else the evening might bring.

Inside, the artist went back to his canvas—the voices of his visitors fading, drowned by the opera still playing from the speakers. He'd been asked a favor: get close to Jake, find out what's happening, see what he knows. He liked these missions. They made life more interesting.

27. Permian M&A

The bar hummed with a subdued elegance, the sort of dark-paneled haven coveted by Manhattan's dealmakers. Low light fell on well-used booths, and murmured conversations vanished into the dark wood.

Jake Laskin sat in the shadows of a corner booth, a beer in one hand. It was a corner in which deals had been born and dynasties undone; Jake knew such spaces well. He wore a pinstripe suit—a uniform of old power—and sat with the poise of a man used to snapping decisions into place.

On the other side, with an air of relaxed confidence, sat Alex Volkoff, the Chairman of Albemarle Holdings. He wore dark, casual pants and a white shirt, its collar open, beneath a tailored light-brown jacket. Jake guessed that Alex was older by a few years and that he was making a deliberate show of informality to heighten the impression of power and authority.

Between them on the table was a glass of whiskey, which Alex had yet to pick up, and a business card embossed with his name and title. Its gold letters shone in the semi-darkness. Alex offered a measured smile. "You know," he said, his tone hinting at long experience, "there's something about this city. Billions of dollars flow through it. But the real money, the kind that shifts the earth beneath our feet: it does not scream—it whispers."

Jake answered with a faint tilt of his glass, acknowledging the point. "So you're here to share a whisper with me?"

A glimmer of amusement danced across Alex's features. "Let's not pretend generosity. I'm here because I respect the way you operate—fast, focused, decisive. That's what this... situation calls for." He paused and settled back with an ease that suggested deep pockets and deeper secrets.

Jake took a long swig of his beer before returning his gaze to Alex. "Then whisper, Alex. I'm listening."

A low chuckle escaped as Alex traced one finger along the rim of his glass. "The Permian Basin," he said, letting the name hang there like an open door. "I think you know the region's seen better days. However, interesting cracks in the market are appearing—bigger than you might suspect. And breaks are where fortunes can be made."

Jake's poker face held, but the flicker in his eyes betrayed curiosity. "You're late. Plenty have already combed the Basin for bargains, picking the bones of the smaller operators. Now the sector's crowded with inflated valuations."

"Late?" Alex repeated with mild disbelief. "On the contrary. Some major player is bleeding. They just don't know how visible their trail is. No, the scraps are gone, but it's the bigger kill that's stumbling."

Jake's lips tightened as he took another sip. "What makes you so sure?"

Alex stopped moving, his eyes sharpening. "I've spent a career in corners where men talk too freely. It's not rumor; it's actionable intelligence. I got my M&A analyst to check a few data points. But it needs someone who can swoop in, handle it boldly. That's your reputation, Jake—cutting to the heart of a deal, no committees stalling you."

Jake considered him, silence soaking up the long pause. Finally, he spoke. "If you're right, it's game-changing. If you're wrong, I'll look like an idiot."

Alex inclined his head. "I've never been known to mistake opportunities. That's your gamble, though. I'm offering you first dibs, because you can close quickly. If you're intrigued, follow the scent. If not, I'll move on to someone else."

Jake said nothing, weighing the man's confidence. "What's your angle? No one does freebies."

Alex betrayed a knowing smile. "We'll talk terms if you decide to move. I expect the chance to participate in some of your other ventures. I believe you're a man of both imagination and execution. I like that combination. It's rare. I will achieve results in America faster alongside someone like you." Alex paused. "However, you should confirm my tip first. I doubt it will stay hidden forever."

He stood, his whiskey still untouched, and adjusted his jacket with a certain nonchalance. "You're a smart man," he said again, turning to leave. "Smart enough to work out if something's worth chasing."

Jake remained seated as Alex departed. Booths weren't convenient for talks that depended on formalities. Once alone, Jake fingered the edge of Alex's business card. Their conversation reverberated in his mind. He had enough skill to identify sincerity, even when laced with cunning. Jake pulled out his phone, tapped a contact. The call connected with a faint beep.

"Get me everything you can pull on the Permian Basin—especially insolvency rumors," he said, voice low. "Major players first. Focus on data from the last six months."

He ended the call, letting the phone slip back into his pocket. He leaned back in the leather booth, beer temporarily forgotten. His mind raced two steps ahead, sifting potential targets. A single slip by a giant operator, an unexpected meltdown in the Basin—and PanEnergy could seize a once-in-a-lifetime advantage.

Jake was still at the bar, with another beer in front of him, when one of his team called back with a partial verification: a major could indeed be teetering. The rumor had been building in certain corners of the energy sector. Trouble was, no one knew the target's identity for certain.

Jake didn't like uncertainty, it gnawed at him. He refused to be left guessing. Reaching for his phone again, Jake fired off a text to his executive adviser: *Monica, get Peter from Blackhawk Executive Search to call me. My personal line. It's urgent.* The headhunter had a nose for gleaning secrets under the guise of recruitment. *And an organization chart of Albemarle's M&A team.*

Within minutes, Peter Worthington was on the line, voice smooth as ever. "Jake. Always a pleasure. How can Blackhawk help PanEnergy tonight?"

Jake went straight to the point. "I need an approach. Discreet. Albemarle Holdings has an analyst who might have leads on a big move. I want her talking—voluntarily. Her name is Emma Callahan. She's sharp and—I'm guessing—loyal, but loyalty can be... persuaded."

Peter gave a low chuckle. "Consider it done. But you know how this works, yes? A delicate dance. If I tip my hand too early, she'll clam up."

Jake allowed a rare half-smile. "I trust your methods, Peter. Just get me the intel. We have to confirm if there's an acquisition wave about to break. Be subtle, but get me what I need."

"Understood, Jake."

The line went dead, leaving Jake to finish his beer, an enjoyable thread of speculation swirling in his head. If Albemarle's people had a clue about the shaky giant, they might have pegged either Palisade Resources or Granite Petroleum. Or it could be an entirely different target. But time was short.

A plush, semi-private lounge was set back from the entrance lobby of The Sinclair Hotel, all tufted leather seats and gilded lamps. Emma Callahan—progressing as a mid-level analyst at Albemarle—had arrived at Blackhawk's invitation. She wasn't actively seeking a new job. Yet the prospect of an "informational lunch" piqued her curiosity. She knew big opportunities often hid behind unlikely invitations.

Peter Worthington stood to greet her. Functionally attired in a black suit, he exuded an air of polished charm, his handshake firm. "Emma, thank you for coming."

She settled into a deep leather armchair, adjusting her blazer neatly. "Your assistant was... persistent," she admitted, half-laughing. "I'm curious what this is all about."

Peter poured on a cordial smile. "I'll be candid: I've been watching your rise at Albemarle. You're well-regarded, and your insights have shaped more than one successful deal. I believe you're due for something bigger—if you're open to a conversation."

Emma brightened at the flattery. "I appreciate that. Albemarle's been good to me, though. I'm not desperate to leave."

Peter spread his hands, an artful gesture. "No one's saying you're unhappy. But the energy sector is in flux, isn't it? And if you have a special vantage on these changes, you might flourish in an environment that is more decisive, more able to take action—some place with the will and means to move fast and secure the result. The kind that would treasure precisely your abilities."

Emma inclined her head, carefully. "The sector's definitely more complex now. Public sentiment's shifting, oil isn't the golden goose it once was, and investor patience is wearing thin. Some firms have almost ruined themselves chasing first one feel-good story then another—ignoring their genuine assets, their raison d'être, along the way. But there's still money to be made if you know where to look."

Peter nodded. "And you've had a front-row seat on that, yes? Overseeing or supporting analysis into the Permian Basin, analyzing possibilities. Dare I say it, you might know which players are interesting for acquisition, which best to avoid?"

Emma suppressed a laugh. "You make it sound dramatic. In reality, it's a swarm of mid-tier operators trying to outlast the price cycle. They can't all win."

Peter let the conversation flow into smoother terrain, ordering drinks, speaking of hypothetical roles she might fill at an unnamed but "globally expanding" enterprise. The artfulness in his voice betrayed a hidden motive—Jake Laskin's, in fact—but Emma sensed only part of the picture, feeling she didn't need to understand more. She was intrigued by the scenario Peter was laying in front of her.

After their short lunch, as they exchanged polite goodbyes, Peter walked away with enough intelligence to confirm Jake's hunch: the rumored meltdown pointed to Palisade Resources. Meanwhile, Emma, enthralled by the promise of a bigger stage with more concrete outcomes, began to consider if she might indeed be ready for a new role in a rapidly changing energy market.

* * *

Back at PanEnergy, Jake Laskin pored over the findings. Emma's glimpses, as reported by Peter, pointed to Palisade: decent acreage, rumored deeper reserves. For some reason, certain corners of the market believed they sat on a potential jackpot—if the technology or capital to exploit it emerged. They pictured Palisade like Barrick Gold in its early incarnation—simply in the oil space.

Palisade's finances were fragile, their expansion strategy half-baked, and a big-enough shock could topple them. An attractive target for a takeover if done right.

Jake allowed a tight-lipped grin. *So that's the whale, or at least the big fish.* His phone buzzed on the desk. Another call. "Adrian here" came a senior geologist's voice, "We have more on Palisade's deeper formations. Might be high-risk, but if it pans out, it's huge." Another confirmation. The puzzle pieces were slotting into place.

He pushed back from his desk. The sky outside had dimmed to a hazy purple, city lights flickering to life. If Palisade truly owned a hidden asset waiting to be monetized, or believed they did, the opening to strike was short. He'd gamble, pounce. Or watch a competitor like Albemarle better organize itself, step in, and snap up the opportunity. And he sure as hell wasn't going to let that happen.

* * *

The next morning Jake arrived at his office earlier than usual, the silence of the floor broken only by the faint hum of computers coming to life. As he entered his office suite, the oversize news screen mounted on the wall caught his attention. A headline, bold and glaring, stretched across the top: "Rival Firm Eyes Palisade Resources for Acquisition; Shares Soar Pre-Market." He cursed under his breath, dropping his briefcase on the desk.

The chart below the headline showed Palisade's stock price, a vertical spike lighting up the graph as trading anticipation surged. Someone had made the first move. "Monica," he barked into the intercom. "Get the M&A team into the conference room. Now."

Minutes later, his executive adviser, a model of efficiency, had gathered the key players in PanEnergy's boardroom. Jake entered, exuding the controlled urgency that had become his trademark.

"You've all seen the news," he began without preamble, gesturing toward the wall screen in the conference room. "Palisade's in play. We can't sit flat-footed on the sidelines. I need to know whether we're going to take action."

Jake sat down and leaned forward, a model of propulsive intensity—so severe sometimes that others mistook it for anger. His top M&A lieutenant, Vince Kramer, fidgeted with a stack of papers, aware that Jake had no tolerance for tin-can strategies.

Adopting his usual direct approach, Jake said, "All right, Vince. The Palisade rumor's out in the open. We can't pretend we have the only intel. Someone's bid for them. Now we see who else steps up. What have you got?"

Vince flipped to a graph showing Palisade's stock price, which had indeed spiked precipitously. "We can make a preliminary offer, not binding, simply to gauge reaction. Their board's not cowering after the initial bid. A release said they'd study their 'strategic options' and entertain 'alternative proposals,' which means they're playing for time."

Jake offered a humorless smile. "And time is not something we want to give them. Let them scramble with their PR spin, divestitures, cost-cutting. The more they flail, the more we exploit the confusion. At least they don't have the financial strength to try a preemptive acquisition of their own."

Vince placed a tablet on the table, bringing up some financial models. "A bunch of hedge funds are piling in, thinking Palisade may have value there under the Permian. That speculation is artificially pumping the share price. If we let them keep the hype going, we'll have to pay a fortune."

"Right. We can't let the share price run away from us." Jake's eyes narrowed. "So we need to either confirm those reserves or sow enough doubt that they can't ramp the price too high."

A twinge of anxiety passed across Vince's features. "We could up the offer, show seriousness, then negotiate down if the geologists find holes in the document room. Or we could orchestrate a line of questioning—just enough to rattle investors, push the price down, then move in."

Jake weighed the options. "Either approach has risk. Overpaying could sink PanEnergy if the reserves aren't real. Undercutting means risking seller interest and corporate goodwill. It can backfire if we misjudge—especially if we miss the deal of a lifetime. We have to be agile. I want Palisade's best assets—and those rumored deeper formations. We can discard what doesn't complement our business."

An uneasy silence followed. Then Jake rose from his chair, stepping over to the wide windows. "All right, Vince," he said, his voice echoing in the quiet. "We keep a foot on each pedal—due diligence on one side, a mild push to rock the market's confidence on the other. If Palisade begin to panic, they might offer up some business at a discount. And if they hold out, we have an idea how much to sweeten the pot—within reason."

Vince exhaled, relieved. "Yes, sir."

Jake turned, eyes gleaming. "We're playing cat and mouse here. And we're not the mouse. Don't forget that." He paused. "Now, let's finalize our next moves. I want face-to-face time with all the big shareholders in Palisade as soon as possible. They'll love the chance to exit if we make it worth their while."

"Then," he concluded, "let's watch the company's announcements. The moment Palisade slips up, we pounce."

Late that evening, Jake convened a smaller strategy session with Vince, CFO Carla Nguyen, and a couple of close trusted advisers, including Monica. They hashed out a schedule for discreet calls to top Palisade investors. The plan was to needle them about whether management had any real path forward or if it was all a bluff. How could a team that had underperformed suddenly change and outperform?

The hum of conversation in his suite carried an unusual charge, a sense that each word might pivot the entire negotiation. Carla, scanning a complex spreadsheet, addressed the group. "If we can't confirm Palisade's rumored assets, or if we are unable to source the tech to develop them, we risk an enormous outlay for uncertain returns. The market's already skeptical about big oil expansions. If we fail, we'll be hammered—by the press and by our stakeholders."

Jake's eyes flicked to Vince. "We've never been averse to risk. But this is next-level. Let's mitigate it. Base any offer on unrestricted access to a comprehensive data room. If Palisade wants a lifeline, they'll entertain it. If not—and some competitor picks them up without doing their full due diligence—then they can flail together."

Vince nodded, scribbling notes. The sense of a plan took shape: a balanced mix of aggression and caution. For Jake, it was reminiscent of deals in earlier days—he had always thrived on the adrenaline rush of a complicated buyout. But this time, the stakes felt higher, a reflection of PanEnergy's new identity, changing persona.

At midnight, Jake found himself still in his 65th-floor office. The day's swirl of market rumors, phone calls, and strategy sessions had left him exhausted, though not spent. A bottle of Peroni sat on the desk, untouched. His phone dinged with a message from Vince: *"We're set for tomorrow's calls. Expect fireworks."*

Jake tapped out a single reply: *"Good."*

Rising, he paced to the window. It reflected back a man who had built his brand on cunning deals and unstoppable will. Alex Volkoff's tip about a wounded giant might have led him there—to Palisade—but Jake was prepared to strike alone.

After all, speed and focus would net Palisade and a golden opportunity to enter the Permian. Random combinations simply slowed things down while impetuous partnerships, Jake felt, often came back to haunt you.

Yet beneath it all, a sliver of uncertainty gnawed at him: what if the rumored deeper formations fizzled, or Palisade's finances proved irredeemably dire? He grimaced, forcing the doubt away. If he had second-guessed every major leap in his career, he'd have remained a minor functionary at some mid-tier outfit.

Flicking off the lid, he drank the Peroni in a single, determined swallow, slamming the empty bottle down on the table. Another day would dawn soon, and with it, the game plan. It was first and ten. Time now to march downfield.

Outside, Manhattan's lights gleamed oblivious—focused on other deals, other interactions—while inside Jake steeled himself for the cat-and-mouse game he was about to unleash upon a sizeable competitor.

28. Russia Trouble

Jake Laskin stepped into his Upper East Side penthouse, thirty-six sleepless hours weighing on his shoulders. Though he carried the burden well—his pressed suit showing only the faintest wrinkles—Jake felt the tension, while his mind refused to stop churning over the day and its outcomes.

From the 47th floor, he had a rare view of both the East River and Central Park—a fantastic spectacle he treasured. He paused at the threshold.

The subtle fragrance of leather and his own cologne hung in the air, a quiet testament to his territory. He closed the door with a soft click, and the patter of nails on polished hardwood heralded his welcoming committee: three black Labradors—Brutus, Max, and Diesel—walking toward him much like shadows come to life, their fur shining in the ambient glow.

"Hey, big fellas," Jake greeted, kneeling enough to ruffle their gleaming coats. "Miss me?" Their wagging tails slammed rhythmically against his shins or the floor. "We'll get you that new walker soon, guys. Word is he's top-notch. No more scaring random strangers." The dogs all panted in response, biting his hands in play.

"Welcome home, conqueror," came a teasing voice from farther inside the penthouse. The words carried a mix of jest and possession—the tone of someone who both adored and resented the empire she'd helped to build.

Jake straightened, turning to see Eve in the open-plan kitchen. She wore a red slip dress with a lace bodice—an ensemble balancing provocation with comfort. The fine lace floral detailing added a romantic touch; its intricate design catching the eye and adding depth.

The slip accentuated Eve's elegant legs, which Jake had always appreciated. Eve still looked amazing in her late forties. Sometimes he had to recall just how long they'd been together.

He liked Eve's element of boldness. Her choices had, in part, reflected his own passions. Sometimes, the resulting chemistry had proven explosive.

Though worried, even then, whether it could be sustained, Jake had focused on the now leaving the longer-term to take care of itself. He was still surprised that they had endured fourteen years.

A single black choker completed Eve's outfit, its dark surface absorbing the apartment light, its meaning ambiguous. In one hand, Eve carried a half-full champagne flute; in the other, she held a pair of stilettos.

"You're early," she said, her eyes skimming him, judging his mood. "I thought you'd be at the office until much later, plotting your next global takeover."

She came over and pecked his cheek. "Welcome home," she whispered. The slip and her body seemed to move at right angles as Eve walked.

Jake gave a low chuckle. "Tonight, I needed to see my own four walls," he said. His voice had picked up a gravelly edge, the product of no real sleep. "The last thirty-six hours were a beast—there's only so long I can push before I crack."

Eve took a sip of champagne. "Shame. I liked you on the edge." She looked at her hand with the shoes. "These suddenly feel impossible," she complained. "Can you help a second? I don't know if it's my feet or what..." Eve dropped her shoes gently onto the entrance floor.

Jake felt the last of his energy abandon him. However, Eve implored and, still feeling some guilt, he kneeled to hold them as she pushed her feet inside. Her perfume, a mix of jasmine and vanilla, reached him as he did so, stirring memories of that wilder time in their relationship—days he found himself indulging less and less.

"I hear the rumors," Eve said. "Your Permian bid? You're unstoppable—the whole Street's buzzing."

Jake only gave a curt nod, letting the dogs bound off as he returned upright and shrugged out of his suit jacket. "We'll see. It's a step in the right direction, or so I keep telling the board. The real challenge is keeping the momentum."

"You're so calm when you say it," she murmured. "But it's this focus that helps you end up on top."

Jake allowed himself a faint, tired smirk. "You know me. Quick, aggressive moves, minimal regret. Anyway, I'm beat." He raked a hand through his hair, which was nearing its limit of hair gel and stress.

"Beat enough to skip out on a real welcome?" Eve purred, pressing closer so the warm satin of her dress brushed his shirtfront. For a moment, Jake closed his eyes, battling the swirl of conflicting urges. He inhaled the exotic scent clinging to her skin and recalled nights in Moscow. Yet tonight, it seemed like a distant memory from another lifetime. "Eve," he began, voice low, "I'm not sure I can—"

Hearing the change in tone, the three Labradors suddenly stopped their random gyrations and stood attentive, ears pricked, uncertain whether to bound over or stay in place. Eve cast them an amused glance. "See? Even the dogs sense the tension."

Jake extricated himself gently, stepping to the side. He held up his hand in a silent apology. "Give me a minute, yeah? I need to get out of this suit and maybe catch the news." His expression tightened as he caught the burst of dissatisfaction on Eve's face.

She sighed, shaking out her hair. "So you want the TV more than me, is that it? You're impossible, Jake."

"I just saw something teased about the sabotage of undersea pipelines," Jake said, walking across to the living area and forgetting about his desire to change. "Russia, sabotage, some CEN documentary. I have to watch—check whether it implies any new risk for us."

Eve rolled her eyes and took another sip of champagne. "Fine," she said, letting her unoccupied hand slide over her hip. "I'll humor you. Yet more talk about Russia. My favorite."

Jake turned on the large wall-mounted television with a press of the remote. Instantly, the room filled with the sound of a polished, relentlessly serious voice. The dogs circled behind, still uncertain whether to keep watch or lie down.

Jake stood for a moment to focus on the screen as the TV anchor continued their introduction: "Up next, our exclusive segment on Russia's evolving energy strategy and potential for renewed sabotage in the Baltic. Stay with us for this CEN Special Report."

Eve gestured to the couch. "I'll come and get comfy," she said, moving to join Jake there. At least then they would be together. She caught a faint outline of her leg against the glass as she came across—sharper than she'd expected.

Jake paused, watching Eve, wondering, then lowered himself onto the plush sofa. Eve sank next to him and slid close enough that he felt the heat radiating from her skin. Jake flicked up the volume a few notches higher, ignoring the pull of Eve's presence, keen to deter more conversation.

"I need to see this," was all he said.

Eve made a show of crossing her legs, the satin riding up a fraction. "This is exactly the foreplay I imagined earlier today as I was getting myself in the mood," she muttered, sarcasm lacing her tone. But she didn't leave. Instead she angled her head back and rested it against Jake's lap.

The documentary began. It was mostly ominous narration, voiced over scenes related to Russia's energy sector: "In the high-stakes world of global energy, Russia remains a formidable player. However, as the Kremlin tightens its grip on oil and gas, in pursuit of reclaiming its sovereignty, the impact ripples far beyond the country's borders..."

A sweeping montage of edited shots followed: drones capturing snowbound Siberian rigs, the silhouettes of pipelines hugging frosty tundra, pictures of LNG projects in Sakhalin, views of Moscow with the domes of the Kremlin looming in the background. Somber music underlined the gravity of each shot.

Jake stiffened as a picture filled the screen of alleged sabotage along three of the four Baltic Stream pipelines. The footage cut to watery undersea shots—twisted metal, curled and misshapen as if from explosions. Captions about willful damage scrolled along the bottom of the screen. Eve noticed Jake's brief distraction and leaned up.

"Jake," she whispered, brushing her lips near his earlobe, "we can watch this tomorrow. Let's not waste tonight on gloom and doom."

He cupped her chin absentmindedly, barely taking his eyes away from the broadcast. "Eve, this isn't gloom and doom—this is the backdrop for every deal I'm pursuing. Russia's energy maneuvers can shift markets and all our fortunes in a heartbeat. It matters."

She pulled back slightly, resentment flaring in her gaze, but she let him focus, sipping her champagne again in silence. On-screen, the documentary cut to an interview with a German energy analyst discussing the effect on Europe's precarious energy supply of both Russian sanctions and the sabotage. Scenes accompanied this footage, drawn from Germany and Italy.

Jake scowled, tugging lightly at his tie as though expecting this would all end badly. *Could the sabotage in the Baltic or talk of restricted exports hamper PanEnergy's own ambitions?* The narrator pivoted to coverage of tensions in NATO, between member countries, and suspicion swirling about Moscow's real intentions—as if the actions were not a message in themselves.

Eve pretended to yawn, but her catlike posture told another story. She shifted on the sofa, letting the dogs meander over to nudge her. As she scratched Diesel's ears with one hand, she used the other to stroke Jake's thigh. He didn't push her away, but his body remained unyielding, his attention resolutely fixed to the screen. If she'd hoped for a moment of spontaneous passion, she found none.

The TV anchor returned and continued the story in a similarly portentous manner: "At home, the rise of Republican candidates advocating a more aggressive 'Focus U.S.' energy policy could further complicate the precarious balance that we have achieved..."

There was a brief cut to an interview with protesting students on a university campus. "What they are really saying to the outside world," one protester explained so that viewers could understand the true gravity of the situation, "is F.U."

Jake gave a dry smile. "Classy." The student evidently thought so—grinning, pleased with his wordplay. "No wonder Russia responds as it does," he continued, sharing his insight. "The country is simply taking the world as it finds it."

Jake's jaw tensed. The program then scrolled through a series of short takes: a headstrong American female politician shouting at a convention flanked either side by star-spangled banners; footage of frazzled European heads of state looking chaotic—apparently trying to stave off crisis; and ending with shots of war in Ukraine.

Jake's gut started making noises. Perhaps it was his sense of alarm... In a world destabilized, he felt that uncertainties were only increasing. Russia was again promoting the idea of sovereign birthright. America was caught between continued *laissez-faire*—or drift as some called it—and strident nationalism.

The documentary faded out with an aerial shot of a Russian oil platform ablaze in the Arctic sun. The narrator's voice draped itself over this final scene: "The question remains: Can the world adapt peacefully to the new realities, or have we set ourselves upon a collision course with expanded conflict?"

Jake muted the screen, the narrator's question echoing in his head longer than he wanted to admit. The credits rolled, and the news desk returned.

"Jake?" Eve's voice sounded languid. Still next to him, she extended a hand lazily to stroke his face, but Jake hardly registered. Instead, he was staring blankly at the screen, wondering how geopolitics might blindside the firm's own efforts, whether their direct investments in oil & gas or their dealings with foreign partners—especially in Moscow. Jake shook his head, stiffness returning to his shoulders.

When he did eventually look down at Eve, he saw she'd closed her eyes and drifted into a doze. She must have grown bored waiting for him to respond. Another pang of guilt caught him. *Am I so consumed,* he wondered—not for the first time, *that she's a second thought?*

He watched her for an instant; her features looked softer in sleep—sweeter. The tension behind her earlier seductive ploy had dissolved. Gently, he rose from the couch, letting her head rest against a cushion. He tugged a blanket from the couch's back and draped it over her, more from growing habit than tenderness.

"Sorry," he murmured under his breath, though she couldn't hear. The dogs padded forward, each sniffing the air uncertainly, worried something was wrong. Jake slid a hand over Max's glossy head. "Bedtime, buddy," he said. Then he stepped away, glancing at the screen and its post-news chatter.

Draining the last of the champagne in Eve's flute, he refilled it and carried the glass with him toward the bedroom. The day's events still occupied his mind—the looming Permian acquisition, the swirling rumors of sabotage, the specter of Russian unpredictability.

It all felt more urgent than anything else. The idea of intimacy with Eve, of that old spark, felt increasingly distant, overwhelmed by the demands of business, expansions, and deals.

He paused at the start of the darkened hallway leading to the bedrooms and looked back at the couch. Eve lay curled beneath her blanket, the dogs quietly settling near her feet, which were still in stiletto heels. She was a vision of unrequited temptation, a reminder of nights when his desire for her was unstoppable.

With a half-shrug, Jake turned off the living room lights, leaving only the glow from the windows and the television. "We'll talk tomorrow," he said—

although experience now suggested otherwise. Had he ever meant it? he suddenly mused.

Claire's office projected quiet strength—clean lines, muted tones, the faint hum of climate control. She stood behind her desk, hands resting lightly upon her tall chair, while her key staffers—Lisa, Rafiq, and another pair of senior analysts—waited.

"Let's go over Ivan," she said, voice clipped but measured. "What have we learned since last week?" Her tone carried the calm of someone who never had to raise her voice—a habit long perfected.

Lisa, Claire's lead researcher on this task and the type of analyst who could find a hidden angle in a grocery list, consulted her tablet. "Immigrated with his parents, unremarkable U.S. childhood—father died young in a car crash. Then the mother passed away after Ivan's imprisonment in Russia."

Claire let a small frown crease her brow. "Any irregularities with the father's accident?"

Lisa shrugged, tapping the screen. "Nothing conclusive. Neighbors guessed emotional distress—he died on the anniversary of their emigration from Russia. But no official sign of foul play. Meanwhile, Ivan's two sisters are alive; they mention him in the past tense, no expectation he may be alive after the Siberian labor camp. They have kids who are now largely grown up. That's about it."

Claire's mouth set in a line. "So the family angle is a dead end. It doesn't explain any particular reasons for Ivan's move to Moscow—nor how he finished up behind bars." She drew a controlled breath, letting the hush expand. "What of Alex?"

The tension in the room sharpened. Rafiq, the desk head for Central Asia operations, cleared his throat. "We've got almost nothing on him from the web. However, discussion on the ground is he got mixed up in politics after too much immediate success and paid the price."

"Collateral damage was his online presence. It all resembled the Stalin era—only cleaner, more digital," he explained. "Now, he has more or less reemerged as a wealthy Azerbaijani entrepreneur—just without any traceable upbringing, no typical stepping stones. It's as though he arrived fully developed into the business world."

Lisa cut in, "We do have one interesting point. Some years ago, Alex Volkoff attended two events in Europe and wound up in the orbit of President Cooper's son."

Claire arched a brow at the reference to the U.S. President proud of her open spirit. "That's new. Do we have specifics?"

Lisa nodded. "One event in Geneva—some private investment conference—another at a tech forum in London. The son was dabbling in business then, but eventually left that sphere for philanthropic pursuits and his beloved art."

Claire's eyes lit up. "Does it connect to any official project or private deal?"

"Not obviously," Rafiq said. "No direct correlation. They were large-scale professional gatherings, standard meet-and-greets. Simply both parties were present, so we took note."

Claire let a beat pass. She angled her gaze away from her team, focusing on the large windows along one side of her room and the green visible through the blinds.

"We're still left with serious puzzles to resolve: how did Alex and Ivan cross; and which of them was the one to emerge—or escape?"

She turned back, hands lifting from the chair. "We keep recording possible sightings of Alex around the country, but notes that he occasionally uses American idioms, suggesting it might be Ivan. Or is that misdirection? We need to confirm who's here—and whether the other one's alive or dead."

Lisa's expression shifted. "Ivan was imprisoned for commercial espionage and data misuse under Russian law. Officially straightforward, but documentation feels... selective. He was tried two more times—effectively for lèse-majesté and treason, ending up in the gulag."

"It's possible, even likely," she continued, "that the affair was orchestrated at high levels in the government, though we've yet to uncover which figures had a stake in burying him."

"Russians don't need airtight evidence," Claire said evenly. "They just need the impetus. That impetus might tie to PanEnergy or some conflict Ivan got himself tangled in." Claire let the weight of it all sink in. "So the question is: who gains from letting Ivan out to take on the persona of Alex?"

The small group exchanged glances. The dryness in the air told them that this was a riddle with no simple thread to pull—yet.

Claire's shoulders squared. "I want everything rechecked. Keep tapping your contacts, Rafiq, for any slip in Baku or the broader labyrinth of Russian enclaves outside Moscow. Lisa, keep digging into the old PanEnergy records. We must see if a switch was set in motion."

A subtle wave of nods moved around the table. The two additional analysts—Morgan and Chang—quietly typed notes on their laptops, finalizing the tasks.

"Thank you all," Claire said. "I need immediate alerts on any fresh lead. This is not a puzzle we can linger over."

They dispersed, gathering tablets, pens, and files. As the door clicked shut behind them, Claire took one last glance out the windows. The agency sometimes felt that it was a silent guardian of democracy. Within its walls, decisions were indeed made that shaped corners of the globe. The business of Alex Volkoff, or Ivan Asimov, lay in one of those corners—small but, she felt, deeply consequential.

She shook her head, feeling something was gravely amiss. More was at stake than two men's destinies. She worried the tangle might facilitate conspiracies, undermine national interests. If Alex were locked away and Ivan out making moves—why? And how had Russia pulled off this ruse—merging such distinct identities?

Claire's eyes glanced at a file on her desk labeled "ASIMOV/VOLKOFF—Confidential." The edges were already dog-eared, a testament to repeated searches for clarity. She let her fingertips rest on the file again.

A vow formed in her mind that no illusions from Moscow would, or indeed could, stay hidden indefinitely. She was sure of that, and she had built her career on piecing the improbable into the undeniable.

She lifted the file and tucked it under her arm. Another meeting beckoned, but her mind stayed on the puzzle of two men, one fate. In a city like Washington D.C., built on formalities and declared allegiances, ambiguity was power—and Claire meant to learn exactly who was wielding it.

The ballroom buzzed, the hum of polished chatter rising above the soft clink of glassware. Beneath crystal chandeliers spilling with golden light, fifty round tables stretched in neat rows, dressed in white linens.

And on each table stood four unlabeled wine bottles—two white and two red—flanked by piles of tasting sheets awaiting the sure scribbles of connoisseurs and amateurs alike. The entire scene pulsed with a mix of lighthearted fun and fierce competition, typical of society fundraisers.

At one table near the center, Kaisa—now in her mid-thirties and more poised—oversaw a small crew of friends and acquaintances. She eyed them: Jessica, Phil, Patricia, Mark, James, Martha, and Cavil (Kaisa corrected herself *Ambassador Lane*). Two unknowns were still missing. It was a tale of her life in America distilled into nine people.

Kaisa leaned over the table, scanning the row of four bottles, an anticipatory gleam in her eye. A faint swirl of excitement coursed through her. She'd grown used to public events, standing gracefully beside her husband—Senator Caleb Warren, a rising star in politics. But tonight she intended to indulge—to focus more on the wine and the contest itself.

Of course, she still had a hostess role to play, especially concerning the two late-arriving guests her husband considered "very important." But for the moment, she could relish the promise of fun that four mystery wines offered.

She checked her phone discreetly—no new messages. *Maybe Caleb's too busy to update me,* she thought. Kaisa stowed the phone back inside her clutch, and looked up. "All right," she said. "Shall we do some damage?"

Phil, early forties but already gray, smirked and raised his well-used leather tasting notebook. "Are we here just to enjoy ourselves—or to win?"

Jessica, the youngest, still in her twenties, rolled her eyes good-naturedly. "You're the one who always lectures us to savor, not compete." She jabbed a finger at his notebook. "Yet you're the only one with gear."

Phil laughed, unashamed. "I'm a contradiction. Embrace it."

Patricia and Jessica exchanged winks. Kaisa grinned, letting out a soft laugh. She was just about to comment on how she, too, loved winning—but her phone buzzed. She felt slightly annoyed—having put it away seconds earlier. Perhaps she'd have to leave it on the table.

The alert was an incoming text from her husband: *Hope all good there. Have our new guests showed up yet? Keep me posted if they do. Thx."*

Her brow furrowed momentarily. She texted back: *No sign. We're about to start. The turnout is great, though. Well done!*

She put the phone down and refocused on the swirl of conversation at her table. Kaisa was determined to have an enjoyable evening.

A tall MC, dressed in a sharply cut tuxedo ascended the small, well-lit dais at the front of the room.

"Ladies and gentlemen," he began, his resonant voice echoing across the wide hall, "welcome to our Annual Wine-Tasting Challenge—our main entertainment at tonight's fundraiser for the esteemed Senator Warren." He lifted a wine glass dramatically, demanding the attention of the crowd.

"You'll each have two whites and two reds." He glanced around. "And a bunch of tasting sheets." He gestured at the sea of white-draped tables, nodding at the eager faces. "Your mission: identify the grape or grapes, name the region, and if you're daring, call out a vintage and producer."

Excited whispers floated around the room. Kaisa darted a glance at Phil, who was already poised to scribble notes.

"But let me offer a cautionary tale," the MC continued. "Sometimes we think we've nailed it, say, a Malbec from Mendoza—yet it turns out a Monastrell from Jumilla, a 2019 Bodega El Silencio with black fruit, spice, and a rustic edge. Surprises abound! So keep those minds open, my friends."

Laughter rippled through the room. Kaisa caught Jessica's wry grin at the mention of random outcomes in blind tastings.

"Each table makes one combined entry—teamwork, even for you alpha types." Another burst of laugh arose, mostly but not only from the men. "How do we win?" a guy shouted out, already in the alpha spirit.

"Indeed. What if you get the same results for the grape and region? The winner is the table with the most detail correct. You're welcome to add as much detail as you feel you know in the comments space."

"We're going to win this," Phil told the table, "No doubt."

"Of course, as the statisticians here know... Do we have any statisticians here?" No one raised their hand. A ripple of laughter followed.

"Of course as you investors will know—and I won't ask how many of you are investors—as you'll know, it just encourages our innate biases, not least overconfidence." At this the MC concluded, raising his glass, "To good wine, to spirited guesses, and to supporting Senator Warren. Cheers!"

A brief lull was quickly replaced by the hustle of eager conversation. The competition was on, and Kaisa would be right into it.

However, the two empty chairs distracted her. In the hush before the server poured the first wine, Kaisa wondered. *Who were these people? And where did they come from?*

She'd gleaned from Caleb they were new to the States, an entrepreneur and his younger partner, possibly someone with close ties to business—someone who could prove helpful in future campaigns whether for networking or, in some way, for financing.

Caleb never spelled it out too plainly—indeed he would find it gauche, she thought. However, she sensed their significance. *They'd better arrive soon...*

The server at Kaisa's table arrived, and deftly poured the first wine into each glass. The wine had a lighter hue.

"All right," Phil declared, sniffing the wine and letting out a long, satisfied hum. "This one's serious. Pale yellow color—but something with oak. You can smell it—vanilla, maybe even a touch of spice. Not overdone."

Jessica, who'd already started to scribble notes on her tasting sheet, narrowed her eyes. "Oak, sure, and—as you say—not so much given the lightish color. But there's a lot going on here. I'm getting apple—maybe even baked apple. And then some floral notes—I'd say jasmine."

Phil shot her a patronizing smile. "Floral? Jasmine? Are you sure you're not mistaking that for a whiff of the centerpiece?" He gestured to the ornate bouquet in the middle of the table, its extravagant roses and lilies spilling over.

Jessica didn't even flinch. "Trust me, Phil, I know the difference between flowers in a glass and flowers in a vase. Maybe your cologne's hiding it," she teased back good-naturedly.

She swirled her wine again and gave it a sip. "There's a hint of richness there. Maybe a Bordeaux-style white blend? Or it could be Tuscan—Trebbiano and Malvasia, but done with real finesse."

"Tuscan?" Phil barked out a laugh. "No way. This has Old World written all over it. Maybe even Alsace. Fairly recent vintage. 2020, 2021—somewhere in there."

Kaisa took a small sip, rolling the wine over her tongue. Undeniably it had a certain richness, with a layered complexity that lingered. "I'm not sure Italy is exactly New World..." she noted, returning to Phil's earlier statement. "I'm getting honey, for sure," she murmured, more to herself. "It's balanced. Not cloying."

"Exactly," Phil pounced. "That sophistication means it's not Italian—too refined, too elegant. Alsace, no doubt. If it's not something like Condrieu."

"I don't know," Mark chimed in, hesitant but thoughtful. "It's different from most Alsace wines I've tried; not fruity enough. Could it be from California—Napa Valley, maybe?"

Jessica groaned audibly. "Napa?"

"It's not a crazy thought," James interjected, his tone measured. "You know California's doing some interesting things with Rhone varieties these days. Viognier, Roussanne—they could produce this kind of texture and richness, especially if it's a small producer who's not overdoing the oak."

Kaisa glanced at James, surprised. He rarely spoke up, but when he did, his comments carried a quiet authority.

"Okay, let's play devil's advocate," Kaisa said, wanting to mix things up a bit. "What about a wine from Australia? Margaret River? They're known for doing elegant whites—maybe a Sémillon-Sauvignon Blanc blend, but aged to give it that honeyed depth?"

Phil groaned. "Margaret River? In Western Australia? Please. Australia is best doing commercial wine. *Yellow Tail*—which I guarantee won't feature tonight."

Jessica bristled. "You're such a snob, Phil. Just because a wine doesn't have a French label doesn't mean it's not world-class. What about New Zealand?"

Kaisa took another sip of her own glass, trying to focus on the wine itself. It was rich but not overly, dry rather than unctuous, with layers of flavor that unfurled like a slow wave—honey, baked apple or pear, even something more tropical. Aromas of white blossoms complemented the whole ensemble.

She let her mind wander, picturing sunlit vineyards, cool cellars, winemakers meticulously crafting blends that would end up on tables like this. The wine was remarkably enjoyable; which meant that there had to be a good level of acidity.

The two empty seats caught her eye again. She wondered if her husband's surprise guests would know their wine. Kaisa doubted it, somehow. Important men rarely came to drink—they came to be seen, to test the room, to measure what might be bought.

"Kaisa?" Jessica's voice snapped her out of her thoughts.

"Hmm?"

"What's your call on this one?"

Kaisa set her glass down carefully. "I think it's complex enough to make everyone second-guess themselves. My gut says Old World, though not Alsace. I'm sorry Phil. Maybe a Bordeaux Blanc? Sémillon and Sauvignon with some age on it?"

Phil rolled his eyes. "Bold move, but wrong. The taste profile suggests Alsace."

Jessica shook her head. "I'd bet on Tuscany before Alsace. Or even California."

Kaisa smiled, jotting down her notes. "What do you say Ambassador Lane, given all your international experience?"

"Ah," he replied, "I just enjoy drinking. This is really nice," he said, lifting his glass. "Not like our usual fare at embassy functions. In proper glasses too..."

Where was his notorious ego? Kaisa thought.

The wine remained a mystery demanding respect, but the truth would reveal itself soon enough. In any case, she noticed that the source of conflict wasn't really the wine's origins, but everyone's self-image and their varying instincts. The unspoken contest was to be the sharpest palate at the table.

"Okay, Phil," Martha said graciously for them all. "You can have Alsace. Put down the grape and any other details, and we can move onto the next wine."

In a brief lull before they proceeded to the second wine, Kaisa glanced at her phone. No new texts—should she check on Caleb's progress? She typed him a short message: *All good here. Guests still haven't arrived. We liked the first wine. How's it going at your end?"*

The empty seats had thrown a small shadow over her table's energy. "Latecomers always miss the best part," she muttered. But Kaisa was determined not to let it ruin her evening. Phil launched into another discussion, this time about the geography of Chablis.

She smiled to herself. It was a good mix. Phil's posturing. Jessica's defiant intellect. The ambassador, always formal, and his wife, Martha. And she—Kaisa, the high-flying senator's wife—so often performing as hostess while inwardly wondering whether this was the life she wanted.

Really, she thought, looking around the room. *How much did the unending rotation of self-important strangers contribute to her life?* Her mind wandered yet again to the missing couple. A foreign entrepreneur. Plus long-term partner, younger. The various fragments swirled in her mind—incomplete pieces of a puzzle she hadn't yet seen but was already trying to work out.

Entrepreneur. These days that meant tech... But could it be something else, still glamorous, like venture capital or private equity. Or was it something more traditional—more essential—like energy, materials, or even shipping?

And the partner—"younger." It felt such a loaded word, especially coming from her husband. Did it mean wide-eyed and ingénue-like, or sharper and self-directed? Was she arm-candy or an equal? Did it mean the guy was a Matt Damon-type, an Al Pacino, or someone more straightforward? Strom Thurmond came to mind.

Was she a first partner, like MacKenzie Scott, or a second, like Lauren Sánchez? Or a later partner, like Wendi Deng. Kaisa was interested to see.

The waiter reappeared, now picking up the second white, this one having a richer golden tone. Kaisa refocused. She could feel the energy around the room shifting. Her own table was back in its tasting posture, swirling glasses with fresh intensity.

Around her pockets of voices rose and fell. Tables appeared to progress at their own speeds. Some were still lost among the nuances of the first wine, swirling and sniffing like chemists forever on the verge of discovery. Others were already onto the reds.

She saw one table debating with a fervor she'd seen in amateur courtroom dramas. *Twelve Angry Men* came to mind. For a second she could almost picture someone saying, "Here's an idea. Let's... run it up the flagpole and see if anyone salutes it."

She wondered, in an amused fashion, what drama might best describe her table. *My Cousin Vinny* perhaps. She laughed, and Jessica glanced her way, startled by the sudden noise.

Kaisa quickly took a sip of her wine, letting it wash over her tongue. "All right," she said after swallowing. "Stone fruit—peach, definitely. A bit of citrus. Perhaps even pineapple on the finish."

Jessica nodded. "And there's something creamy again," she added, "that buttery character."

"What do you call it, Phil?" she asked with a little hesitation, goading him.

He missed the gibe. "Malolactic fermentation."

"Ah yes, thank you," she replied. "MLF, not to be mistaken for any other acronyms. At least I hope not..." Suddenly interested, she gave the room a quick survey.

Phil didn't notice. He was swirling his glass with a focus bordering on the theatrical. "You're overcomplicating it. This is a French Chardonnay.

Burgundy—I'd say Côte de Beaune. 2019. Maybe 2018 if we're being generous."

Jessica, her attention returned to the table, lifted an eyebrow. "Generous? How very magnanimous of you, Phil."

As Phil and Jessica restarted their playful yet somehow serious antagonism, Kaisa noticed another table a few rows away where the server was delivering a fresh bottle of the first white. The group there was highly animated—less concerned with the rules of the game than with enjoying the wine itself. They raised their glasses as laughter erupted, and Kaisa saw a man pitch his head back for a long, enthusiastic swill.

She chuckled. Not everyone was here to play sommelier. Some were here just for the sheer indulgence—a chance to drink expensive wine in a lavish setting without worrying too much about provenance or vintage.

Back at her table, Phil's tone had become more professorial. "See, Burgundy whites are all about minerality. You're getting that flinty quality, right? It's subtle, but it's there. I think also some oak. French oak, specifically. Lightly toasted. Very refined."

Kaisa blinked, unsure. Swirling her glass again, she sniffed deeply and took a sip, trying to detect the minerality Phil asserted was there.

"I don't know," Jessica said, hesitant but firm. "It's brighter than I'd expect from Burgundy. The acidity feels sharper, fresher. And that tropical note—it doesn't scream France to me. It's...

Mark interrupted her, "California. Santa Barbara or Sonoma Coast—maybe even Russian River Valley."

Phil shook his head. "No, no, no," he said. "This is elegance in a glass. We know chardonnays from California; we've all had them. They are big, over-oaked butter bombs."

Jessica's eyes narrowed. "Not all California Chardonnays are oak monsters, you know. And Russian River can make wines just as complex as the best

Burgundy. The coastal fog cools the vines, so you get acidity along with the ripeness. This bright character? I think it's Sonoma."

Across the table, Patricia interrupted, feeling she needed to support her husband. "I think this is too restrained. I'd also say it's Old World."

"Thanks, darling," Phil replied, toasting her.

Kaisa leaned back, her brow furrowed. She turned again to Ambassador Lane. "What do you think?"

"You know," he replied, "they say women are better tasters than men; just naturally better at it."

"I'd say!" Jessica interrupted.

"It's partly about the taste buds and partly about the ego," Cavil continued. "Martha, dearest," he turned to his wife, "what are your thoughts?"

"Yes, men do have inflated egos." Everyone laughed. After a pause she continued, "I do taste, however, something tropical. Can it be pineapple?"

"Exactly," said Kaisa. "Peach, pineapple—hot-climate flavors."

James continued, "If it's Burgundy, wouldn't we be getting more green apple or pear?"

Phil sighed—the kind of sigh implying he was again having to shoulder the burden of educating the room. "Not necessarily. A warm year could give those riper fruit characteristics. 2018, for instance, was warm in Burgundy. That could easily explain the tropical notes."

Jessica was about to respond when Mark interrupted. "What about Margaret River?" Everyone turned to him, startled.

"Margaret River?" Phil gave an incredulous look. "You're messing with me—like Kaisa, right? That's the kind of game she likes to play. Do your head in with clever ideas." Phil gave a snort. "I mean, for the love of God, can we stop pretending that Australia is even going to make an appearance in this room?"

"Why not?" James asked, shrugging. "They make incredible Chardonnays there. They're kind of like a midpoint between Burgundy and California—powerful fruit but with that clean, almost saline quality. And their oak use is restrained.

"Yes," concurred Mark. "That tropical note could definitely be Margaret River."

Jessica nodded slowly, considering. "That's not a bad call. They get a lot of ocean influence there, after all. And their Chardonnays are well-balanced."

Phil shook his head. "Margaret River isn't even in the same league as Burgundy. Sure, it's good *for Australia,* but this wine? It's complex and layered. It's Burgundy."

Jessica crossed her arms. "You find any excuse, so long as France comes out on top."

"I have this colleague at the hedge fund," she went on. "A top manager promoted really fast. He said to me once, 'I should warn you, I'm a connoisseur. I drink only Bordeaux and Burgundy, and just occasionally Opus One.' I mean..."

Phil smirked. "But he's right. And it's not about prestige—it's about centuries of tradition and craftsmanship. California doesn't have that history." He paused. "And Margaret River? It's still trying to catch up with America, who inspired them. What was it—fifty years ago when Mondavi went across? Australia's still just trying to figure out what kind of Chardonnay to produce."

"Ugh, you're impossible," Jessica muttered, swirling her glass.

Kaisa sighed, trying to tune out all the noise. She took another sniff of her wine, keen to focus simply on the aromas: ripe stone fruit, the hint of citrus. She took a sip, letting the wine coat her palate.

"I'm still stuck on that acidity," Kaisa said finally. "It's just so bright and sharp. It doesn't feel Old World to me."

Phil waved his hand dismissively. "Kaisa, that brightness is exactly what makes it Burgundy. They balance acidity with oak perfectly. New World, sadly, doesn't have that finesse."

Jessica leaned forward, eyes blazing. "Finesse? Have you even *had* a Ramey or a Kistler from Sonoma? They're every bit as nuanced as Burgundy, and sometimes more exciting."

Phil was ready with a retort, but Kaisa held up her hand. "All right, let's focus. We need a consensus."

"I say Burgundy," Phil said firmly.

"Sonoma," Jessica countered.

"Margaret River," Mark added, shrugging again.

Kaisa sighed, scribbling notes on a tasting sheet. "Fine. You can have it, Phil. But if it's not a Burgundy, you owe the table an apology. And if it's Sonoma or Margaret River, then you are buying us each a bottle."

Phil smirked. "Deal. But don't worry—you'll see I'm right."

Around the room, a few other tables were deep in similar arguments, their voices carrying the same mix of passion and certainty. Kaisa glanced once more at the empty chairs beside her. They were missing this charged debate. They'd hear all the arguments again, of course, along with the post-mortem. However, it wasn't the same as being present at the time.

Wine wasn't just wine tonight. It was intuition, ego, and identity poured into a glass. And when discussions became charged, it wasn't about which region the wine came from—it was about who would decide the table's answer.

The hustle continued. Kaisa's phone buzzed again. She got up and went to the wall so as not to disturb the others. It was a message from Caleb. *"In good shape here. Donors are happy. Newcomers called—ETA maybe 15-20 min. They're new but I believe important for the future. Thx for hosting them properly."*

Kaisa typed back: *"Got it. We just finished the second white. Will keep them engaged."*

So they are coming, she thought. *Better late than never.* She had no idea how much their arrival would change the course of her evening—as well as everything to follow.

The server lifted the first red bottle and began to pour. The wine shimmered in the glasses, a pale ruby hue, which immediately triggered excitement around the table. Kaisa swirled hers delicately, letting the aromas rise. Her eyes danced with speculation.

Jessica was the first to speak. "The color's so light–rules out Bordeaux or Syrah. I wonder..." Jessica's voice trailed off. She swirled the glass, took in the bouquet. Another swirl and she gave it a sip. "Definitely not Barolo–there are no monstrous tannins."

Mark had gone straight to drinking the wine; after all he preferred red. "Agreed," he said. "Barolo would have that dry grip. This is too soft for Nebbiolo."

"What about Chianti?" Phil offered, feeling he had perhaps overplayed his defense of French wine earlier. His tone lacked conviction. "Sangiovese can sometimes be lightish."

"It's missing that black tea character," Mark countered. "Chianti always has that dryness which offsets the tart cherry pucker. This feels more rounded."

"It's Pinot," Jessica declared confidently. "We're thinking too hard this time. The real question is where it's from."

Kaisa nodded. "Pinot makes the most sense. But narrowing it down–well, that's where it gets interesting. France? Oregon? New Zealand? Germany? Australia? Even England's in the game now."

Phil sought to keep his expression neutral, continuing his effort to stay away from France for at least one discussion. "California?"

"Too delicate," Jessica said. "Most California Pinots are more fruit-forward, bigger in style."

Mark raised a finger. "But not all of them. The cooler regions, like Santa Barbara, make some incredibly elegant Pinots. You remember that film?" Everyone groaned.

Kaisa turned to Cavil, as before trying to keep the ambassadorial couple involved in the table's activity as much as possible. "What do you think, Ambassador Lane?"

Cavil gave a small deprecating smile, setting his glass down. "I think that Jessica's on form. And Mark's comment about California is worth considering—it all depends on the region. Your mention of Australia is interesting, too. We were posted there. It could be like Victoria or Tasmania. Cool climate, restrained fruit… it fits."

"What a lovely place Tasmania is," added Martha. "So wild and untamed."

Jessica grinned. "You're very diplomatic, Ambassador… All right, let's focus. If it's Pinot, where's it from? Burgundy seems too restrained—our wine's got more brightness."

Phil tilted his head, Jessica's nonchalant rejection of Burgundy's capabilities breaking down the last of his self-restraint. "Burgundy can be bright, depending on the village. Volnay, for example, can produce wines like this—light, elegant, with a bit of red fruit."

"But this doesn't have the depth of Volnay," James said. "It's a bit too straightforward for Burgundy."

"New Zealand, then?" Mark suggested. "They make Pinots with this kind of vibrancy."

Jessica leaned forward. "Could be, but I still think it's Oregon. It has that perfect balance of ripe fruit and earthiness—what the Pacific Northwest is known for."

Ambassador Lane swirled his glass, getting a bit more into the spirit of things. "Germany's Spätburgunder might fit. I was stationed there too. Spätburgunder can have that soft fruit character. But this doesn't have the floral notes. No violets, no roses."

Martha offered quietly, "The brightness in the fruit does lean more New World than Old."

Jessica nodded vigorously. "See? New world. I'm sticking with Oregon."

Mark hesitated. "It's not impossible."

Phil raised his glass in a mock toast. "All right. Let's hope you're right." He wrote his own thoughts down in his notebook so that he wouldn't forget later.

The table agreed, and Jessica eagerly scrawled "Oregon Pinot Noir" on their tasting sheet.

The table buzzed with a loosened energy as they approached the final wine of the evening. Bread rolls, plain biscuits, and cubes of cheese were passed around, their simplicity a counterpoint to what would later be a substantial meal. Water glasses were kept full by the ever-attentive waiters, but few here or elsewhere were interested.

As the fourth wine was poured, all eyes were on the dark red liquid now swirling into their glasses—a wine of undeniable presence. Jessica held her glass up to the light. "Now, this is serious. No delicate Pinot here."

"No shrinking Spätburgunder," offered Martha, but no one laughed and she wondered if they'd missed the oblique reference to the violets her husband had mentioned.

* * *

Just as they were about to analyze the second red, Kaisa spotted a slight stir at the ballroom's entrance. Two figures approached a staff member who pointed them toward Kaisa's table. She felt a dart of apprehension. *They've arrived.* This had to be Caleb's important guests. Conversation faded; footsteps approached.

Kaisa's heart raced. She recognized the reaction she had at the gala. Her body seemed to respond as her mind froze. The tall man wore a tailored silver-gray suit with a light pastel-blue shirt, his hair combed. But it was his face—the jawline, the eyes—something about it made her stomach flip.

His companion was a striking woman in a peach-orange evening gown. Her hair was gathered low and clean—a single knot, fastened with a bronze pin. Kaisa set her glass down, and mustered her composure. She rose, greeting them: "Hello! You must be Caleb's friends. We've been expecting you."

The man offered a handshake, his gaze lingering on her face for a beat. "I'm Alex Volkoff, and this is Anisa, my partner. So sorry we're late. We ran into traffic snags." He looked down, smiling apologetically.

Anisa gave a gracious nod. "The city can be unforgiving, especially for newcomers like us."

Kaisa's mind whirled: *Volkoff? So that's his name? Or was it? The embassy guy at the lake cabin had talked about an Alex. This guy?* His appearance unsettled her—and she realized it threatened to unwrap the careful structures she'd placed around her past.

Nevertheless, she managed a bright smile. "We're glad you made it. I'm Kaisa Warren, Caleb's partner. Welcome to our table." She gestured around her and then to the two empty chairs. *The same face from that fleeting moment at the Gala,* she thought, *but older than she had calculated, and older than Ivan should be.*

The rest of the table introduced themselves eagerly, making room for Alex and Anisa to join the swirl of conversation. The staff quickly poured them a glass of the first red so they could catch up if they wished.

Phil launched into an explanation: "We've already guessed the two whites—a Riesling from Alsace, then a Burgundy. But we might be wrong, who knows." He laughed. "And we've completed the first red, which Jessica pegged as an Oregon Pinot."

Anisa sipped her wine and nodded. "It's lovely. I'm not well-versed, but I do enjoy a red like this. I hadn't expected a wine tasting."

Kaisa chuckled, meeting Anisa's gaze. "Surprises are what make evenings like this memorable, don't you think?" Kaisa noted the newcomer's poise.

Anisa inclined her head, her eyes sparkling. "Absolutely. Though, in my experience, surprises can be—double-edged." The words hung, sharp and layered, as if Anisa sensed Kaisa's suspicions about Alex.

Kaisa felt a prickle of intrigue. She studied Alex's reaction as he sipped the first red wine. His expression betrayed little. "The fruit is quite forward, lovely strawberry with soft tannins," he commented. "That fits your guess, Jessica." He bowed his head in appreciation—noncommittal and polite.

Kaisa's thoughts spun. *He's so guarded.* She felt compelled to confirm—or disprove—what her heart was whispering. She couldn't relax until she'd put her doubts to bed.

"Alex," she said lightly, "I've been picking your brain all night in absentia—my husband said you have common interests? I'm sure that he hopes you'll find synergy with some of our folks here."

Alex gave a quiet smile. "Yes, the senator was kind enough to invite us. We might have some overlapping ambitions, for example in the energy arena. It is always good to find new ideas and explore new potential, yes?"

Kaisa forced a chuckle. "He'll be thrilled to hear that." *So that's the link—he's in the energy sector, just as Ivan once dreamed. This can't be coincidence.* She recalled how Ivan had a passion for oil and gas years ago.

Attention turned back to the second red. This wine poured thickly, deeper than the previous one. Kaisa's table had perked up with fresh excitement.

"Look at the depth of color," Jessica said again.

"It's opaque," Mark added, already sounding confident. "This is something with structure. A bold red, clearly. Cabernet Sauvignon?"

Phil, back to his old habits, scoffed. "Too easy. Cabernet, Bordeaux, is an obvious choice, which makes me think it's a trick. Maybe one of the other component grapes: Malbec or Petit Verdot? Or something else completely—Mourvèdre?"

Kaisa smiled, her fingers resting lightly on the stem of her glass. "And the possibilities go on... It could be a Syrah, or maybe a Zinfandel—if they're feeling in the mood."

James offered his own observation. "It's got that inky color you'd expect from Syrah. And a slight smokiness on the nose—which is again typical for Northern Rhône styles, no?"

Jessica tilted her head, considering. "True, but does it have the peppery bite of a Syrah? I'm not sure."

"Let's not forget Grenache," Kaisa said, continuing to expand the list of options. "The color's darker than some, but the alcohol on the nose could fit. Still along the Rhône. Maybe Châteauneuf-du-Pape?"

Phil laughed, a bit too loudly. "You're dreaming, Kaisa. This isn't Grenache. It's got way more tannin."

Kaisa caught Alex's eye and decided to prod. "What do you think, Alex? I'm sure you're a detail kind of guy. What do you notice?"

Alex poured a glass of the second red for Anisa and himself, then gave it a sip. "My immediate observation tells me," he said with a small smile, "that your guesses are better than mine."

Jessica rolled her eyes. "Oh, come on, Alex. You're sounding like the Ambassador now." Cavil laughed.

"I'm afraid whiskey's more my thing," he said simply.

"But you must have an opinion. Give us something."

Alex raised his glass again and slowly deliberated over the wine as the table watched. "I'd say you've all made compelling arguments."

The table erupted in laughter, Phil shaking his head. "You're impossible, man. What do you think, Anisa?"

Anisa, who had been enjoying her wine quietly, smiled. "Yes, he's careful with his words. I, on the other hand, know that this is delicious. I'm amazed by everyone's experience."

Kaisa interjected at this point. "You and Alex make quite a pair," she said, keen to seize the moment and probe a little deeper. "Where did you two meet, if you don't mind my asking?"

Anisa's gaze flicked to Alex, then back to Kaisa, her smile softening but her eyes sharp. "In Baku, actually. I was working at a mission there—an orphanage, where I'd been since losing my parents young. Alex was... let's say, a generous visitor."

She turned and smiled at Alex, her eyes alight. "He has a way of turning up where you least expect."

Kaisa's heart skipped. Anisa's words were full of ambiguity, hinting at hidden chapters in Alex's past. Were they messages—or simply coincidences? Kaisa tried to keep her tone light and direct in an effort to match Anisa's poise. "A mission in Baku? That's a long way from Manhattan's ballrooms. You must have so many stories to tell, ones that put ours to shame."

Anisa laughed. "So many stories." Briefly her face clouded over. "Some are not so happy, not so frivolous. Others—in contrast—are wonderful: like the day I first saw Alex," she glanced at him again, "so grand, so determined as he entered our orphanage."

Anisa paused. "Many of these stories, however, are still unfinished. Their evolution is like a good wine." She picked up her glass and looked at it closely. "Each with its own trajectory. In time, the story arrives at a natural ending, which is rich and complex for having taken time." She smiled, perhaps a little too gaily.

Jessica understood. "Something," she said, "that true connoisseurs here—knowledgeable about origin, vintage, and conditions—would appreciate. Right, Phil?" He smiled, more alert now to Jessica's barbs.

"And Alex," Kaisa asked, not to be distracted. "Why was he there in Baku?"

"Alex?" Anisa replied almost as if weighing the word. "I think because... he's always been drawn to lost causes." She glanced at Alex one more time with a mix of tenderness and gratitude. Then she gazed at Kaisa, as if daring her to dig deeper.

Kaisa opened her mouth to respond, but the buzz of laughter from another table broke the spell. And then the table interrupted. The contest was nearly finished, and they wanted to complete their tasting note.

The tension, whatever had developed, now eased. But Kaisa filed away their exchange: the discussion suggested that Anisa was more than just a companion—maybe even a participant in whatever game Alex was running.

And while the others debated and argued, Kaisa kept her focus sharp—especially on Alex. She noted how he scanned the room, as if cautious.

More than that, she saw the way he ran his finger along the rim of his glass—the way, occasionally, he gave an apologetic glance downward. Increasingly she wondered that he might, indeed, be the man she'd agreed to marry. He preferred whiskey. He was into oil and gas.

The conversation at the table resumed its liveliness, with jokes and good-natured gibes flying as the group narrowed their choices. Jessica finally leaned forward, pen poised over the tasting sheet. "Right, final votes. Syrah, Cabernet, or Grenache?"

"Syrah," James said firmly.

"Mourvèdre," Phil countered.

Jessica turned to Kaisa. "What do you think?"

Kaisa hesitated, glancing at Alex before answering. "Syrah. There is, as James points out, that smokiness which feels unmistakable."

Jessica grinned, scribbling it down. "Syrah it is. Northern Rhône. Year? I'll put 2018."

The decision made, the waiter swooped in to collect the sheet, and the group largely relaxed into the easy camaraderie that comes from finishing a task together. Kaisa, however, felt anything but relaxed. She studied Alex as he reached for a piece of cheese, his movements deliberate, his demeanor unflappable.

"So, Alex," she started again lightly, her tone deceptively casual, "have you always been so good at avoiding questions? Or is that a skill you've picked up recently?"

He looked at her, his dark eyes unreadable. "Avoiding questions? I prefer to think of it as listening carefully."

Kaisa laughed, but it didn't reach her eyes. "Well, you're excellent at it. Almost too good."

Alex inclined his head. "Thank you. I'll take that as a compliment."

The rest of the table had moved onto more lighthearted chatter, but Kaisa couldn't let go. Her mind was spinning. It really could be him. The resemblance was striking; the subtle mannerisms were not unfamiliar. Yet his name, his story, his apparent detachment from the past—his age!—they pointed to a different man entirely.

But if it *were* him, why was he here? Why had he come back, and why now? She shuddered at what it might mean for her present life. She had built a comfortable world based around her career, Caleb's political ambitions, and their home together. The sight of Alex now raised the tough prospect of reconsidering all that she had lost years ago and what it meant for her current world.

The wine glasses on the table seemed to dim as Kaisa's thoughts turned inward. The memories she'd carefully packed away for years, the explanations she'd painfully organized, were suddenly falling out, colliding with the present and threatening to unmoor her entirely.

By the time the last cork was pulled, the night had changed course. About that much Kaisa was certain. However, she wondered. Had it also broken open the conflict existing from the start, when she encountered Caleb and realized his interest in her—the contradiction she knew was there, but had deliberately embraced?

Kaisa sighed, letting the ambient noise envelop her. She knew the truth lay hidden somewhere behind Alex's calm façade. She needed, one way or another, to bring it to the surface.

If Alex had rung the bell in a fight for her heart, it was hardly a fair contest: on one side, stability and surety—a relationship that functioned and had a clear trajectory; on the other, something darker and unfinished, a connection that had never had the opportunity to live, whose potential was completely unknown.

The evening she sensed, had become a warm-up for a far more serious game—and one that might ultimately break her in half.

32. The Hamptons

As Kaisa stepped into the Manhattan night, the event's success was clear. People were leaving happy and committed.

Among the many cars pulling up at the same time to collect guests and take them back home, a Mercedes-Maybach S680 parked a bit farther down the road, its polished black exterior seeming to fully absorb the city's neon glow.

To the casual observer, it was just another sedan in a city accustomed to excess. But to those who understood the nuance, the car's understated elegance signaled membership in a rarefied echelon of power.

The rear door opened with a whisper, revealing a dimly lit, spacious interior. Alex slid in first. Anisa followed, her slender frame settling beside him. She was someone who had long ago mastered the art of graceful composure. The door closed behind them with a satisfying thunk, and sealed them within a cocoon of unassuming luxury.

Inside, the atmosphere was one of quiet refinement. The leather seats in soft caramel tones molded effortlessly to the body. A trace of cedar lingered in the air. Ambient lighting cast a golden hue, accentuating the smooth lines of the overall design.

A bald, seasoned driver sat beside Alex's young assistant, David—clean-shaven and sharp-eyed. David's tailored jacket and neatly pressed shirt were all business, but the way his eyes moved suggested a constant, instinctive vigilance. He was scrolling through his tablet, scanning emails and updates, but paused briefly to nod at Alex before resuming his work.

Alex looked out the window and caught sight of Kaisa taking a moment to wind down following what must have been a long evening. His expression was unreadable. After a second he settled into the seat and rested his elbow on the door armrest. "Home," he said quietly.

"To the Hamptons," the driver confirmed, steering the car smoothly away from the curb. For a moment, there was silence, then Alex addressed David. "Have you arranged to be the dog walker?"

David looked up from his tablet. "Yes. All in hand—as you requested."

"Eve's nice," Alex continued. "You'll like her."

Silence fell again and stretched as no one felt the urge to speak further. The muted hum of the car's powerful engine and the faint vibration of the road filled the space. Outside, the city lights blurred, gold and white streaks against the tinted windows. Alex's gaze lingered there, distant, unfocused, as though trying to catch hold of something in the rush of the passing streets.

Anisa shifted slightly, her head inclining as she studied him. "The evening went well." Her voice broke the silence—but gently. "The event, the wines, and—" she hesitated for an instant, "the encounter with Kaisa."

Alex turned his head toward her, his expression unreadable. A long pause, then a slow exhale—part sigh, part release. "It did," he said finally, his voice low. "At least, it went as well as it could. In the scheme of things."

Anisa waited, sensing that he was still working through his thoughts. His gaze returned to the window, his brow furrowing slightly. "But I didn't—I didn't anticipate how difficult it would be: sitting there, saying nothing." His fingers curled slightly against the seam of his trousers. "Not hinting or letting on..."

His voice trailed off, his mind somewhere else. Back in St. Petersburg, the gilded halls of the Hermitage, where he was Ivan, catching glimpses of a possible future with Kaisa—one that never came. The memory of their third encounter weighing on him—when hope was realized and then so cruelly shredded.

Briefly his anger flared. He was a man betrayed. Anisa remained silent—her presence steady, her gaze unwavering. Alex moved his hand absentmindedly along the seat beside him and found Anisa's. "The life I could have had," he murmured, almost to himself, his voice cracking. "The life I didn't have."

Anisa didn't speak right away. Instead, she reached out and grasped his hand with both hers, cradled it, and held it in her lap—a quiet anchor in the drifting storm of his emotions. "We can only move forward," she said, her tone calm and certain, a point of clarity to pierce his introspection before it became too dark.

Alex turned to Anisa, his eyes meeting hers. For a moment, their gaze held, unspoken understanding and gratitude passing between them. Then he nodded, slow and deliberate, as if agreeing not just with her but with himself. "Forward is all that's left," he echoed, the words heavier on his tongue.

Anisa offered a faint smile, her thumb brushing lightly against the back of his hand. Alex shifted his gaze forward, his posture relaxing slightly as the car glided effortlessly through the city's veins. Gradually, the chaos of Manhattan dissolved into quieter roads, the heartbeat of the city fading behind them.

The limousine carried them onward. Anisa leaned back in the protective intimacy of the moving car, her hands still lightly holding his. The past had happened. The future, however, was still theirs to decide.

The S680 rolled to a stop in the long gravel driveway, the soft, intentional crunch of tires the only sound breaking the Hamptons night. The house before them was a study in modern style—glass and stone blending together seamlessly into the coastal landscape, illuminated subtly to emphasize the mansion's clean lines with minimal ostentation despite the near preposterous size.

David stepped out first, his gaze sweeping across the grounds in a quick, practiced scan before moving to open the back door. Anisa emerged, her heels clicking lightly on the gravel as she pulled her shawl around her shoulders, bracing against the cool ocean breeze. Alex followed, stretching slightly as if to shake off the weight of the evening.

The driver gave a small nod through the windshield before easing the Maybach down the driveway, its presence vanishing into the darkness.

Anisa looked at Alex. "I'll say goodnight," she said. There was a gentleness in her voice, an understanding. Alex was still elsewhere, his mind preoccupied. "Try not to stay up too late this time," she added with a faint smile.

"Goodnight, Anisa," Alex replied, his tone soft—thankful but nevertheless distant.

She nodded, her shawl fluttering slightly in the breeze as she ascended the stone steps, disappearing inside. David remained by Alex's side, his tablet tucked under one arm, waiting. The ocean's rhythmic crash filled the silence.

Alex stood still for a long while, his jaw tight, his mind churning over Kaisa, the weight of a past he could neither reclaim nor escape. How liberating it would be to choose one or the other, rather than living in this no man's land.

At last he turned to David, his voice low but edged. "How did we get here, David?" He breathed in the ocean, which smelled faintly of iron and salt. "Really. How did I end up in that prison?" His words were a demand, as if saying them aloud could unravel the knot of his past.

His eyes, dark and piercing, locked onto David's, as though he could set the air alight with his contained fury. "Tell me again—every detail. I need to hear it."

David's sharp eyes briefly softened, a rare show of feeling, but he quickly disguised the slip—Alex didn't want or like sympathy. David gestured to the stone bench overlooking the sea, and they sat.

"It began with a charge of data espionage," David recounted, his voice steady but loaded with the weight of truth. "Moscow, a full fourteen years ago now. You were Ivan then, climbing the executive ranks at PanEnergy, forging deals for the Arctic. You upset various people in the process—each in their own fashion. The catalyst—what unknowingly set everything alight—was your well-known intransigence over the deal celebrations."

Alex's jaw clenched, his fingers digging into the bench's edge. "Naivety," he murmured, the words raw. "Thought I could make the world perfect."

David nodded, his gaze fixed on the horizon. "You reported it to Yulia—and she protected the machine. She spoke with others: Evelyn, Jake himself, even Dmitry. Jake saw you as a threat, resented you. Evelyn was upset and so grabbed a chance to give you a slap in the face. Dmitry saw an opening—possibly a chance to tip the power balance, to get someone more amenable. Maybe there was a certain animosity toward who you represented.

As David talked, the night's chill began to seep into their clothes but neither of them noticed. "So in combination," David continued, "actively or not, they framed you—planted data on your system, made it look as if you were collecting sensitive material—not clearly commercial, difficult to explain."

Alex's eyes darkened. The memory of Evelyn's laughter at the Moscow party flashed through his mind—her attentions. "She should have spoken up," he said, his voice a low growl. "She should have defended me when everything spiraled out of control."

David's eyes flicked across to Alex, acknowledging the pain. "It wasn't just her," David continued. "There were others who could've vouched for you, pressured Moscow to investigate fairly. Indeed, there was the prisoner swap several years later, as we discovered. Instead, they all turned away—let the narrative take hold: Ivan, the ambitious upstart, collecting data for country or for profit. Your birth in Russia simply made the situation worse. On both sides. America abandoned you."

Alex almost sobbed recollecting the pain of those first years in the prison system, desolate and bewildered. David continued relentlessly. "The FSB arrested you. The charges were relatively small at first, but then escalated."

"Treason," Alex spat, the word venomous, his fury reignited. "They turned it into treason."

David nodded grimly. "You crossed paths with Navalny before he was sent to the corrective colony FKU IK-3, the one in Kharp. You two became friendly. Of course, the Russian courts didn't care about truth. They were concerned about the optics. You were sentenced to the same treatment, stripped of everything. Two years in a cell, then the transfer to that hellhole in Siberia."

David paused a moment, worrying he was feeding Alex's anger, pushing his desire for revenge to levels of madness. "Who was to know different?" he reasoned.

Alex's hands curled into fists, the tattoo on his arm—a jagged scar of ink from prison—pulsed. "I trusted the world," he said, his voice barely above a whisper. "Eve most of all, but also Yulia and, I suppose, Dmitry—I thought they'd have a certain principle, a certain honor. I thought..." Alex's voice broke, the weight of combined betrayal a raw wound that continued to fester.

"And to make it all worse—infinitely worse," he added, "I thought that, somehow, Kaisa would know. She would know and fight. Or at least," hesitating again, "know and wait."

David's gaze softened again, but he pressed on, unforgiving. "Kaisa was kept in the dark. Yulia fed her lies—told her you didn't want her caught up in your shame."

David looked at Alex carefully as he pushed toward the conclusion. "Yulia told Kaisa you'd abandoned her—partly shame, partly cowardice. Yulia emphasized there was no future for the two of you given what had happened, that Kaisa had to accept the consequences of your actions."

He paused. "And not long after, Caleb arrived on a congressional mission—young, charismatic, a man with a vision. By the time you were in Siberia, Kaisa had moved on, married—perhaps as a way to manage the pain. No one told her the truth. So no one fought for you."

Alex stared toward the sea, the waves crashing there in the dark like his own fractured memories. "And you?" he asked, his voice raw, probing. "How did you find me? How did we get *here*?"

David leaned forward, his tone steady. "We met later. You had tried to find salvation in Tobolsk, at the seminary—trained to become a priest adopting the name Alex Volkoff. You had sought to rebuild yourself from the ashes of Ivan."

David looked into Alex's eyes to check that he wanted him to continue, that it wasn't too painful. "You completed your pastoral formation in Paris, where you began as a presbyter."

Alex nodded at the recollection. "Yet, it was all hopeless. I couldn't forget."

"You started wandering."

"Yes, I was tormented."

"You spent time in Baku where you served at the Cathedral of the Holy Myrrh-Bearing Women. You found Anisa there—who calmed you down, turned you into someone who could be presentable in society once more. Tried to curb your bloodlust."

David now permitted himself a smile. "Eventually you arrived in Israel and the Church of St Mary Magdalene at Gethsemane."

"Where I met you."

"Indeed. You had changed by then. You were sharper, harder; but you were also more willing to engage, to be pragmatic. You'd started creating a plan."

Alex's eyes glinted, resolve surfacing and hardening his features. "A plan," he echoed, the phrase a vow. "Jake, Yulia, Dmitry. They'll pay." He hesitated—long enough that David wondered if mercy could have established a toehold.

But Alex continued. "And Evelyn. All those complicit. I'll make them feel my pain." His voice was sharp, the anger crystallizing. Revenge, not redemption—that was the creed of a man who'd once believed in both.

David nodded, his fingers already moving across his tablet. "Steps are in motion. Jake's the first target—his PanEnergy moves are sloppy, exposed."

Alex stood, his figure dark against the moonlit horizon. "Ramp it up," he said, his voice cold. "No mistakes." David gave a curt nod, sending the next set of instructions as Alex turned to enter the house.

The heavy door swung shut behind the two of them, the ocean's roar fading. But the storm within Alex—within Ivan—still burned bright, fueled by a betrayal he could not forget—and by the treacherous comfort of mistaking vengeance for justice.

33. Poison Pill

Rain streaked against the glass walls of PanEnergy's tower block, the clouds outside a churning storm mirroring the pressure inside. The overhead lights cast a subdued glow on the black conference table and leather chairs.

Jake stood at the window, hands deep in his pockets, his gaze fixed on the storm. Behind him, Vince—head of M&A—dropped a stack of reports on the conference table and sat down. He opened the topmost folder with a loud clack. Without turning his head, Jake spoke, his tone calm but almost to the point of menace. "You've had a week, Vince. I want something worthwhile—or I go."

Vince steeled himself. "We are on it. The divestiture list from Palisade is shaping up nicely. We've identified a handful of assets they might offload that we'd want to pick up ourselves—a few that could really strengthen our position. Permian remains the crown jewel, of course. And their overseas properties might be flipped for a profit."

He paused, waiting for an interjection. When none came, he continued. "They're toying with a poison pill."

"That's a desperate gambit," Jake said, his tone sharpening. "They think they can bluff me out of the ring?"

"It's the usual approach," Vince said, laying out the next steps with forced composure. "They'll flood the market if we cross the threshold—total dilution. It's not subtle. But it'll buy them time."

He watched Jake cross to the table—his Italian leather shoes echoing in the stillness before the next peal of thunder. Jake grabbed a report, scanned it, set it down. "So we're supposed to simply sit and let them jerk us around? You know me better than that, Vince! What's our response?"

Vince nodded, mentally rehearsing what he had. "We can challenge the pill in court. Argue that it violates shareholder interests, that management's only protecting themselves. Courts sometimes side with aggressive buyers in these cases—when it's clear the board is stalling."

There was another brief silence. "Legal recourse, sure," Jake replied. "But that's slow, and they can string us out with appeals. Next."

Vince continued, "We can skirt the threshold. Buy up positions via proxies, covertly gather shares below the trigger level. Simultaneously, we work the institutional investors behind the scenes, building a hidden coalition of votes. By the time the board realizes it, we've effectively secured the outcome."

"I like that." Jake rolled his shoulders. "But I hate playing by their rules. I'm not happy to play by anyone's rules. They want to dance? Fine. Then, we'll tap-dance on their grave. What else?"

A moment's hesitation passed through Vince. He inhaled, then forged ahead. "We can go on the offensive. Leak some of their negative data. Show the market their weaknesses—ballooning debt, debatable expansions, challenging resources. We shift the narrative so shareholders blame the board, not us. They start clamoring for a savior—which *would* be us."

Vince watched Jake tap the table with a single fingertip—each strike precise. "Risky, but effective," Jake concluded. "I'd prefer not to get caught in a public mudslinging. But if they adopt the pill, we push back." Straightening up, he paced once more, the storm flickering behind him. Each flash of lightning captured his angular profile.

He pursed his lips with a mark of satisfaction. "Then we make them bleed first. We sue them—hard and fast, summons by morning. Also you begin working those covert channels to accumulate positions—quietly. Keep under the threshold until we're ready to pounce."

He returned to the window, the storm-lashed glass a fierce accompaniment to his words, brimming with urgency. "And we stir trouble. Talk to one or two activist funds—let them know we offer a route to fix Palisade's meltdown if the board takes its role seriously. That'll rattle management. The CEO could have a mutiny on his hands if he can't find a way to rebuild confidence in his approach."

Jake looked at Vince. "There's nothing wrong with building redundancy into our strategy," he continued.

Vince's pen scratched across his notepad, capturing each directive. "Yes, sir. I'll have a refined strategy for you in the next twelve hours." Vince snapped his folder shut. "I'll start immediately," he said, getting up to leave with all his material.

A burst of sheet lightning created an eerie halo behind Jake's head. "Make it six, Vince," he said. "Every hour we hesitate, we lose ground. Palisade's board is betting we'll blink. They're wrong." A low rumble of thunder shook the building. The thrill of a new battle line excited Jake. He knew from experience the bigger the challenge, the more intense he felt the adrenaline hit.

Alone again as the door shut, Jake looked at the weather. Raindrops collided with the glass in relentless waves, streaking downward in silver rivulets. A small grimace set on his lips. He enjoyed these storms—they came before a change.

His phone buzzed with an incoming text—likely from his legal team about the imminent lawsuit. *Let Palisade scramble,* Jake thought. *Let them throw poison pills and Hail Marys. I've seen it all. We'll shut them down. They don't have the skills to make it work.*

* * *

Later that evening, the office's overhead lights dimmed as the building's after-hours system kicked in. The streaks of water outside only sparkled more brightly. Jake was still there, tie discarded, the top button of his shirt undone.

On the desktop computer, multiple screens displayed M&A documents, share price charts, and chat windows including half a dozen consultants as well as inside teams working on one issue or another.

A knock interrupted Jake's thoughts. The door opened slightly, and Monica—Jake's ever-efficient assistant—entered. She quietly took in the disheveled state of the normally immaculate office.

"Mr. Laskin," she said. "All the key points for the lawsuit are ready. Vince wants your final okay on the wording. He's also arranged a 9 a.m. call with Redwood Equity, one of the large hedge funds. They're eager to hear what you have to say about Palisade."

Jake nodded slowly. "Perfect. Let Redwood think we're offering an inside track. They'll jump at the chance to pressure Palisade for a speedy resolution. It'll give the fund a nice return in short order, a quick hit for their books. That's the synergy we need."

Monica nodded. "Anything else?"

He paused before answering. "Not tonight, Monica. Just keep an eye out for anything from their side. The moment you spot a rumor alert me—especially anything about Palisade's board position or their poison pill strategy."

"Of course," Monica said, slipping out as quietly as she arrived.

The door shut, leaving Jake once more in the semi-darkness, surrounded by polished wood and steel. He rubbed a hand across the back of his neck, feeling the stiffness that only unrelenting focus could bring. Outside, thunder rolled but farther into the distance now.

Jake angled behind his desk, scanning a final email before shutting down his computer. The faint reflection of his face showed hard lines etched by ambition and lack of sleep. Another deal, another whirlwind. But in reality he loved it. He thrived on the game—a cat-and-mouse scenario where he liked to play the cat, pressing advantage after advantage until the prey simply gave up in exhaustion.

A small ping indicated a message—from Vince with the draft of their lawsuit. Jake toggled it open on his phone, eyes skimming the legal jargon. He read the headline message. *We'll challenge the board's fiduciary responsibility... hamper the poison-pill triggers... then call for an emergency shareholders' meeting...*

His lips curled in satisfaction. If Palisade's management thought they could stall him indefinitely, they were about to learn otherwise. He would exploit every angle—legal, financial, psychological—and either force them to the table or break them. He'd crushed people before. *No one underestimated Jake Laskin twice.*

34. GSx Consulting

Early morning, well before dawn, Jake got up from his couch in the corner of the room. The storm hadn't moved on—just changed color, from black to charcoal gray. He had a few hours now before the call with Redwood. Alone, and back behind his desk, he scanned a trove of diligence reports about the Permian acquisition target. A single, unfamiliar name halted him.

He leaned against his desk to confirm. *GSx Consulting*. The letters, just ordinary type, seemed to pulse on the page. Indeed the name itself was unremarkable, perched amid the shadows of his deal documents. Yet it triggered an instinctive alarm.

After so many years in the high-stakes world of boardroom takeovers and hidden alliances, anything he didn't recognize signaled trouble—or opportunity. He set the pages aside, drew a measured breath, and pressed the intercom.

"Monica," he said in a low, commanding tone, "I need you here."

Monica was always first in the office each morning. She entered at once, dark hair pinned back, tablet in hand. Jake found her formidable competence—her ability to get things done—seductive. He enjoyed working with her more than anyone else at the company.

Jake rarely betrayed tension, but today the lines around his eyes revealed the weight of too many sleepless hours and too few certainties. He watched Monica walk across the room, then picked up a due-diligence file resting under a highlighter.

"Take a look. GSx Consulting—they're listed as the primary advisor for this Permian Basin outfit we've been circling." He paused. "Ring any bells for you?"

Monica shook her head, stepping closer to the pool of light cast by his desk lamp. "Never heard of them. And that's unusual." Her gaze skimmed the text. "They're not one of the typical boutique advisors or usual M&A shops that appear in these deals. We certainly have no background with them, no previous interactions."

Jake nodded grimly. "Exactly. It's as if they materialized from nowhere. I've scoured a half-dozen of our past transactions, and not one mentions GSx. It suggests either a brand-new outfit or, more worryingly, a front. We need to know everything about them, from day one to now."

He half-smiled. "And, of course, I wanted it yesterday."

Monica offered a faint, knowing smile in return—she recognized, even admired, the old spark in Jake's voice.

"I'll start immediately," she said. "Where do we focus first? Corporate records? Their signatories? Possibly foreign registries if they're based offshore?"

"All of it," Jake replied. "No half measures. No gaps. If they're a legitimate consultancy, we'll find a trail of prior clients or a series of license filings. But if they're something else... well, I want that uncovered, too."

Jake recalled his talk with Vince just the previous evening—asset buys, poison pills, the next stage of a corporate battle. Yet GSx Consulting looked like a different breed of problem altogether, something that signaled deeper games.

Monica flipped through some pages of M&A documentation, eyes scanning for clues. "Would you like me to coordinate with our legal or due diligence teams?"

Jake shook his head. "Keep it close for now. No external queries. If we raise a flag with the usual law firms, someone'll tip off GSx we're suspicious. I want the element of surprise. Keep Vince in the loop. He'll need to know if there's a hidden force behind this company. We may have to adjust our entire approach." A flash of lightning briefly illuminated the office. Monica looked out at the storm now into its second day.

"You think they're a front, perhaps associated with the target's real owners?" she asked.

Jake considered this. "Could be. Or maybe they're the ones truly pulling the strings—some shadow investor with ulterior plans or some actor who wants to turn this second-tier Permian firm into, I don't know, a stalking horse. Hell, for all we know, they might be connected to another major."

Monica nodded, checking her notes. "Understood. I'll dig. Bank records, offshore leads, industry news, social media for the staff, if any. If the firm hides, the people may leave a trace."

Jake allowed the ghost of a smile. "Precisely. Everyone leaves footprints. And we're good at finding them, aren't we?"

With that, Monica gathered the various documents, half in admiration, half in concern for Jake's relentlessness, and headed for the door. She hesitated before exiting. "Expect a preliminary memo by this evening. You'd better get ready for the meeting with Redwood."

Jake almost regretted the little sleep he did get—it was a luxury he couldn't afford with so much happening. Now there was GSx, an unknown entity operating in a field where he prided himself on omniscience. He shook his head. A new piece of the jigsaw had appeared. However, its place and its purpose were tough to understand.

Jake shifted in his chair, feeling his exasperation building again. "Who are you, GSx?" he asked aloud, jabbing the paper in front of him. The words echoed in the briefly still room.

He couldn't pinpoint why it got under his skin, why the situation felt off this time. Usually Jake thrived on challenges. He felt energized. However, these three letters—sleek and silent—felt unprecedented, as if something genuinely malevolent were watching from the dark.

He shook his head—pushed away his concerns. If the firm had secrets, he'd pry them open and leverage the information. No shadow was going to slow him down.

35. Home Cooking

The same morning had arrived across town. By the time daylight broke, the storm had ebbed, and by the time Eve woke, late, a muted shine had spread over the Manhattan skyline. Eve found the penthouse silent again—no signs that Jake had returned at all.

She tied her silk robe loosely at the waist and made her way to the kitchen. Even in her solitude she moved as if someone might be watching—grace as habit, not so much as performance.

A discreet knock at the front door echoed through the spacious hallway just as she was getting out a mug. Opening it, she found a young man with an athletic build and dark, friendly eyes. He wore cargo pants and black T-shirt, rainwater beading on his forearms, catching the light like tiny sparks. He smiled, a soft grin revealing immaculate teeth.

"Hi," he said easily. "David. Here for the dogs."

For a moment, Eve blinked, then remembered Jake's mention of a new dog walker. "Right, of course," she said. "The new guy. Come on in."

Behind her, three large black Labradors appeared, sleek coats and powerful frames giving them an imposing yet endearing presence. David's face lit up. "Wow," he said, "these are the 'puppies' I've been warned about? Guess I'd better keep my wits about me."

Eve laughed, leaning against the doorframe. "They're sweet but headstrong, especially when chasing squirrels. Our last walker nearly got yanked off his feet a few times before Hollywood called him up." David reached out, letting them sniff his hand before patting each head in turn.

"They're a handful," Eve teased. "Our last walker couldn't leave fast enough to progress his acting career. Let's hope you won't vanish on similarly short notice."

David chuckled. "I don't see Hollywood calling me anytime soon, so you should be safe. Besides, dogs are easier critics than casting directors."

Eve smiled in amusement. "I guess that's right. So, David...? The plan?"

"Central Park," he replied with a self-assured nod. "We'll do a couple of circuits, see if we can spot some squirrels, give them a proper run. I'll have them back in two hours—suitably tired."

She watched him clip their leashes, the Labradors looking eager to bolt out the door. "All right," she said, playful but stern. "But do return them in one piece."

"Count on it," he said, stepping into the corridor. With a final wave, he guided the dogs to the elevator. Eve's gaze lingered on his confident stride. Then she headed back inside, shaking her head at the novelty of it all.

* * *

A few hours later, the rhythmic click of dog nails on marble signaled David's return. Eve opened the door, and in padded the Labradors, their energy sapped by an evidently thrilling excursion.

"All safe and sound," David announced, offering a friendly grin. "They had a blast in the park. We did Sheep Meadow, then The Ramble."

Eve greeted the dogs with fond pats, then turned to David. "Thank you so much. They look happy and tired. I meant to ask: next time you're out, could you pick up some saffron? I plan to cook tonight, and I can't find any here. I'm sure I had a bit."

He gave an easy shrug. "No problem. Saffron's an unusual request, but it's part of the service, right? I'm pleased to help out."

Eve smiled, relieved. "Excellent. I'll pay you back, of course."

"No worries at all," he replied, winking. "Besides, I'm a big believer in going the extra mile. Happy clients make for good business. I'll see you later."

He departed with a relaxed wave, and Eve shut the door. She felt a sense of anticipation at having a new ally, even if only in a small domestic way.

That evening, David returned from another dog-walking session, saffron in hand. Eve opened the door, and a sweet mélange of aromas—rich spices, simmering chicken—rolled warmly into the hallway. "Welcome back," she said, taking the packet. "You're a lifesaver."

David looked inquiringly across to the kitchen. "I'm making some Persian-inspired dishes," Eve explained. "Saffron rice, a tangy barberry chicken, and cucumber-yogurt dip with mint."

David inhaled the rich aromas. "Smells incredible," he said, stepping into the penthouse. "You must be quite the cook."

Eve laughed gently. In her mind, she pictured Jake negotiating his next conquest while she tackled rice and saffron. "I try. I'd be thrilled to share, but I assume you're—"

David smiled. "Actually, if you don't mind some company, I'd love a taste."

"Wonderful, I've cooked enough for an army—and I'm not thrilled about dining alone. My husband, yet again, is caught up in work."

David's face dropped, "But I can't show up empty-handed..." He thought a moment. "I'll join but only on one condition."

"Oh?" Eve asked, raising an eyebrow. David grinned. "If there's some good chocolate in that kitchen of yours, some eggs and sugar, I make a mean chocolate mousse for dessert. And if there's a decent red wine around, I'd say we've got the perfect meal."

Eve laughed, the day suddenly looking different and fun. "Chocolate and red wine? You're speaking my language. I know just the bottle." She raced off to get it from the temperature-controlled wine cellar. Returning and brandishing the bottle in triumph, Eve's face turned quizzical. "Don't you need cream for chocolate mousse?"

Another boyish grin lit David's face. "Not in my recipe," he assured her. "It's something I picked up from a French roommate at college. Let me start now with the chocolate mousse so it's ready in time for dessert—if that's okay," he said after a brief pause.

Eve's eyes gleamed. "By all means. Let me fetch the ingredients."

Within minutes, David set to work in the spacious, state-of-the-art kitchen. The dogs trotted around curiously, sniffing at the chocolate aroma. "I'm afraid you can't have any. I know it smells delicious but," David cautioned, "it's not good for dogs."

He melted and whisked with a confidence that impressed Eve, who hovered around the island, monitoring her dishes. "How often do you do this?" she teased.

He flashed a grin, now layering the liquid chocolate into whipped egg whites. "Whenever the urge hits. Cooking is a great creative outlet, that is when I'm not walking dogs or writing."

"Writing?" Eve asked, intrigued. "What do you write?"

"Fiction, mostly." David shrugged, still folding. "I'm drawn to the period from 1860 to say 1900 at the latest: Victorian Gothic, especially if it has romantic overtones. Christina Rossetti, for example. I never get over how she weaves beauty and darkness together in *Goblin Market.* Some of her lines still live with me."

Eve glanced at him, her eyes brightening. "You know *Goblin Market*? I studied it briefly when I was doing my college degree. It's eerie and yet mesmerizing." She didn't realize until too late—that she'd had almost the same thought twice that day: now about the poem, earlier about the man.

David set aside the whisk, and his voice fell into a soft recital. "Morning and evening / Maids heard the goblins cry: / Come buy our orchard fruits, / Come buy, come buy." He paused. "Could quote it all night." He smiled. "Sorry—old habit when the words hit close to home."

Eve shook her head, evidently pleased. "Not at all. I love how it flirts with themes of temptation and sisterhood. People often reduce it to a moral fable, but there's so much more under the surface."

David nodded. "Absolutely."

Eve continued, "I remember the professor saying that Rossetti's layering of spiritual tension with erotic undertones was groundbreaking—certainly for the Victorian era."

David nodded again and recited another passage, voice glowing with passion: "Apples and quinces, / Lemons and oranges / Plump unpeck'd cherries..." David's voice trailed off as he closed his eyes to savor some memory. Then he looked at Eve, slightly bashful. "I get carried away."

Eve felt a warmth that wasn't just from the stove. "You bring it alive. I'm impressed, David—very impressed."

He let out a subdued laugh, returning to his mousse. "Time for a quick chill," he said, sliding the mixture into the refrigerator. "Should be ready after dinner."

Dinner was a cozy affair: aromatic, candlelit, the dogs dozing nearby. Over plates of saffron rice and barberry-strewn chicken, they talked about everything: dog-walking mishaps, the intricacies of *Goblin Market*, David's passion for travel. He mentioned his dream of returning to Bhutan.

"Bhutan," Eve mused, sipping a modest pour of red wine. "Isn't that the place which measures Gross National Happiness?"

David's eyes shone. "Exactly. It's mountainous, culturally rich, and the people seem able to maintain their heritage despite the pressures of modernity. I've been twice, never for long enough. You should watch the film, *Travellers and Magicians*. Quite something."

She smiled, tipping her wineglass. "Jake's always in some corner of the world, but rarely for pleasure. I envy your wanderlust."

"And I admire your cooking," David said lightly, finishing off a final bite of the chicken. "My wanderlust doesn't pay the bills, though. Hence, the dog walking for now."

Eve's expression turned momentarily wistful. "Jake's out conquering deals. I'm left here to cultivate saffron dinners."

David set down his utensils, understanding in his gaze. "Well… at least you have company tonight." He rose to get the mousse from the fridge, garnishing it with some fresh mint and a strawberry that he'd seen there. "Voilà—a quick but potent dessert."

Eve's gaze widened at the luscious texture. Tasting a spoonful, she closed her eyes. "This is divine. You're not just a dog walker, you're a magician. Maybe that film's about you."

He laughed, the sound oddly intimate. "Maybe. But the mousse—amazing, right? My roommate said it was his family's secret recipe. Without cream. You see?"

Eve savored another spoonful. "You might've found your calling. I'm beyond impressed, David, by both your cooking and your sense of adventure."

"I'm afraid the mousse is all I can do—my one party trick. Otherwise I just experiment. I prefer to eat and enjoy, especially when the cooking is as good as yours."

They lingered over mousse and residual conversation, the skyline twinkling outside like a living tapestry. Eventually, the clock pushed toward midnight, and David excused himself, collecting his jacket from a nearby chair.

"Thanks for dinner," he said. "And for letting me share that poem. It's rare I find someone who appreciates *Goblin Market*—or even knows it."

Eve smiled. "Thanks for the saffron. And for cooking. Definitely made my night less lonely."

"Anytime," David replied. "Seriously—just text me." He offered a final nod before the door shut softly behind him.

As the door closed, the apartment suddenly felt quiet. Eve contemplated the deep warmth she'd felt that evening—the unexpected camaraderie. Usually, her nights ended in solitude; Jake away somewhere wrestling with business.

Tonight was different, unplanned, genuinely pleasant. It felt like a hinge turning—the first click of something Eve couldn't name, not as yet. She returned to the table, tidying plates in comfortable silence, her thoughts for once positive and bright.

Chocolate lingered in the air. She thought about David. He listened to her as Jake had once done. How nice it was to be heard and appreciated. The evening reminded her that life still possessed flavors beyond ambition. How many times had she sought a world richer than performance, only to find disappointment?

She refused to repeat her parents' mistake—achievement could be as stifling and colorless as apathy. Eve believed they had missed so much in life—the adventures that remained possible even as time moved on. Tonight she felt a renewed hunger, a wish to taste everything that might still be possible. Eve wondered if she could break the mold—or if another effort would undo her.

A few pale streaks of sun did little to lift the somber mood in Jake's high-rise office at PanEnergy. The thick gray clouds, low and threatening, had slowly disappeared, allowing streaks of sun to filter through the full-length windows.

Standing at the window after his talk with Redwood, his hands buried in his pockets, Jake let his gaze drift over the teeming streets below. The city moved with its usual frenetic yet somehow mechanical rhythm. GSx Consulting weighed on his mind—a cipher in the system, intangible and vexing. This wasn't *The Matrix*, he reminded himself.

Behind him, Monica, his unflinchingly loyal assistant, entered with a pile of documents for the Permian deal and reports associated with GSx, which she left on the desk before exiting again.

Monica had reached out to her contacts, combed through public records collecting dust on the internet, and cross-referenced any snippet of rumor that might illuminate this stealth-like consultancy.

She noted other deals in her search where the firm had made cameo appearances—but always peripheral, never central. Each discovery led nowhere and each new dead end simply deepened her resolve.

"Anyone heard of GSx?" she asked over a call to Dave, a broker whose knack for networking was matched by an occasional flair for speculation.

"GSx?" he echoed, skepticism coloring his tone. "Heard of them. Total ghost. They slip in, do their thing, slip out. Folks don't seem to have much to do with them."

Monica jotted down his wary remarks, feeling a swell of frustration as she ended the call. *A ghost indeed.* Everything about GSx was exasperatingly elusive, their online presence no more than a minimalist site with a blank-faced logo and boilerplate text. *Which consulting firm operated like that?*

Its social feed simply repackaged headlines, news items, and cute pictures. Even her cat's social presence, she thought wryly, had more substance.

Jake returned to his desk and went through the new documents about the Permian deal. As he turned the pages, he saw scope for significant gains, yet found nothing there or in Monica's other reports that solved the riddle of GSx. The name lingered only on the margins, feeling anything but irrelevant.

A brief rain shower spattered the glass, gone almost before it began, snapping Jake's focus. He got up to prowl around the office, agitation building. He'd built a career on understanding all the pieces involved in the corporate game, forging quick, incisive moves.

Every instinct behind his empire was against uncertainty; yet uncertainty was all GSx offered. There was no playbook for phantoms. The idea of an adversary operating unseen, beneath the ground, upset him—as if they had produced a hairline crack in his empire's foundation that would fatally undermine the whole edifice.

"Monica," he called through the intercom, again, his voice taut. She popped her head around the door. "Any more luck?" he asked, scanning her face.

She shook her head, her usually composed features betraying frustration. "I've consulted everyone I trust. No one has solid intel. GSx show up in a few deals—like rumors in the shadows—but vanish without the spotlight ever finding them."

A sharp knock sounded from behind Monica, and Eugenia, the firm's Head of Investor and Government Relations entered, carrying a file. Her brisk, confident manner stood out in the unusually strained atmosphere. "Jake, I've got news: more local groups are mobilizing against the pipeline. Grassroots pushback is spreading."

Jake's eyes flashed. *Poison pills, GSx, and now an expanding pipeline fight.* He could almost sense a hidden hand orchestrating chaos from a distance. Could GSx be fueling these protests as leverage within some bigger scheme?

He let the half-formed thought circle in his mind. "Orchestrated mischief, perhaps. You think someone is behind it?" His frustration was starting to break through.

Monica and Eugenia exchanged glances. "Hard to say," Eugenia replied. "It's consistent with sabotage tactics—unofficial, untraceable, but crippling enough to disrupt progress. However, there doesn't have to be a formal organization. Activists are tremendously well-prepared these days and well-resourced."

Jake's pulse throbbed at his temple. He felt a vein on his forehead bulging, as it occasionally did. If GSx were truly engineering these flank attacks, he needed to snuff it out. He wanted names, faces, motivations. "We have to identify who they are," he said, voice low but full of intent. "We can't bring down a ghost."

Monica gave a quick nod. "I'm already diving deeper into corporate registries and offshore listings. I've hired a cybersleuth to track online presence—anything. GSx has to leave traces somewhere."

Eugenia rested the folder on Jake's desk. "I'll find out which activists might be involved. Whether or not your new group is behind this set of protests, the reality is we're fighting on multiple fronts to contain the opposition."

Jake grimaced. "Keep at it. Both of you. I want every angle covered." He paused, letting the tension swirl before adding, "I've dealt with illusions before. They always have names."

Monica read the urgency in his posture. She understood Jake and his world: a place where ignorance was the only unforgivable sin, and where controlling the unknown was vital, if not sufficient, for ensuring victory. "Yes, Jake," she said. "We'll find the thread." They would find this phantom and turn it into flesh.

With that, she retreated—going back to her workstation. Eugenia lingered an instant more, as if deciding whether they needed to discuss further, then chose to follow Monica out, leaving Jake alone with his simmering thoughts.

The lack of knowledge disturbed him. A new adversary. Shadows stacked on shadows. Such obscurity offended Jake's deep-seated need to master every variable. He went over and picked up his pen, but let it drop as impatience got the better of him.

Even now, phone calls buzzed in the background, fresh demands for his attention. Yet Jake remained fixated on GSx—like a hunter who had glimpsed a single paw-print and refused to rest until he'd tracked the beast.

In the corridor outside, Monica's fingers flew over her keyboard. Each tap hammered at the digital labyrinth that shielded GSx, each query defying the entity's vanishing act. Vince, who always orchestrated acquisitions with such bravado, had quietly worried about the task to her. They lacked, he'd said, the time to properly unravel all the threads before things simply moved on regardless.

The day continued in this fashion. The sun rose and set without shedding any new light on their elusive target in the dark.

As evening arrived Jake turned on more lights to battle the gloom. He stood near the window once more, phone in hand, scanning the updated notes Monica had forwarded. *No new leads. Another broker raised his eyebrows but had no facts.*

A single conviction crystallized in Jake's thoughts: whoever GSx was, they threatened his vision, his next big move. He returned to his desk, fired off a bunch of directives to Eugenia, Vince, and Monica; telling them to dig deeper still, call in more contacts, speak to local intelligence. He wanted them to chase down every lead.

The day's end neared. Jake let the final ring of his phone echo in the usually comforting stillness. Tomorrow would bring fresh opportunities—or fresh complications. Either way, Jake would pursue an answer. He didn't accept illusions—not since he was twelve, and his father promised that yet another move would be great for the family. Illusions held no place in his world, only results.

The estate sprawled across the Hamptons coastline like an empire made flesh, its lights shimmering in the salt-laden breeze. A symphony of excess swirled into the night, champagne flutes clinking in a crystalline harmony. Somewhere, beyond the laughter—and the crinkle of old money mingling with the pulse of new—the roar of the Atlantic reminded everyone where they were and who they were supposed to be.

Alex, the host, had materialized in New York out of nowhere, as though some mythical figure conjured by Wall Street gossip and tabloid dreams—impossible to ignore.

Rumored to have made his billions first in oil fields then in telecoms, he now stood at the center of this gilded hurricane. A thin, taut man with a wolfish smile and dark eyes that seemed to glint with private amusement, he moved through the crowd like a fiendish conductor, orchestrating moments that would be whispered about for weeks among Manhattan's corridors of power.

Caleb was there—the youthful senator whose political trajectory was as ambitious and upward as his hero's rockets. He worked the crowd with the wisdom of someone who understood that politics, like wealth, was a game played on shifting sands. Alex's support—or the suggestion of it—would prove valuable in time, if not at once.

At his side stood his wife, Kaisa, her Nordic poise clear—her profile so entrancing she resembled nothing more than an ode to Bronzino. She had lost none of the voluptuous charm that had first caught Ivan's eye. Her aquamarine gown shone in the light like the heirloom of a forgotten royalty, her smile cool and immovable.

Near the illuminated pool, its heat creating a faint mist in the evening air, Jake, the pugnacious CEO of PanEnergy, dominated a cluster of men in suits, tailored so finely they seemed to bend physics. His voice, loud and confident, cut through the ambient hum, drawing laughs that felt easy and rehearsed. They were arguing political history, members of the group all parading their knowledge of presidential lore ahead of the election.

Jake's wife, Evelyn, was beside the pool, her long polished hair cascading down the deep open back of a sequined dress that exposed as much as elegance would allow. She could turn eyes even as she approached fifty. Eve bent to brush the water with her fingertips. *So inviting.*

Eve loved the social world—the interaction, the small talk. *You didn't even need to understand the conversation to own it,* she remembered telling a friend at one point. And it had come to mean more over time. She sparkled with every exaggerated laugh as acquaintances came over to say hello.

The party itself was an exercise in engineered awe. The fountains spewed streams of prosecco; a band, flown in from Paris, played classical string quartets on a rotunda; a choir was singing a cappella near the front entrance.

A whole section of the enormous garden had been transformed into a piece of living art—with performers and installations. Peacocks strutted between illuminated sculptures—everything in such a way that the garden seemed to breathe and move.

For those needing a respite from the extravagance, a private yacht anchored just off the shore ferried them to a quieter slice of the evening—a beach lit by hundreds of burning lanterns where little cabanas had been placed and caviar-topped hors d'oeuvres were served alongside shots of Azerbaijani vodka.

Amid all the grandeur, there were occasional cracks in the façade. Evelyn's laughter sometimes grew shrill. Kaisa's watchful gaze occasionally darted toward her husband with a hint of awkwardness or an edge of distaste. And Jake, accustomed to commanding rooms, bristled as guests circled Alex—Caleb, the golden boy, among them—appearing like moths drawn to a new flame.

Alex himself—dressed in a tuxedo, always smiling, always charming—seemed to radiate an odd, unnamable strain, as if the world that he'd created for the night, his own conception, were somehow unsavory, challenging. But as the champagne flowed and oysters emerged, resting on top of miniature carved ice sculptures, no one cared. Joviality and laughter echoed across the lawn, disappearing over the water.

And as the hours wore on, the entertainment seemed only to crescendo. A troupe of aerialists fell from wires extended above, their bodies twisting and twirling in glittering costumes that reflected the light like falling stars.

Acrobats jumped over the lawn, drawing gasps from the audience, as their white costumes fluoresced in the UV light. And dancers clad in a shimmering gold wove through the crowd—their movements synchronized to a beat pulsating from hidden speakers.

Food stations multiplied like magic, chefs flambéing rare delicacies as eager guests lined up to film the spectacle. Bright-colored sushi appeared and disappeared among clouds of dry ice. Dessert came in the form of an entire patisserie—rows of macarons, towers of spun sugar.

Floodlights illuminated a chocolate waterfall taller than any guest feeding into a marble pond. One guest, already too drunk, wandered under and laughed in hysterics.

Eventually the music's tempo quickened as a DJ took over—unleashing a relentless rhythm to match the beating hearts of the revelers. The lawn transformed into a natural dance floor. Shoes were abandoned, laughter soared, and the air buzzed with a kind of electric abandon.

Then, as if summoned by some unspoken signal, the sky erupted. Fireworks exploded over the ocean in a symphony of light and color. Golds and silvers cascaded like exploding stars, reds and blues bloomed like celestial flowers, and an iridescent green comet streaked across the heavens before dissolving into a shower of sparks.

The sea and sky, the emerging mist, all reflected the display, doubling and multiplying its brilliance, while the crowd, silent for the first time all night, stopped dancing and stood awestruck.

The final explosion lit up the coastline, a kaleidoscope of shimmering light, a chameleon display that seemed to linger in people's eyes long after it had gone. In that moment, the evening seemed to reach a peak, a climactic burst of beauty leaving everyone breathless. Glasses were raised, arms entwined, and for one brief, overwhelming instant, everyone felt deeply and mystically united.

The memory of that climax, that impossible culmination, would linger in every heart like a secret. The party would now live on in whispers, each retelling more vivid, more impossible.

And then, as the last ember faded into the blackness of the sky, the spell broke. Conversations resumed, laughter rippled back through the crowd, and the night began its slow, inevitable descent.

By the early hours of the morning, as the first streaks of light began to thread their way over the horizon, the crowd thinned to a mere handful. Alex, ever the enigmatic host, stood alone and motionless on the lawn looking out—his tuxedo jacket discarded, his bow tie hanging loose.

Around him, staff members were already clearing away the night's debris, their movements quiet and efficient. Among the guests remaining were Caleb and Kaisa, Jake and Evelyn, as well as Cavil and Martha—their energy subdued, but their eyes still alight with the lingering magic of the evening.

"Let's greet the new day properly," Alex announced suddenly, his voice breaking the silence with a note of exhilaration. Without waiting for a response, he began unbuttoning his shirt, shrugging it off to reveal a lean, sun-bronzed torso.

It was surprisingly muscled, the physique more of a street fighter than of an office worker—lean and wiry. It bore the many scars of his victories. The faint pink traces of an old slash ran across his back; and deeper marks, a thick puncture scar on his outer thigh, hinting at a past life dangerously close to the edge.

Most striking of all to Kaisa, as she watched unable to look away, was a huge tattoo that covered his back: a web of Orthodox icons intertwined with darker sigils—an intimidating, hypnotic mix that once spotted sucked the viewer in.

Kaisa, who had thought she was beginning to get a handle on Alex, let out a sharp breath. Her hand fluttered to her throat, her mind racing to process this new, rawer dimension of the man she'd been puzzling over. The tattoo looked less like spontaneity or art, more like affiliation—something out of a foreign mafia.

For a moment, the only sound was the hiss of the surf. The other guests, it seemed as Kaisa looked around, were too far gone, too focused on the moment to linger much on the revelation. The combination of fatigue and alcohol slowed their curiosity while the prospect of a cold, shocking sea absorbed what remained of their attention.

Alex kicked off his shoes, stripped, and strode confidently toward the water. *It must be cold,* Kaisa thought, *barely sixty degrees.* For a beat, no one moved. Then abruptly a few laughed, shrugging their shoulders, and began to follow.

Shoes, pants, and dresses were abandoned on the sand, and soon a small procession made its way into the cool embrace of the Atlantic. Jake was among the first—whooping as he ran in and dove headfirst below the waves. Kaisa followed, her typical composure giving way to an almost childlike delight as she entered and the water lapped around her. Indeed, it was not so different from her dips around Klovharu when growing up.

Evelyn, laughing and shivering, joined them, playfully splashing Jake as they moved out, further from the shore. This was the sense of adventure—the spontaneity—she had been missing for several years now. Caleb stayed back, his arms crossed, watching the scene unfold with an inscrutable smile. Cavil did too. However, Martha felt no restraint. "Thank goodness you've retired!" was all she said in explanation to Cavil's questioning look.

Screams of shock at the sharp cold, then of bravado in defiance, hoopla and cheers, echoed in the receding darkness as swimmers reveled in their impromptu communion with the sea. "Now *this* is the way to live!" someone shouted, their voice ringing out over the water.

Alex floated on his back, gazing up at the lightening sky. "To beginnings," he murmured to no one in particular, his voice lost in the gentle crash of the waves. As the first rays of sunlight kissed the horizon, it seemed, for a fleeting instant, that anything was possible.

And Kaisa, as she watched Alex floating—still trying to understand him—let her mind slip back to the last time she had been with Ivan, similarly exposed to the world. It was more than a decade ago, at the dacha in Russia. She screamed again now, her cry lost among the others—but whether she yelled from the shock of intense cold or from the pain of a resurrected past, she couldn't tell.

38. GSx and Alex

A salty breeze lingered as dawn broke, the last notes of laughter dissolving into the surf. Waiting at the edge of the dune, Alex's staff stood at the ready, offering soft towels and steaming cocoa to each of the swimmers.

Jake Laskin, still catching his breath from the bracing early morning chill of the Atlantic, thanked Alex for his hospitality. "I appreciate the invite," he said, wrapping the towel around his shoulders. "It's not every day I get to end a party like this."

Alex, casual with his towel wrapped around him and an unbuttoned shirt over his back, grinned. "You're always welcome, Jake. Do you need a ride back? I can have someone drop you off, or send for a car if you prefer."

Jake shook his head, the remains of saltwater in his hair glistening under the new sun. "No, I'm fine. My driver's here. I'll grab my things and go." He paused for a beat, looking around the now quiet beach. He was sad to see the party end. "Thanks again, Alex. Really."

With that, he made his way across the manicured lawn—still debris-strewn despite the work already done—stepping into the house through sliding glass doors. As he headed for the front entrance, Jake caught sight of a spacious living room: a fire flickering against the morning chill in a large stone hearth.

Above it hung a portrait of Anisa wearing an ash-blue dress cinched with a rose copper sash—her figure rendered in a fashion at once alluring and powerful. The light from the fire danced over the artwork, bringing it to life, as if Anisa's spirit were inside while her physical body was outside, having just emerged from the sea and now striding purposefully along the beach to join Alex.

He meant to leave but, intrigued, drifted in for a closer look. The hush of the room, its serene layout, soothed him—until a stack of papers on a low coffee table drew his attention. The top page bore a header: GSx Consulting.

Jake halted mid-step. The sight punched through his fatigue like a live current. GSx had cropped up in his world so many times in only a few weeks. And it was always under mysterious or provocative circumstances.

He bent down for a careful look at the documents: charts and analyses of the U.S. energy sector, strategic overviews, lists of perceived weaknesses. It was an unsettling trove of information—less like consultancy work and more like reconnaissance, an industry forensically dissected.

The implications raced through his mind. Why did Alex have these, and why was he apparently so familiar with GSx?

Jake paused, glancing over his shoulder toward the patio door—Alex was still outside, saying farewell to the others, Anisa by his side. A suspicion stirred within him: perhaps Alex was not simply a friendly host but someone with a deeper interest in the energy world—not necessarily in Jake's favor.

He replaced the documents where he'd found them, but a touch of unease lingered in his chest. Casting one more look at the portrait of Anisa, he exhaled slowly, then headed back toward the front door. The hush of the house was suddenly sinister, the once-inviting space now layered with questions. When he reached his car, he felt a renewed determination settle over him: maybe he had discovered the first real clue about GSx's reach.

Alex wasn't a friend. He was a player—and the game, Jake suddenly intuited, had begun when he arrived.

The morning sun cast a slight haze over the Hamptons estate, its rays filtering through the tall windows of the terrace where just five of last night's party were gathered for a post-celebration breakfast. The scent of sea water mixed with the aroma of freshly brewed coffee, and everything felt unassuming—almost jarring in its simplicity given the preceding extravaganza. The ocean's rumble offered the only real connection—a bridging melody between the frenzied night and the new morning.

Alex—now dressed in casual pants, white shirt, and linen jacket—continued to play the gracious host, directing staff to offer plates of fresh fruit, pastries, scrambled eggs, smoked salmon, coffee or juice—whatever his guests desired.

Seated at the teak table were the former Ambassador Lane and his wife Martha, still buzzing with excitement. She had enjoyed the final dip, momentarily free of the diplomatic life her husband had chosen for them—a life that had constrained her behavior and her options for decades.

Kaisa was the third guest, sitting quietly opposite Alex, gently rubbing her throat between her thumb and forefinger—her cool demeanor masking a storm of suspicions that never ceased despite her efforts at control.

The swim had left everyone invigorated, but Kaisa couldn't shake the image of Alex's tattoo—a raw, severe symbol that clashed with her memories of Ivan and fueled her paranoia about this new arrival in New York. Over the years, in a search for meaning she'd built diverse myths around Ivan—some of them with the help of a therapist. She had sought to make sense of events. Alex's party threatened to shatter all these endeavors and undo her hard-won calm.

Martha, ever the vibrant soul, broke the comfortable silence as she speared a piece of mango. "Thank you so much for lending us these clothes. You and Anisa have quite a wardrobe. I'll have to show Cavil—if you don't mind. I can see that we are shopping in the wrong districts." She looked in admiration at Anisa, who was now dressed in a fine wool gray top over garnet-colored linen pants.

Anisa bowed her head in encouragement. "Please do. I think sometimes men don't get women's fashion—women's need to shine—to be singled out from the crowd as someone special and desirable."

"Exactly," interjected Kaisa. She, however, was wearing a dark blue tracksuit, slightly too big. "Women deserve to be cherished and remembered—to feel important. For if they are not treasured, what is the point?"

"Yes," Martha responded. "Did you hear that, Cavil? I hope you are taking notes."

She laughed. "What a night! That swim was so exhilarating—wild and freeing. I haven't had so much fun since I talked with President Cooper's son about reading and his favorite books." She looked at Alex. "You throw a party like no one else. We must do it again—perhaps next year, though I'm not sure I can wait that long..."

Cavil nodded, his ambassadorial poise intact despite the early hour. "Indeed. It's been ages since we've had so much fun. Speaking of which..." He paused with a sudden thought, glancing at his wife. "Why don't you all come over to our home for dinner next week? Nothing extravagant—a barbecue, a bottle of wine—straightforward... What do you say?"

Martha beamed, clapping her hands. "Oh, yes! Let's make it Friday. We can grill some fresh seafood—keep the ocean theme going."

Alex chuckled, his dark eyes wrinkling with amusement. "We'd be delighted. Anisa and I might contribute the wine, if you permit. I will bring some white from my cellar."

Anisa smiled gracefully. "Yes. How wonderful. I would love to deepen my acquaintance with everyone." Her gaze took in both Martha and Kaisa. "Somehow, when functions become too grand, they leave no scope for real dialogue."

"I know what you mean," Martha said. "I got quite a different impression of Cooper's boy when I sat next to him that occasion. In my whole time with

Cavil, he was the only one—the only high-profile guest, I mean—who actually spoke to me as if I were interesting and worth a serious conversation." She grew silent for a second. "I've never forgotten, and will always respect him for that. I still have his number in my contact list."

Kaisa smiled. "I really look forward to learning more about Baku."

"There's lots to tell," Anisa replied. "It was certainly a tough episode. I had little hope and even fewer ambitions. Then Alex turned up." The pause between her words was short but heavy, as if the arrival had rewritten her life.

She glanced at Alex once more. "Anyway, I'm sure we all have exploits that we could discuss next Friday—the Ambassador and Martha leading the way."

"Yes, indeed," asserted Cavil. "My career was quite colorful."

Kaisa smiled. "I often wonder what draws two people together—whether it is fate or calculation. And then, perhaps more significantly, what keeps them together."

"That is a discussion for the ages," Alex interjected. "And perhaps again we should seek guidance from the Ambassador next Friday. How has he, despite circumstances, kept Martha by his side for—what is it now—more than forty years?"

Cavil laughed. "Forty-six!" he exclaimed proudly. "We are the only couple left standing among those we know."

Anisa laughed. "Fate's a romantic notion." She paused. "In my experience, the best connections are the ones you don't see coming—serendipity rather than destiny. The sudden encounters that take you by surprise and grip you in ways you could never dream. Wouldn't you agree?"

She looked at Kaisa, but it was Martha who replied. "Oh, yes," she said, her eyes twinkling. "I saw Cavil on the dance floor, and I knew—he was the one."

The table chuckled, easing any strain. Yet Kaisa felt Alex and Anisa were too careful, by half, in their words. Her suspicions just grew each time she encountered them. However, there was no way to pursue anything further.

Cavil steered the conversation back to dinner plans, finalizing details for Friday. As breakfast wrapped up, Kaisa exchanged polite goodbyes, her mind churning over the new pieces of the puzzle she had collected: Alex's tattoo, Anisa's past, their clever wordplay.

The dinner invitation would give her another opportunity—another chance to dig deeper. And if that failed, then she still had a final card to play.

Charlotte arrived in a deep green town car outside PanEnergy's gleaming headquarters, the glass façade reflecting the softer but clearer sunlight of the season. Gone was the summer haze.

Stepping onto the marble pavement, she adjusted her oversized sunglasses and pulled tighter her Venetian red cashmere coat. Every click of her stilettos sounded like a deliberate announcement to the world that she had arrived.

Inside, the lobby hummed with the discreet, focused energy of a Fortune 500 operation—assistants hustling by with wireless earbuds, a receptionist snapping to attention the moment Charlotte approached. But before the poor man could welcome her, Jake appeared.

Tall, broad-shouldered, he radiated that quiet alpha confidence of a business executive seldom denied—even though he did occasionally realize its cost. "Charlotte," he greeted. "Glad you could make it."

She slipped off her sunglasses, giving him a frosty stare that managed to be both dismissive and, somehow, coquettish. "Naturally," she replied. "I was informed," she said with a slight flirtation, "that your new empire's aesthetics were in desperate need of salvation. I couldn't possibly say no."

Jake let out a low rumble of laughter. "Your wit's as sharp as ever. Let's hope the art we chose together can do the trick."

Charlotte smiled. "The truck's around the side, at the service entrance," she said, gliding past him. "My team will hang the pieces. Of course, the main installation, the *pièce de résistance* for your office gets my personal attention. You still want it above the desk?"

Jake nodded, keeping pace with her as she headed for the elevators. "I hope the work looks as good in natural light as it did in the warehouse," he said, briefly nervous about his decisions. Art was not the same as business, and he felt slightly out of his depth.

Charlotte halted abruptly and turned to him, amusement lighting her eyes. "Jake, do you think I've built my gallery's reputation on anything less than perfection? The lighting here will only enhance the collection. Let me assure you: Each piece aligns with your...ambitions."

He studied her for a moment, then gave a brief nod. "All right. I'll leave it in your hands. I know they are more than capable."

Without another word, she pivoted and stepped into the elevator. Just before the doors closed, Charlotte looked back, her voice smooth and unhurried. "One more thing," she said. "The artist will visit once everything's hung. He insists on making sure the placement is perfect. I told him you'd appreciate the special attention."

Jake raised an eyebrow, faint surprise mingling with curiosity. "That's... thoughtful."

"He's a perfectionist too," Charlotte replied with an enigmatic half-smile. "Much like all of us." And with that, the doors slid shut.

Smiling, Jake let out a breath and, glancing at the receptionist, stated simply, "She's terrific, isn't she? Or, should I say terrifying?"

Inside the elevator, Charlotte permitted herself the faintest smirk as she caught the parting words. *Yes*, she thought, *'terrifying' would do just fine.*

A few days later, Jake stood by the main entrance, watching the lobby staff go about their routines while he waited for the artist. When Theo arrived—tall, wiry, hands stained from nonstop painting—he exuded the same raw energy as before, the same vitality evident in his work.

"Mr. Laskin," Theo said, extending a hand in greeting. His voice was calm yet carried the slightest edge of curiosity.

Jake greeted Theo and then gestured toward the huge open lobby. "Theo. Thanks for coming. Charlotte's team did the initial hang, but if you see anything that needs tweaking, speak up."

Theo's gaze scanned the space as they walked. He paused before the sweeping triptych now dominating the entry wall, swiveling his head to appreciate once again the impressive set of brushstrokes.

"This piece thrives on motion," he remarked quietly. "All these brushstrokes loop in on themselves, like they're trying not to be pinned down. It's bold, even a bit volatile, but balanced by an underlying rhythm. It draws attention without shouting for it."

Jake shoved his hands into his pockets. "It matches the energy of this place. You think it works for a lobby?"

Theo nodded, stepping in closer to admire the textural detail. "Absolutely. A lobby is like a handshake—it sets the tone. First impressions decide whether people feel welcome and uplifted, or instead depressed. This piece promises movement and progress—everything my work and yours represents."

Jake allowed himself a smile. "That's exactly what I was hoping."

They moved down the corridor, smaller artworks punctuating the space. Theo pointed out the layered paint over vintage maps. "These act like punctuation marks. They are multi-functional pieces." He looked at Jake, before explaining.

"They break up the monotony of the walls. They encourage visitors with an artistic sensibility to pause. And yet they move along others, less interested, like crossties on a railroad."

Jake glanced at the series of pieces as though seeing them anew. "Charlotte said these pieces would work well here."

"Precisely," Theo agreed. "They are subtle, but effective."

In the boardroom, a large painting commanded the wall, deep blues slashed through by shimmering gold. Theo took a moment, arms folded, absorbing the piece in silence.

"It's a masterstroke," he said at last. "The blues pull you in, and the gold strikes like lightning through a storm. Turbulent, but with a hint of reassurance—like the promise of calm and renewed energy after chaos. It's ambitious. A boardroom should feel that way, right? It's where decisions happen."

Jake leaned against the conference table. "You think it's not too much?"

"It's meant to be almost too much," Theo replied with a small grin. "Safe art fades into the background. This painting demands engagement—like I'm sure you do when you're at the head of this table."

Jake smirked but said nothing, following Theo out toward his personal office.

Inside, Theo stopped short. Mounted behind Jake's desk was a sprawling burst of color—reds, whites, blacks, and gold layered in almost sculptural thickness. It seemed alive, ready to leap from the wall.

"This," Theo said in awe, "is the heart of your collection." His pulse quickened just looking at the work. Not simply because he'd made a masterpiece, something that might etch his name in posterity.

"It's so raw and primal," he explained, "the palette capturing ambition, triumph, power—no apologies. It transforms the room rather than just decorating it. And yet, it frames you—the person behind the desk—rather than overshadowing you."

Theo tried to calm his emotion. "Corporate art shouldn't just sit there; it should enhance the owner and challenge the viewer." He went up closer, as if admiring one last time.

As requested—he had placed a tiny device in the canvas. A single, almost invisible speck—smaller than a poppy seed—nestled in the wet-on-wet mingling of a brushstroke, now masquerading as a fleck of dried pigment.

From a foot away it was just texture. Matte black in color to drink the light. There was no glint, no bulge, no telltale seam. Even he couldn't pinpoint it without careful examination.

From six inches it was, he knew, a pinhole lens and a hair-thin diaphragm. The dot breathed with the canvas, flexing imperceptibly when the frame shifted, its microphone tuned to catch a whisper across the room and its lens wide enough to frame the desk and almost the entire sofa.

Jake behind him seemed uncharacteristically pensive. Theo wondered for a split second whether he could possibly notice. "You've got a way with art. I'll grant you that," Jake said at last, clearly pleased.

Theo felt a sudden relief, which he covered with a grin. "I'm not just making it up. Art like this shapes the space and the story. It becomes part of who you are, part of the myth."

Jake gave a slow nod, eyes still on the painting. "I can see that now."

"That's why I do this," Theo said, stepping back once more. "I want to connect and shape the story." Even he wasn't sure why those words rang truer than he intended.

Back in the lobby, Jake and Theo exchanged a firm handshake in front of the towering triptych, Jake clearly impressed by both Theo's vision and Charlotte's curation. Then Jake's tone shifted, as it did on their last meeting.

"How's your mom doing?" he asked.

Theo offered a knowing smile and adjusted his blazer. "She's handling it all well—busier than ever. Polls are... interesting. We've got a few good breaks, but the overall narrative is still tighter than we'd like."

Jake hummed, thoughtful. "Sometimes those outliers are more accurate than people think. Internal polls show any difference?"

Theo nodded, his face turning more serious. "They're a bit better, actually. Young voters and suburban women are trending our way—especially on renewable energy, abortion rights, and DEI issues. It's definitely resonating, and with the upcoming family event, we're hoping to spotlight her achievements."

"Sounds good," Jake said. "Feels like people are finally seeing the bigger picture—the longer-term prospects. Our future's not in fossils. And your mom's approach to progress—social issues, the environment—is forward-thinking. What's the opposition up to?"

Theo huffed a short laugh. "Leaning on old-school fear and nostalgia. It fires up their base but doesn't help them grow any. We stick to the more inclusive picture. Voters want stability and solutions, not disruptive slogans that do no more than stir up emotions."

Jake paused and admired again the triptych in his lobby. "Is that approach clicking? Connecting all the dots, I mean?"

Theo noted Jake's gaze—the admiration for his artwork. He smiled. "It is, but the campaign's a marathon. You have to keep showing, not just telling. The program can't get too intellectual." He looked at his triptych. He was almost sorry to part with it.

"It's like assembling layers of paint into a cohesive piece—the physicality matters, the detail matters. The bystander has to feel pulled in, engaged."

Jake nodded. "Which brings us to the volunteers. You feeling comfortable on that front now—enough to bus around wherever needed? I have a sense that some of the states will be quite close."

Theo smiled. "We're increasingly well resourced. We've lots of young people signing up—partly because of abortion rights and climate action."

Jake nodded. "It's better to avoid close runs, like 1960 or 2000."

"Don't worry. Our emphasis on women's rights and social justice will mobilize voters. People feel they have skin in the game. The choice is obvious."

Jake looked at the individuals on the sidewalk outside, bustling past the office lobby. Were they going to vote—would New York swing the outcome one way or another? "I suppose funding remains key," Jake said, his voice low. "Last time you felt a need for more."

Theo smiled again. "There's always room for more, but we're holding our own. Those who believe in the platform are stepping up."

Jake folded his arms. "Your mom has real vision. She's not just talking about the future; she's actively building it. She has my full support, especially where renewables are concerned. That's not just politics; it's survival."

Theo's expression softened, gratitude evident. "She's always said it's about what you do once you win, not just winning. She wants to finish two terms, leaving a better world for all of us—a world that the next generation can enjoy as well."

Jake nodded. "Here's hoping she keeps her position. If the other side wins..."

Theo nodded solemnly. "We lose ground on everything—renewables, abortion rights, immigration reform; dare I say it, democracy. It all goes backward."

Jake's voice dropped. "Let's do what we can to make sure it doesn't happen. I'm on board."

Theo's grin turned lighter. "You've already been a huge help. Just keep doing what you're doing—amplifying the message, supporting the cause. It makes a difference."

They strolled to the front doors in companionable silence before Theo added, "Besides, Charlotte would never let me live it down. You've done so much, and we appreciate everything."

Jake smirked, picturing Charlotte's arch expression. "She'd have my head if I didn't step up, and you know it." The two men shared a quick laugh. With other business waiting and the new backdrop now in place, Jake bid farewell.

But, Theo knew, the art was more than a backdrop. He would find out what was happening at PanEnergy, work out what Jake was thinking—what he was up to—and then report back. He hadn't done anything so fun in a long time.

41. Scientific Report

Outside Jake Laskin's office block traffic pulsed through the city's arteries. Inside, the man himself stood by his desk, nursing a growing weariness that pooled behind his eyes.

A knock at the door dragged him out of his thoughts. His assistant, Monica, popped her head around, looking unusually hesitant. "Dr. Sylvia Reed is here for her appointment."

Jake's grip on his coffee mug tightened—Sylvia never came bearing good news. "Send her in," he said, setting his shoulders. He felt a flash of annoyance, but also the familiar readiness of a man who'd made his career by confronting challenges head-on.

Sylvia Reed entered with a confidence that belied her simplicity of dress. A tailored blazer, dark jeans, and scuffed boots suggested she was equally at home in corporate boardrooms and on protest lines. She spared no time on pleasantries. "Jake," she greeted, slapping a worn manila folder on his desk. "Let's skip the small talk." Sylvia called her tactics 'shock and awe.'

He offered the polite smile he reserved for adversaries. "Sylvia. To what do I owe the pleasure?"

"Cultural survey," she said, tapping the folder. "Or maybe I should call it a red light. Your proposed pipeline route runs right across land sacred to Indigenous people on the Thunder Creek Reservation."

Jake flipped open the folder and skimmed the contents: historical references, signed expert testimonies, and some tribal endorsements. He sighed, wishing he could dismiss it out of hand. "We've heard cultural objections before," he said carefully. "But you're implying it's more than just some local pushback."

Sylvia stared hard. "Pushback? That's your word for it?" She stepped closer. "This is existential. What you're doing is desecration. This land is bound to creation stories that go back to the first inhabitation of this country. And with the full backing of Indigenous advocacy groups, we have already notified the regulators and served your lawyers."

Jake closed the folder and went to sit down, the leather creaking slightly. "You realize the scale of this project—billions in investment, thousands of jobs. We won't just walk away."

"Then be prepared for a legal war," Sylvia shot back. "It could drag on for years. Actually decades. If you think you can spin this as just another PR hiccup, good luck. Public opinion hardly supports corporations that trample over the environment. Much less do they accept corporations that trample over Indigenous rights."

Jake gave her a thin, tired smile. He was in his element, but he could feel a subtle ache behind his temples. "I've weathered my share of storms, Sylvia. You're tenacious, I'll give you that. But don't expect PanEnergy to roll over."

Jake got up again and came around his desk to face Sylvia. "I think we'll have to let the courts settle this." He proffered his hand to close the discussion.

Sylvia looked down at the extended hand and refused to take it. "We both know how this goes. I'm giving you the opportunity to do the right thing—reroute if you can, or scrap the pipeline entirely." Jake shook his head in a display of superficial bewilderment.

"You won't like what comes next," Sylvia continued. "You'll be stuck in the courts forever. Thanks to the priorities of the current administration—who actually understand the need for justice—our funding is becoming effectively limitless. And in the end, you'll have to cease work and pay reparations."

Sylvia pivoted and left, her boots thudding across the floor. Jake watched her go, anger and fatigue mingling in his chest. He glanced again at the file, its worn cover telling him this was more than just a single shot fired randomly—it was part of a long-running battle of attrition. He was getting too old, he felt, for this routine, yet such fights were the only ones he knew.

He idly flicked through the report again, more slowly this time, before calling his legal team. He glanced at damning headlines, quotes of Indigenous elders, cultural claims woven tightly within a broader narrative of neglect and exploitation, the logical positions of fervent activists, and complementary testimony from an expert at a leading non-profit.

People always equate non-profits with non-biased, he thought. A sense of ennui washed over him. Until he saw the logo of GSx Consulting in the list of research organizations. Instantly his attention was aroused, and a jolt of suspicion coursed through his veins, as if another puzzle piece had clicked into place.

GSx was no ordinary consulting firm; and he wondered again whether they specialized in orchestrating political and environmental pressure on behalf of undisclosed clients.

He buzzed in Monica. She was not just his longtime assistant but also his de facto first-line crisis manager. Monica hurried in with her tablet and some other documents. The concern in her expression matched his.

"I've been looking at my copy of the new file," she said, taking a seat. "Sylvia left me one. She said in case you threw yours away... I guess you've noticed that GSx is mentioned there. They may be offering more than just research."

Jake ran a hand over his face. "So Sylvia's complaint might be valid—or it might be orchestrated."

Monica nodded, "GSx seems to be wherever waters are becoming muddied. Do you recall that fiasco overseas last year? The maritime case?" She flipped through the papers she had. "Some of my contacts say GSx backed a group opposing deep-sea drilling. They used various environmental regulations and cultural reviews to stall that project indefinitely."

Jake nodded. "I remember some headline or other in the industry press."

Monica continued, "The result was a total blockade. The company had no choice but to withdraw. GSx never appeared publicly, but my contacts say they were involved. I can't verify."

Jake tapped Sylvia's file. "So now they might be pulling the same stunt with our pipeline. Indigenous rights are a powerful lever. If GSx can paint us as villains, they won't need to challenge us in open court—the public narrative does the damage for them."

Monica grunted, a mix of concern and resolve. She felt the last thing Jake needed was another fight. "We have to respond. If GSx is behind this, there's more going on than meets the eye. Nevertheless, if the Reservation's claims are genuine, we can't just ignore them."

"I don't plan to disregard any legitimate concerns," Jake said, his voice taut. "But I won't let GSx manipulate us either. First, talk with our legal team. Then, let's ask someone who knows about that maritime fiasco overseas you mentioned. Given their experience, they're sure to have suggestions about how to approach this matter."

She made a note. "And you, Jake?"

He closed the file and stood, fixing his tie. The Manhattan skyline beyond the window had turned deep orange in the setting sun, skyscrapers cutting dramatic shapes against the fiery sky. "I'll tap into my own contacts," he said. "They might have intel on who's really funding the entity. If GSx thinks it can sabotage us while staying behind the scenes, it's in for a rude awakening."

A tremor of excitement undercut his weariness. Jake was a fighter; and adversity only sharpened his resolve. He grabbed his phone and scrolled through a list of private numbers.

Monica hesitated. "Just be careful. If GSx is well-connected, we might be walking straight into a damaging brawl."

Jake looked up, eyes determined. "Let them hide in the shadows if they can. I've navigated darker corners before. Information is power, and I plan to load up. We'll address legitimate claims through the proper channels, but if there's a conspiracy at play, we're not going to lie down and let it unfold."

He smiled as Monica nodded. "I'll call the legal team," she said and headed out. Alone, Jake stared outside. The day had begun so well, with all his new art. If it had ended badly, it wasn't in the way he'd expected.

A potential clash with Sylvia was, in many ways, tough but straightforward. A fight with some cunning adversary still hiding in the shadows would be more complex.

He drained the last of his coffee, savoring the mouthful. The taste lingered, bitter and dark, like his mood. But he was ready for the fight. This was his life, after all—and if GSx wanted a war, Jake Laskin would bring it to them.

Claire leaned back in her chair. The atmosphere in the small meeting room was somber—a temporary fan the only sound before she broke the silence. "All right, let's get started. What do we have on Alex?"

Colonel James Calloway, her adjutant, nodded to Lisa, the analyst who had been coordinating the investigation. Lisa stood, tablet in hand. "Ma'am, the situation is escalating. Alex's arrival has stirred up significant activity, and not all of it is easily explainable."

"Go on."

Lisa clicked a button, pulling up a digital dossier on the screen in front of her with images and timelines. "First, the facial recognition data. We're still holding at a similarity score in the low sixties with Asimov, the American sent to a Russian labor camp over a decade ago. It's not a high-confidence or automated match, but combined with everything else we've uncovered, it's troubling."

"Define 'everything else.'"

"Let's start with Kaisa Warren," Lisa said, shifting to a photo of a striking woman in her mid-thirties. "Ivan's fiancée at the time of his arrest. She is now married to the senior American senator from Wyoming, but already she's been seen with Alex twice. Once at a fundraising gala for the ballet in Manhattan, and again at a private party at Alex's newly acquired estate in the Hamptons." Lisa paused.

"She's reputed to be a person not easily spooked; and yet her movements have become... more erratic."

Claire's expression darkened. "Coincidence?"

"Perhaps," Lisa said, "but then there's the cabin."

Lisa pulled up a satellite image. "An old shack in the Finger Lakes region, previously owned by Ivan's father. It's been dormant for years. Recently, we've picked up signs of activity via satellite—vehicles coming and going. Could be nothing, but given the timing it's worth noting."

Claire tapped a pen on the desk, her mind calculating. "What about his connections?"

"That's where it gets even murkier," Lisa replied. "Jake Laskin, current CEO of PanEnergy and a former colleague of Ivan's when he worked business development in Russia, is now asking about Alex through back channels. Jake thinks he's being subtle, but his queries have been logged through the system. He's nervous—that much is clear from his behavior."

"PanEnergy," Claire murmured. "That's a name with plenty of Russian entanglements."

"Exactly," Lisa said. "And speaking of Russia, both the FSB and one of the country's mafia groups are circling Alex. The FSB's movements suggest they're trying to confirm his intentions in America, while the mafia's efforts seem more... territorial. They're worried—we've been told—that his operations might intrude on theirs. How they're related to this whole situation is unclear."

"So we have a man who looks like a ghost from the past, who's connected to powerful figures, and who's drawing attention from both state actors and criminals. Am I missing anything?"

Lisa hesitated before replying. "No."

Claire uncapped her pen and wrote a few notes. "Whoever he is," she said, "he's deeply enmeshed in networks that present a danger to the country." She leaned forward, her voice now low. "Strengthen our surveillance on Alex 24/7. Every move he makes, every contact he has. I want deeper dives on Kaisa, Jake, and anyone else from Ivan's past now in Alex's orbit. And that cabin... I want boots on the ground there. Quietly."

"Understood," Lisa said, nodding.

Calloway cleared his throat. "Ma'am, if this is Ivan, the implications could be huge. A sleeper resurfacing after decades? It would be the first time since 2010."

"And if it's not Ivan?" Claire asked, fixing him with a piercing stare.

"Then we've got an entirely different kind of problem on our hands," Calloway replied.

Claire nodded slowly, her mind racing. "Either way, Alex is bad news. Let's make sure we're ready for whatever comes next." She closed her notebook. The unknown never frightened her; it only demanded better questions.

Elusive figures—untrustworthy characters—had a tendency to reshape history. There were so many examples... Now she had to decide, like others in her position before, whether this one had value. Or whether, learning from past outcomes, he was better neutralized. As the team filtered out of the room, Claire stayed seated, her gaze fixed on the screen where Alex's face lingered.

Ghost or not, he was feeding a storm that would eventually break—and, like a storm chaser, she intended to be present and ready when it did.

43. Jordanville

It was still dark outside when Alex hurried into the foyer of his Hamptons residence, calling for the others. They emerged quickly—Anisa adjusting a scarf on her shoulders, David carrying a slim leather-bound diary. "We're going to be late," Alex reminded them, his voice calm yet insistent.

Outside, a sleek Maybach awaited, engine purring quietly. The chauffeur held the door open for Alex. "The Russian Orthodox church in Jordanville?" the chauffeur double-checked as Alex clambered inside.

"Yes, please!" he replied.

The car glided away from the estate, its engine barely audible, and wound along roads still quiet in the early morning. Before long, it merged onto the highway that led through the city and out the other side.

Anisa glanced at the passing landscape, first dark then ombré, while David looked at their schedule, ensuring they remained on track.

As they approached Jordanville, the monastery's golden domes caught the first full light of morning—an island of ritual calm in a restless land. The church and its monastery complex stood out amid the bright green grass and turning leaves. Instead of entering through the ornate front doors, Alex guided them to a side entrance. Frankincense hung in the air as they made their way to the vestry.

David and Anisa stood by as Alex swiftly removed his casual weekend attire. From a tall simple wooden wardrobe, he took out his gold vestments. He slipped them on quickly and efficiently. Anisa wondered, as she often did, whether Alex believed they purified him—or just hid him.

A knock came at the door. "Father Alex," the deacon muttered in his deep voice, "we're ready to begin."

"Just a second," Alex replied, tying the final sash. He steadied his breathing, feeling the familiar calm descend.

Shortly, he would step through the royal doors—the deacon a little behind and to his right, censer already swinging, the incense rising in slow clouds. The deacon would thunder across the nave: "*Blagoslovi, vladyko!*" and Alex would lift his hand in blessing toward the altar, answering: "*Blagoslovenno Tsarstvo...*"

"Are you two joining today?" he asked as he finished vesting. Anisa nodded, but David shook his head. "I've got to walk the dogs. If it's okay, I'll take the car." Alex waved in agreement. Straightening his posture, he looked at Anisa, and together they headed out.

Anisa took her place with the congregants, pulling her scarf over her head, aware of the subtle shift in atmosphere. Here, in the sacred calm of the church, Alex shed the role of Hamptons host and instead became part of the monastery team leading parishioners in the Divine Liturgy.

Here, Anisa guessed, he could safely surface both sides of himself—faith and justice—without spinning out of control.

44. Complications

Alex stepped back from the ambo, his words still resonating in his ears, the echoes of his sermon mingling with the faint rustle of the congregation. He had spoken from the heart, recalling personal scars etched deep in his soul—scars of betrayal, of loss, of hard lessons learned in the brutal confines of a Siberian prison. Yet, as he now scanned the congregation, his heart jumped.

Kaisa.

Her presence jolted him. She stood near the back, poised and elegant, wisps of blonde hair escaping her head-covering—catching the light. Time had softened her features. However, her spirit, the aura that had first attracted his attention, was untouched.

Even now, fifteen years since they met, he felt moved. And yet... the years had placed a tremendous chasm between them. Kaisa, the woman with whom he had once dreamed of sharing a life, was now Ms. Warren, wife of the prominent American senator.

His mind churned. What was Kaisa doing here? Did she know? And more importantly, would she confront him? He hoped not. However, a plan was necessary. There would be an opportunity to speak only after he'd handed out the antidoron and venerated the Gospel. He'd slip back into the vestry when the last parishioner had kissed the cross, when the nave had begun to empty, and shut the door behind him.

He got to the vestry, and his fingers were already loosening the sash of his vestments when the door slammed open with a force that shook the small room. For a second, he wondered—bizarrely in hindsight—whether it was Kaisa. But before he could better formulate his thoughts, a pair of strong hands seized his shoulders and drove him hard against the wooden cabinet.

"Govno," snarled a voice in Russian, thick with the guttural slang of prisons.

A second assailant moved into sight, a wiry man with a nasty grin and tattoos peeking from his shirt cuffs. Alex recognized the patterns instantly—the stars on the neck, the skull inked on the hand. These men were Vory v Zakone, thieves-in-law. Russian mafia, as old and ruthless as the system birthing them.

"You've been busy, Father," the nasty one sneered, his accent thick and mocking. "But not busy enough to avoid us."

Alex reacted instinctively. A quick twist broke the first grip, but the second man lunged, slamming him into the cabinet again. He felt the sharp edge of a shelf dig into his back as the two gangsters pressed their advantage. They were strong, their moves coordinated, their attack well-honed. But they had underestimated him.

Years in the gulag had taught Alex a lot. Pain was a teacher, and survival was a skill honed under the harshest conditions. These men might have the element of surprise, but Alex—determined to survive—had developed the instincts of a predator.

He drove an elbow into the gut of the larger man, the one pinning his left arm. The thug grunted, stumbling back, but the nasty one was already reaching for something. Alex caught the glint of metal as the man grabbed a brass candlestick from the vestry shelf.

The blow came fast, aimed at his head. Alex ducked, the candlestick grazing his shoulder. He pivoted, using the momentum to grab a wooden cross from the wall. The man lunged again, and Alex swung the cross in a wide arc, the heavy wood connecting with the man's temple. The attacker went down with a painful thud, but the larger gangster was back, pulling a knife from his boot.

"Priests shouldn't fight," the man hissed in Russian, advancing.

"And Russians shouldn't spill blood in a holy place," Alex shot back, icily.

The gangster lunged, the blade aimed for Alex's stomach. He sidestepped, grabbing the man's wrist and twisting hard. The knife clattered to the floor. A swift knee to the thug's midsection followed, and the man staggered. Before he could recover, Alex seized a chalice and struck hard—the dull metal rang out.

The larger man crumpled, groaning, but Alex didn't stop. He knew better than to leave an opponent merely dazed. Two swift strikes to the head ensured he wouldn't get up again.

The vestry was a mess. The table was overturned, religious artifacts from the shelves lay scattered, a smear of blood marred the white linen of a rumpled altar cloth. Alex stood amid the chaos, breathing hard, his vestments stained and torn. He hadn't even managed to lift off his phelonion.

He stared at the two bodies on the floor, his mind racing. The larger one was dead, his head at an unnatural angle. The thinner one groaned faintly, momentarily stunned and alive—for now. Alex knelt by him, gripping his collar. "Who sent you?" he demanded, his voice low and dangerous.

The man spat blood, grinning through broken teeth, slightly disoriented. "You think this ends here, Father? We know. We'll come for you. For her."

Her.

Kaisa? Or her, Anisa?

Alex's blood turned cold. He released the man with a shove, quickly getting up. Grabbing his coat, he sought to hide the worst of the damage. As he turned to leave, he snapped the remaining thug's neck with a precise, brutal kick. He couldn't afford to waste time. The crack echoed once and then disappeared beneath the hum of the sanctuary lights.

He went back through the church. The congregation was gone, but he saw Anisa waiting outside the front entrance talking on her cellphone. As he approached, she looked up; smiling at first until she noticed his state. "What happened?" she asked after breaking short her chat.

"Hmm. Call David and have him send some cleaners. It's a mess in there. He doesn't need to join." Anisa nodded, and Alex quickly turned his attention to Kaisa. *Was she okay?* Scanning the grounds, he saw a familiar figure over near the monastery.

The past and present collided each time he saw her. But now, more than ever, he knew their reunion wouldn't be the peaceful one he'd imagined. The wolves were circling, and he had to act fast.

A sharp fall wind cut across the grounds around the church, reflecting the more volatile weather of the season, whipping Alex's exposed face as he stared at Kaisa.

His pulse quickened as he saw another woman approach and engage her in earnest conversation. Kaisa leaned over to hear and respond, her hand moving up to rest on her collarbone. The two were close, but the exchange looked formal—their stances rigid, their gestures measured. From this distance, it was impossible to hear the conversation or read its intentions. It couldn't be good.

Alex's instincts, suspicious after years of surviving treachery and deception, began to stir. Who was the woman? A curious parishioner, perhaps? Or someone with more serious designs? He shifted slightly in the shadows of the church's doorway, careful to avoid distracting their attention.

He caught a glimpse of the stranger's face and recognized her. She had been there at the Divine Liturgy. A middle-aged parishioner with a heavy coat, chestnut brown hair, and an ingratiating smile. Kaisa had recognized her too, but she now detected a kind of serious curiosity that bordered on probing.

"I don't think I've seen you here before," the parishioner had begun, her voice casual and relaxed. As she turned her face toward Kaisa, the light picked out Nadia's features. She had recently traveled across from Paris in pursuit of Irina's research.

"It's not often we have foreigners at our divine services. I have read that more Americans are growing interested in Orthodox Christianity. The notion still surprises me. Are you interested in the faith? Do you plan to attend more often?"

Kaisa answered as curtly as she could without rudeness. "I am interested. I attended the Divine Liturgy as a child in Helsinki—at Uspenski Cathedral. My mother was Orthodox." The admission introduced a hint of something—

nostalgia, perhaps—to her voice. "I'm not sure if I'll attend more often. It's a long drive." She paused. "The service was... meaningful. It brought back memories." Too many, she thought, and none that she could safely vocalize.

Nadia angled her head, studying Kaisa with a glimmer of something Alex couldn't place from his distance. "The priest? What did you think of him?"

Kaisa hesitated before speaking. "He's an imposing figure. The sermon today was powerful. It seemed deeply personal to him."

"Do you know him?" the woman pressed, her tone shifting slightly, though still casual enough to feign innocence. "Does he know you? I noticed he stared in your direction at one point—intently. Almost as if he recognized you."

Kaisa's expression tightened, biting back a sharper retort. "It's the first time I've come here," she said with finality, her voice colder now. "The priest is new to me. I guess I stood out among the usual faces."

Kaisa's tone had an edge now. She wanted the conversation finished. "I really must go," she said abruptly, sidestepping the woman. Her pace quickened, her steps deliberate and almost hurried as she made her way into the parking lot.

Alex's heart sank as he realized the speed of her departure left him no chance to follow without drawing attention or attracting questions with tough answers. Not that he could have pursued Kaisa anyway—not with the parishioner now watching him so closely. He must have stepped out a little too far in order see better.

The faint betrayal of recognition in the woman's gaze as she spotted him was unsettling. And her expression—she appeared pleased at the way things had gone.

Alex stepped back into the shadowed recess of the doorway, his mind racing. The wolves were closer than he feared—and worse, not all of them came with knives.

A hush blanketed the conference room, as if a trading floor waiting for the FRB to release its decision. Jake sat at the head of the long, polished table, his fingers steepled beneath his chin—his eyes fixed on Vince, his Head of M&A.

The overhead lights threw stark angles over Jake's features, accentuating the hard line of his jaw. Across from him, Vince looked exhausted, a stack of bulging dossiers under his hand—the latest salvo in PanEnergy's attempts to acquire its target in the Permian Basin.

Jake broke the silence with a voice honed to slice through comfort. "All right, Vince," he said, "why am I suddenly hearing now about senators and statehouses meddling in my deal?"

Vince looked at his pile of documents and flipped open the top folder to reveal a thick sheaf of policy briefs, emails, and press statements. "They're going big on the political front," he said, his tone matter-of-fact. "Talking about patriotism—lobbying federal and state officials anywhere they've got operations."

He tapped the first page, where the bold words 'CONGRESSIONAL HEARINGS' were highlighted. "They want a federal review of the takeover, framing us as a risk to energy security. Their argument is that once we acquire these fields, we'll pivot too hard toward renewables—jeopardizing America's hydrocarbon independence and contributing to inflation."

Jake let out a low, humorless laugh. "Energy security? We're one of the largest energy companies in the country. We're doing oil, gas, wind—you name it."

Vince nodded. "Yes. So, at the same time, they're floating the idea of asking the FTC to broaden its antitrust review—with the goal of slowing us down." Jake gave a look of disgust.

Vince continued. "They're not aiming at the facts; they're aiming at headlines and sound bites. They claim we're more interested in feel-good stories and cocktail hours in Manhattan rather than the prosaic realities of everyday life—like the cost of gasoline or electricity."

Jake's lips curled. "I suppose there's more?"

Vince flipped to another page. "They're mobilizing at the state level, tackling the governor, legislators, regulatory boards—the usual suspects. Can you believe it?—even the Texas Railroad Commission is sniffing around. I guess somebody's got to them." He shook his head.

"Anway, they're stoking partisan flames, labeling us as an 'elitist East Coast firm' that cozies up to Democrats. Meanwhile, they're posing as 'salt of the earth' operators who keep red-state America employed."

Jake's smile vanished, replaced by a cold light in his eye. "When logic fails, wave a flag, right?" He'd seen this play before—men dressing greed in the colors of patriotism. It never failed to move markets or mobs. He tapped a middle finger on the table. "So how do we fight back?"

Vince sat up a little straighter. "Publicly, we lean on facts. We highlight job creation, our operational track record, our balanced energy portfolio. We show we're not city slickers in some financial equivalent of an ivory-tower—we're the real deal, who can maximize production and keep the lights on."

Jake arched an eyebrow. "And privately?"

Vince hesitated, only for a beat. "We use our contacts—lobbyists, PACs, sympathetic members of Congress. We push them to block or stall any hearings and to undermine state-level opposition. We remind the right people a strong PanEnergy means a stronger America on the global stage."

Jake gave a curt nod. He'd always known influence was the cleanest form of violence. "Who's on our side?"

"I'm compiling a list," Vince replied, tapping the stack of folders. "We've got folks on key committees who owe us favors, or at least see the wider picture. I'll have a full list of names by morning."

Jake's gaze sharpened. "And those who don't see it our way?"

Vince cleared his throat. "We turn up the heat—donations, influence, back channels. If they're on the fence, we push them off. If they're hostile, we look for leverage. Maybe they have vulnerabilities. Almost everyone does. Maybe they just need a reminder of how deep our pockets go."

Jake leaned back, a faint smile curling on his lips like a predator who's caught the scent of victory. "Good. That's how I like it."

He looked Vince deep in the eyes. "*Now* you're making sense. Push hard but keep it quiet. No need to hand the media another headline."

Vince closed the top dossier, then paused. "Should we also run a campaign against the target? Leak details about their debt, their questionable board oversight—force them to defend their own record instead of attacking ours."

Jake's smirk returned, sharper this time. "That's the spirit. We can frame it as concern for shareholders' best interests. We're not mudslinging—we're 'protecting value.' Get our PR team started immediately. Talk with Eugenia."

Vince nodded, already mentally mapping out the next steps. Jake rose from the table, striding to the window with the kind of confidence that came from years of aggressive, but calculated moves.

He spoke as if to the city through the glass. "They can bring their senators, their governors, their red-white-and-blue speeches." His tone was soft but edged with steel. "Let them play politics if it makes them feel stronger. I'm only interested in winning, and that means applying pressure where it truly works."

He cast one last look at the shimmering skyline, then turned back to Vince. The fight was coming. But if Jake Laskin had his way, the outcome was not in doubt.

46. Classic Mercenaries

Monica's desk was more like a command post than a workspace, scattered with paper and printouts. Gray filing cabinets had been shoved aside to accommodate corkboards crowded with photos, clippings, business filings, notes with rumors—some credible, others less so.

Jake returned from the conference room still vibrating with adrenaline, the kind that came from steering a multi-billion-dollar storm. But he came to a stop next to Monica's chair when his gaze caught the collage in front of him. "You did this today?" he asked, eyebrows lifting, quietly impressed.

It had been a marathon day. He loosened his tie. His expression showed anticipation despite the fatigue.

Monica looked up and smiled. Her eyes were increasingly shadowed by the extended series of late nights. "Jake," she said quietly, "you need to see this." She beckoned him closer with a jerk of her chin, and returned her focus to the computer screen in front of her.

He took a long drink at the water fountain. The mineral tang helped wash away some of the day's weight. Still holding his paper cup, he approached Monica, stepping around the desk to see her screen. "Lay it on me," he said. He could detect a hint of excitement—the same look she had whenever she achieved something big. Or found something troubling.

She tapped the keyboard, bringing up a dedicated folder in which she had saved corporate registries, annotated charts of business relationships, legal documents.

"GSx Consulting," she began, "isn't just a bunch of local fixers. They appear to be international—offices in Europe, some presence in Asia. It's tough to pin down their true scale." She looked up at Jake. "But they're not some all-powerful Goliath."

"Their track record," she continued, "shows that they force their way into specific industries—oil and gas, minerals—and work within legally gray areas to create a sharp, momentary disconnect between perception and value."

Jake leaned over the data. "So they present a challenge to our ambitions—we just don't know how big or intentional," he said.

"That's exactly what's bugging me," Monica said, flipping to another window that displayed names—corporate and individual—tied to GSx. Some were vague placeholders with little more than an email address, others were mid-level attorneys or PR specialists. "Are they here to sabotage a firm like us specifically? Or is it broader, like trying to position themselves to influence U.S. energy policy?"

Jake grimaced. "Considering our run-in with them, I'm guessing they're at least laser-focused on us for the time being. But if they're also tangling with other operators, who knows what their endgame is?" He paused to think, his eyes drifting to a list pinned on one corner of Monica's corkboard. "What's that?"

Monica swiveled her chair around, following his gaze. "That's a partial guide to the companies GSx has advised over the last two years. You see some big oil and gas names, a couple of shipping outfits, even a few renewables. They seem willing to go wherever benefits them."

Jake snorted. "Classic mercenaries." He leaned a hand on the desk, scanning the timeline. "So that explains the rumors of them fueling public controversies in one area, while championing energy projects in another. Keep everything off-balance, watch for the best payout."

Monica gave a wry nod. "Could be. Their moves certainly fit into a series of lucrative side hustles. Yet do these moves build into a grand strategy? They seem to keep everything so... random, almost spontaneous."

Jake glanced at her. "I suppose the other question is: do they operate as a hired gun, or do they have their own agenda?"

She shrugged, frustration creasing her brow. "We don't know. But the fact we can't figure it out... that worries me."

"And me," concurred Jake, throwing his paper cup into the wastebasket. "And me," he repeated after a pause.

Monica wheeled in a whiteboard and wrote down the names of connected parties—GSx staffers, known clients, rumored associates. She circled one name in bold red: Alex Volkoff. A glossy photo pinned to the corkboard showed Alex, full-length, smiling for the camera at some society function. His well-tailored, serious look suggested ambition.

The lines on Jake's forehead tightened. "I still can't wrap my head around what Alex wants—what he's after. He's an Azerbaijani entrepreneur, maybe two months in America."

Monica folded her arms. "From the little we've gathered, he's made a splash quickly. Some investments, including real estate, a few social connections—enough to get him invited to the right parties. And then your run-in with him at the Hamptons..."

Jake nodded, recalling the memory as though it were an epiphany. "He hosted an obscene party followed by a dawn swim at his place—though 'place' is an understatement. An enormous mansion by the water. The man has money, that's for sure. As I was leaving through the house, I spotted the GSx document in his living room. Didn't have time to read much, but I got a sense it wasn't just random."

Monica glanced back at her screen. "Didn't you confront him about it later, at that industry dinner in Manhattan?"

"Yeah." Jake pursed his lips, thinking back on the conversation. "He didn't exactly deny knowing them. He said something vague about 'navigating capitalist webs'—a line that could mean anything." The phrase had stuck with Jake—it sounded as though it belonged to a different world, another life. "When I pressed him, Alex pivoted to small talk. Shook me off with ease."

Jake's mind wandered to that industry dinner in Midtown a few days earlier. Alex had arrived wearing a bright smile, shaking hands like a man who intended to collect as many influential friends as possible. The minute Jake raised GSx, Alex's attitude changed. A hint of discomfort, a forced laugh, then a quick deflection toward safer topics. For some newcomer to the U.S., he navigated the whole evening like a seasoned pro.

Jake remembered watching Alex mingle with the crowd—feeling uneasy. Was Alex capable of grand-scale maneuvering—or more likely, was he some cog, a functionary, in a larger operation?

Monica clicked on a file labeled *Volkoff: Background*, scanning the meager bullet points. "We still have no clue if he's a client of GSx, or an associate, or just a new friend crossing paths with them. It could all be pure coincidence. But given how new he is to the States, it's suspicious he's so well-connected, so fast."

Jake rapped his knuckles on the desk. "I hired Grant—a private investigator—to dig into Alex. Maybe we'll find something—determine whether he's just a regular hustler, a charming importer of Caspian crude, or whether he's got more sinister ties."

Monica nodded. "I hope so. But even Grant might be chasing whispers if GSx keeps its public profile so low. The firm's certainly adept at burying its tracks."

Jake took a slow breath, scanning the various boards and then again the computer screen. "So let's not bank on a single lead. We do this from multiple angles. We follow the money, the politics, the paper trails. We watch for activist groups suddenly noisy, regulators suddenly eager to intervene." Monica nodded.

"In any case we check our own flanks," Jake said. "They could be burrowing into our vulnerabilities as we speak."

He leaned forward, scanning again the many threads of commentary. "We just don't know if they're truly powerful, or if they're trying to punch above their weight."

"We won't resolve much tonight," sighed Monica. "Meanwhile, I guess we unfold our own strategy and keep sight of our own goals." She looked at Jake. "We mustn't get distracted or, worse, second-guess every move now."

Jake nodded. "Very sensible," he said, giving Monica a long, appraising look up and down. "You're quite something."

Monica hesitated. "So what's the plan, concretely?"

Jake straightened, eyes sharp. "Most importantly, we don't panic. If GSx is targeting us, we need to fortify our position: keep our partnerships solid, keep regulators on side, and lean on our record of successful operations."

"Second," he continued, "we pursue relentlessly—Grant on Alex, sure, but also a more thorough inside look at GSx's deals. If they're messing with us specifically, we'll try to work out their game plan, their endpoint."

"And if it's bigger than us?"

"We make sure we're not caught in the crossfire. And if it's about American energy security... well, we bring that to the right political allies. Let CFIUS or the Feds worry about potential foreign meddling."

Monica smiled. "Sounds like a great plan."

Jake returned the gesture, though his eyes remained somber. "This is a high-stakes game, Monica, and I don't intend to lose. Not to some half-shadow group whose motives we can barely guess, and certainly not to some wildcard newcomer like Alex Volkoff."

She nodded, flipping a page in her notebook. "Then let's keep digging."

They spent the next hour or so refining a plan of attack—drawing up a list of contacts to call, angles to exploit, questions to answer. By the time Jake stepped out of Monica's room and had a quick look along the corridor, no one but the cleaning staff seemed present.

For all his confidence, a tiny worm of doubt gnawed at him: GSx's size might be relatively contained, but their methods were sophisticated enough to sow chaos. And Alex, friendly on the surface, was an unknown variable, possibly harboring his own hidden agenda.

Yet, if there was one thing Jake Laskin excelled at, it was navigating potential threats. He thrived on the precarious edge where every decision could reshuffle power. With PanEnergy at stake, he had no choice but to confront these uncertainties head-on—and uncover the truth about GSx, no matter where it led or how deep it went.

Monica was still at her desk. Jake nodded once, an unspoken signal that it was time to move on. Shoulders set, he returned to his office.

He would brace himself for the coming showdown. If GSx wanted to tangle with him—be it for a narrow objective or as part of some wider conspiracy—he'd be ready to meet them, blow for blow, until the last round was all played out.

47. Horse Riding

Morning light spilled across the glass and leather surfaces of Eve's apartment, picking out furniture that seemed to hover above the park and river below. Once, Eve had dreamed of this—success made visible in skyline and design. Now the apartment felt constricting, its perfection stifling, claustrophobic.

She rubbed her temples as she shuffled from the bedroom to the kitchen, the remnants of a sleepless night weighing on her. A sigh escaped as she poured herself a cup of artisanal coffee, another vestige of an ambitious past. Each sip was bitter, and she found no pleasure in it.

It reminded her not of the rich, satisfying life she had imagined and later been promised, but of the unchanging routine that she worried was slowly suffocating her spirit.

The morning hours blended together, a predictable loop of mundane tasks and unfulfilling activities. She flipped through magazines filled with glamorous lives, chatted with friends over text about fashion—necklines, hemlines, no lines. And her aspirations were increasingly confined to drinking cocktails in the evening, talking about the latest show on Broadway.

Today, she planned another lunch with her girlfriends at some trending location. The outing promised to be fun, but as she glanced at the silver fridge, Eve barely recognized the woman reflected back. In particular, her eyes, once bright and lively, now seemed dull.

Tucking a strand of hair behind her ear, Eve thought of Jake. He had been so convincing in weaving tales of business success, shared adventures, and exhilarating travels. Yet all she had seen of him lately were the tailored suits he wore to meetings and the shadows he left behind as he rushed out the door those mornings he bothered even to return. His world seemed to spin at an accelerating pace, while hers had come to a grinding halt.

The doorbell rang, its sound jangling. She set her coffee down on the marble countertop and walked to the door. Opening it she found David, the new dog walker, standing there with an easy smile and a nonchalant posture that made her momentarily forget her weariness.

“Hey there, Eve,” he greeted, letting the dogs bound joyfully around him. “How’s it going this morning?”

“Just another day in paradise,” she replied with a slight laugh, trying to keep the weariness from spilling over. Having watched the BBC series the previous night, she almost said ‘just another death in paradise,’ but had recovered in time. “And you?”

“Same old—except today feels like it has potential,” he remarked, an elusive twinkle in his eyes that hinted at mischief.

Eve raised an eyebrow, intrigued. “Oh? How’s that?”

David chuckled, his tone relaxed yet engaging. “I was thinking of taking the dogs to the stables for a bit of excitement. There’s a kennel yard there with an attendant. Care to join?”

She hesitated, momentarily pulled back to nostalgic memories of summers spent out in the country. Those memories felt distant now, almost another world. “I’ve never actually ridden a horse before, you know,” she confessed.

“Hey, we all start somewhere,” he said, shrugging casually as if it were the most natural thing in the world. “I’ll teach you the basics. You might discover a knack for it. Or at least a good story to tell.”

His words hung in the air, weaving a thread of curiosity that tugged at her. She could step outside her well-ordered existence, if only for a day. “You really think so?” she asked, her tone wary but intrigued.

“Absolutely. And even if you hate it, at least you’ll have a new excuse to complain, right?” His laughter was light, infectious.

Eve bit her lip, trying to suppress a smile. “I don’t know... What if I fall?” It felt childish to ask, but she hadn’t dared anything in so long.

David stepped closer, his expression earnest. "You won't. I listen to this podcast, and it tells me all the time life's about attitude. Bad things only happen when you believe they will."

Although Eve didn't know whether she agreed, she felt a stir of defiance in her. She had spent too long trapped in a predictable cycle—her horizons narrowing until no bigger than a small triangle of New York. Today could be different. She could reclaim a piece of that spirit which had fueled her rebellious early years.

"All right," she finally said, her resolve strengthening. "Let's see what this is all about." Eve slipped into a pair of sturdy sneakers, grabbed a light jacket. *I guess they've got gear*, she briefly reflected. She felt excited.

When they reached the basement parking garage, the air was colder, crisper. David was trying to load the dogs into his beat-up Jeep. His casual attitude and relaxed demeanor radiated an ease she hadn't enjoyed in a long time.

Eve sought to suppress the flutter in her stomach. "So, how did you end up walking dogs?" she asked as the dogs finally jumped in and moved around until they had found a comfortable position.

"Oh, a favor turned into another turned into a gig," he answered lightly, opening the door for Eve to clamber inside and then getting behind the steering wheel.

"To Storm King Stables," David instructed the GPS on his phone as he started the car. It still needed an old-fashioned key. He tapped on *Google Maps*, and the voice directions began.

They headed into the Hudson Valley and the countryside. Eve sat next to David, looking out the window. Everywhere she saw vibrant color: golds, reds, browns. It was a landscape designed to push away hesitation and arouse the spirit.

Seeing a group of tourists outside a bar, she suddenly recalled her friends. Eve texted them, apologizing that something had come up—she couldn't make lunch. That something was David, and as the Jeep navigated winding roads, she asked about the day's outing.

"Storm King is one of my favorite spots," David explained, glancing at her with a genuine smile. "I hope you're ready for a little adventure."

"Adventure is perfect," Eve replied, watching the trees streak past, feeling a sense of anticipation blossom in her chest. It was strange, how easily the tension gripping her for so long began to dissipate in the new surroundings, replaced by a sense of freedom.

Arriving at the stables, she noticed at once the air—different, fresh, carrying the scents of hay and leather. It was somehow invigorating. David took out the Labradors and led them across to the daycare facility with its kennels and off-leash play area.

He came back holding two helmets. "Here this should fit," he said. As he gave one to Eve, his fingers brushed against hers inadvertently, and she felt a warmth spread through her. "Safety first," he said with a grin, the playful gleam in his eyes encouraging. "There are some boots across the yard," he said pointing.

As they mounted their horses, Eve took a moment to absorb it all: the stables nestled between rolling hills, the sweeping pastures stretching out under an expanse of blue sky, the horses magnificent and powerful—radiating a force she found intoxicating.

"Just relax your grip and loosen the reins," David advised as they began their ride. "You don't want to pull too hard. Let the horse feel how you move."

As they set off along the trail, Eve followed David, trying to match his ease. The rhythmic sound of hooves against the packed earth created a hypnotic melody.

They rode past fields dotted with wildflowers swaying gently in the breeze—asters, goldenrods, various weeds. The meandering Hudson River and the stunning backdrop of distant hills took her breath away. Occasionally, she felt a need to push the horse around some obstacle or another, until David suggested that the horse could look after itself.

And as they progressed, Eve's apprehension faded. Each stride thudded like freedom itself—a rhythm her life had forgotten. As they entered some woods she laughed, a light buoyant sound that ricocheted through the trees. "This is incredible!" she called out.

David turned back, a bright smile on his face. "I knew you'd love it." His tone was full of enthusiasm. The moment was so beguiling, Eve felt her breath catch.

As they rode deeper among the trees, sunlight filtered past the multicolored canopy above and painted dappled spots on the forest floor. It was a magical scene.

After some time spent following the trail, David guided their horses toward a clearing. "There's something I've been wanting to show you," he said, dismounting effortlessly. Eve followed, but a little more clumsily. David pointed to a view of the Storm King Art Center.

The sprawling sculpture park stretched before them, with artworks emerging magnificently from the landscape. Eve's eyes widened as she spotted a massive steel sculpture rising against the backdrop of the hills, its form at once commanding yet harmonious in the setting.

"Isn't it stunning?" David asked, watching her reaction. "I love how the artists have managed to integrate their work into nature. It feels like a genuine, constructive dialogue between the human imagination and our landscape."

Eve looked at him, surprised. "I've never seen anything like it. This place is breathtaking!" she said.

"We'll return our horses and come back," David suggested.

* * *

The return seemed a lot quicker, and it felt almost no time before they were back inside the park itself. Eve wandered close to a towering piece, feeling the cool metal beneath her fingers, marveling at the way it seemed to interact with the light and the surrounding trees.

David moved beside her. "That one," he said, pointing farther away, "is my favorite: *Storm King Wavefield*." He glanced at Eve. "It's meant to reflect the movement of wind and water. You can almost feel the lifeforce within it, can't you?"

He blushed slightly. "I get carried away here."

Eve nodded, captivated. She too was struck by the scale of the place—the mix of beauty and vision. The valley was enchanting. She felt overwhelmingly grateful that she had accepted the proposal and agreed to join the expedition.

David saw her look. "You can spend a lifetime searching the world and still find something new right beside you," he said. "That's existence—always changing, always waiting to be noticed." He gestured toward the hills. "You just have to engage with it."

The words were powerful. But, for a second, Eve wasn't sure whether David meant the art or something else. David looked at her and noticed she'd gone quiet. Suddenly diffident, he apologized. "Sorry, I'm rambling as always."

"Not at all..." she replied. "I just recalled something I wrote in my journal as a teenager. *To stop desiring is to stop living.*"

48. M&A Victory

Outside Jake's office the sun was heading down past the tallest towers. Inside the air was still and charged, the silence broken only by the soft buzz of the speakerphone on Jake's desk. He leaned back, smiling—his hand resting on the armrest as if holding court.

On the other end of the line was Palisade's CEO, betraying a mix of weariness and resignation.

"We've reviewed the situation, Jake," the CEO said, his tone measured but edged with defeat. "You've made your point, and we've come to the conclusion that a prolonged fight isn't in anyone's best interests. So here's the deal: we'll stand down. You get the acquisition you've been chasing. But..." There was a pause, deliberate, heavy with meaning. "We need certain assurances."

Jake's smirk widened as he sat up slightly, his eyes gleaming with triumph. "I'm listening."

The CEO continued, his voice steady. "First, financial packages for the management team. Call it golden parachutes, call it what you want, but payouts need to be attractive—sufficient to get everyone to sign off without hesitation."

"Second, protections for our existing operations. No gutting regional offices or mothballing key projects just because they're ours rather than yours. And third, assurances for employees. They're worried, Jake. They need to know they're not heading into a bloodbath. Otherwise, there'll be a huge exodus."

Jake's fingers drummed on the desk—a slow, deliberate rhythm. "Reasonable enough," he said. The tone made it clear Jake was weighing each word for leverage. "What else?"

"That's it," the CEO replied. "In return, we'll cooperate. No more poison pills, no political interference. Just a clean path to closing. We'll let the lawyers hammer out the specifics. But there's one non-negotiable clause: a hefty break fee. If you pull out, you're paying for the privilege."

Jake's laugh was low and sharp, like a blade sliding into its sheath. "You're a shrewd one. I'll give you that. Fine. We'll make sure everyone comes out of this looking good. But let's be clear—this is *my* deal now. Your management team's golden parachutes don't include a second act. Once we close, they're done."

"Understood," the CEO said, the weight of the concession clear even over the phone. "Let's get our lawyers on it."

Jake leaned forward, his voice dropping to a conspiratorial tone. "You're making the right call. Dragging this out would've only hurt shareholders—tarnishing your excellent legacy. Let's end this clean."

"Agreed," the CEO said. "I'll have my team reach out first thing tomorrow."

Jake ended the call, the predatory grin widening across his face. He picked up the phone again and dialed internal. It rang twice before his CFO, Carla, answered.

"Get the financing ready," Jake said without preamble. "We're closing this deal. Have everything lined up—bridge loans, syndicates, whatever it takes. I want no delays."

Carla's voice stayed calm, alert. "Understood. Should I loop in the treasury team tonight?"

"Yes," Jake agreed. "And make sure they understand—this needs to be airtight. The lawyers are about to draft the agreement, and I'm not paying a break fee because someone dropped the ball."

"Got it," the CFO replied. "Congratulations, Jake."

Jake leaned back again, his eyes on the skyline. "Save it for when the ink's dry. Call me if anything comes up."

He ended the call and let the silence of the room settle around him. The city outside his office was thinning into early dusk, its towers faintly mauve against a sky now going silver at the edges. Monica entered. "Anything you need me to do?" she asked.

"Yes, let's get the team together—party at *The Nines* tonight. Thanks!"

Monica nodded. "Great idea. Everyone will enjoy the chance to celebrate the result and let their hair down." She exited, closing the door behind her.

Jake loosened his tie, the day's excitement refusing to settle. He looked at his phone, thought for a second, then dialed.

"Jake?" Eve's voice came quickly, warm. "I was just thinking of you."

He smiled. "Good instinct. We closed it."

"That's wonderful," she said. "You must be exhausted. Have you—"

"Not yet... We cornered them. Textbook. You'd have loved it."

Eve gave a small laugh that didn't quite land. "I'd have been in the way."

Jake turned his chair toward the window, the reflection of his own jubilant grin faint on the glass. "It was clinical," he said. "Beautifully clinical."

"That's good," Eve said after a moment. "You deserve that."

Jake heard something small and careful in her tone but ignored it. He went on, "We're celebrating at *The Nines*. I don't know how late we'll be."

"Of course. You should go party," she said. "I'll see you later, then."

Jake hesitated, thumb still resting on the phone as though there were more to say, but the silence on the line was steady and complete.

Eve put the phone down. The sun outside the penthouse was almost gone, and the kitchen smelled of the dinner she'd started preparing. She lingered for an instant, listening to the faint hum of the fridge—then pressed play on her podcast. David had put her onto it. Esther Perel started talking, quietly.

Back at the office, Jake was back onto his computer—putting away old files, opening up new ones. The game was won. Now he was thinking about the next one. Victory never tasted like rest—it was just a silence between moves.

49. Grilled Fish

The Ambassador's home in the Hamptons was smaller than Alex's but just as curated. It breathed a quiet elegance. Outside, it was typical with its verandas open to the sea breeze. Inside, it was unusual—the walls lined with photos of diplomatic postings: Martha in Germany holding up a stein of beer, Cavil in Australia, wearing his fluorescent cycle gear, out riding with the Prime Minister.

The air here, as at Alex's, carried the salty tang of the Atlantic. However, it now mingled with the smoky promise of the grill where Cavil overlooked newly caught striped bass, swordfish steaks, and an entire halibut, their skins crisping over open flames.

Kaisa arrived with Caleb, her heart feeling tight. She wondered whether this evening could unravel everything—or nothing. She had chosen her outfit carefully: a simple navy dress that both accentuated her Nordic heritage, and echoed—if just faintly—her outfit all those years ago at the dacha.

And on her right hand gleamed the antique engagement ring Ivan had given her that evening together—a delicate band with a diamond. She wore it not on her left hand, to avoid questions from Caleb, but as a talisman, a probe to flush out Alex's identity. The move felt almost theatrical. However, it was necessary to match the brutal reality that she faced. Ivan may have returned.

The ring would prove it—provoke some sort of recognition or confession if he were Ivan, but appear as no more than interesting jewelry if he were not.

Still, when she'd slid it on, her fingers had trembled with the memories it recalled. The ache of loss, she realized, remained—even if the years had cauterized its sharpest edges.

Worse, she wasn't sure she truly wanted the truth—if there was something to find out. How would confirmation help? And what would it cost? Any revelation that Ivan was back would dramatically complicate her life with Caleb.

Her husband, oblivious to the war in her head and the anxiety in her heart, gently kissed her cheek as they stepped up and onto the veranda at the Ambassador's home. "You look stunning," he commented. "Elegant as the first day we met. No wonder everyone is charmed when they see you."

Kaisa smiled. *Charming isn't the goal tonight*, she thought. However, she replied simply, "I try my best," keeping her voice steady.

Cavil greeted them with a bear hug, his ambassadorial charm undimmed in retirement—maybe it had even become more stylized. "Caleb! Kaisa! Come, the grill's just heating up. Martha's inside mixing her famous mojitos—with Dominican rum in memory of our short, early posting to Santo Domingo."

Kaisa guessed Cavil had never spent more than a year in Washington. She'd heard there were more officers than desks in D.C. now. With the relentless surge in expeditionary platforms—plus the rightsizing across local bureaus—a full Washington tour had become a prize, something officers might see only once or twice in an entire career.

Martha emerged and hugged Kaisa tightly. "Darling, so glad you could come. And look at that ring." She noticed it instantly and picked up Kaisa's right hand to have a closer look. "Stunning! I would marry again just for that ring," she declared. "Unlock myself from Cavil, whom I love dearly—but we've been together so long—for the chance of experiencing fresh exploits with new partners." She laughed as Cavil raised his eyebrows.

"Did you just get the ring?" she asked. Kaisa's pulse quickened. She hadn't prepared for such questions. "It's a family heirloom," she said, keeping her tone light. "I felt like wearing something special today."

Alex and Anisa arrived shortly after—Alex again in a linen shirt, though this time better ironed, and Anisa in a white dress that evoked Mediterranean grace. Alex shook hands with Cavil, his wolfish smile in place. "Ambassador, Martha—thank you so much for the invitation."

He looked at the preparations, which signaled a relaxed home meal. "After our wild swim the other night, this feels like a much more civilized sequel."

Anisa nodded. "Indeed," she agreed. "Although I suspect the conversation will be just as spirited." Her sharp eyes met Kaisa's with a silent greeting.

The group settled around a long, weathered table on the veranda, its blue-white paint fashionably worn. The barbecue's sizzle provided a homely backdrop, while the staff—discreet holdovers from Cavil's diplomatic life—started to serve.

Martha had arranged a nice selection of chilled white wine and appetizers: oysters on the half-shell, marinated octopus, and grilled prawns with lemon aioli. The sun dipped low, casting its hue over the sea.

As the grilled fish arrived—bass flaky with herbs; swordfish seared to a nice perfection, not too dry; and halibut stuffed with garlic and lemon—the talk turned to international affairs, prompted by Cavil's casual remark.

"With the election heating up, Caleb, what's your take on the Middle East? Oil prices are volatile again—Russia's embroiled in Ukraine, China's economy has lost its way, Israel is a challenge that activists can't seem to let alone. There's no sign of peace."

Caleb leaned forward, senator-mode engaged. "It's a powder keg. Sanctions on Russia aren't biting hard enough; they're rerouting exports through proxies, whether in the Gulf region or Asia. We need to build alliances—but in a fashion that makes sense for everyone including us." Cavil nodded—neutral in a way that diplomats had perfected over centuries of international exchange.

"We can't always subsidize NATO," Caleb continued. "At some point, Europe has to take responsibility for its own security—as adults. On the other hand, we shouldn't reject out of hand the chance to get better results by aligning with parties in the Middle East, for example some big pacts with the Saudis—bolster their status, bring them more into the international fold."

Caleb sipped his wine, before adding some more thoughts. "Alliances are fragile, Ambassador, and credibility is all we've got at the end of the day. Take Baku—Anisa's old stomping grounds. Azerbaijan's pipelines are key to bypassing Russia. The BTC oil pipeline and the Southern Gas Corridor were explicitly built to give Europe access to non-Russian hydrocarbons. Yet, with Armenia tensions and Turkish influence, it's still a chess game. One wrong move, and Europe freezes."

Cavil nodded, impressed. "Spot on. I was briefly in Ankara when Nagorno-Karabakh flared up—calculated brinkmanship at its finest. I recall visiting Georgia at the time, hearing the missiles as if they were from the next valley."

He paused and turned to Alex. "You've got oil roots. What's the play for independents here—such as PanEnergy in the U.S.? I see Jake Laskin's been vocal about renewables while also pushing Arctic drilling among other traditional projects. How can we manage geopolitical concerns on the one hand and environmental pressures on the other?"

Alex gently leaned forward, his tone measured but authoritative, seeking to measure up to Cavil's global expertise.

"The Arctic's a gamble—melting ice opens routes, tightening laws close them. PanEnergy's hedging with renewables, but the real game might be elsewhere. In Africa, Congo has most of the world's readily accessible cobalt for EVs. In Asia, China has most of its rare earths. Neither resource is locked in. I feel the U.S. was perhaps a decade late to fully realize the strategic implications."

He paused before making a final point. "Government attitudes here will have a serious impact on how the future is put together. Talk about sanctions is growing, and new approaches could unsettle everything. The story is always about leverage—the question is who has it and how it will be used. The rest, even though the media might obsess over it, is just noise."

Anisa interjected smoothly, but her voice sounded unusually tense. "Don't forget the human cost. In Baku, missions like the one where I was often deal with refugees from 'quiet deals' or 'turned eyes'—people who are displaced by projects, pipelines, or politics. Africa may be the next frontier, but without ethics, it's yet another cycle of exploitation."

Alex reached out and briefly held Anisa's hand. "Ultimately we need to see that equity is served and justice is realized. Nothing stands the test of time if done purely out of greed and self-interest."

Martha smiled, keen to steer the conversation toward smoother waters. "Anisa's right. We saw it in Delhi—corporate gains fueling inequality, accidents causing mayhem. But Alex, your telecom ventures—there are rumors that you're eyeing satellite networks for remote regions. Will it change the situation for global connectivity? Are you taking on Elon Musk?"

Alex's smile sharpened. "Satellites democratize data, but they're weapons too—facilitating espionage, exposing cyber vulnerabilities. Russia's jamming signals in Ukraine; China's building a proprietary constellation. The U.S. must counter with its own efforts—its own ventures. I applaud Elon's push. Whatever people say, he is doing what needs to be done."

Cavil chuckled. "You sound as if you could manage the State Department."

He turned to Caleb again. "What's your take on the Pacific? Taiwan tensions rising—Belt and Road encircling allies. China setting itself up in strategic posts such as Papua New Guinea, the Solomon Islands, and even in Darwin at the top of Australia."

Caleb loved the attention the Ambassador was giving him, asking his views. Indeed Caleb had high aspirations for his role on the Senate Foreign Relations Committee, given his party did not adhere strictly to committee seniority.

"The Pacific's a flashpoint," Caleb now said. "The U.S. should benefit from the AUKUS expansion—maybe include others. But it can't be just a PR exercise for America's partners. Countries such as Australia must participate sincerely and wholeheartedly, otherwise they will end up like Europe—doubted and dismissed, rated as unreliable or, worse, quixotic." Again Cavil nodded

"But economically," Cavil asked, "how does one decouple from China without crashing markets—without sending the world into stagflation?"

"Indeed," interjected Martha, getting a little bored of the conversation—the kind she'd heard for forty years or so. "It seems that business has answered that by going all in with AI."

Kaisa, recognizing Martha's intent, followed her lead. "Anisa, do you like art? I read there are some great exhibitions now showing in New York. Here, let me see." She fished out her cell phone from the clutch purse. "I haven't yet got to them, but I intend to."

Her ring caught the light as she scrolled through the phone. Alex's eyes flickered, a shadow crossing his face, or did Kaisa just imagine it? "Here." Kaisa leaned across to show Anisa the list of exhibitions.

Alex's gaze followed the ring, but it was Anisa who responded. "How lovely!" she cried, spotting the band. "You know, I think this is Russian—maybe even Imperial, pre-Revolution."

That caught Kaisa by surprise. And Alex. "Let me take a look. Do you mind?" Anisa asked.

"Not at all," she replied taking off the ring.

Anisa turned it around carefully. "It truly is beautiful—simple but lovely. I only hope the man who finally proposes to me offers such a fine declaration of his love."

Kaisa smiled, saying nothing. Her hand went up to rub the base of her throat as she looked at Alex. Anisa smiled and handed it back. "Actually, I could end up more attached to a ring like this than the man who gave it to me," she joked.

"How could it be otherwise?" Martha chuckled.

Anisa laughed too. "As I keep saying, love is for romantics." She watched while Kaisa slipped the token back on.

Alex's gaze lingered on the ring and then on Kaisa herself. Was it a twinge of recognition—a hint of sadness? Or was her paranoia just playing tricks? Kaisa couldn't tell. She felt briefly cross. *Plans couldn't work if you weren't able to read the signs.*

It was Cavil who now shifted topics, praising the fish. "Perfectly grilled," he noted.

"But you did it yourself," Martha replied. "You can't praise your own work." Everyone laughed again, although Kaisa's mind remained elsewhere. A sea breeze picked up, carrying the faint scent of char and sugar.

Dessert arrived—grilled peaches with honey and burrata. Martha apologized slightly. "I know burrata is everywhere these days. You can hardly eat at a restaurant without being served this decadent progeny of the mozzarella. It's like truffles in Italian restaurants—everywhere, servers constantly trying to upgrade your order. However, I so adore this dish—I couldn't help making it."

Kaisa returned her attention to the table. "The dessert looks amazing. What a great combination."

"Yes," said Anisa. "The dish looks familiar, the original is well-known." She tasted a mouthful. "But then somehow the sweet is transformed. It becomes something new and marvelous—demanding our attention."

"You are so right," Martha enthused. "We are forced to consider what we are tasting, decide if the transformation is truly better or not."

Kaisa had a spoonful as well. "Yes," she said. "It's a good question. Are transformations good or bad? Do we approve—or do we resist and stick forever with the original?"

The evening ended, at Alex's suggestion, with a few toasts, but Kaisa had little to cheer. The ring seemed to have worked. She saw that Alex had reacted. But was it a crack—a hairline fault threatening to break his façade? Or was she no more than creating situations into which she could read anything?

Picking up her cell phone, she saw the exhibition list there from her chat with Anisa. Almost unconsciously she suggested, "Let's go see the Frick." She looked up at everyone. "I saw the renovation got lots of praise. I'll fix a date that works for us all, perhaps later in November—when we've settled down after the election."

This, she hoped, would flush out Alex's true identity. She wouldn't need to use her trump card. It might well work but it would put everything at risk—all she had worked so hard to achieve, including her happiness.

50. Pipeline Research

The highway shimmered under the noon heat when Jake finally got a signal. He called Eve. "Hey," he said. "Just checking in. I'll be off-grid most of the weekend. Meeting the elders, making sure the pipeline goes ahead—maybe a sweat lodge, maybe a hunt."

There was a pause—the faint hum of the kitchen in the background, a bark or two from the dogs who somehow guessed the caller. "That sounds good for you," Eve said softly. "Grounding."

Jake smiled at the windshield. "Diplomatic, mostly. Everyone likes a show of respect."

"You always did sweat for politics." Eve's tone was light but tired, the kind that came from too many polite goodbyes. "Will you call after?" she asked.

"If the reception holds."

Static took over, and then the line dropped. Jake left the phone face-down on the console.

The late afternoon sun cast long shadows across Thunder Creek Reservation when Jake finally stepped out of the SUV. He took a moment to adjust to the stark beauty of the landscape—rolling hills, the distant glint of the river. A landscape that demanded respect. Jake understood the gravity of his visit.

The driver, Meredith Black, PanEnergy's Head of Indigenous Affairs, jumped out after him. "Chief Ben Stonefeather and the council will be ready for us," she said, gesturing toward a building up the slope, a modern interpretation of Frank Lloyd Wright—something that seemed to reflect the nature and spirit of its location.

Jake nodded, adjusting his windbreaker as they neared the stylish building. They were met at the entrance by an elder who shook hands and led them inside. "All materials from the area," he commented as they walked through the foyer.

As Jake entered the corner room, he noted the magnificent views down the valley but kept his focus on Chief Ben Stonefeather, instantly distinctive in his turquoise necklace.

With him were several tribal council members and two academic experts—they had taken part in the initial cultural survey on behalf of PanEnergy. Expressions around the room varied, from reserved to cautious, and Jake knew this was no simple courtesy call.

"Mr. Laskin, Ms. Black," Chief Ben Stonefeather said, his voice steady but guarded as he extended his hand, exposing his silver bracelet. "Welcome back to Thunder Creek."

"Thank you, Chief," Jake replied, matching his firm handshake. "I really do appreciate the opportunity to meet again. This project is important to all of us." He meant it—in the way men have faith when they still believe in control.

The group sat around a table covered with maps, documents, and a few ceremonial items that seemed placed as reminders of the land's significance. After brief introductions, Meredith began.

"As you know, Chief, PanEnergy conducted an extensive survey of cultural and environmental issues a few years ago, in the pre-feasibility stage. We worked closely with your council. Our expert team, including Dr. Simmons and Dr. Alvarez, sought to map out a pipeline route that avoided areas of cultural or spiritual importance." She looked at the Chief.

"We wanted to confirm with you today that there have been no discoveries or new concerns raised since that time."

Dr. Simmons, a cultural anthropologist, added, "The research was thorough. We consulted tribal elders, reviewed historical records, and conducted multiple field studies. The findings indicated no sites of obvious significant cultural or spiritual importance along the proposed route."

Stonefeather listened, his expression unreadable. After a pause, he leaned forward. "I won't dispute the findings of your survey or the process you've followed, but you should know this: not everyone agrees with the council's position. There are agitators in our community, some who've got outside backing, who see this as an opportunity to stir dissent."

Jake tilted his head slightly. "We assumed opposition might arise," he said carefully. "We're committed to addressing any concerns with transparency and respect, as we've done here."

Stonefeather's sharp gaze met Jake's. "Transparency and respect are a start, but they're not always enough to keep the peace. Our community needs tangible benefits we can list—continued investment in our schools, healthcare, and infrastructure."

"What we've negotiated so far," he continued, "has been meaningful, but if you want to ensure that dissent doesn't gain momentum, the commitment needs to be clear and sustained; one that constantly emphasizes the benefits."

Grace Talltree, one of the senior council members, cut in. "The pipeline project could be transformative for our community if handled right. But without ongoing support, it's easy for outside voices to exploit dissatisfaction. We've seen it before."

Jake exchanged a glance with Meredith. "Chief," she said, "the agreement we've negotiated includes annual reviews and additional funding tied to certain milestones. PanEnergy is open to discussing enhancements to that framework, provided that the terms are mutually beneficial."

Stonefeather nodded slowly but did not relax his posture. "It's not just about money. It's about ensuring our voice is heard and respected at every stage of the process."

"If you want to set a precedent for future cooperation, you'll need to show this isn't just another corporate promise. We've seen how well big companies honor their promises to the national government. How much, then, do you think we trust similar vows to a mere reservation?"

Jake responded, his tone measured but firm. "I hear you, Chief. PanEnergy isn't looking to walk away from our commitments after the pipeline is built.

We want to create a longer-term partnership beneficial to both sides. If that means revisiting the deal to address new worries or strengthen our pledges, we're willing to do so." Jake paused.

"We have, as you know, created an advisory committee for the pipeline company—on which various members from the reservation sit, including your son."

Dr. Alvarez, one of the academic experts, spoke up. "If PanEnergy meets its promises and the project works, the agreement could indeed set a precedent for future ventures. Collaboration with Indigenous communities is rare, but it doesn't have to be."

Stonefeather finally allowed a faint smile, even though his voice remained cautious. "We'll hold you to your word, Mr. Laskin. The council is largely supportive of this project, but only so long as that support brings real benefits and respects our sovereignty. Keep that in mind."

"I understand, Chief." Jake nodded. "We'll do our bit to make this partnership work."

One of the council members, who had been silent until now, spoke. "A purification lodge has been prepared for tomorrow night." He looked at Jake, then across to Meredith. "You may enter separately—or together if you'd like."

Jake looked out the window and down the valley. He hesitated a moment. "Together," he said at last, looking at Meredith. A small silence followed. The councilman nodded, "together it is."

As Jake walked back to the SUV, the rich light of the setting sun deepened the shadows around him. He glanced over at Meredith. "That wasn't exactly a thumping endorsement," he said.

Meredith shrugged. "It was a realistic one. The elders are largely onboard, but as the Chief said, outside voices can stir trouble. We'll need to keep a close eye on things."

"What I can't believe," Jake said, looking back at the building where the council members were still gathered, "is that they'd jeopardize a project creating more than forty thousand jobs at its peak. As if they didn't want the opportunity..."

He shook his head. "Anyway, if we manage this right," he said after a pause, "it could be more than just a project. We need an effective model for how we do similar business in future." Maybe he was chasing a pipe dream. More often than not partnerships started with good hopes and ended in forensic audits.

Meredith gave him a small nod, as if reading his silent concerns. "Let's just hope the future doesn't hold any surprises." Jake didn't respond; yet as they drove away, he couldn't shake the feeling that surprises were inevitable.

The SUV hummed quietly, winding its way out of Thunder Creek along the dusty roads. Jake leaned back in his seat, staring out the window at the sprawling plains, his expression pensive. Beside him, Meredith had her hand on the wheel, her elbow on the window ledge.

Jake broke the silence. "Meredith, I need us to get ahead of this. If there's one thing I've learned in business, it's that the battle isn't just in the boardroom or even in the courtroom. It's in the narrative. I want you to dig into this opposition. Specifically, the people behind that report Sylvia dropped in my office."

Meredith turned to him for a second, her expression sharpening. "You think it's worth pursuing? It might just be noise, a desperate ploy to stall us."

"Maybe," Jake replied, his tone measured. "But there was something about the way she presented it. Sylvia's too smart to throw a weak punch. I want to know who's feeding her the information and why."

Meredith nodded. "We know Sylvia is the public face of Clear Horizons—a well-funded environmental advocacy organization. The report she handed you had multiple authors, including GSx. I'll investigate some of the others: their credentials, past work, affiliations."

"Good," Jake said. "And don't stop there. I want to know how the report was put together. How any consultation was done. Were their methods thorough and scientifically sound, or was it simply an exercise designed to sow doubt?"

Meredith nodded again. "That'll give us insight into their strategy. If the report has holes, we can dismantle it. If it's solid, we'll know where we need to counter."

Jake turned to her, his expression serious. "And don't shy away from using legal channels. If they've filed this with regulators, we have every right to pursue discovery. I want access to their communications—their emails, drafts, anything that shows how this came together."

"That might raise eyebrows," Meredith said cautiously. "But we can frame it as part of our due diligence. It's our responsibility to verify claims that could halt a ten-billion-dollar project."

"Exactly," Jake replied. "If their assertions hold up, fine—we'll deal with them head-on. But if they're simply raising possibilities without concrete evidence, we need to expose that. This isn't just about a pipeline, Meredith. It's about setting the tone for every project we, or others, pursue in the future."

Meredith nodded, her mind already working on the logistics. "Understood. I'll start with the report itself and trace it back to the source. If we need court orders for anything, I'll loop in legal."

"Good," Jake said, glancing out the window as the reservation faded into the distance. "This project is too important to let an argument derail progress, especially if it turns out not to have merit. Let's make sure we're prepared for anything they throw at us."

Meredith's voice was calm but resolute. "We'll get to the bottom of it, Jake. One way or another, we'll know exactly what we're up against."

Jake looked at the horizon as the SUV sped down the highway. The sun had just about set, casting a final deep-red glow. Their hotel was famous for its home-made s'mores. Jake looked forward to enjoying a few in the outdoor courtyard, drinking some wine, relaxing with Meredith around the big fire that the hotel lit there each evening.

He could take his mind off the battles ahead for a couple of hours. No one was able to stop him getting what he wanted—not these days.

51. Early Morning

A few weeks had passed since that exhilarating trip to Storm King, and Eve's days had taken on a different hue. Her encounters with David had brightened her mornings, each little conversation stirring something in her—a renewed zest to be in the world.

On this Saturday morning, the sunlight poured in through the tall windows of her apartment, filling it with warmth and beckoning her to embrace the day. She poured a mug of coffee, savoring again the ritual. David's familiar knock broke the silence.

She opened the door, mug still in hand, and there he stood, casually dressed in a fitted flannel shirt and rugged jeans, a now familiar hint of adventure in his eyes. The dogs surged forward, tails wagging, claws scrabbling against the floor as they sought grip.

"Good morning, Eve!" he greeted with infectious enthusiasm. "Ready for another day of the dog show?"

"Always!" she smiled, trying to ignore the quick lift in her chest, unexpected but impossible to deny. "Jake is away again for the weekend, making sure his treasured pipeline does not get ensnared in tribal politics." David nodded in sympathy.

He glanced at Eve's coffee. "You know, I was listening to another podcast. Some kind of TED talk. They contrasted Vienna, where revolutions began over coffee, with Moscow," he continued, "where they were let go for cafés." He caught Eve's smirk. "Yes. I thought it was rather cute too."

He paused. "It got me thinking—it could be like a window into people, their desire for comfort or revolution. For example, your coffee," he asked, "what does it represent?"

Eve considered the question. "Habit, I suppose—and some days, survival."

"Yes. So why not wake up differently? That's what I try to do, if not always successfully. I want to have a constant sense of revolution. I want each day...

to bring something new." He paused. "Of course, it doesn't..." And, for a second, he lost his smile.

"Whose revolution do you propose?" Eve replied. "Freud, Klimt, Trotsky, Wittgenstein? I remember seeing once that all were in Vienna around the same time."

"Which kind of revolutionary is most appealing to you?" David asked.

"Klimt," Eve said without hesitation. "He painted hunger and desire without shame."

"That's a lovely choice," David agreed.

"Yes," Eve affirmed. "Freud would have made coffee a symptom, and Trotsky, a program."

She smiled. "I guess you would have liked Wittgenstein. He would've dismantled the original question." David laughed.

Eve thought back to her first dinner with David—their discussion of *Goblin Market.* She always preferred Laura in Rossetti's poem—the sister who embraced life until her lips were sore. Something in the idea of revolution—and David's voice perhaps—now stirred up old feelings.

For a moment, neither spoke while the sudden hiss of the espresso machine cleaning itself filled the space like a breathing animal. At last Eve spoke up. "What's on the agenda for you today?"

"Not much today. But tomorrow... Tomorrow, I'm heading out to tackle the Bull Hill Loop," he said, his face lighting up with excitement. "I've got big plans for breakfast at the first summit!"

Eve raised an eyebrow, half smiling. "Breakfast at the summit?"

"And," he continued, "If I can manage it, I'll also take on Breakneck Ridge afterward."

"How will you do breakfast?"

He grinned widely, his passion surfacing. "I'll take some heating equipment, brew myself a fresh Italian coffee. I have this lovely small Bialetti moka pot. Then I'll make myself a breakfast burger."

"Which is?"

"Sour-dough bun, eggs, bacon, avocado, the whole works. Sometimes I mix it up, swap the avocado for some beetroot. There's nothing quite like eating a hearty meal while gazing out at the dawn rising over the valley."

"I remember having an egg-and-bacon roll once. I bit into it—and the egg burst, going everywhere. So funny!" Eve dwelled a second on the memory. Then her mind moved onto more practical challenges. "How do you even start walking in the dark?"

David leaned casually on the doorframe. "I use headlamps. It's a different world out there before dawn. Everything feels so alive yet still, like nature is holding its breath. The shadows shift and mutate, and as the darkness starts to give way to light, there's this magical moment when everything grays and then, all at once, blooms into color." Eve pictured the sunrise lighting up the landscape, releasing a spectacular view from the peak.

"You see the outlines of the mountains and the trees," David explained, "and then suddenly, the sun leaps over the horizon, and the whole world appears in detail, which seems all the more saturated for being revealed the first time that day."

Eve found herself captivated. The Storm King expedition had awakened her to the possibilities that she'd been missing—all the beauty that was out there, beyond the city. Still she hesitated.

"Maybe I'll just stick to my coffee and the gym," she said, her voice trailing off, feeling the tug of her comfortable routine. How her world had closed in around her within the space of a decade!

"Or you could join me." David urged gently, his eyes bright with enthusiasm. "It'd be another adventure! One time I reached the second summit just after dawn—turned the corner and found a choir singing; their voices just cascaded across the mountain tops. It was magical!"

The prospect he painted—demanding a simple leap of faith—lingered in the air. "I suppose it would be fun," Eve mused, "just once to witness the world waking up, all while enjoying a delicious breakfast al fresco." She lifted her cup, the steam veiling her face.

"And in honor of *Goblin Market*—temptation dressed as fruit—I'll bring some cherries for the hike. Not temptation though, just snacks with literary pedigree." He paused, amused by Eve's half smile.

"Cherries?" she replied. "Aren't they out of season?"

"Yes. But I'll find some good ones if I can."

"I think you'd better, since they are meant to be *sweet to tongue and sound to eye.*"

Eve found David's call for spontaneity hard to ignore. As Robin Williams famously put it: *carpe diem.* She'd been a devoted admirer of Peter Weir and his films long before he vanished to Palm Beach. Life, travel—these weren't things you just read about in books. They weren't dreams. They were experiences you shaped, realities you brought into being.

"All right, you've convinced me," she said, surprising herself with the suddenness of her decision. "Yes, please—I'd love to join!"

David's expression lit up, his joy palpable. "Great! I'll come at 4 a.m., pick you up. And don't worry; I'll bring an extra headlamp."

"4 a.m.? Is it really necessary to start that early?" Eve laughed, a mixture of disbelief and excitement bubbling within her.

"Trust me, it'll be worth it," he assured her, his smile infectious. "The early morning works a miracle all its own."

"Okay, then," she said, feeling a sudden rush of anticipation. "I'll see you before dawn."

"Looking forward to it!" he replied, flashing her one last grin before waving goodbye and heading out to walk the dogs. They swarmed the corridor, eager to bolt before being leashed—more mischievous now, having learned David's weak spots.

As the door closed behind him, Eve leaned against it, her pulse alive with a beat she hadn't felt in years. This new expedition would give her a chance to reclaim the dawn as something hopeful. It felt like a turn she should have made long ago—one she'd kept postponing. What had she been avoiding—was it fear or the truth?

With a newfound determination, she brewed another coffee, watching the steam billowing up. She pictured the sunrise over Bull Hill, mountains all around—the sense of freedom and adventure. For the second time in a long while, a hint of possibility—a feeling of renewal—engulfed her. Eve couldn't wait. The world was opening again.

52. Court Decision

The courtroom filled to capacity, the high stakes of the decision drawing journalists, activists, and industry insiders alike. Jake Laskin, CEO of PanEnergy, sat with his team, a portrait of confidence forged by years of high-stakes negotiations and courtroom battles.

Across the aisle, Dr. Sylvia Reed sat quietly, her demeanor calm but her fingers unconsciously gripping the table's edge.

Judge Amy Herrera took her seat, the gavel's sharp crack silencing the room. "In the matter of *Clear Horizons v. PanEnergy*," she began, "this court has reviewed the evidence, testimony, and legal arguments presented during the course of this trial."

Her gaze swept the room—deliberate and unblinking. "The plaintiffs have argued that the proposed pipeline would traverse land sacred to people on the Thunder Creek Reservation, causing irreparable cultural and spiritual harm. At the heart of their case are the figures of Tohska, the Life Bearer, and Niyówa, the Earth Watcher—central to local creation stories and tied intrinsically to the land in question." She paused.

"The plaintiffs contend that disrupting this land would sever an essential connection between the community and their cultural heritage."

Jake glanced at his lead counsel, who gave a small, almost imperceptible nod.

"The plaintiffs further argue," the judge continued, "that recognizing Indigenous claims to sacred land is not just a moral imperative but a legal one." She looked up.

"They have called upon this court to acknowledge that cultural heritage cannot be subordinated to profit or convenience without significant harm to a community's identity and rights."

Sylvia lifted her head slightly, the weight of the argument filling the room.

"However," Judge Herrera said, her tone sharpening, "the court has also considered the arguments and evidence presented by the defense. PanEnergy asserts that the pipeline project has undergone rigorous environmental and regulatory review and complies with all relevant laws."

"Moreover, the defense has highlighted the community benefits of the project, including the creation of thousands of jobs and the potential to strengthen energy independence—a matter of national interest as defined under the Mineral Leasing Act."

She paused, her expression neutral but her words cutting. "The defense also raised serious concerns regarding the plaintiffs' evidence. Testimony from the plaintiffs relied heavily on a single expert. His methodology and findings have been credibly challenged." Those listening shuffled slightly.

"Furthermore, the cultural mapping exercise cited by the plaintiffs showed insufficient consultation with the broader community around the Reservation. These deficiencies significantly undermine the weight of the claims."

Sylvia's heart sank as the judge continued.

"This court must also weigh the timing of this lawsuit," Herrera said. "Filed mere days before construction was set to commence, it appears designed to obstruct rather than to protect." The Judge stopped to emphasize her final words.

"While the court deeply respects the need to preserve Indigenous culture and heritage, the claims in this case lack the substantiation required to justify halting a project of this magnitude."

Sylvia stared at her attorney, who whispered, "We'll appeal. Don't worry. And we have other, more administrative, channels—less exposed to public politics."

"In light of these findings," the judge concluded, "this court rules in favor of the defendant, PanEnergy. The plaintiffs are ordered to cover the full legal expenses incurred by the defense plus other costs and interest. The total is set at $9,042,093.05."

The gavel's strike echoed like a final blow. Sylvia felt its sound like a train-wreck inside her chest.

As the room emptied, Jake approached Sylvia, who didn't attempt to get up. He stopped a respectful distance away. The echo of the gavel still pulsed in the air between them. "It didn't have to end this way," he said quietly.

Sylvia met his gaze, defiance edged with regret. "The fight for what's right is never easy."

"True," Jake replied, his voice suddenly quiet, "but it must be fought with integrity."

"We'll see who's right on appeal, Jake. Our truth will be recognized."

Jake smiled wanly, turned and walked away, his team falling in behind him. Sylvia remained seated, the courtroom emptying around her. Her gaze fell to the manila folder–its contents those she'd handed Jake in his office. This battle had been lost, but she knew the war was far from over. The land and its stories were worth it.

53. Kismet Bar

Jake was back at the office when his phone vibrated on the table, startling him. Sometimes the silence around him was too profound. The message on the phone was blunt and cryptic in a way insiders communicated when the stakes were high and the risks even higher. *Meet me at Kismet Bar. 9 p.m. This may be what you suspected.*

Jake had been chasing shadows for weeks, fixated on the group called GSx Consulting. He'd pieced together an incomplete but troubling picture. If Grant was being this cautious, it meant new information. Possibly a weapon to use against GSx. Jake was never one to turn down an advantage.

***

At 9 p.m. sharp, Jake stepped out of a black sedan into a side street off the East Side, where the Kismet Bar was located. A soft drizzle had begun, turning the neon reflections on the pavement into liquid ribbons of color. The establishment wore a veneer of old-world grandeur: stained-glass windows, crimson drapes, and heavy wooden doors—all of which seemed increasingly out of place among the city's modern high-rises and latest exclusive developments.

Dim light, low voices, the soft clink of glass—it had an ambiance of secrets. A waiter in a starched white apron guided Jake down a narrow hallway to a private alcove, separated from the main dining area by an ornate partition. A faulty light illuminated a booth where a lone figure waited: Grant.

"Jake!" he welcomed, but keeping his voice just above a whisper.

Jake nodded, slipping into the seat opposite him. He did a quick scan of the area: no obvious security cameras, just fire alarms and a couple of motion sensors flashing a brief red light when picking up movement. Budget sensors.

"You have new intel on GSx," Jake said, leaning forward—a statement rather than a question. "Let's hear it."

Grant looked like a man stitched together by sleepless nights—Jake knew the feeling. "I've been tracking them for a while," Grant began, his voice steady but frayed.

"They're not all-powerful, but they have reach—especially now that they've expanded to the U.S. They come from old networks in the former Soviet states, where lines are blurred, and business has—almost literally—a razor's edge. Over there, as you know, alliances form and crumble quickly. GSx thrives in that environment. Here, they seem to have latched onto energy as a bridgehead."

Jake's brow furrowed. "So it's about oil and gas, or something bigger?"

"It doesn't appear so simple," Grant replied. "They seem to dig their hooks into any target: energy deals, green lobbying, policy negotiations—anything that can move markets. Then, once they've carved out their share, they walk away and leave the carcasses swinging in the air."

Jake let out a slow breath, recalling the uneasy rumors he'd picked up—that GSx was poking around American energy firms, forging odd alliances to either promote or bog down projects. "So they are playing the field across multiple fronts," he said, half to himself.

Grant cleared his throat and went on. "They've potent networks that reach into all the right circles—the corporate world, the political arena, the nonprofit sphere. They've access to the administrative bubble in D.C." He paused. "They can orchestrate grassroots protests, regulatory hurdles, or political fever almost on demand. They're chameleons."

Grant lowered his voice until Jake strained to hear. "They're experts at sowing confusion. They like to keep everyone off-balance—fighting each other. They create an environment of uncertainty and suspicion, where everybody is second-guessing."

"In part because they don't seem unstoppable, people underestimate them—but that's their trick. They move in, capitalize on a specific project or crisis, and then vanish before anyone knows who really pulled the strings. Rumor says they're zeroing in on bigger fish here." Grant stopped a moment before coming to the crux of the matter.

"Right now, your name is floating around in those circles. I can't tell if you're a target to be knocked down or recruited. But either way, they're interested."

An unsteady tension clenched in Jake's gut. The idea of being recruited by a rogue consulting firm with ties to the former Soviet Union and the ability to shape U.S. markets was absurd. Yet also—somehow—frighteningly believable. "Who's behind GSx? Is there a single figure calling the shots?"

Grant's gaze flicked toward the shadows behind Jake, as though checking for eavesdroppers. "No one's certain. Some say it's a cadre of ex-officials with deep pockets, others claim it's a private syndicate that lobbies from behind a tangle of shell companies. Some even link it to the President. But they all come from that hazy world where business, politics, and organized crime can nudge up against one another."

He paused. "Did you ever read that book, *Young Stalin*, by Simon Sebag Montefiore?" He looked at Jake, who shook his head.

"Anyway, they now see opportunities here."

Jake tapped a finger on the table, thinking of the myriad deals PanEnergy had in play—from domestic drilling rights to global import agreements. If GSx was messing around in that space, it could sabotage everything he had built. "Any particular leads I should follow?"

Grant shrugged. "Not without stepping on landmines. If you ask me, you'll need more specialized intelligence, someone who can navigate those old Soviet corridors. Maybe someone you know from your days in Moscow. I recall you had certain connections that you liked using."

"In any case, GSx didn't just materialize out of thin air; they've been refining their tactics for decades, and they're adept at hiding their tracks."

Jake nodded. He pulled out a thick envelope and slid it over the table. "This is yours." Grant flipped the envelope open, though he knew what was inside:

cash—enough to prove Jake took the tip seriously, but not so much as to look desperate.

"Before I go, anything else you can tell me?"

A glimmer of thanks passed across Grant's face as he pocketed the cash. "Just... watch your flank. I wouldn't underestimate them." Then he stood, gave Jake a stiff nod, and disappeared into the gloom.

...

Jake stepped outside onto the sidewalk. City lights refracted off the puddles underfoot, and a cold wind rustled the edges of his coat. He made his way back to the car. Leaning against the rear door, he took a moment to let the conversation sink in.

GSx was no unstoppable juggernaut, but they had a cunning approach, it seemed, that could destabilize entire markets if wielded effectively. He thought of the endless calls that PanEnergy had fielded from "concerned citizens," the new nonprofits that had contested his drilling projects or pipeline expansions. Now it all could fit a larger pattern.

He climbed in the back seat and asked the driver to head for PanEnergy's headquarters. Through the window, Manhattan's lights bled into each other as the car navigated its way through the remnants of the day's traffic. Jake's mind raced, piece by piece assembling a jigsaw that looked more ominous with each new revelation.

If GSx wasn't after PanEnergy alone, then the threat could extend to the energy sector as a whole—even beyond that if they forged the right alliances with activists or policy makers.

...

Back at his high-rise headquarters, Jake strode to his desk. He sank into the leather chair and unlocked his computer. Various windows opened on his screen, showing competitor reviews, legal updates, risk analyses. He pulled out one of the burner phones he kept in his drawer.

"I've got a location in the Hamptons," he wrote, tapping the keys with a typical economy. "Need some thorough reconnaissance—quietly. I have reason to believe an out-of-town operator with ties to the former Soviet Union is connected to GSx. I want to know what's there, who's involved, whether it links back to me."

He read the text once more before hitting send, aware that any digital footprint he created might be monitored. Yet time was critical. GSx's expansion into American markets was only a year or two old, but if they'd managed to nestle themselves within the domestic establishment, they already had a strong position. PanEnergy could be a hit, and Jake Laskin wouldn't sit idly by and let that happen.

He leaned back, exhaling slowly. Seeing his reflection on the computer, he thought of a general planning his war. He was engaged in a high-stakes battle—a game that straddled the line between commerce and espionage. The legality might be questionable, but the tactics GSx employed were not typical. They came from a place where the rules were different, where alliances shifted overnight, and everything had a price. A world, in fact, Jake knew well and had learned to manage.

He glanced at his watch. The hour was late, but he felt more energized than earlier. This was no time to rest. He needed to marshal his resources, gather intelligence, and prepare for a confrontation that might upend more than just PanEnergy's bottom line.

In his mind, he pictured the next day's board meeting—half of them blissfully unaware of the storm brewing, the other half already suspecting something was off. He'd have to walk a tightrope: keep them calm, keep the share price stable, and quietly fortify the company's defenses.

He stood up again and walked to the window to stare out at the luminous sprawl below. He let the tension settle in his shoulders, a familiar weight. GSx might not be unstoppable, but they were dangerous enough to spark upheaval if left unchecked.

Well, let them come. He was no stranger to dealing with rivals or Russians. Jake was willing to hit back from an unsuspected angle and twice as hard when cornered. He'd taken down bigger adversaries before through a mix of grit, strategy, and guile—whatever victory demanded.

Pushing aside the swirl of thoughts, he picked up his phone again. There were more calls to make.

Let GSx slink in the shadows for now. He would shine a glaring spotlight on them, and he had every intention of rooting them out before their actions turned into a stranglehold on his—or America's—energy future. Some wars, he realized, began not with declarations but with meetings in bars.

The scent of beeswax candles mingled with the heady aroma of incense, spiraling upward as though bearing prayers to the divine. The modest Russian Orthodox church rose around the congregation, its dome painted with heavenly visions, its walls lined with the steadfast gaze of saints.

The parishioners, a diverse mix of life stages and dispositions, stood in reverence as was their custom—eyes fixed forward, hearts turned inward.

The trisagion began, the choir's voices intertwining like golden threads in a celestial tapestry. "Holy God, Holy Mighty, Holy Immortal, have mercy on us," they chanted in solemn harmony.

The congregation responded, bowing their heads and making the sign of the cross, their murmurs forming a soft undercurrent. The air seemed to expand, to thicken with sanctity. The church itself seemed alive at that moment with the Spirit.

After the trisagion, Deacon Pavel approached the ambo with deliberate steps, bearing the Gospel book as if it were a jewel on a cushion. He intoned the familiar words, "Wisdom! Let us be attentive!" The faithful stood even straighter, their focus sharpening. Father Alex, resplendent in vestments of emerald and gold, took the book and began the Gospel reading. His baritone voice, rich and deliberate, filled the space with the passage from Matthew: "Blessed are the peacemakers, for they shall be called children of God."

The words landed with the weight of ancient authority, and all listened as he read of Christ's teachings on humility, forgiveness, and love in the face of cruelty. The text, though timeless, seemed startlingly modern in its relevance.

With the reading concluded, Father Alex kissed the Gospel book reverently and handed it back to the deacon. Then he turned to face the congregation, his hands spread wide in a gesture that encompassed them all. His eyes, dark and piercing, interrogated the room as if searching out every shadow of sin and suffering.

Once more he saw Kaisa in the congregation. She had been present now most Sundays, usually leaving before the service ended. He paused this time, uncertain whether to go on. His topic today might reveal too much to her—about him, about what had happened. He took a breath and pressed on. He knew Kaisa couldn't begin to imagine the world that lay behind his words.

"Brothers and sisters," he began, his voice now carrying an edge that demanded attention, "we live in a world fraught with cruelty. It may whisper in the schoolyard or shout in the marketplace; it may hide behind indifference or strike with violence. But know this: cruelty, in all its forms, is a sin against God and against our shared humanity."

A murmur rippled across the congregation, not of dissent but of recognition. The priest's words cut some to the quick—for who had not suffered or seen suffering inflicted by another?

"Our Lord," he continued, "teaches us to be peacemakers. But he does not call us to passivity in the face of injustice, but to active love. To confront cruelty with courage. To bear one another's burdens. To speak the truth with love if possible, with sincerity when love cannot yet take root."

He raised his voice. "As it is written: *The Lord detests the proud of heart. Know this: they will not go unpunished.*"

His gaze fell upon Kaisa, who met his look with steady, unblinking attention. He turned to the children near the front pews. Some showed a mixture of curiosity and trepidation about their surroundings, others had their wide eyes fixed intently on him. A few were fidgeting or had zoned out completely.

"And you, little ones," he said, softening for a moment, "must remember that every cruel word, every selfish act, is a seed. What you plant in your hearts today will grow into the tree of your life. Will it bear fruit of kindness and courage, or of bitterness and harm?"

Father Alex straightened, his voice resuming its fiery tone. "Cruelty is not just a failure of kindness; it is a rebellion against the divine image in another. It diminishes the tormentor as much as the victim. And let us not be deceived: no society can thrive where cruelty is allowed to fester." He looked around.

"If we are to be the Body of Christ, we must excise this cancer. Remember the words of Saint Paul: 'Let no corrupting talk come out of your mouths, but only such as is good for building up, as fits the occasion, that it may give grace to those who hear.'"

The congregation stood silent, the weight of his words settling over them like a heavy mantle. From her position, Kaisa felt each word as both a blessing and accusation. Alex's expression hardened again as he raised his hands in a gesture of invocation.

"How do we respond to cruelty that leaves scars? The first concern of the Hebrew prophets was not sentiment, but justice—the restoration of moral balance. Before mercy could heal, truth had to be named." Alex looked at the congregation, his eyes tightening.

"When Deuteronomy speaks of vengeance, *nāqām*, it does not mean revenge born of spite; it means the act of setting right what hands have twisted. Beside it stands another word, *yadīn*—'he will judge.' In the prophets, this judgment is not a burst of rage. It is the fire that burns away cruelty so that justice can live again."

The priest's words lingered in the air as he stepped forward. "When the tormented child cries for justice, that cry is not sin—it echoes the prophets. Anger is not always a failure of love; it is a refusal to tolerate injustice."

Kaisa looked around and saw that the sermon had stirred the congregation. A woman balled her hand into a tight fist, as if recalling some event.

"Throughout the prophets—Amos, Micah, Isaiah—wrath is always tethered to restoration. Amos thunders: 'Let justice roll down like waters.' Isaiah speaks of the fire that refines silver." Alex paused. He could feel heat rising beneath his collar, though the church itself was cold.

"The Old Testament saw judgment as re-creation, not annihilation. When evil rends the fabric of creation, vengeance reweaves it. In the Fathers we read that God's wrath is His love burning away what harms His children."

There was a slight shuffling among the listeners as they grasped the unfamiliar direction of the sermon.

"The Church carried forward the vision of these Hebrew prophets. But in much Western Christianity forgiveness is pictured as immediate release: to forgive is to let go, to move on, even if justice never comes. The Orthodox vision—preserved in Russian and Byzantine spirituality—is different. We are taught to hold mercy and truth together."

Alex raised the Bible he held in his left hand and clasped it with his right to emphasize the final point.

"For Orthodoxy, forgiveness and judgment are one movement of God. In every icon of Christ Pantocrator we see both tenderness and exactitude—the same Lord who forgives the repentant and judges the unrepentant."

"Where the West often separates God's wrath from His love, Orthodoxy insists: they are two sides of the same divine energy. The fire burning the sinner is the same fire warming the saint—what differs is the heart receiving it."

Alex looked across the congregation a last time, meeting Kaisa's gaze, then stepped back, bowing before the altar. The choir resumed its chant, the ancient melodies lifting the hearts of the faithful. Some even wiped away tears or stood as though rooted, pondering the sermon's challenge.

Outside, an early winter wind howled as Kaisa exited. She wiped a tear that squeezed out of her eye. She wasn't sure whether it was the wind or a sense, somehow, that the priest had spoken truly—from the heart. If so, the gulf that stood in front of her was huge indeed.

Alex finished his sermon, the words drifting up into the church's vaulted dome. He had never imagined his life might twist so brutally. What should have been a new beginning with Kaisa had shattered, replaced by the stark reality of a Siberian labor camp—the first step in a harrowing, soul-eroding descent to the very edges of human endurance.

He was an American, though not quite an outsider—shipped across Russia by forces, whether political or personal, hard to fathom. Yet, there he found himself, locked in the walls of a crumbling concrete and steel relic, caught in the maws of a brutal system where strength, intimidation, and raw cunning determined who survived the day.

It was no ordinary prison. The camp had an official title, but the inmates gave it other, darker names: *The Freezer, The Wolves' Den, Hell.* It sprawled on the edge of a desolate steppe, ringed by fences topped with razor wire. The climate was harsh—bitter winters that froze the marrow, scorching summers that left men delirious, and always, the relentless threat of violence from within.

* * *

Alex recalled how his new life had truly started: at lunch one midday in the prison's mess hall. The room was a particularly treacherous island in gulag life. Endless waves of clanking trays, dragging boots, and grizzled complaints lapped at its shores.

Light from high windows fell in dusty columns across the worn linoleum. Some days, the guards were so indifferent they might as well have been wraiths floating among the convicts. Other days, they loomed with a sour presence, using arbitrary authority to break up quarrels or incite them at whim.

Once he'd been a man of tailored suits and Washington dinners. Now, he wore tatters, and the canteen's watery gruel made him gag daily. Hunger overcame revulsion. Soon enough he was forcing down each spoonful. But it was scarcely an existence. His mind could not let go of Kaisa—what might have been, what should have been.

He was still Ivan then, and love had defined his final moments. He clung to the memory of Kaisa not just as a beacon but as the last element of his identity that mattered. It helped him get up each day, protected his sanity, made him want to survive.

However, he remained physically exposed. His tactic to stay alive comprised solely of keeping his head down—like a student avoiding a teacher's eyes. Ivan sat in a corner, a lonely figure among the sea of hardened men. It took weeks to find a seat where he thought he might remain unseen.

The alliances and rivalries in this place still baffled him. The last thing he wanted was to provoke a confrontation by accidentally encroaching on a group's unspoken territory. He had seen enough American movies. On this particular day, it became clear his efforts to stay invisible had failed. The result was disastrous.

He had been dreaming of Kaisa—of their last and only night together. He hadn't even noticed the hush that rippled across the hall. He almost felt it before he saw it—like the drop in air pressure before a storm. The rowdy chatter petered out, utensils paused midair, and men tensed. A figure had entered the hall who commanded absolute attention by mere presence.

"*Yuri,*" someone hissed under his breath. In that single name, Ivan sensed a thousand unspoken warnings.

Well over six feet, Yuri carried the thick, coiled power of a heavyweight boxer turned feral. His face was all hard angles—jaw carved like a cinder block, eyes the color of gunmetal and bright with predatory amusement.

His arms, roped with muscle, bore scars and cryptic tattoos testifying to a past steeped in violence. The men parted for him, either out of respect or fear, until the giant arrived at Ivan's table and stood over him like an eclipse.

Ivan looked up, heart hammering. Yuri's lips twisted into a grin that did not reach his eyes. "Mind if I join?" he asked in Russian, an almost genial lilt in his voice.

The question felt rhetorical. He didn't wait for an answer before dropping onto the bench opposite Ivan, causing the old wood to creak in protest. Inmates at neighboring tables turned away in case somehow they might end up involved. Even the guards exchanged uneasy glances.

Ivan forced himself to speak. "Sure," he mumbled, though his throat felt as if sand had filled it.

Yuri leaned across the table. Up close, the man smelled of sweat, tobacco, and stale vodka. But there was something else—something primal Ivan couldn't name. It set him on edge, simultaneously repulsed and mesmerized.

"You're American, yes?" Yuri asked, still in Russian, his accent thick. "I can see it in your posture."

Ivan nodded. He'd known Russian since birth, and he'd picked up some gulag slang since his arrest, enough to get by, though conversations still presented traps for him. "I—I got arrested... it was a misunderstanding," he started to say, but Yuri waved a dismissive hand.

"Misunderstanding, or perhaps you just stumbled too far into business that wasn't yours," Yuri said with disarming acceptance. Then he laid a massive hand over Ivan's forearm with a proprietary air.

The pressure was slight, but in a place like this, the contact held tremendous implications. The warmth of Yuri's skin hinted at a violence barely leashed. "In this place," Yuri continued, "you must learn whose side you want to be on. Prison is... cruel."

Ivan tried to withdraw, but the man's grip tightened. The mildness in Yuri's tone contrasted with the steely glare in his eyes—a predator's promise. "You're not suited to this environment," Yuri noted, looking Ivan up and down. "I can help you. Or I can destroy you. It depends, little American."

Despite the fear prickling his spine, Ivan felt a surge of indignation. He swallowed it. Silence was the best shield he had.

After a long moment, Yuri released him, stood, and exhaled a theatrical sigh. He glanced around the hall, as though claiming it by right. "Remember," he said, "the wolves here will circle you, and you must decide: are you the prey, or do you want to hunt?"

With that, Yuri strode away, leaving Ivan shaken, his half-finished soup now forgotten. All around, inmates cautiously returned to their chatter, but for Ivan there was no returning. He had been marked—willingly or not, he had stepped onto Yuri's radar.

That evening, the cell block felt more than usually cold and claustrophobic. Each cell—barely large enough for a narrow bed and a stool—was a stage where men struggled against despair. It was a struggle that cost most inmates. Tonight would be one when some eventually lost.

A flickering light bulb controlled by a switch outside provided an anemic illumination that made every shadow appear sinister. Ivan sat on his bunk, shoulders hunched, trying to gather the tatters of his composure.

What do I do now? he wondered. He had no illusions that Yuri's interest had ended with a conversation in the canteen. The man had singled him out, and if Yuri truly ran the place—if the rumors of him controlling the guards and orchestrating the internal gangs were true—then trouble was only a matter of time.

Sure enough, trouble arrived quickly.

A metallic clang reverberated through the corridor—a cell door was being unlocked. Ivan's pulse jumped. Footsteps approached. A guard swung wide the door of Ivan's own cell and briefly checked out the tiny space, before stepping back to reveal Yuri's hulking silhouette. Ivan sensed the inevitability of it all as the guard locked the two of them together.

"Hello again, little American," Yuri said. His accent sharpened the edges of his words. "You look nervous. Are you worried about your safety?"

Ivan rose, hating how easily fear could make man an animal. He clenched his fists determined not to succumb. "Get out," he spat, a surge of defiance spilling out. "I don't want any trouble."

Yuri's lips curled. "That's adorable," he drawled, stepping closer. "But trouble wants you."

The confrontation escalated with frightening speed. His anger snapping, and fear spiking, Ivan swung a fist. Pure desperation powered his effort. The blow landed on Yuri's jaw—one that might have floored a smaller man. Yuri merely grunted.

"That was cute," Yuri said, massaging his chin in mock appreciation. Then he responded in kind, fists slamming into Ivan's ribs, an explosive barrage that took the air out of his lungs. Ivan crumpled, vision swimming, too dazed to defend himself.

Yuri lifted him, effortlessly pinned him to the wall. Yuri struck again. Blow after blow hammered him, each a deliberate lesson. The man's fists felt like granite. A helplessness roiled in Ivan's gut. It was a methodical beating that delivered a single message: *You cannot fight me. You are nothing here.*

At last, Yuri let him collapse on the cold concrete floor. "Know your place," he growled, looming over him. "I am the *pakhan,* and you... you're just learning the rules." He spat on Ivan's face, a final gesture of contempt. "This is only the beginning, little American."

He left the cell, the metal door grinding shut behind him. The guards had turned a blind eye. Ivan remained curled up on the floor, gasping for breath, battered in body and spirit, a thin smear of blood on the ground. He was surprised the blood was so little. In the hours that followed, Ivan drifted into and out of consciousness, the agony of each bruise and contusion a bleak reminder that Yuri had singled him out as a personal project.

But the night was not finished with him. Sometime after midnight, well after the lights had been turned off, the door opened again, rattling Ivan from a pained half-sleep. Yuri returned—this time with two henchmen in tow. Their eyes gleamed with malicious excitement, as though they'd come to watch a show.

"You look comfortable," Yuri said, as though delivering a punchline to a joke only he understood. Ivan sat up, wincing. His entire torso throbbed. The glare in Yuri's eyes told him to expect no mercy. "What do you want?" he managed.

Yuri glanced at his companions and made a subtle hand gesture. They each hefted a bucket, rank with the smell of old cabbage, moldy bread, rotting scraps. "A gift," Yuri announced. "I realized you had no house warming. I wanted to make sure you felt properly welcome—so I brought with me a present, something to remind you of... *home.*" He upturned the first bucket onto Ivan's bunk. Congealed slop splattered onto the sheets, a nauseating mess of spoiled food and greasy residue.

"This should make you homesick," one of the goons cackled as a second bucket followed, doubling the vile spew. The stench hit Ivan's nostrils, and he choked back bile, his mind reeling. A noxious cloud filled the cell.

"Clean it up," Yuri sneered. "Or sleep in it. I don't care. However, you must embrace your new reality, little American—it's not going to get any better." Then Yuri leaned down, and his voice dropped to a purr. "Are you one of the prey, or do you wish to roam with the wolves?"

Rage flared in Ivan's chest, hot and desperate, but it collided with the brutal logic of his situation. The guards sanctioned Yuri's cruelty. No one would intervene. With a trembling hand, Ivan struggled upright. "You are... you're nothing but a coward," he exploded, his heart hammering at the risk such words provoked.

Yuri's eyebrows rose, then he smirked. "It's a bold statement. But empty." He jerked his head at his henchmen. Satisfied grins plastered on their faces, they withdrew, taking the buckets with them. "This will do for now," Yuri muttered, stepping back. "It is no good holding onto the past." With that, he and the pair vanished into the corridor.

The cell door clanged shut. Silence returned, broken only by the drip of foul liquid from the bunk to the floor. Ivan sagged against the wall, trembling with fury and fatigue.

Yet he'd avoided worse possibilities, and the actions had, he realized, ignited something new in him: a desire to resist—to show he would not be cowed. *I won't forget what happened. One day,* he thought, *I'll find a way out of this hell, and I'll remember.* It was the first night he didn't dream of Kaisa.

Over the following weeks, rumor spread like wildfire that Yuri had singled out an American—some said for amusement, others whispered for more personal reasons. Whichever the case, Ivan found himself ostracized, the other inmates leaving him to navigate the morass alone.

One respite came in the prison yard—an expanse of cracked concrete and hardy weeds. Exercise benches, old and rusted, decorated the far corner.

On good days, the sun baked everything to a sweltering heat. On bad days, a bone-chilling wind whipped through from the steppe. Regardless, the men always came out to posture and test. The yard was where inmates flexed their muscles and weighed alliances.

Ivan took to lifting weights there, not out of vanity, but to build any edge he could. He was no stranger to exercise—he had tried to keep fit in his old life—but this was different. Here, every muscle built was an investment in survival. The plates were battered, dented from years of abuse, and the barbell's grip was so eroded it cut into his palms. However, every rep made him a fraction stronger, a fraction more confident.

In theory, Ivan should have remained unobtrusive, coming out before the others, lying flat on the bench. But Yuri's gaze always found him. The big man would come out and stand at one end of the yard, surrounded by a ring of admirers, many of them large men who weighed well over two hundred pounds. Yuri would always look for Ivan and smirk—a grin visible even from fifty feet away.

Despite an instinct to flee, Ivan would force himself to keep bench-pressing. Fear could smell like blood in the water. If he showed weakness, it would only spur Yuri on. So Ivan would keep his breathing steady and try to ignore the tension coiling in his belly.

This day he didn't have to wait long before Yuri sauntered across. The slowness of the approach was designed to intimidate. Men parted before Yuri like weeds bending before an uncaring boot. And by the time he reached Ivan's bench, a hush had fallen all around. The bar hovered over Ivan's chest, loaded with what meager weight he could manage.

Yuri's voice was deceptively pleasant. "You've been working out, little American. Good. Maybe you won't break so easily next time."

Ivan racked the bar and sat up, sweat trickling down his forehead. "I can handle more than you think," he replied, aiming for a confident edge. However, his voice wavered.

Yuri turned, flagged down two of his men, and they hauled over giant plates of iron. With an effortless motion, Yuri stacked them onto the bar. The steel clanged like a bell, magnifying the gravity of the challenge. "Lift this," he said, "I'll spot you." The crowd rustled with anticipation.

Ivan eyed the barbell. It was a weight beyond his abilities. Yet to balk now would invite immediate humiliation. So he wiped his hands over his uniform, lay down, and gripped the bar, every muscle taut. He slowed his breath and sought to focus on the lift. The other inmates watched with undisguised glee.

He managed to raise the bar an inch, maybe, off the stand—his arms on fire, quivering violently. His heart pounded. He tried to complete the lift, his chest tearing apart. The weight was monstrous, and his underfed, battered body screamed in protest.

Yuri watched calmly. "Not bad," he murmured close to his ear. "But is that all you have, little American?"

Ivan tried to push further, but the bar drifted dangerously to one side. He felt his muscles fail, the weight crashing down onto the safety bars an inch above his chest. Gasps sounded in the yard. He lay there, pinned beneath the oppressive mass, face flushing with indignation.

With casual ease Yuri grabbed the bar and lifted it off Ivan, tossing it aside. The clang reverberated across the open space. Then, in a sudden motion, he seized Ivan's shirt—a thin prison-issue garment—and tore it open. The cloth shredded beneath his fingers like paper, leaving Ivan's torso exposed to the baking sun.

"Clothes here are privileges," Yuri sneered. "And you... you haven't earned them." He gestured to the rest of Ivan's attire. "Take it off."

Ivan's mind whirled. Stripping in front of the entire yard? A sense of shame washed over him. The circle of onlookers quietened, enthralled—some sported half-smiles, others averted their eyes in sympathy. But no one dared to intervene.

Yuri stepped closer. "I said, take it off."

Ivan's felt his resistance flare up. *He can beat me, but he won't break me*, he told himself. Yet the memory of the cell beatings, of the night with the slop poured onto his bunk, reminded him how far Yuri would go to demonstrate power.

Grinding his teeth, Ivan stood up—his arms still shaking from his effort at the bench press—and unfastened the thin, torn jeans. He stripped them off, leaving just threadbare underwear barely preserving his dignity. Every muscle in his body tensed as he stood before the ring of leering men and their judgmental stares—a mess of shame and defiance surging through his veins.

Yuri sat down on the vacated bench and regarded Ivan as a lion surveying a gazelle. "Look at me," he said, and he waited until Ivan was facing him. "This is your reality." His arm swept around the prison yard. "Remember it the next time you think about challenging me."

Yuri lifted up his foot, and Ivan stared at it blankly, uncomprehending. He noticed how the prison-yard grit had fused over time with the hard skin to form a dark, crusted sole. Then with his big toe, almost larger than life, Yuri hooked onto Ivan's underwear and pulled it sharply down.

Ivan's eyes flashed. But even in this final humiliation, he clung to some scrap of rebellion that he had found the other night. He stood there, making no attempt to cover himself. "You can humiliate me, but I'm not giving up," he said, his voice tight.

That earned him a faint chuckle from Yuri. "We'll see," he muttered. The big man turned to the yard at large. "This is what happens when a man doesn't know his place." Then he got up and stalked off, leaving Ivan as he was, in front of the assembled prison. As Ivan bent down to pick up his clothes, Yuri caught the motion out of the corner of his eye. He turned. "Not this time, you don't," he cautioned.

The bell rang and the guards came out to usher everyone back in. They pushed Ivan along with the others.

***

Ivan's humiliation in the yard became the stuff of instant legend. Whispers circulated about how Yuri stripped the American down to remind inmates who really held power. Everyone continued to give Ivan a wide berth, unsure if even talking to him meant crossing Yuri's unstoppable wrath.

But prison had a way of forging resilience. If you didn't collapse, before long you got stronger, and Ivan refused to give in. He discovered other pockets of routine that allowed him to train away from prying eyes—the quiet corners in his cell, or early mornings in the shower room.

On a good day, he survived unnoticed for a few precious moments, enough to build his stamina and hone his reflexes. Over time, his old dreams of

Kaisa faded, and new dreams took their place—of fighting back, of exacting judgment.

And that was how he ended up in the shower on a rare morning when the water steamed, providing a thick veil of anonymity. The place was a bleak chamber of dripping pipes and cracked tiles. Water from overhead faucets leaked constantly, echoing off tiles like rain on stone. That morning Ivan lathered up fast, keen to move on with the day.

His body had changed. Gone was the softness he had brought from the outside world. Now his frame was wiry, defined by necessity. His arms and torso bore large bruises—purple reminders of nights spent restless and in pain. However, they also testified to an endurance that had grown stronger with each beating. Surviving, after all, meant adapting.

As his mind started to drift, the steam parted and Yuri entered, even more horrendous for being unclothed. Thick cords of muscle dominated his entire form, while scars ran across his chest and arms, each a testament to some past battle. His legs were like pylons. Yuri paused as he caught sight of Ivan through the haze. Immediately the air tensed.

"Well, if it isn't my new pet project," Yuri purred, stepping forward so that the water cascaded over his powerful shoulders. "Found yourself a private corner this morning, little American?" The small lines at the edge of his eyes tightened in pleasant anticipation.

Ivan braced himself. "I'm not afraid of you," he said. "I never have been." The water dripped off his chin, but his words carried a desperate resolve.

Yuri loomed closer, a mountain in the swirling steam. "Your bravery, as always, is commendable," he said. "But bravery without strength is foolish. Are you truly stronger now? Or is that just an illusion?" He felt Ivan's arm.

In a flash, the tension exploded. Ivan lunged, jabbing Yuri's ribs with quick punches. Here, stripped of all pretense, it was raw man against man. They slid on the wet tiles, each man grappling for some advantage. Water splashed at their feet, turning the floor into a slick hazard. A ring of curious inmates, attracted by the commotion, gathered at the shower entrance. There was no sign of prison guards. No one saw value in intervening.

For a moment, Ivan's speed gave him an edge. He evaded Yuri's enormous arms and landed a few decent hits. Yuri grunted, stumbling, but quickly recovered. A backhanded blow sent Ivan reeling, and nearly cost him his footing. Then Yuri advanced again, fists swinging with lethal precision, powerful blows raining down on Ivan's torso.

Still, Ivan refused to yield. He pivoted, letting Yuri's momentum carry him forward, then slammed an elbow into Yuri's side. The big man hissed in pain. That slight sound of weakness spurred Ivan's hopes. He pressed on, launching a flurry of strikes at Yuri's lower body—his liver, solar plexus—targets that could cripple even the mightiest if Ivan managed to hit correctly.

But Yuri was no stranger to brutality. The shower recess became a primeval arena with watchers lined around the periphery like hungry ghosts. Yuri bided his time, absorbing the hits until an opening emerged. Then, with a thunderous roar, he swung a ferocious hook that caught Ivan's side. Pain exploded along Ivan's ribs, and he slid down on one knee, water pounding his shoulders.

Yuri seized the moment and stepped back to gesture at one of his men, who slipped out of the crowd. The henchman tossed something into the mist: a blade, a *finka*—its steel flaring as it bounced and slid across the floor. Ivan's blood ran cold.

Yuri grinned, showing teeth. "Time to end this farce. You're no wolf," he growled, picking up and brandishing the knife. Droplets on the blade shimmered, each one a miniature reflection of the hell about to unfold. The watchers murmured, fear and anticipation rippling through them like an intoxicated shiver.

Ivan's mind raced. He spotted a towel lying on the floor near the wall. In a desperate improvisation, he snatched the damp cloth. It was a pitiful shield, but better than nothing. He whipped it in front of him, hoping to entangle Yuri's blade.

The giant came on, each slash a potentially lethal blur. Water hissed off Yuri's body as he moved with a speed that now seemed terrifying. Ivan ducked, wrapping the towel around Yuri's forearm. For a second, he thought he had it, but his opponent wrenched free, nearly tearing the cloth in half. One slash nicked Ivan's bicep, leaving a jagged, stinging line.

The fight devolved into a savage dance of lunge and retreat. Yuri slashed again, the knife scoring a shallow line across Ivan's thigh. A vivid, terrible red mingled with the shower water, swirling hot down the drain. Gasping, Ivan stumbled backward, his mind ablaze with pain and the primal fear of death. Yuri advanced, eyes alight with triumph.

Somewhere at the edges of his mind, Ivan realized the watchers were silent, completely rapt. The hierarchy of the prison was at stake, but there was no question. Yuri would emerge victorious, and once again his dominion would be unassailable. If by some miracle Ivan survived, it would be as a broken man.

Yuri's next thrust found its mark with brutal efficiency, burying the knife deep into Ivan's left leg. The agony was immediate, searing through nerve endings. Ivan collapsed, choking on a scream. Blood oozed out from the embedded blade, a horrifying sight that made the onlookers recoil.

A hush fell. Yuri towered over Ivan, the steam swirling about him like smoke around some nightmarish genie. "You never stood a chance, little American," he said as he pressed a grimy foot down on Ivan's chest. "I told you from the start: I decide who lives or dies here."

Ivan felt a scorching wave of despair. The giant stepped back to parade in front of the spectators—his face showing a mix of unrequited rage and pleasure. In the swirl of half-lit steam, as pain clouded Ivan's vision and blood flowed from his leg, it seemed clear that Yuri had won.

But some grim desire for survival persisted in Ivan's chest. Summoning the last vestiges of strength, he gritted his teeth and gripped the knife's handle. The bar of steel was still lodged in his thigh, but if he could just—

In a burst of adrenaline, he pulled the knife free from his own flesh. Bolts of pain ripped through him, dark spots dancing at the edge of his sight. Yuri saw the motion, and his eyes widened in surprise. He hadn't expected Ivan to be that bold—or, indeed, so reckless.

As the giant returned to finish him off, Ivan channeled all his desperation into a single thrust, stabbing up and piercing Yuri's inner thigh. The blade sank deep and, without any intention on Ivan's part, cut the femoral artery. Yuri's face contorted in astonished pain and he staggered back, releasing a profound guttural sob.

The watchers inhaled sharply, almost as one, a ripple of confusion and disbelief coursing through them. Yuri, the unstoppable juggernaut, had been wounded. They could see his legs struggling, his chest heaving. Some inmates who'd lingered behind the front now stepped up, newly interested.

The towering figure that had terrorized them for so long was keeling over, blood pouring from his thigh. Yuri pressed a hand on the floor, too stunned to speak.

Ivan lurched across and grabbed the knife a second time, twisted it, and pulled it out. The gush of blood widened into a thick stream. He forced himself upright, half-crawling. His own leg felt like molten lava.

His blood and Yuri's streamed into the shower well, pooling and coalescing in a watery swirl. A wild determination fueled him. He refused to let Yuri recover. Sucking in a breath, he raised a trembling fist and landed it square on Yuri's jaw.

The blow wasn't the strongest, but Yuri was off-balance. He toppled back, his face contorted in fury and confusion. For an instant Ivan thought Yuri might collapse entirely, but the man steadied himself. Realizing victory wasn't possible today, he grabbed the towel Ivan had used and pressed it hard up against his leg, eyes blazing with a new and profound hatred.

A tremor of uncertainty snaked through the crowd. Yuri was not gone—certainly not yet. He was down and bleeding profusely, but not finished. They looked on as both men panted, wasted, the shower's water pouring over them like a waterfall in a savage wilderness.

"I can kill you," Ivan rasped, brandishing the knife. It was bluff. Shock was the only thing keeping him upright. But he needed Yuri to believe it, at least for a second.

"You... might," Yuri admitted, a grimace twisting his face. "But I doubt it."

In that moment, the shower block had never been quieter. Even the noise of running water seemed to fade. Every inmate recognized the future had reached a crossroads. Would Ivan deliver a final blow, or would Yuri rally to exact his revenge?

Ivan stared at the blood on his hands, the swirl of red around his feet. He had trouble breathing. Air came in ragged painful gasps. His leg burned and fresh waves of agony pulsed with every heartbeat. In the back of his mind, alarm bells rang. If he crossed this line, killed Yuri, it meant no going back. And yet, if he didn't, Yuri would surely retaliate.

He looked across at Yuri, who remained slumped, paling rapidly. A newly discovered corner of Ivan's spirit, savage and vengeful, demanded he end this bully's rein once and for all. Yuri's eyes stared back, daring Ivan to try. But another voice—was it Kaisa's?—held him in check.

Seconds passed like hours. Then, torch lights and urgent shouts broke the spell. The guards—hearing an end to the fighting—burst into the shower block, brandishing batons and barking orders. They waded into the ring of inmates, scattering them like crows. The sudden chaos yanked everyone back to reality.

Two guards grabbed Ivan, punching him in the stomach, forcing him to drop the knife. Another group surrounded Yuri, hauling him up. Blood dripped everywhere onto the tiles as a senior guard ordered prisoners to stand down and return to their cells.

And just like that, the fight was over. Ivan found himself dragged through corridors, pain hammering his body as he tried to keep his head high. Consciousness wavered, and as darkness started to descend, he saw Yuri's defeated scowl one last time in his mind. Had he tamed the unstoppable beast or was it just another beginning?

For Ivan, it didn't matter. He'd crossed a threshold. No longer just the prey, he had proven capable of fighting back. Though battered and exhausted, he felt a sense of triumph as the world went black.

* * *

The aftermath of the shower-room fight crashed through the prison like a tidal wave. Yuri did not recover but bled out. His cronies now dispersed, unsure where to put their allegiances. Meanwhile, Ivan recuperated under surly medical attention, leg bandaged and throbbing, but spirit intact. The guards had informed him he would visit the *kartser* for two weeks once he had sufficiently recovered.

Prison life continued, but the atmosphere had changed. A man who'd once lorded over the yard without question had been removed. Yuri was no longer there and a new leader had to emerge—and would do so before long. The power structures of the prison would shift to fill the void and align behind one side or another.

As for Ivan, he felt the precarious nature of his position. One fight did not overturn a hierarchy, and the thirst among some prisoners for dominance had not miraculously disappeared. Still, the weight in his chest felt lighter. He had survived and shown that he was no man's victim.

Word even spread around some corners of the prison that "the little American" might prove a useful ally—he had been resourceful and unyielding in the face of brutality. But, if some saw Ivan as a possible source of empowerment, others saw him as a threat—and resented his rattling the status quo. Violence raged below the surface regardless, waiting for a spark.

But in a place where hope was in short supply, Ivan dared to embrace his slender victory. He'd endured a savage humiliation, faced nights of terror, and come within inches of death. Yet, each scar etched upon his skin felt like some testament to a real, unbreakable core that he hadn't known existed.

He thought of his mother's sermons when he was younger—of mercy as strength—and wondered if such faith could survive in a place like this. Perhaps, in time, his reserve would guide him to something resembling freedom—if not literal, then at least a freedom of spirit and movement.

Whatever the case, he knew as he gazed at the ceiling that he had found a determination which he could scarcely have imagined on arriving. *I won't let them bury me here.*

A faint but grim smile lifted his features. Yuri had taught him a hard truth. In a world governed by fear, a man who showed strength and defiance could change things. Ivan had decided, for better or worse, to be that man. And yet the question remained: what would he change?

The New York skyline shimmered through the floor-to-ceiling windows of the boardroom, but this time Jake barely noticed. His fingers drummed a relentless rhythm on the table as the silence stretched. The CFO, Carla, sat to his right, stiff but not betraying a tremor. Eugenia, the firm's Head of Investor and Government Relations, sat next to Carla, arms crossed, her face carefully neutral.

Jake finally spoke, his voice cutting through the air like a whip crack. "A tax compliance investigation?"

"Yes," Carla replied, her words as sharp as her gray blazer. "The Federal Tax Service delivered the notice this morning to our Moscow office. They claim irregularities in our reports. Backdated several years."

Jake's drumming stopped. He leaned forward, his icy blue eyes boring into hers. "This isn't about taxes. It's about control. They want us out, don't they?"

Eugenia cleared her throat nervously. "Jake, we've seen this play before. They'll weaponize regulations, make operations hell until we yield."

"And what they want," Jake barked, "is our damn venture holdings and infrastructure."

"They'll call it 'national interest,'" Carla said, shrugging. "A few well-placed headlines about an 'uncooperative American firm,' and they'll look like heroes while they gut us."

Jake slapped his hand on the table, rattling the water glasses. "We've done no wrong! We're playing by their rules. Hell, probably better than most of those oligarch-owned outfits. Eugenia, the numbers—tell me they're clean."

"As clean as you'd expect in Russia," Eugenia said cautiously. "We followed the law—better than most. If anything, we're the poster child for compliance."

"And yet here we are," Jake muttered, his tone like acid.

Carla leaned forward with an intensity that matched Jake's. "This isn't about what we've done. It's about what we are—foreign. They're targeting us because they can. And because someone in Moscow sees an opportunity to score points."

Jake's laugh was bitter. "Or someone sees an opportunity to make a grab. This stinks of Gazneft, doesn't it? Someone whispering in the right ears to squeeze us out."

"It's possible," Carla admitted. "Or it's simpler than that. The Kremlin doesn't like foreigners profiting from what they see as their birthright."

Eugenia shifted uneasily in her seat. "We need to think about damage control. What's our exposure if this escalates?"

Jake's eyes snapped at her. "No. What we need is leverage. Eugenia, you've got contacts—use them. Find out who's really behind this. And Carla, I want a full forensic audit. If they're going to make this a war, we're not going down without a fight."

Carla raised an eyebrow. "Fighting might not be the best strategy. This is Russia, Jake. Sometimes, it's not about fighting—it's about knowing when to deal."

Jake stood, a fist clenched. He had a sense of déjà vu. "We'll deal when it's on our terms, not theirs." Again he thought of his father—of that willingness to accept bad outcomes as if they were fate. Not recognizing they were simply the decisions and choices of other individuals, often flawed or self-serving. As if they were his due regardless of merit—a burden his father had to accept.

"Until then, I want every angle covered. If they're seeking a war, they'll learn who built the playbook." The room fell silent as Jake stormed out, leaving Eugenia and Carla exchanging a wary glance.

"God help us," Eugenia muttered.

Carla smirked, a trace of grim amusement in her expression. "God? In Moscow? Good luck finding Him."

It was past midnight, and New York seemed particularly active with promise as the networks called the election. Jake had been gazing out at the city from high above in a private suite of PanEnergy's corporate headquarters. A hush fell across the room, punctuated by the clink of champagne flutes.

A red banner scrolled across the muted television: REPUBLICAN VICTORY: ELIZABETH HAWTHORNE BECOMES FIRST GOP WOMAN ELECTED PRESIDENT.

For a second, nobody moved. Then cheers erupted—assembled executives reacting like they'd just seen their stock portfolios double in real time. Jake turned from the window, his sharp blue eyes capturing the moment. At forty-nine, with well-barbered hair, he radiated the self-assurance of a man who knew how to succeed in any circumstance.

Jake thought of the French proclamation in medieval times—adapted for this night. *The queen is dead, long live the queen!* A cool smile tugged at his lips as he raised his glass. "Well," he stated, voice quiet but resonant, "the game's changed. Let's make sure we're still running the board."

Early the next morning, Jake visited his trading floor. The space was a nerve center of sleek desks and glowing monitors, a multi-million-dollar operation that could sell oil futures in Dubai while shorting carbon credits in Berlin—if it suited the bottom line.

Phones rang incessantly, red and green lights flickered across massive screens, and his team spoke to counterparts with manic urgency. Hawthorne's victory had jolted the markets like a Red Bull shot straight to the heart.

On one battered old TV screen in a corner looped coverage: *"President-Elect Hawthorne's energy platform is poised to transform U.S. domestic production, sending hydrocarbon stocks to record highs."* On a newer big screen along the main side-wall, PanEnergy's ticker symbol blinked in bold green, each uptick further boosting the company's market capitalization.

Jake paused by a young analyst hunched over her desk. The glow of six Bloomberg screens on stands painted the analyst's face in patterns of changing color. "What's the read?" Jake asked, looking over the woman's shoulders.

The analyst jolted upright, adrenaline coursing through her at the CEO's presence. She tapped a key, pulling up a map of the Permian Basin. "Sir, it's huge. Resource stock valuations just soared. With Hawthorne in office, regulation on drilling is expected to ease—Permian output might double by 2030. Supply constraints from Russia and Iran are expected to drive up global oil prices regardless. PanEnergy is—"

She stumbled a bit as she spoke, nerves getting to her. Jake just gave a brief nod. "So we're riding the wave."

"Absolutely. Wind and solar took a hit this morning, but it's not a total bloodbath. Some big money still believes in renewables, just... not as enthusiastically."

Jake spotted Kat, his Head of Business Development, stepping out of the elevator. He motioned her over. "Kat, line up a meeting with our LNG export partners," he said, his voice carrying the terse authority everyone had come to expect. "Hawthorne wants to flex American energy muscle. If we can flood Europe and Asia with our LNG, we undercut Russian gas, reduce Iranian leverage—win-win."

Kat's eyes showed concern. "I don't think it's that simple. We've got a wave of protests forming outside Capitol Hill. They accuse the new administration of ignoring environmental justice and setting the climate agenda back twenty years." Her words carried the fatigue of someone who'd read too many death threats in her inbox.

Jake let out a dry chuckle. "Noise. The market's already decided where the money's flowing." He turned on his heel, leaving the analyst to her work. In the world of PanEnergy, the agenda never stopped. And with the political winds now at their back, Jake had no intention of allowing their plans to slow down.

By mid-afternoon, Jake was on the company jet, a sleek Gulfstream that soared above the gray clouds. His destination: Midland, Texas. In the plush interior cabin, he flicked through a file of documents on the imminent merger with Palisade Resources—a deal that would produce an entity with a combined market cap well over one hundred billion dollars and cement PanEnergy's status in the Permian Basin.

Four hours later, he stood on the sun-scorched tarmac outside Midland's small airport. Palisade's Chairman, an affable Texan named Roy Tucker, greeted him in a white Stetson and bolo tie. Together, they drove through dusty fields to a private ranch, courtesy of Roy's vintage pickup.

Once there, they sat in cane chairs on a wrapround porch, each nursing a tumbler of bourbon and ice. Roy had a sip and grinned, the lines around his eyes deepening. "Gotta say, Jake, your timing couldn't be better. With Hawthorne in the White House, Washington's rolling out the red carpet for drillers."

Jake picked up his glass, the amber liquid catching the last rays of the desert sun. "Elizabeth Hawthorne's not just a politician," Jake said, swirling his drink. "She's a CEO. And her business is America."

Roy laughed. "Damn, you sound like you wrote her campaign speech."

Jake just smiled, a calculating glint in his eyes. "Can't take credit for that, but I can capitalize on it."

They clinked glasses. The Permian Basin stretched out before them—millions of barrels waiting to be tapped, enough profit to shape the next decade of U.S. energy. The future was bright, and Jake Laskin intended to own as much of it as possible.

Jake returned to PanEnergy's Manhattan offices the next evening to find the boardroom buzzing with several of his top strategists and their various assistants. The space had been transformed into a war room. One wall now displayed an oversized map of U.S. oil and gas fields; another showed shipping lanes for LNG tankers crisscrossing the Atlantic and Pacific. A giant touchscreen sat on the center table, dotted with icons representing rigs, pipelines, refining hubs, and prospective acquisitions.

Kat stood near the map, reading from a tablet. "The latest strategic updates from the Middle East indicate political tensions might escalate. That pushes oil prices higher, so we're good." Jake smiled.

"But," Kat cautioned, "the ESG contingent is screaming murder on social media. Like Extinction Rebellion. Non-partisan groups and NGOs are labeling Hawthorne's policies an environmental disaster, arguing that she will lead us straight off the climate cliff. There's talk of lawsuits and investor pressure."

"They'll take their opposition to the courts," she continued, "leveraging the latest appointees. You remember *Juliana v. United States.*"

Jake lifted a hand, silencing her. "I respect the ESG crowd, Kat, but I'm not letting them scuttle our play."

"You realize," Kat went on, unphased, "that the outgoing President has done an excellent job with the Senate, stacking the benches—even better than her predecessor. It's become a priority these days, given litigation trends—almost overshadowing other business."

"And yet," Jake said, "the world does need energy. We answer that need."

One of the strategy directors—Frank, a former Capitol Hill staffer—spoke up. "Still we must have a plan for them. Even if it's simply a gesture. There's a world out there. The IUCN is adopting a motion to recognize ecocide, and state actors are pushing the idea of climate imperialism."

Jake exhaled. "Fine. Quietly boost a couple of green pilot projects in states that are heavy on renewables. California! Give us some cover, where it's going to cost us the least." Frank nodded.

"However, don't go too far simply for cosmetics and ruin our returns. Otherwise, we'll get caught on the other side." Jake shook his head.

"We'll have some activist fund meddling in our affairs. The kind of mess you see in Europe from all their foggy thinking. Our focus stays resolutely on oil, gas, maybe—" He tapped the map, "coal. Hawthorne's AI ambitions require gigawatts of cheap juice. Coal may be taboo, but it's economic and America's got it. We can't ignore that."

"Sure!" Frank nodded again. "A kind of butterfly option in the real world."

But no one was really listening. The excitement in the room was palpable. Even if these were men and women who thrived daily on the cutthroat competition of energy markets, they could sense the unusual scale of Jake's next move. He was going all-in.

Jake pointed to the board. "We are not just out to beat the competition. We are out to redraw the map. For too long Russia and Iran have held Europe hostage with their energy. Let's help the old world."

Jake looked around the room. "Why rely on exposed pipelines from dubious sources that need to cross a continent whose boundaries are increasingly porous and uncertain when they can just get LNG from us?"

He stepped closer to the group, eyes fierce. "Infrastructure is key: more pipelines, more terminals, more shipping capacity. No half-measures. PanEnergy must be the first name on every deal from Berlin to Bangkok."

The excitement was contagious. Heads nodded around the table. Kat's grin widened, Frank scribbled notes. They could practically taste the victory—and the money.

A week later, Jake found himself in a sleek, high-rise conference room that belonged to a boutique financial firm in Lower Manhattan. The place radiated wealth: polished glass floors, minimalist furniture, panoramic views of the city's skyline. And a faint hum of futuristic electronics pulsed underneath the hush.

Across from him sat Tim Harland, a venture capitalist known for spotting unicorns before anyone else. Projected in holographic form between them was a conceptual grid of the United States with clusters of data centers sprouting like mushrooms—each requiring massive gigawatts of electricity.

Tim rubbed his jaw, eyeing the projection. "So you want PanEnergy to transform from an oil giant into a power utility for AI data centers? That's a pivot."

Jake shrugged. "Why do we extract oil and gas in the ground? Because we monetize it. Electricity is the next currency—especially for advanced computing. If we're the ones fueling AI's exponential growth, guess who reaps the rewards? Like in the old days, suppliers at the goldfields."

Tim brushed his hair back with his hand. "It's not a crazy idea," he said. "But you're stepping onto the turf of utilities—regulated markets, stable and boring, definitely not sexy. Are you comfortable with that?"

Jake smirked. "Utilities used to be stable and boring. That changes when every major tech player demands power to run AI clusters. We feed that hunger, we become indispensable. Boring? Try *essential.*"

"What about developments like DeepSeek? Doesn't that change everything—in terms of model compression, energy efficiency?"

"Not really," Jake replied. "The possibilities it raises just further promote AI and accelerate its diffusion. Power is going to invade every aspect of our life. AI, EVs, mobile technology: our relationship with electricity is going to alter. Completely!"

Tim raised a brow, a shimmer of intrigue lighting his gaze. "And you think Hawthorne's administration is on board with nuclear too? You sure about that?"

Jake nodded. "They want America to control its energy future. Not just that. Electricity is going to become a strategic lever, a competitive resource, like never before. Nuclear is the final piece—clean, consistent, perfectly matched for AI's appetite. SMRs—small modular reactors—are the future. Less red tape, cheaper to deploy, and they pair seamlessly with the decentralized data center model."

A grin tugged at Tim's mouth. "So you're going to corner the AI power market? That's a bold claim."

Jake edged forward, hands on the table, brimming with conviction. "I'm not cornering it alone; we'll need partnerships, joint ventures. I'd prefer to be asset-lean. But I'm not standing idle while other companies figure it out for themselves. This is the direction the wind is blowing—I'm just hoisting the sail."

Tim offered his hand, a gleam in his eye. "I'm in. But you'd better move fast because big tech is already scouting for energy deals."

Jake's handshake was firm. "Fast is the only speed I know."

It was nearly midnight by the time Jake returned once again to PanEnergy. The city's lights flickered like so many fireflies below, and from his office, Jake saw only possibilities.

He sank into a leather chair and poured a double shot of single-malt whisky; Ardbeg—one of his favorites, prized for its strong peaty character. Lagavulin was like Bordeaux—for those with money who had no sense of individuality or exploration; the many, sorry conformists of the luxury world. He tipped a good pour into his tumbler.

Usually, victory celebrations were done publicly—big deals demanded big headlines. But tonight, after the swirl of deals, the election results, and the behind-scenes talk of nuclear expansions, Jake wanted a moment to think.

On his desk lay a dossier marked *CONFIDENTIAL*. Inside were spreadsheets projecting PanEnergy's new trajectory:

- Hydrocarbons as the cash engine, growing with the pro-industry policies from President Hawthorne.
- LNG exports bridging immediate demand in Europe and Asia.
- Coal as the short-term power source for factories and data centers.
- Nuclear (SMRs) as the moonshot, the pivot that would catapult PanEnergy into the trillion-dollar stratosphere if pulled off correctly. Or simply if investors believed they could.

He lifted the tumbler, swirling the deep brown-gold liquid. For a fleeting moment, doubt nibbled at the edges of his mind: was he overextending? Oil, gas, coal, nuclear—plus a total rebrand toward powering the AI revolution. The scale was enormous, and the stakes soared beyond anything PanEnergy had ever undertaken.

But that was the point. Fortune favored the bold. Especially in a world where a single election victory could shift market sentiment overnight, turning last week's long shot into tomorrow's gold mine. How different, he thought, his approach from that of other companies like BP.

He raised the tumbler to his lips, a wry grin forming as he recalled Tim Harland's parting words. *Boring, my ass!* thought Jake. Indeed, if his plan succeeded, PanEnergy would be anything but.

Across the cityscape, the skyline flickered with other giants—corporate behemoths, rival energy firms, political players. Were they sleeping, or were they awake too?

If they were sleeping, they would wake up to a reality where Jake Laskin held a seat at the table of power, a blueprint in his hand that spanned from oilfields in Texas to AI server farms in Seattle, from midwestern coal plants to next-gen nuclear stations. And still, he noted wryly, with a foot in the renewables camp.

He finished his whisky in a single motion. Tomorrow, the noise of protestors and climate activists would ring louder. Tomorrow, financial reporters would hound him for quotes on energy strategies. Tomorrow, the tectonic shifts in Washington could produce new obstacles. But tonight, he allowed himself one moment of pure triumph.

In the hush of his office, Jake set the tumbler down. A fleeting image of Eve on the couch arose, unbidden and unwelcome, in his thoughts. He pushed it aside. The personal could wait; the strategic never could.

He opened a new sheet on his laptop, which he titled simply: "NEXT STEPS." He wrote a quick series of bullet points:

1. Permian Integration – Fix synergy targets for the Palisade merger.
2. International LNG Partnerships – Identify top-tier shipping and offloading terminals worldwide.
3. Coal Assets – Quiet dialogue over key assets; avoid public scrutiny.
4. Nuclear R&D – Accelerate SMR feasibility and secure federal support under Hawthorne's new policies.
5. AI Power Supply – Fast-track expansions of data-center electricity nodes in strategic states.

He stared at the list, exhaling slowly. Each point carried complications—lobbying, local politics, engineering challenges. Yet each also represented a step closer to the mammoth empire he envisioned.

Jake flicked off the desk lamp. He leaned back, closing his eyes. Power. Influence. Dominance. He could feel all three coursing in his veins, amplified by the knowledge that this moment—right now—was the hinge on which PanEnergy's future would swing.

His phone on the desk buzzed. The screen read: *New York Times.* He ignored it for the moment. Let them wait. He had a chapter to write—his own, rising through the noise of a new presidency.

From his quiet vantage in the Manhattan night, Jake Laskin was certain of one thing: this was just another beginning. The city was poised on the precipice of another transformation. It just waited to be plugged in, and the future would arrive.

58. Pipeline Leak

The sleek steel-and-glass interiors channeled the afternoon light onto Jake as his finger gently tapped the conference table—steady and precise, the sound of thought and control.

Across from him sat Logan Briggs, the company's sharp and relentlessly efficient Managing Director of Pipeline Operations. They'd been dissecting the implications of the new president's policies—specifically, how her unpredictable stance toward Canada could ripple through the company's operations.

"She's pro-hydrocarbons," Logan was saying, flipping through a stack of briefing notes, "but this Canada situation is tricky. If she imposes punitive tariffs and they retaliate, both could affect resource trade, tightening margins for our pipeline expansion."

Jake smirked. "We've faced worse. We'll carve out an exception. We always do. This pipeline is too important to fail, Logan."

Logan opened his mouth to respond, but his phone buzzed loudly on the table. He glanced at the caller ID, his face darkening. Without hesitation, he swiped to answer.

"Logan Briggs," he stated.

"Logan, it's Mark up in Alberta," came the voice, tense and hurried. Mark Barnes, General Manager of Pipeline Operations in Canada, rarely called without good reason.

"What's going on?" Logan asked, his tone sharpening.

"We've got a problem with the pipeline," Mark said. "There's a leak."

Logan froze for half a second before switching the call to speakerphone. Jake straightened in his chair, his focus narrowing.

"How bad is it?" Logan demanded.

Mark hesitated, and the line crackled faintly. "The leak itself isn't massive. Pressure is stable so far, but we're losing measurable volume. Too early to estimate total flow. And we haven't pinpointed the source yet. Technically, the situation appears manageable."

Jake cut in, his voice calm but edged with authority. "Then why the hell do you sound like someone just died, Mark?"

Mark exhaled sharply. "Because of where it is. The leak's in one of the protected zones—right near the Athabasca watershed. Sensitive as hell."

Logan swore under his breath. "And if it crosses into First Nations territory, the political cost triples," he murmured.

Jake's jaw tightened, but he kept his tone steady. "What's the immediate action plan?"

"We've shut down that section for now," Mark replied. "However, to do a thorough inspection and satisfy the regulators, we'll need to shut down the entire pipeline for an indeterminate period. And there's more."

"Go on," Jake said.

Mark's voice dropped a notch. "The environmentalists were already on our backs about this expansion; and the guarantees we gave the regulators—that there'd be no impact on sensitive areas—are going to bite us. The Canadian government is going to seize on this, especially with their renewables agenda. And if it hits the press..."

The room fell silent for a beat, tension coiling in the air. Logan broke it with a bitter laugh. "Well, let's hope we don't end up like some of our American peers."

Jake's eyes flashed with annoyance. "We're not some aircraft manufacturer. We fix problems; we don't wallow in them."

Mark's voice came back, hesitant. "Still, worst-case scenario... they could shut us down permanently. And you know Ottawa doesn't need much of an excuse to tighten the screws on the U.S. these days."

Jake leaned forward, his elbows on the table, his voice dropping to a low, deliberate tone. "Listen to me, Mark. You're going to handle this, and you're going to handle it fast. Get boots on the ground, find the source, and come up with a solution that's airtight—not just for the regulators but for the media and the activists too. I don't care how much it costs or who you have to bring in. Understood?"

"Yes, sir," Mark said, the weight of the conversation audible in his voice.

Jake ended the call and sat back. For years, he'd conquered markets, not mud. Oil, though, had a way of reminding men where power began—and where it ended. Jake ran a hand over his hair. He'd begun dyeing it to hide the gray. Logan looked at him, his expression unreadable.

"Damage control plan?" he asked.

"First, we keep this out of the press for as long as possible," Jake said. "Leak containment needs to be the focus, but we have to control the narrative. If the activists get wind of this, they'll weaponize it. We need to have our story waterproof before it hits the news cycle."

Logan nodded, already making notes. "And the Canadian government? This is going to play right into their hands. If they decide to act on this publicly, to grandstand, it'll be a hell of a lot harder to control the story."

Jake's lips curved into a cold smile. "We'll handle Ottawa the way we always do—reminding them who needs whom more. They can't posture forever without risking their economy. But we'll need to tread carefully. Their green agenda makes this a PR minefield, as does recent polling that suggests the PM is seen as too soft." Logan didn't respond.

"These Old-World democracies—with their Westminster-style systems... I find they have increasingly odd ways of managing the task of government." Logan looked at Jake, puzzled, but remained quiet. It wasn't really his thing.

"Canada, Britain—these countries," Jake explained, "their policy formation is all over the place. You no longer know what is possible, where the line in the sand is." Jake shook his head.

"Their leadership's become almost passive-aggressive. They hide when it's difficult, but decisions are needed; show force when resistance is minimal, but tough action adds little value. That's what our pipeline is to them right there." Jake saw Logan's eyes glazing over.

"There is no internal compass. At least Hawthorne has that. You can't say you don't know what's coming." He tapped the table.

"Well, enough of politics. Let's get ahead of it. Start reaching out through the usual back channels. We need to know how hard the government is going to push. We don't want to overreact."

Logan nodded and rose from his chair. As he headed for the door, his steel-toed work boots thudded against the polished floor—a field man in a room built for strategy.

Jake stared at the door as it closed. Crises were currency in this business—what mattered was how you spent them, he reminded himself. How you turned them into opportunities.

Yet, as he stared, a nagging thought lingered in the back of his mind. This wasn't just a logistical problem. It was an environmental and political powder keg, one that could blow up in ways even he couldn't predict. For the first time in years, Jake felt something he wasn't used to. Not fear, exactly. But the unmistakable prickle of unease.

59. The Frick Collection

The quiet elegance of the Frick Collection on Fifth, its limestone façade ensconced along the avenue's Museum Mile, felt almost a rebuke these days to Manhattan's frenetic pulse. Kaisa hesitated in front of the entrance, around the side on 70th—her breath clouding in the November chill, her navy coat cinched tight.

She had invited everyone on a whim during the grilled fish dinner at the Ambassador's home—unexpected words, but calculated ones. They'd all accepted—including Alex with his swift, wolfish grin she'd come to recognize.

However, Kaisa felt a tightness in her chest. This was no mere outing. It was a mirror to her Hermitage excursion years ago in St. Petersburg, when Ivan had listened so intently to her tales of art under gilded ceilings. If her hunch was correct, this visit could, at last, break open Alex's charade. If not, Kaisa was—as in other, previous episodes—conjuring ghosts from a heartbreak that lingered like a widow's wail.

She passed through the lobby into the Garden Court, where they'd agreed to meet. It welcomed her with its marble serenity—fountains murmuring, light filtering through skylights, the air heavy with the scent of polished wood and history.

Alex arrived in a tailored gray suit, lean and composed. His dark eyes met hers, flashing with a private amusement she couldn't read. She wore, once again, Ivan's engagement ring. In fact, she wore it all the time now, much to Caleb's surprise at the change in habits.

"Shall we?" Kaisa said when they'd all assembled, gesturing to the grand residence surrounding them. Her voice was calm and smooth, but she'd calculated every step. If Ivan lurked within Alex, she'd flush him out.

The group began in the West Gallery. However, gradually they dispersed as each member established their own speed and routine.

With a certain pleased surprise, Kaisa saw Anisa head off with Cavil on her arm, while Martha charted an independent course. She noted that, as usual, Caleb found himself unable to disengage himself from the phone.

That left her with Alex. They stood in front of Holbein's *Sir Thomas More*, who gazed down on them with stoic resolve. Kaisa paused, her tone measured, setting the theme she had prepared. It had taken some time to work out her plan of attack.

"When I was young," she started, "my mother used to play a game when we entered galleries to keep us engaged—to make sure we left having learned something. It adjusted over the years," she continued, "but the idea was so good I still use it today." Alex looked at Kaisa, intrigued.

"The first game involved going into a room and, without looking at any of the labels or plaques or descriptions, choosing your favorite picture. Often it was not the famous one."

Alex laughed. "That sounds like great fun," he said.

"The second game, as I grew older, involved choosing a theme—any topic, random but interesting—and trying to relate specific artworks to the theme. We found the exercise frequently raised new ideas, different perspectives."

"Now there's an interesting challenge!" he nodded with appreciation. "So which one are we playing today?"

"The second," Kaisa said. "We are really too old and knowledgeable to play the first."

Alex nodded again. "Do you have something in mind, then?" he asked.

"Yes. I read a question recently," she said, "one that stuck with me: 'Do you think a man can suffer so long and yet remain human?' I thought we might start off here, in front of More's martyrdom. It feels fitting, don't you think?"

She looked at Alex. "His principles cost him everything. Does trial undo a man—does suffering strip away humanity? Or do these challenges forge it?"

Alex's eyes narrowed, a hint of something—recognition, unease?—passing across his face. "Suffering's a crucible," he replied, his voice unusually intense. "It can burn away the superfluous, leave only what's essential. But too long, and it risks breaking the soul entirely." He stared at the picture.

"Sir Thomas More held fast," Alex continued after a pause. "But not everyone does." Kaisa's heart quickened—her plan was having an effect. However, what did the response mean?

She pressed on, guiding them to Bellini's *St. Francis in the Desert,* its golden light evoking spiritual torment. "St. Francis chose suffering—asceticism, isolation. But can a man endure external torments, like imprisonment, and still emerge... himself?" Her words were a scalpel, slicing toward Ivan's arrest, cutting away the scar tissue that had built up over time, seeking out the original wound.

Alex lowered his head. "Imprisonment tries the core," he whispered as his countenance clouded over. "Some men rebuild themselves, there in the dark. Others... they shatter. It depends on what they carry inside." Alex's eyes met hers, steady but piercing, as if he now understood her objective.

"I can see you are taken with the question, Kaisa. Is there something personal behind it?"

Her pulse spiked, but she deflected the question with a smile. "Maybe I'm just curious about resilience. You strike me as a person who's faced storms. What's the worst you've endured and still come out human?"

Alex chuckled now. His eyes picked out her ring, lingering for a moment—maybe too long. "Storms, yes. Let's say I've navigated rough seas—oil fields, boardrooms, places where trust is a currency that you can't afford to spend lightly."

They began to walk again and this time paused before Goya's *The Forge*, its muscular figures hammering iron in fiery light. "This painting reminds me about the art of survival—raw and unrelenting," Alex said. "Suffering doesn't always destroy; sometimes it shapes a new identity, one with a sharper edge."

Kaisa's instincts flared—his words seemed to echo Ivan's old musings about ambition's cost, but were they deliberate or accidental?

She headed over to Turner's *Harbor of Dieppe* and its shimmering waves. "This feels like freedom after confinement," she said, her voice soft. "After suffering, can man reclaim his past, or is he forever changed? There are so many related questions: is the past reclaimable at all—should we try to bring it back, to relive it? Personally, I doubt we can recapture moments once lost."

Alex's jaw tightened, a spasm of raw emotion breaking through the polished surface. "The past is a ghost," he murmured. "You can chase it, but if you reach out for it the vision slips through your fingers. A man can stay human, but not unchanged—suffering rewrites the soul."

Alex's eyes dropped to the ring again, a muscle twitching in his cheek. *Was it recognition?* Kaisa's heart pounded. The Hermitage flashed in her mind, its gilded halls—Ivan's presence next to hers, like Alex's now. G*hosts only haunt the living*, her therapist had said.

They drifted across to the East side, which had only reopened in April, to the Fragonard Room, its rich rococo panels and large-scale pictures bursting with decadent romance. The style, the mood—she was hoping it would all resonate with that winter palace fifteen years ago. How appropriately named, she now thought in passing.

Kaisa seized the moment to probe a little further. "Fragonard's lovers reveal no adversity. However, real love—does it not experience pressure, can it not survive torment?" She watched for Alex's reaction as she caressed the gilded armrest of a Louis XVI chair.

He smiled, although tightly. His stance seemed more wary. "Love's not immune. And suffering can twist it—turn devotion into nostalgia, trust to fear. Yet, the strongest bonds should endure—even if they scar." His voice softened, becoming almost intimate, as he studied Kaisa. "Your ring—I was intrigued to know better how you got it."

Kaisa's breath caught. "It was a gift from a man who promised eternity, then vanished. But I think even the strong don't heal from some wounds, Alex."

They headed into other parts of the mansion, towards the southwest, which was the family's private quarters and found themselves in Henry Frick's bedroom—now the Walnut Room. In front of them they saw Ingres and his *Comtesse d'Haussonville*. The noblewoman's poise seemed, somehow, apposite given Kaisa's own guarded dance.

"I wonder," Kaisa said. "When sitting, did the Comtesse seek to present the woman she had been—or the one she was becoming. Which life did she choose to protect for posterity?" She looked at Alex. "What do you think?"

"It's difficult to tell now without knowing the whole person, all the history."

"I feel," Kaisa said after a moment, "that we still haven't answered the basic question: about whether suffering is what makes us human, or what undoes us."

Alex looked at the portrait. "Suffering makes us more human," he replied, "if it teaches compassion. Less, if it breeds bitterness." He turned to Kaisa. "And the many scars become marks of history—yours, mine, the countess's here." His eyes dropped to the ring.

Once more Kaisa's heart skipped a beat. He was deflecting, but the ring had landed. She could see a tremor of unease in his eyes—a shadow, she thought, of the old Ivan.

Kaisa smiled, keeping her tone playful but pointed. "Art does that—brings the past alive. I like to scrutinize memory—my own private recollections as well as more public memorials. This place, today, reminds me of another time in a gallery far away with someone else."

Alex's expression hardened briefly, then softened into a wry grin. "Which gallery can compare to this? It is unique in its way."

They slowly moved on and reached another small gallery near the Living Hall, where Vermeer's *Mistress and Maid* was temporarily displayed. Its quiet tension seemed to mirror their own.

Kaisa pressed again from a new angle. "Vermeer uses light to reveal secrets. Personal suffering, too, hints at hidden truths. But it can become circular: a man once hurt may use that same pain to hide—to conceal, if not reject, his origins for fear of being wounded again."

"Is it not like Rembrandt's *Return of the Prodigal Son*? The figure must risk vulnerability once more if he hopes to feel again the love he lost. Hiding cannot do that. Perhaps the type of light matters—Vermeer's exposing clarity or Caravaggio's dramatic chiaroscuro has a different effect compared with Rembrandt's warm, embracing glow."

Alex's gaze darkened; he became momentarily still. His mind returned to their discussion so long ago at the Hermitage. "A man can hide, but not forever," he said quietly. "Suffering strips old masks and builds new ones. The question is whether a core remains—something that can return." He stepped closer. "You're searching for something, Kaisa, and maybe it's not found simply in these paintings."

Her pulse thundered; her face felt hot. The ring, the gallery—together they had worked, or almost. Alex's words, his glances—they echoed Ivan too closely. Yet ambiguity lingered. Was he playing her, or was the past now bleeding through?

"Maybe I'm searching for truth," she said, her voice steady but sharp. "Art reveals it, sometimes. Classical paintings are an old form of promise—to display the world as it is." Alex took in a deep breath at the words and noted, perhaps for the first time that day, the faintest aroma of mint.

For a second he felt dizzy—as he had that day in front of Matisse's *Dance*. He recovered, reminding himself all the possibility of that moment had crumbled under the devastating repudiation that followed. He forced a smile, enigmatic as ever.

"Truth," he said, "is a dangerous pursuit. Love reshapes us, pain scars us—but truth..." His gaze held hers. "Truth decides what is real."

Alex laughed to dispel the sudden dark turn. "Shall we go into the courtyard once more?" he suggested. "Wait for the others there?" He held out his arm for Kaisa in a form of old-fashioned gallantry.

"This visit," Alex said as they walked arm in arm. "I'm really pleased you proposed it. Thank you so much for going to the trouble of getting us all here today. I've enjoyed the collection immensely. And our talk," he said as they entered the Garden Court. "It has made me reconsider my attitudes about life and relationships: what keeps us going, what we should hold dear."

He smiled warmly. "Sometimes I do forget," he concluded.

Kaisa nodded, in a way pleased. But her heart remained heavy, full of unanswered questions. The day had sparked something—recognition, humanity—but it had not given her certainty.

They waited for the others in the courtyard before going into the museum shop. All agreed that the outing was magnificent—the Frick's renovation a grand success. They couldn't wait to see the final layout.

As they parted on Fifth Avenue, the city quickly swallowed them up. Kaisa felt as if her world remained under siege: Alex was either Ivan rebuilt through suffering, or a stranger wearing his shadow. Either way, the Frick had been a battlefield, and the war for truth was a long way from over. The sunlight ignited her ring like a small, defiant flame.

60. The Environment

Jake stood by the massive windows of his corner office, staring out across the snow-dusted Manhattan skyline. He liked their location near Hudson Yards. Behind him, the air was heavy, punctuated by the occasional rustle of papers.

Carla Nguyen sat in one of the sleek leather chairs, her expression calm but her eyes sharp. Across the table, Dick Harrington, the head of Exploration and Development, was flipping through a file with the kind of nervous energy Jake despised.

"All right," Jake said finally, turning around. "What the hell's going on in the Arctic?"

Dick looked up, startled. "Sir?"

"You heard me," Jake snapped. "The Russians are sniffing around our exploration permits, saying we're in violation of their environmental regs. I want to know—are they right?"

Dick hesitated, pushing his glasses up the bridge of his nose. "Jake, it's not that simple. Their regulations are vague, and they change the goalposts whenever it suits them. What we were doing last year was fine, but now they're saying it's not."

Jake folded his arms, his gaze pinning Dick in place. "That's not what I asked. I asked if we've done anything that could give them ammo. Are we compliant, or are we not?"

"We've followed every guideline to the letter," Dick said, his voice defensive. "At least, as far as anyone can tell. But you have to understand, this is the Russian Arctic we're talking about. The rules are opaque, enforcement is arbitrary, and there's always someone looking for an excuse to shut you down if it benefits them."

Carla spoke up, her voice smooth and even. "Jake, this is the same playbook they used in Sakhalin. They're leveraging environmental concerns to squeeze us into a weaker position. The question isn't whether we're compliant—it's whether they want us to stay."

Jake stepped closer to the table, his tone lower, more dangerous. "Dick, I need certainty. I can't fight these bastards without it. I want a full audit of every operation we've conducted up there. Every permit, every report, every inspection. If there's even a hint of non-compliance, I need to know now, not when they're using it to skewer us in court."

Dick nodded, swallowing hard. His thumb had worried a crease in the file. "Understood. I'll get my team on it immediately."

"You'd better," Jake said coldly. "If we've handed them a loaded gun, Dick, I want to know before they pull the trigger. Your head will be the first one out of the trench."

Carla leaned forward, her gaze steady on Jake. "And if the audit comes back clean? What then?"

"Then we prove it," Jake said, his jaw tightening. "We push back hard. I'm not letting them bulldoze us out of this project."

She arched an eyebrow. "You do realize, Jake, that in Moscow, being right doesn't always mean winning?"

Jake's laugh was humorless. "Let them come. They'll find out what it's like to fight someone who doesn't fold."

The room went quiet again, the tension palpable. Dick gathered his file and papers, muttering something about getting started on the audit, and hurried out. Carla lingered, watching Jake as he stared back out the window.

After a beat, Carla added, "This isn't some TV show set in Montana, Jake." She waited for a reaction. "It isn't a cowboy shootout. It's a chess match. And the Russians? They've been playing it for centuries."

Jake didn't turn; his voice stayed low and hard. "Good. Then I'll throw the board at them." He wished his mother had done that: had just once shown her feelings, drawn attention to the injustice done to her.

Jake's father had wronged her through his weakness of will—and through insisting on being the breadwinner. It had boxed her in and kept her from shaping a life beyond the home. Society had contributed—challenging her right to give full expression to her drive. Even other women had consciously kept her back with their quiet, clipped advice—their eagerness to enforce conformity: "It's just not done."

He wasn't going to repeat the mistake. He had seen where it led. As Carla watched Jake flare she wondered, for the first time, who'd still be standing when the pieces fell.

The message pinged on Eve's phone late in the evening, catching her by surprise as she tidied the living room. Picking it up, she saw David's name and opened the text with mild curiosity: *I'm leaving for Bhutan tomorrow. I've arranged for my friend, Auguste, to walk your dogs—no need to worry. You can always join me if you want! (jk)*

Eve blinked at the screen, a brief shock of excitement at the message, which she tried to dismiss. She caught herself almost smiling. "Why not?" she muttered under her breath before shaking her head. "Don't be crazy," she replied, scolding herself.

Still, she couldn't shake the rush of excitement that followed. She typed back a quick response: *Have fun! The dogs are going to miss you! LOL.*

Moments later, her phone buzzed again. *I'll be on Singapore Airlines, leaving at 5 a.m. I'll send some photos when I finally get to Paro.*

Eve stared at the message, her mind whirring. The idea of Bhutan, of setting off without a clear purpose, was liberating—almost intoxicating. She glanced at the empty penthouse, her mood dampened by Jake's unrelenting absence. The table where they'd shared meals now felt like a relic from another age, and the once-vibrant apartment seemed devoid of life.

She poured herself a glass of wine and tried to banish the thought. But it lingered, hovering at the edge of her mind while she drained the glass and poured herself another. "What's stopping me?" she wondered.

Jake was busy as ever, his work taking precedence over everything, including her. Why shouldn't she take a break, have an adventure, experience something new? Maybe she could start afresh—recalibrate her life, cast off the shackles she had accepted, somehow unwittingly.

By the time she stumbled into bed, the wine had dulled her restless thoughts, but her sleep was fitful. She dreamed of winding mountain paths, vibrant prayer flags fluttering in the wind, deep valleys, stunning vistas. The images teased Eve through the night. When she finally woke, sun was streaming through the curtains—the clock on her bedside table read well past 9:00 a.m.

She recalled the film David had mentioned: *Travellers and Magicians*. She had watched it, been mesmerized not just by Bhutan's beauty but by the film's insight. *Was Bhutan a place where you could get clarity and rediscover meaning?*

Eve turned her head to check Jake's side of the bed—it was untouched. At the sound of movement the Labradors came bounding in. Eve scarcely noticed. There was no note, no message, no indication of when Jake might return. A familiar, hollow ache of loneliness spread in her chest as she stared.

"Why not?" she said aloud, her voice firmer this time. Swinging her legs out of bed, she grabbed a small suitcase. She was still in her negligee, and Eve knew it reflected a life that no longer existed—a past she had lost, an idea she had clung to.

Maybe she'd been lured by nostalgia. Maybe she'd been afraid to recognize yet another dead end. However, she'd lose no more days. She wasn't even fifty and her desires mattered. Eve still had a vision for her life, and this was not it.

A current of anticipation coursed through her. What to take? She opened all her drawers: scarves, blouses, pants, cosmetics, velvet bags, perfumes, boxes of various sizes. She ran her hands along the dresses and skirts, looked at her shoes, amused by how many she had once felt necessary. She began tossing items into the suitcase—moving on instinct.

The dogs showed excitement at all the activity, which usually meant a trip for them. Eve added some dresses before swapping them out for jeans and skirts. She went to the living room to grab some books she'd always meant to read, but never got around to even opening. The Labradors followed her, scampering down the corridor and in between her legs as she leaned across to pick out first one book, then another.

Next came her passport, which she retrieved from the wall safe—her hands surprisingly steady. Impulsively, but keen to make a statement, she placed her negligee in the safe where the passport had been—a quiet message Jake would understand. One day. He had treasured her presence but neglected her spirit. She was taking action to restore the balance.

Jake would eventually recognize the emptiness she had left, even if he might not understand the hurt he'd caused—but that no longer concerned her. She believed, for the first time in ages, that there was the possibility of reclaiming herself.

Taken with the idea of renaissance, she went back to the bedroom and walk-in closet to find new clothes from among those she'd bought but rarely used: a pair of coral-colored pants tucked away in a bottom drawer, a cream blouse from the garment rack.

She loosely tied her hair back, letting a few strands escape. She added some designer jewelry—handcrafted gold pieces that she'd bought but that had spent most of the time hidden away. By the end, as she zipped shut the bag, her mind felt lighter—as if the weight of indecision had melted away.

Eve headed for the door—then hesitated. She should write something to Jake. Getting out a piece of paper from the printer in the study and an envelope, which she found in a drawer for greeting cards, she scrawled out a longer note. She rested it against a bottle of wine on the counter, then headed for the front door. *This is it,* she thought. *My chance to create a new story.*

She paused at the entranceway, the leash rack catching her eye. A pang of guilt flickered through her as she saw the Labradors there, looking expectantly. But David had made arrangements, hadn't he? They'd be fine. She crouched and stroked their heads, whispering a quick apology, promising she'd be back soon. She gave Diesel a quick kiss on the forehead. "If only things had gone differently," Eve sighed. And she watched—surprised—as a tear dropped from her eye onto his black fur and burst into little beads.

As if to dispel the hint of weakness, she got out her phone and texted Jake: *Taking some time for myself. Don't worry about the dogs—everything's covered. I'll be in touch.* She hesitated before hitting Send, but eventually pressed the button and slipped the phone back into her bag.

She stepped out of the apartment, closing the door firmly behind. The click of the lock sounded final—a last punctuation mark ending a long, convoluted sentence.

"Living requires adventure," she murmured. "And I want to live. There is still so much to experience—so much I haven't let myself enjoy." At the curb, a cab pulled in just as she was stepping out—as if fate had intervened. "JFK, please," she said. She'd figure out the logistics on the way—there were always seats somewhere, even if it meant multiple stopovers.

The cab sped off, the bracing air making everything seem fresh. Eve allowed herself to smile, really smile. It was the first time in months. For once, she wasn't waiting for someone else to make her feel happy. She was taking the leap on her own. And, on this occasion, she felt sure the path ahead would open.

62. Inauguration Day

Despite the brittle chill outside, Jake's penthouse stayed warm inside, bathed in the glow of dozens of recessed lights. The apartment radiated luxury—high ceilings, hardwood floors. The sophistication of modern design meant there was no condensation or fog to mask its view across Manhattan, which even a jaded New Yorker would envy. However, Jake was completely engrossed by the flat-screen TV mounted on his wall as it broadcast history in the making.

The screen televised a cold, windswept Washington, D.C., where the new Republican President—having taken her oath at midday to succeed another trailblazing female leader—was speaking to the nation on the West Front of the Capitol. Jake watched in silence, swirling a glass of red wine in one hand, his posture surprisingly relaxed for a man usually wound so tight.

He caught a glimpse of himself in the reflective edge of the screen: the sharp, perpetual focus in his eyes, the faint lines of stress etched around them, softened only slightly by this moment of solitude. Out of the corner of his eye, he caught sight of Eve's message still on the marble counter, a silent reminder of her sudden departure, weeks back, to Bhutan. He had no idea when—or if—she would be back. He'd left the negligee, too—the one he'd found inside the safe. Some souvenirs, he decided, were best left out of sight.

For all the light in the room, he felt oddly surrounded by shadow. Perhaps that suited him. There were no deals to close, no negotiations, simply the quiet acceptance that sometimes even he couldn't chart all the outcomes.

A soft ring from the doorbell echoed through the apartment. With a hint of impatience, Jake set his wine aside and walked to the entrance. Standing there in a puffy winter coat, cheeks flushed from the cold, was Auguste—the new dogwalker.

"*Bonjour, Monsieur.* Mr. J... Jake," she corrected herself with a polite smile, a little unsure of herself. She pronounced all the 'j's like the 's' in pleasure. The French accent hovered delicately in the entranceway. "I'm so sorry to interrupt, but I'm here to walk *les chiens*, the Labs."

Jake stepped aside, letting her in. His three black Labradors bounded across the polished floor, tails wagging furiously at the sight of Auguste. She dropped to her knees with genuine delight, scratching behind their ears and baby-talking in French. The dogs were in heaven, nudging her hands with their wet noses for more affection.

Jake watched her, his mood unexpectedly lifting at the sight of someone so young and full of life—someone for whom the world still seemed wide open. In her knit hat, scarf, and heavy boots, she radiated an effortless charm. She glanced up at him with an unsure smile, as if she sensed his gaze.

"You have quite a view, *Monsieur* Jake," she said, glancing briefly at the enormous windows, not attempting to fix the 'j'.

He offered a measured grin, nodding. "Yeah. It's something. Even for the most jaded." Their eyes met for an extra moment.

"And these dogs," she continued, "these three beautiful dogs, so *charmants.*"

Standing, Auguste brushed a stray lock of hair from her forehead. "Shall I bring them back in an hour?"

"That'd be good," Jake replied, slipping a hand into his trouser pocket. "And, uh... dress warmly. Weather's brutal."

She laughed, a light, musical sound. "I will. *Merci.*" She clicked her tongue for the dogs, and they trotted after her, obediently close by her heels. Jake noted that she seemed to have the dogs more under control than David did.

He watched the doors close behind Auguste, the faint echo of her departure leaving him strangely aware of how expansive his apartment was—especially without Eve. Perhaps it was good to have space right now, he told himself, to breathe and consider his next moves without distraction.

He poured himself another glass of red wine. It was the bottle against which Eve had rested her letter—a wine bold and expensive, like everything else in his life. Jake returned to the living room.

The new President's speech was reaching its crescendo, the crowd clapping in appreciation. Jake sank into a leather armchair, swirled the wine in his glass again, then took a slow, thoughtful sip.

He totted up the balance. On the one hand, an M&A deal agreed, a pipeline venture defended in court but entangled in its execution, and an unexpected shift in the country's leadership, favoring traditional resources.

On the other hand, pressure on his JV in Russia and a personal void left by Eve's departure. In the comfort of his penthouse, a pour of deep red in his glass, he felt nothing but calm. The results tilted in his favor.

He raised the wine to his lips, eyes half-lidded, and let the President's final words drift over him. There would be another day—with new power plays and further deals. For now, however, there was only the stillness around him, the wine, and the city outside his window—waiting, Jake believed, for him to decide his next move.

...

The reverie didn't last. The sharp trill of his phone shattered the stillness. He glanced at the screen, his brow furrowing as he saw the caller ID: Dick Harrington, head of Exploration & Development. Jake hesitated for only a moment, then picked up.

"Dick," Jake said, his voice steady but edged with warning. "This had better be good if you're calling me on Inauguration Day."

"Apologies for the timing, Jake," Dick began, his tone tense and apologetic. "I figured you'd want to hear as soon as possible."

Jake sat up straighter, setting the wine glass down on the table in front of him. "Go on."

"Well," Dick continued, "I was using this moment to dig deeper into the data we've gotten since the acquisition. Specifically, the reserves in the Permian. I've been reviewing the latest appraisal results, and, uh... it's not great news."

Jake's jaw tightened, his grip on the phone firm. "Define 'not great.'"

Dick shuffled audibly, clearly uncomfortable with what he was about to say. "The reserves are a lot more complicated than we originally thought. The resource formation—it's not as straightforward as we assumed in the due diligence phase. It's layered, fractured, inconsistent. Extraction's going to require significantly more investment, and even then, output is likely to be variable, not steady."

"What about their technology?"

"Their technology, well, it's scarcely at the stage of scaling up, let alone commercialization."

Jake leaned back in his chair, running a hand through his hair, his eyes narrowing as he processed the information. "How much more investment are we talking?"

"It's hard to say exactly without more testing," Dick replied, "but we're looking at a major hit to margins. Best-case scenario, we barely break even for the next few years. Worst-case... it's a money pit."

Jake's face darkened. "And we paid top dollar for it."

"Yes," Dick admitted nervously. "We're sitting on something that's about to under-deliver just when we need it to perform. The business was already overextended—their finances stretched. This... well, this complicates things, to put it mildly."

Jake stood and walked to the window—the skyline, once calming, suddenly suffocating. "Unbelievable," he muttered, more to himself than to Dick. "They sold us a dream, and we bought it."

"I'm sorry, Jake," Dick said, his voice heavy. "I thought you needed to know ASAP."

Jake turned back to the room, his expression hard, his mind already racing. "Here's what we're going to do: I'm convening an executive meeting first thing tomorrow morning. We'll review every project on the books, including this deal, and figure out how to get ahead of this mess. Be ready to present everything you've got—the numbers, the risks, the contingencies."

Jake paused before reiterating the obvious. "I want solutions, Dick, not just problems."

"Understood," Dick said. "I'll have everything prepared."

"Yes," Jake said firmly, "you will." He paused. "And Dick—don't let this news spread. If word gets out before we have a plan..."

"Got it. I'll see you in the morning."

Jake ended the call and stared at the phone for an instant, his hand now gripping it as if to extract answers. He let out a sharp breath, grasped his glass, and drained the wine in one swallow—nothing left to savor. Victory suddenly tasted stale.

There was no time for regret, no place for second-guessing or self-pity—simply the next move. Jake knew better than anyone: he wasn't playing to lose—not now, not ever.

63. A Son Is Born

January wind knifed across the Capitol's West Front, carrying hints of snow and history. Washington D.C. pulsed with the fervor of Inauguration Day, the crowd's cheers swelling like a tide beneath the gray sky.

The new Republican President—a woman succeeding another trailblazer—stood at the podium, her voice resolute, weaving promises of unity and strength into the frigid air. Kaisa stood there on a reserved platform among dignitaries, her navy wool coat cinched tightly, the diamond ring glinting.

Beside her, Caleb stood sharp in a tailored overcoat, enjoying the ceremony and the crowd with a senator's ease, his hand holding hers in a show of unity.

The President's speech drew to a close, with applause thundering across the National Mall. Caleb leaned close to Kaisa, his breath warm against her ear. "She's set the stage for a bold term. Good for our future campaigns." Kaisa nodded, her smile tight, her eyes scanning the sea of faces—congressmen and women, donors, power brokers.

Then, she saw him—a ripple in the crowd exposed a familiar figure cutting through with purpose, approaching them. Alex. Her pulse surged, a sudden fear about her designs constricting her chest. He had Anisa at his side, in a cream coat and fur-lined hat that framed her elegance, her sharp eyes taking in the scene.

"Kaisa, Caleb," Alex greeted, his voice smooth as polished stone, betraying nothing. His now-typical wolfish smile was intact, but his dark eyes held a guarded intensity. "A historic day, isn't it? The nation's turning a new page."

Caleb shook Alex's hand, his grin broad. "Alex, Anisa, great to see you. Quite the spectacle, right? This'll be one for the history books." He gestured to the crowd, oblivious to the undercurrent rippling between the others.

Kaisa seized the moment, her tone light but laced with intent. "Historic, yes. New beginnings, but old promises—always a delicate balance." Her eyes met

Alex's, probing for a crack in his façade. "What do you make of it, Alex? A fresh start, or just another chapter in the same story?"

Alex's gaze wavered. "Fresh starts are rare," he replied. "But every chapter carries echoes of earlier passages. Don't you find?" His eyes held Kaisa's, a wariness beneath the charm, as if he discerned her provocation.

Anisa smiled as she surveyed the staff beginning to reorganize the space, her voice carrying over the general noise. "I think this is a new story with its own trajectory."

Before Kaisa could respond, a lanky figure emerged, weaving through the dignitaries with a teenager's careless grace and indifference. He was a boy in his mid-teens, wearing a dark suit, his blond hair tousled by the wind, his eyes a light brown. "Mom, sorry I'm late," he said, his voice cracking slightly. "The security line was insane."

Kaisa recognized the mix of nonchalance and annoyance that had lately begun to characterize him. "You made it, darling," was all she said.

Her voice was steady, but nervousness was eating her inside. She turned to Alex and Anisa, her maternal instinct taking over. "Let me introduce my son, Matisse Warren. He's fourteen, and here to witness a special day."

Alex's expression froze, a look of shock finally breaking through his polished mask—raw and unguarded. Something in the boy's stance struck him... Alex took in his features: the sharp jaw, the blond hair, and the piercing eyes that could be his own. *Fourteen years.*

Alex considered the two of them—Kaisa and Matisse. The math was obvious: the Hermitage, Moscow, his arrest, the life stolen from him. Caleb wasn't on the scene then—only him. Ivan.

That he might have a child was—despite its possibility—something he'd never considered. The revelation slammed into him, reshaping everything. Yet his face hardened, as he sought to betray nothing and keep his resolve firmly in place.

"Fourteen," Alex echoed, his voice controlled, almost too smooth. "Quite an age to see an inauguration. You must be proud, Kaisa." His gaze lingered on Matisse, studying him—a nose like Kaisa's, a stance like his own as a kid. His heart raced, but he buried it, his discipline now holding firm.

Matisse offered a shy grin, oblivious to the storm he'd ignited. "It's pretty cool," he said, shoving his hands in his pockets. "Mom said it's important to see how things change."

Kaisa's hand rested on Matisse's shoulder, her touch protective but her eyes locked on Alex, watching. "He's my anchor," she said, her voice soft but pointed. "Family matters, doesn't it, Alex? They shape who we become, even when the past is... complicated." Her words continued to test Alex's resolve.

His jaw tightened. "Family's not always so easy," he replied, his tone a little heavy. "They tie you to things you can't always claim. But," he added, trying to strike a lighter note, "they make for interesting stories, don't they?" His eyes fluttered and came to rest on Kaisa's hand. It lay on Matisse's shoulder, the ring in full view. A small muscle in his cheek began to twitch again.

Caleb, sensing the shift but misreading it, clapped Matisse on the back. "This guy's our pride and joy," he said. "Kaisa's brains, my stubborn streak." Caleb laughed.

Anisa stepped in, her voice smooth. "Indeed he's a fine young man. You both must be very proud. In some ways he reminds me of boys in Baku—bright, full of potential. You must cherish him." Her smile was gracious and her eyes gentle.

"We do cherish him. Don't we, Matisse?" she said. He smiled good-naturedly though his mother's expression of love proved irksome. "However," she went on, "Matisse's story is still unfolding. He's had an interesting start, and I don't know where it will lead."

Alex's eyes darkened a touch. "He's going to turn out fine," he said at last and then turned to Caleb. "We'd better keep going." He paused. "I think this election will set you up well for the future. You must be very happy at the results." Caleb smiled.

Alex turned to Matisse. "Nice meeting you. You're fortunate indeed to have such good parents." Then, stepping back and taking hold of Anisa's hand, Alex moved on.

As they melted into the crowd, Kaisa rewound the scene in her mind: Alex's fleeting shock, his guarded statements. It suggested he'd done the math too, and yet betrayed little. His resolve appeared a wall she couldn't definitively breach. Matisse tugged at her sleeve, pointing to the President who was now waving impromptu at the crowds. "Mom, she's awesome."

"She is," Kaisa murmured, her eyes more interested in picking out where Alex had gone. She'd played her trump card. Matisse was her truth. For a little over fourteen years she'd carried this truth alone, while Ivan remained no more than a memory, a shadow.

However, if Alex was now Ivan returned, then the shared blood, their son, would reframe his quest. She had unveiled the truth. Whether it would save or destroy them both no longer mattered.

64. JV Sale

Jake stood by the massive windows of his office, the dying light of a winter afternoon now spilling gray shadows across the room. The jagged Manhattan skyline loomed in the distance, indifferent to his turmoil.

Behind him, the air was still, suffused with a heavy tension that seemed to press against the walls. Michael Sokolov, PanEnergy's country head in Russia, sat across the lacquered walnut desk, his features set in that careful mask Jake had come to associate with unwelcome news.

On the desk itself lay the folder, a slim but weighty testament to the options—or lack thereof—before them.

Jake's hands were in his pockets, clenched into fists so tight he could feel his nails digging into his palms. He stared out at the darkening city as if it might offer him an answer, a way out. However, he already knew there wasn't one. Not this time.

"This is it?" he asked finally, his voice low and sharp, each word carrying the weight of his disbelief.

Michael nodded. "This is it. Alex is the only serious option. I've spoken to the others on the list, but they're not even pretending to be interested. Alex is the only one willing to take the business on. And even then, it's at terms..." He hesitated, choosing his words carefully. "Let's just say, not favorable to us."

Jake turned, his blue eyes narrowing. "Not favorable?" he began icily. "That's putting it mildly. The bastard's offering pennies on the dollar for a venture we spent years building." His voice rose, sharp and bitter.

"We did the groundwork. Built the infrastructure. Navigated every damn labyrinth of bureaucracy they required of us. And now we're supposed to just... hand it over? So Alex can waltz in, with Moscow's blessing, and reap all the rewards while we take the loss?"

Michael didn't flinch. He'd seen Jake's temper before, weathered the storms. It was not a pretty sight. "Jake, they've got us boxed in—the environmental probes, the tax audits. None of it's about compliance. It's about control. If we don't play ball, they'll make sure we bleed out one way or another. They want us gone."

Jake strode to his desk, looming over it as he flipped open the folder. The numbers stared back at him like an insult, cold and undeniable. The price Alex was offering barely covered their sunk costs. It didn't even begin to account for the potential lying untapped beneath the Arctic permafrost. He slammed the folder shut; the sound cracked across the room.

"In better times," he said, his voice quieter now but no less venomous, "this fight might have been winnable. Hell, I'd have taken it all the way to the Kremlin if I had to. But now..." He trailed off, his jaw tightening, the words sticking in his throat. He hated admitting it—to Michael, to himself. "Now I'm running out of time. Out of energy. Too much is coming at us from all directions."

Michael shifted in his chair, his expression cautious. "If we cut this loose, Jake, we can stabilize the rest of the company. The regulators drop the charges, we avoid the fines, and Alex takes on all the risk going forward. It's not ideal, but it's clean. And it's fast."

Jake laughed bitterly, the sound harsh in the stillness. "Clean? Nothing about this is clean. This is blackmail, plain and simple. They want me to fold, and you're telling me to hand over my chips, walk away like a smart foreigner."

"It's not walking away," Michael countered. "It's survival."

Jake stared at him, his shoulders taut, every muscle in his body screaming against the decision that was forming in his mind. For decades, he'd built his empire on aggression, on never backing down, on bulldozing anyone who dared stand in his way. But now, for the first time, he could see the cracks forming, could almost grasp the risk of it all collapsing—leaving him under the debris.

"If I'm not careful," he said, almost to himself, "this could take everything. For the first time, I'm looking at a situation where I might lose it all. And that..." He shook his head, his lips curling into a grim smile. "That's not a gamble I'm willing to take."

Michael said nothing, sensing that this was a rare moment of vulnerability, one that would pass as quickly as it came.

Finally, Jake straightened, pulling himself back into the hardened shell he'd spent a lifetime perfecting. "Fine," he said, the word heavy with reluctance. "Negotiate with Alex. Push him as far as he'll go—get every dollar for every concession."

He paused. "And when the documents are ready, we'll sign them. Find a place—somewhere suitably neutral. Let's get it done." He waved a hand dismissively. "Let's be rid of this whole mess. I've got other fires to put out."

Michael rose, gathering his papers. "I'll get it done."

As the door closed behind him, Jake sat down heavily in his chair, staring at the closed folder on the table. The room felt colder now, the shadows deeper, as if the encroaching night carried the weight of his decision. He closed his eyes, rubbing a hand over his face. He could almost feel the younger man he'd once been—impatient, invincible. He'd always fought—always won. But now, the rules of the game seemed to have changed.

Claire and her team had gathered in a meeting room for another briefing. The strain was beginning to show.

"What's the latest on Alex?" Claire asked, leaning forward.

Lisa cleared her throat. "Ma'am, there's been significant movement. First, Alex has agreed to purchase PanEnergy's joint ventures in Russia. What's more surprising—he's doing so with the support of the Russian government." She paused.

"This is extraordinary. The Kremlin rarely endorses foreign acquisitions without strings attached, and especially given Alex's history. It hints there may be unseen ties or hidden motives at play."

Claire's eyes narrowed. "Go on."

Lisa clicked through a few slides on the screen behind her, bringing up surveillance photos of Alex's estate in the Hamptons. "Second, someone entered Alex's house in the Hamptons last night."

"We observed the break-in but didn't intervene to avoid tipping off third parties. Our team has been monitoring Alex closely, and any interference could have compromised the operation or alerted actors to our presence. The extent of the damage or what, if anything, was taken remains unknown."

Calloway, seated next to her, crossed his arms. "Risky, but you're right—we'd have burned our cover."

"What else?" continued Claire.

Lisa nodded. "Alex is slated to attend the White House reception to thank supporters of the new President. That's scheduled for this Saturday. Interestingly, the CEO of PanEnergy, Jake Laskin, is heading to Moscow at the same time to finalize the JV sale."

Claire's pen tapped the table, rhythmically but quietly, as she processed the information. "What's the latest on our Alex-Ivan connection?"

Lisa hesitated. "The jury's still out. Nothing definitive, but everything about Alex—his moves, his encounters—screams trouble. He's an unknown quantity—one whose actions may have serious implications for American interests. He cannot be ignored."

"Agreed," Claire said sharply. "Will Alex be attending the reception alone?"

Lisa shook her head. "No, ma'am. He's bringing his partner, Anisa. By all accounts, she's a much younger woman of Iraqi background with an international upbringing. Charming, sophisticated, and very private. We're now running deeper checks on her as well."

Claire's expression shifted slightly, a look of resolve taking over. "All right," she said after a moment. "Colonel Calloway, arrange for my partner and me to attend the function—same table as Alex and Anisa. I would like to see Alex firsthand, size him up for myself." She would look into Alex's eyes, and she would separate truth from suspicion.

Calloway nodded. "Understood, ma'am. I'll make it happen."

The room fell silent for a beat, the weight of the situation pressing down on everyone. "This man spells trouble," Claire said. "Let's just make sure we're ready for whatever comes next." She paused for a moment. "That's all, thank you."

As the team filed out, Claire remained seated, her mind working through the pieces of the puzzle. This was no ordinary game, and Alex no ordinary player. She would face him in person and decide for herself what he truly was.

66. JFK Airport

Jake Laskin tightened his grip on the leather portfolio as he strode through the VIP channel. His overcoat brushed his ankles; a hint of weariness shadowed his eyes. His direct flight to Moscow was due to board in less than an hour—a quiet, unpublicized journey to finalize the sale of PanEnergy's Russian assets.

For months, political heat had mounted in Russia, forcing him to disentangle his company from a market once brimming with promise. Now, he was set to offload those interests to the enigmatic and, he was sure, hostile Alex.

At the far end of the same terminal, Irina Kostov stepped off an incoming flight from Paris. Even though she had recently changed her official documents, the family name in her *ФИО,* she cleared immigration swiftly, her diplomatic passport expediting the usual checks.

Dressed in a tailored suit, smoky charcoal in color, over a pale gold silk shirt, Irina projected a cool composure. Yet the lingering stiffness in her posture betrayed not just the flight but her concern. She needed to learn everything about Alex—and what he signified for her. It all remained too vague.

Where did his ambitions cross hers? She savored the chase—the prospect of hunting him down. But to what purpose? She wondered if Alex were simply a step in her career, or if—somehow—he held more meaning.

She thought again about the fortuneteller all those years ago. Irina was sure the prediction had carried a private aspect. Was Alex, in some way, a means to get back at her father?

Another shadow appeared across the glass wall—another form passing over the same light. Jake and Irina crossed each other, moving along parallel corridors of brushed steel and polished glass—so close, yet oblivious to one another. Jake eyed his phone, scanning messages from his attorney. Irina discreetly studied her own intelligence files, memorizing details about Alex's transactions.

Moving in different directions, leading to different outcomes, they were each being pulled by the same person. At the Arrivals hall, Sergei and Nadia waited to greet Irina as she exited—rubbing the old, increasingly smooth cross on her necklace. The chase continued, and she would not be the one to surrender.

67. White House Reception

The State Dining Room of the White House buzzed with the clink of crystal and the murmurs of campaign worthies gathered once more to celebrate the new President and her achievements.

The late January light filtered through the large windows, casting a cold glow on polished hardwood floors, softened by a cream-colored rug, and the round tables draped in ivory linens. Claire navigated the room slowly, her heels tapping softly, her walking stick providing a percussive backing.

She wore a tailored emerald dress—suggesting influence without ostentation. She spotted her assigned table near the podium—close enough to feel the event's weight, discreet enough to observe. This was much more than just a reception, she knew. It was a first pass at who was in and who was out.

At the table, Caleb Warren, the re-elected Wyoming senator, flashed his well-prepared charm, his arm brushing that of his wife, Kaisa—her poise unshaken despite events of the last several months.

Alex sat opposite, his slate suit sharp, his smile masking any unease. Beside him sat Anisa, striking in a crimson dress, her dark eyes surveying the scene, her posture elegant—straight in a way, Claire noted, many young women had lost.

Tom Stephens, the Texas attorney general, alongside his down-to-earth wife, Ellen, were another two, exchanging laughs with General Finley Jones, a grizzled Middle East veteran eyed for Secretary of Defense, and his lawyer wife, Margaret. The table was a crucible of intermittent success, varnished pasts, and unspoken agendas.

Claire reached her seat and lowered herself efficiently but carefully, offering a short apology. "Good afternoon, everyone. My partner, Theodore, is delayed by work, but he'll join us soon." Her smile was wide, but her eyes lingered on Alex, noting the subtle disturbance his presence caused.

She called a waiter over, and gave him her cane to mind for the duration of the meal. Alex watched in quiet understanding. He'd come out of his fight with Yuri troubled by deep bruising, a fever, and nerve trauma. His limp had lasted years and still occasionally reappeared when he was upset. Briefly he wondered about the source of Claire's affliction.

"I'm sorry that Theodore's going to be late," began Caleb. "As you know, work waits for no one in this town, Claire." The table laughed.

Caleb then picked up a glass, his voice ringing quietly. "Now that almost everyone is here, let's toast. To the President, and to four years of prosperity!" The group echoed the cheer. Kaisa's gaze caught Alex's as they knocked glasses.

It wasn't long before everyone was steering conversation down their favored paths. Tom was interested in the likely direction of new policy. "The President's energy agenda—bold, but tricky. Senator Warren, you've been interested in energy policy. How do you see it playing out for oil states?"

Caleb put a hand on the table. "It's a balancing act," he stated with his senator's polish. "I feel we need to be pragmatic—less ideology, more consideration for our unique assets. We need to leverage our advantages versus our competitors overseas." He glanced at Alex. "Don't you agree?"

Alex smiled. "Energy's a volatile game—oil pipelines, renewables, data, power grids. One policy shift, one corporate misstep, and the board alters. Progress and investment requires trust."

General Finley, for his part, launched into anecdotes about past American engagements. He was most interested in Iraq—talking of heroics, airstrikes, victories.

Anisa was caught between the two conversations, which she felt overlapped. "Trust is fragile," she interjected, her fingers tightening around her glass. "Whether in business or war, promises break under pressure." Her accent carried a slight tremor. She gazed at the General, her posture suddenly strained. Anisa masked it, but Claire caught the shift, her instincts telling her something was amiss.

Kaisa seized the opening. "Promises do break, Anisa. However, the past—family, events, inheritance—does keep a hold on us and ultimately forces a reckoning, whether we like it or not." Her eyes again sought to pierce Alex's mind.

Alex looked down. "Yes, the past matters," he replied, his voice low. "And it can resurface when you least expect." His gaze rose and flicked from Kaisa to Anisa. "It's difficult to guess always what it means. The ties can strengthen or they can choke."

General Finley, oblivious, laughed heartily—a laugh that hinted at the weight of men who had seen too much and survived. "Indeed! Just like my old unit—loyalty forged in fire. You can't break that." His war stories resumed, and Anisa's smile again tightened, a silent storm brewing.

Claire noted the whole exchange: Anisa's awkwardness, the sparring between Kaisa and Alex. It all interested her. However, Anisa was the new variable. *She's not just Alex's shadow,* Claire began to think. *She's a player in her own right, with her own scars.*

The conversation grew sharper—Tom pressing Caleb about judicial reform, Caleb countering with infrastructure needs, each testing their own agenda.

Kaisa's focus stayed on Alex. "History's a funny thing," she said. "In writing it, the author chooses the story and, in doing so, hides the inconvenient truths. However, sooner or later the complicating facts emerge—like a son stepping into the light." Her heart pounded at making such an obvious provocation.

The others, of course, did not notice the gibe, but Alex's eyes darkened. "Truths emerge when they're ready," he said, his voice almost intimate. "Timing's everything, Kaisa. Some stories need... patience." He looked at Caleb. "Is politics about haste or patience—what do you think, Senator Warren? Do we limit our ambitions to the timeframe and circumstances?"

Just as the talk was becoming heated, the last member of the table arrived, a little breathless and dressed in an ochre-colored suit. "Sorry I'm late, darling," he said, bending down to kiss Claire's cheek. "Theodore Cooper," he introduced himself, although almost everyone knew him. He nodded toward Alex. "Pleasure to see you again."

Claire smiled, but her focus stayed on the table and Alex in particular, who offered Theodore a polite nod, his composure unshaken. The luncheon slowly progressed—salmon en croûte, roasted vegetables, a choice of wines.

A feeling of unease eddied around the table despite the positive implications of the day. Anisa spent a lot of the meal casting looks at Finley. Kaisa continued to probe Alex, who, for his part, was more interested in Caleb—the senator who, unaware of his wife's concerns, cheerily talked of his ambitions and the prospects awaiting him as a key member of the winning side.

The room around the table glowed with polished light—crystal, silver, smart outfits. Waiters passed among the politicians, donors, campaign leaders, and prospective appointees. Alex at last engaged Caleb, voicing what was gnawing at his mind.

"I enjoyed meeting your son at the inauguration," he said. "He has a sort of poise—something not easily taught."

Caleb laughed lightly, pleased. "Ah, Matisse. He's a good kid. His mother's influence, no doubt. Though he's got a certain fervor—which must be from me."

Kaisa stiffened in her chair. Her eyes seemed to mix anxiety with a sense of anticipation. The shift attracted Claire's attention once more.

Alex's smile was reflective. "Perhaps. Who knows how these traits appear." His gaze lingered for a moment too long, his tone still perfectly polite but edged with something Claire couldn't quite name.

Caleb, still oblivious, nodded. "Well, whoever he takes after, he'll make his mark. He's already talking about politics, would you believe it? Fourteen and certain he'll change the world."

"Fourteen," Alex repeated, turning the stem of his glass. "An age full of discovery. Senator Warren, you must find it rewarding—to see yourself in someone else, to know the line continues."

Caleb chuckled. "Sure, though he's far sharper than I was at his age. Kaisa says he questions everything. Maybe too much."

"Curiosity," Alex said, lifting his glass, "is the mark of a restless mind. And blood—" he paused, smiling faintly, "blood has a way of finding its echo, even when others do not hear it."

Kaisa, from across the table, caught the phrasing and felt her breath tighten. Claire's eyes flicked between them all, measuring.

Caleb only nodded, good-humoredly. "True enough. We're lucky with him. He's our bridge, really—between all this," he gestured at the glittering room, "and something honest."

Alex's smile was cool. "Bridges," he dwelled on the word. "Sometimes they take us where we don't really want to go."

Alex glanced toward Kaisa. "In any case, you've raised a remarkable son. You must cherish him."

Their gazes locked just long enough for Kaisa to feel the tremor of meaning and for Claire to notice. Then Alex turned away as another senator approached. Claire leaned toward Kaisa, her tone barely above a whisper. "He has a way of making small talk sound quite like a confession."

Kaisa's reply was measured, her eyes never leaving Alex. "Maybe it is, of some kind." She shrugged.

As dessert arrived—chocolate tart with gold leaf—Alex turned toward Kaisa. "Kaisa," he said, his voice urgent, a certain rawness breaking through his normally controlled demeanor. "I need to talk." His eyes glanced at her ring, then her face—revealing a mix of pain and desire.

For a second, Kaisa froze—hope and fear colliding. And then something erupted. "If you want to talk, prove it." She'd reached this point after so much effort, but now all she could feel was a sudden anger. "Show me that you mean it."

Before Alex could continue, his phone vibrated, sharp and insistent. He tried to ignore the intrusion, keen to stay focused on Kaisa, to respond properly to her searching eyes and the uncertain flickers of desire he saw emerging. However, the phone buzzed and buzzed again, unrelenting. It shattered the moment.

Alex's expression hardened, his discipline snapping back. He nodded to Kaisa, an unspoken promise, and rose, leaving the room.

Kaisa watched him go, feeling as if yet again nothing had been resolved. She felt newly adrift. Alex had, for the briefest moment, created the opening for some answers—maybe even for some resolution. Now he'd left.

Kaisa looked at Claire. She saw some of her own disappointment mirrored in her neighbor. Both felt bereft of real answers.

However, Claire's head was turning over everything she had seen. Alex. Matisse—was he somehow a pawn? Kaisa. And now increasingly the enigmatic Anisa. What was her role in the whole saga? Was she an obstacle, to be worked around, or the means to some form of solution? In every room, Claire believed, one person held the key. The challenge was finding who—and why. Here, today, the overall picture remained tantalizingly beyond reach.

In the hallway, Alex lifted the phone, his reflection caught in a gilt mirror—a man divided between past and future.

Jake's voice came through, brittle with distance. "I know you're involved. It's not all random." Alex didn't respond.

"Let's finish this," Jake continued, "properly."

"We already have," Alex replied.

He cut the connection and turned to head back. The phone went off again. *Jake, no doubt,* Alex thought. *Persistent to the end.* But it was a message alert—an unidentified sender, encrypted attachment.

He hesitated. He already knew, in part, what it would be. Alex pressed to open the file. There was a rush of code, and then a video sprung to life.

Grainy footage, time-stamped from years before. A dust-choked street, a low compound, soldiers shouting orders. Through the static came the voice he recognized—the General ordering a sweep. The camera jolted—a drone feed, maybe, or a body-cam later stitched into record. Then a door blew inward, and chaos froze into something unbearably clear—the relief center's chapel, the two civilians on the floor, the cross upon the wall. A command. Gunfire.

The feed continued. It panned across faces still visible despite the smoke. He paused the reel before it finished.

Alex had suspected long ago about Anisa's parents. He'd heard fragments from Anisa herself—regarding what she'd lost and how. That night in Baku when they first talked, she'd spoken of mercy as if it were both prayer and weapon. He hadn't corrected her. Some missions required faith to wear the mask of vengeance.

He played the final frames: the General stepping into sunlight, brushing dust from his uniform, crossing himself.

Alex understood what had happened. No one meant for such things to occur—death always accompanied campaigns. The questions lay in the principles adopted, the measures taken—and who ultimately was responsible for checking man's inhumanity to man.

Alex whispered an ancient benediction, half for the dead, half for the living. He typed a short reply: *Message received. Всё ясно—all is clear. Nothing is hidden that will not be revealed.* Then pressed Send.

He wondered why outcomes always twisted—good intentions foundered on execution, past loves strained beneath present vows, personal identity dissolved in the grind of daily living. What was the answer—reconciliation, vengeance, mercy, redemption? He still didn't know.

Instead he defaulted to movement and action. Standing still led nowhere. Squaring his shoulders, Alex walked back into the noise and the day's celebration.

68. Acknowledgments

A large part of the opening chapters was a loosely based, fictional version of my mother's sixtieth birthday and what followed. The year was 2008 rather than 2009. I was asked to chase down Helen Illend, and we have all become great friends since. She and her extended family have visited over the years and stayed with us numerous times. I'm deeply grateful to Helen for allowing me to start my first novel with this story of our encounter and its evolution.

My family lived in Moscow from about 1980 to 1982. I have only a few, but powerful, memories. They have, of course, become romanticized over time. We are big fans of the poetry of Pushkin and Lermontov—descended from the Scottish family of Learmonth. Both poets died too young.

I recall organizing with my family a big party to celebrate the renaming of Leningrad to St. Petersburg in 1991. I was studying Russian history at the time, and we invited everyone with more than a passing interest in the great country. Each guest brought along a souvenir: vodka bottles frozen inside blocks of ice, personal statues of Karl Marx, the poems of Anna Akhmatova.

Once again I thank Debbie Thawley, Katie Isles, Fleur Spriggs, and Rimini FitzGerald for their extraordinary help. Helen Illend too provided strong encouragement and, as always, wonderful insight. All the feedback made this book infinitely better.

I'm particularly grateful to Debbie for her boundless enthusiasm, without which I would have abandoned writing altogether as too hard and out of reach. I have so many stories and so much I want to say. It has changed my life to see something get down on paper.

Storytelling, my mother says, runs in the family. It comes from our side in Wales—the same side that produced Julian Fellowes. Now if only I could write like he does!

69. About the Author

Samuel Thawley is a gold medal-winning olive oil producer in the hills of Umbria, Italy. He has written three novels—this being the third and final to reach the light of day—and is now crafting two biographies.

His journeys have taken him through the great cities of Moscow, New York, Washington D.C., and Helsinki—and through the various corporate worlds that pulse beneath this story. He has no plans to stop adventuring.

Samuel is married to Trina O'Hara, a visual artist whose work moves between paint and photograph.

KAISA
PUBLISHING

Published by

KAISA

A Kaisa Online Project

www.kaisa.online

Printed in Dunstable, United Kingdom

78197728R00255